Praise for Th

~ What authors, bloggers, and readers are saying about *The Samurai's Heart* ~

"As a historical fiction fanatic, there is something extra special about experiencing stories in new-to-me time periods and places!"

~~ Beth Erin, *Faithfully Bookish* blogger and *Diversity Between the Pages* contributor

"The Samurai's Heart (The Heart Of The Samurai Book 1) had everything I could ask for in a story: well- developed characters with compelling internal and external conflict, a sweet romance nurtured along by the story's thoughtful pacing, and an exotic land brought to life with nuanced world-building (Seriously, I found myself craving miso soup and I had to go out and get some)."

~~Marcia Kipp, reader

"A vivid tale of 16th Century Japan. Saturated with historical detail, *The Samurai's Heart* is a timeless story of love, loyalty and faith."

~~ *New York Times* bestselling author Tosca Lee

"Walt Mussell has penned a stunning story of action and adventure, romance and heartbreak, inspiration and intrigue. *The Samurai's Heart* is a beautiful tale that will sweep you into its pages and hold you rapt until the very last sentence."

~~ *Wall Street Journal* bestselling author Melinda Leigh

"Walt Mussell's beautifully crafted story breaks the mold for a romantic adventure, spinning an emotional journey of love and faith put to the test in historic Japan ... and leaves you wanting more. Thankfully, this is only the first book."

~~ *New York Times* bestselling author Dianna Love

"There are so many great things about the story, I couldn't list one favourite. There are many layers that are all expertly woven together. It never seems too complex or too simple, and there's always multiple ways of thinking about the same thing. [. . .] Overall, I highly recommend this story. It's one of the very best I've read in the last few years and I'll buy the next books as soon as they're out.

~~ Russell Rutherford, reader

"It is not a book I would have picked out for myself but having said that, it is still an excellent book. It has deep emotions, suspense, romance, and a clash of religions. A historical fiction done right that left me thinking about it long after finishing the book."

~~ Montzalee Wittmann, reader

THE

SAMURAI'S

HEART

THE

SAMURAI'S

HEART

Walt Mussell

First EDITION

Please Note

This is a work of fiction. Names, characters, places, and incidents either are the product of the author's imagination or are used fictitiously, and any resemblance to actual persons, living or dead, business establishments, events or locales is entirely coincidental.

Cover Design by Rogenna Brewer at Covers by Rogenna

ISBN: 978-0-9992910-0-9
Published by Walter Mussell

DEDICATION

For Motoyo—You make every day of my life special.

Author's Note:

Though actual figures and events from history are mentioned in this book, the book remains a work of fiction.

Western date references are used, as Japan employed a lunar calendar in the late sixteenth century, the time period of this book. This is also used to avoid confusion, as what might be the "third month" on the lunar calendar could refer to April on a Western calendar.

When someone's full name appears in the story, I have followed the Japanese naming convention in which surname comes before given name. Some characters, like the mothers of the two main families in the book, are just called "Mother" with no mentioned name.

Goami: A swordsmith
Goami Sen: Castle servant and younger of Goami's daughters
Goami Haru: Older of Goami's daughters
Jiro: Apprentice swordsmith and Haru's husband
Tokoda Shigehiro: High-ranking samurai at Himeji Castle
Tokoda Ujihiro: Himeji Castle samurai and oldest son of Tokoda Shigehiro
Tokoda Toshihiro: Himeji Castle samurai and middle son of Tokoda Shigehiro
Tokoda Nobuhiro: Swordsmith apprentice and youngest son of Tokoda Shigehiro
Sakichi: Birth/childhood name of Tokoda Nobuhiro
Moto Omi: Castle servant
Akamatsu Fumio: Lord of Haibara Castle
Yoshi: A restaurant owner
Naomi: Yoshi's wife
The Carpenter: A hoodlum for hire
Eijiro: A samurai
Funaki: A samurai
Ishida: A samurai

Kaiken: A samurai
Kitayama: A samurai
Matsubara: A samurai
Michiba: A samurai
Saga: A samurai
Shimoto: A samurai
Yamashiro: A samurai

The following list notes individuals from history mentioned in this book.

Kinoshita Iesada: Lord of Himeji Castle from 1585 to 1600 and during the course of this story

Kuroda Yoshitaka: Former lord of Himeji Castle from 1567 to 1580

Sen no Rikyu: Father of the Japanese tea ceremony

Oda Nobunaga: Feudal lord who unified half of Japan. Assassinated by one of his generals in 1582 (five years before this story begins).

Toyotomi Hideyoshi: Feudal lord who rose to power after Nobunaga's assassination. He was one of Nobunaga's generals and unified Japan, earning the title of *kampaku* (regent) in 1585. He was also the lord of Himeji Castle from 1580 to 1585, under a former name, Hashiba Hideyoshi. He was given the name Toyotomi in 1586 by the Imperial Court.

Tokugawa Ieyasu: Feudal lord who rose to power after the death of Toyotomi in 1598. He earned the title of shogun (military ruler) in 1603 and established a line that ruled for two and a half centuries. He was a general of both Nobunaga and Hideyoshi prior to his rise to shogun.

Prologue

Haibara, Japan—August 1587

"By order of the regent, Christianity has been banned from the nation."

Sen shivered in her light silk kimono, her arms wrapped against her body. The mounted samurai directed his pronouncement toward her master, castle lord and regional governor Fumio Akamatsu. The mounted samurai, flanked by two more men on horseback, swept his icy stare over her and the rest of the servants and samurai. The meaning was clear. The pronouncement applied to everyone at Haibara Castle.

Behind the three horsemen, hundreds of additional samurai advanced on foot in the early sunlight, their long shadows as menacing as their numbers. The samurai were a token of the much larger force outside the gate and an indication of the fate that awaited all the castle servants if they didn't obey.

The three leaders dismounted. All three horsemen wore gray *hakamas*, the seven-pleated skirt of the samurai. A *kiri* flower, the crest of Regent Toyotomi, decorated their flowing blue robes. Did these men despise Christians or were they following orders? Sen bowed low and struggled to maintain a passive face as the men passed. The feelings of these men toward Christians didn't matter.

The samurai stopped in front of Lord Akamatsu, exchanged perfunctory bows with him, and then the tallest samurai pulled out a scroll. "Akamatsu-*sama*, you and your assemblage must renounce your faith."

Sen swallowed hard and glanced at Lord Akamatsu. Dressed in his fine golden kimono for the morning service, his regal bearing exuded confidence and peace. She laced her fingers and pressed her hands to her chin as she stared at the spectacle, drawing her arms in close.

Lord Akamatsu's voice rang across the keep: "I am a servant of Jesus Christ, the Son of God and the human pillar of the one true faith."

Stoic, the leader stared back. "The regent requests you reconsider. He reminds you of your great service to him over many campaigns. He does not wish to see it end."

Lord Akamatsu nodded, but his expression remained impassive. "I am grateful for his recognition. It does not have to end. Still, I am a follower of my God."

Sen's throat constricted as the words caused her heart to swell. The lead samurai's eyes widened. He rolled up the scroll, glancing at both the men with him before focusing on Lord Akamatsu. "Then, you are ordered to surrender your castle and lands."

"And if I refuse?"

The two flanking samurai stepped forward and drew their katanas, crossing the long swords at Lord Akamatsu's neck. "Then our forces will lay siege to your castle, lay waste to your grounds, and lay your Christian followers in their graves. We will eradicate this faith, starting with you."

A trickle of blood oozed from Lord Akamatsu's neck, and Sen gasped.

Lord Akamatsu's lips thinned, but he did not move. His gaze scanned both the servants and his own group of samurai nearby. His eyes conveyed love. "And if I accede? What happens to my people?"

"We will question each one of them. They will be given the same chance as you. Renounce this foreign religion, and they may keep their station for whomever takes over the castle. Refuse, and they will face our judgment. Those we show mercy to may walk away with the clothes they wear. It is over. You are in our power now."

"If you have power over me, it's only because it was granted to you by God. I surrender the castle."

Pride welled inside Sen at Lord Akamatsu's steadfastness, and her arms relaxed as the samurai removed their swords from his neck. They spared him. But Sen's breath caught in her throat as the samurai faced the crowd.

"Line up," the lead man said, pointing in two directions. "Lord Akamatsu's samurai to the left side. His servants over here on the right."

Sen let the movement of the crowd carry her forward with the other servants. She bowed as more samurai passed, and then she headed to the servant line. She closed her eyes briefly. *Lord, please help us.*

A woman screamed, and the sound chilled Sen's soul. She craned her neck to see around the fifty or so people in front of her and watched in horror. A maid from the kitchen—it looked like she'd been first in line—fell to the ground. Blood poured from both sides of her neck. Her body convulsed, then grew still as the life flowed out of her. She was a young woman, only fifteen. Now she lay on the grass, her pale-green servant's kimono stained red.

Sen gulped air but couldn't swallow. She glanced around as best she could without moving her head. All of the servants' shoulders drooped. Would she and everyone in line face the same fate?

She finally managed to swallow, but the truth wouldn't go down so easily. She was so close, so close. One more week, and then she would have left to be with her family. They needed her.

At the thought of her family, Sen reached into her belt and sighed. It was still there, the letter from her mother telling Sen of the death of her sister, Haru. The crinkled feeling of the paper brought sadness. It also reminded her of her duty, the duty of a remaining sibling when an elder child had died. She must find a husband to marry into the family business and to help her look after her parents.

The line moved slowly. Maybe thirty people in front of her now. Sen's feet trembled with each step forward. Some people who had already stood before the samurai now walked free, staring at the ground, their chins tucked against their chests. Why had they been spared? Had they renounced Lord Akamatsu? Had they renounced Jesus? Were they now ashamed? Sen strained to hear, but the voices up front were inaudible despite the silence of the grounds. The samurai obviously meant for no one to listen. Sen leaned left but then righted herself. She would soon learn how the samurai offered mercy.

Another woman and then a man screamed and fell to the ground, blood draining from their necks and streaking their kimonos as they shook and then fell still. Two more people mercilessly slain. More servants walked past Sen, apparently headed to the castle entrance. Dejected with their heads bowed, they carried nothing but shame. Sen looked over at the other line, the line of samurai. Six men lay on the ground, motionless. Just as she might soon be. No screams had come from the samurai. Only the rank smell of death that floated on the air. Christians all, they'd refused suicide. None showed stomach wounds.

Sen craved water to quench her dry mouth. She struggled to breathe, each inhalation and exhalation sounding in her ears.

Could she make the right choice?

Confess God and leave her parents to Him? Renounce God to fulfill her duty to her family? Was that truly the choice set before her?

Sen wrung her hands as she drew closer to the front. More of her fellow Christians fell to the ground. Still, she could not hear their words. Were people confessing God and still surviving?

Only ten people remained ahead of her in line. One of the samurai wiped his blade on a dead servant's kimono, then kicked some of the bodies to the side. Sen's knees and shoulders wobbled as the sun reflected off the metal, stinging her eyes with its harsh light.

A sword. The realization dawned on her. She would die by a sword.

Childhood memories rushed forward like rapids, bringing images of her parents to mind. Her father was the best swordsmith in her hometown of Himeji. He had crafted hundreds of swords over the years.

How would he feel if he were to learn his daughter was slain by one?

Sen grasped her belt and traced the edge of the letter with her fingertips. Duty to God. Duty to family. Her breathing grew steady. Measured. Calm.

She neared the front. One more person, an older woman, was ahead of her. The woman walked toward the three samurai awaiting her and bowed. Two of the samurai crossed their long swords at the woman's neck. The lead samurai's words finally reached Sen's ears. "I will say this once. Renounce your faith."

"I am a servant of Christ," the woman said.

Metal clanked against metal as the samurai completed the cut. The old woman's hands flew to her neck. Retching, she sank to her knees, then fell to the ground.

My turn.

Sen stepped forward and bowed to the three samurai, her gaze fixed on the bodies at her feet. Lives taken, cut down. The old woman before her twitched and inched toward Sen, the last flashes of her life ebbing away as the red spots of blood began to stain the hem of Sen's kimono. The coppery smell of blood filled Sen's nostrils. Bile rose in her throat as she choked back a gag and then straightened to her full height, her eyes focused on the samurai.

The men nodded back, then crossed their long swords at her neck. The cold metal dug into her skin, yet it burned like fire. Sweat poured down her face and back. The leader's face betrayed no mercy. "I will say this once. Renounce your faith."

Sen took in a shallow mouthful of air and exhaled. Tears bit her eyes as images of her parents' faces again rose in her mind.

God, please look after my family.

"I am a servant of Christ."

The blades bit deeper. The clank of swords sounded in Sen's ears as she struggled not to cry out. She scrunched her shoulders, bringing them up to salve the sting. Her head felt light and her knees buckled. Her breathing slowed . . . and then continued. Her dizziness cleared. She reached her hands to her neck and felt the hot liquid. The cuts were deep.

But she would live.

She rose slowly, too fearful to glance at the samurai's face, her eyes fighting tears. She should accept her fate and leave. It wasn't her place to ask, but she had to know. "Forgive me," she said, bowing low. "I beg your indulgence."

The samurai tilted his head, his gaze scanning her up and down. "You're the first to dare question us. You have courage, as misplaced as it may be. You may ask."

"Why?"

The lead samurai smiled. "You paused before you responded. You debated this religion in your mind. There is still hope for you."

Paused? She had paused?

She had prayed before she answered. The samurai had taken it for doubt. Her prayer had saved her.

"Thank you," she responded.

"Let the lesson burn into you. You survived today only by *our* justice. Now leave these grounds. See if your deity protects you."

Sen bowed, glanced once more at the bodies at her feet, and then walked toward the entrance. The castle gate, long a source of comfort, appeared ominous as she approached it. Just a few more strides and she'd be outside. Once outside, she would head for home.

But home was eighty miles away. Could she make it there on her own?

She passed through the gate, took a few steps along the road, and crashed to the ground.

Chapter One

Himeji, Japan—April 1588 (Eight Months Later)

The faint fragrance of cherry blossoms roused Sen from her slumber. It shouldn't have.

A creak from the hallway cut through the snores and wheezes of the other castle attendants sleeping around her. A couple of guards making their rounds? It was early for anyone except samurai.

Closing her eyes, she endeavored to go back to sleep. Yet the scent lingered. It filled her body and raised her spirits. She brought her hands to her neck and traced the scars on each side. Would she wake up every morning and remember that day, a day when samurai murdered twenty of her fellow servants? She clasped her hands under the blanket, remembered her fallen friends, and thanked God again that she had been spared.

Sen savored the minutes of solitude while the other women slept. She sat up and slipped the letter from her mother from her bag of meager belongings, opened the paper, and traced the characters with her fingertips in the moonlight that filtered through the window. Since that tragic day, she had carried the letter with her. A reminder of her sister. A reminder that she needed to go home. After tracing the characters for a few minutes, she put the letter back, looking around to make sure that no one was watching. Tears welled in her eyes as she lay back down, recalling her childhood. *Haru, I wish I could have seen you once more.*

"Wake up, Sen," a woman's voice said.

She opened her eyes and shook her head to clear the blur, seeing the face of her friend and fellow attendant, Moto Omi. Her black hair was pulled taut behind her head and pinned with a red comb that accented her yellow servant's kimono.

"What's wrong?" Sen asked.

"What's wrong?" Omi rolled her eyes. "You're still asleep. Do you want to get in trouble? You've only been here two weeks. You need to be alert. If you lose your position, you'll have no place else to go."

Sen nodded, then rose and dressed in silence. Omi helped her put away her bedroll, wooden pillow, and bag. Sen slid open the door to the room, stepped into the hall, and then stopped. A narrow viewing portal nearby offered a glimpse of the western grounds. The pale pink cherry blossoms on the trees, a sign of spring, shimmered in the receding moonlight. For the first time since Sen's arrival in Himeji, a tiny bud of hope sprouted in her heart.

As she wiped a tear with the back of her hand, a gentle shove broke her thoughts.

Omi glowered at her. "Why did you stop?"

Sen averted her eyes. "The cherry blossoms are in bloom."

Omi glanced out the portal and then stared at Sen. "I see that. Why is that important?"

Sen breathed through her nose, remembering the feeling of a few hours earlier. "Their scent woke me last night. I couldn't sleep for a while."

Omi pushed out her lips, her arms akimbo, reminding Sen of Haru. "You must have been dreaming. Cherry blossoms don't have such a strong fragrance, but that explains why you rolled around so much last night."

Sen opened her mouth to disagree, but her breath caught in her throat. Omi was right, and she was also trying to help. Sen needed to focus. "You must be right. It was only a dream."

Omi nodded and then turned serious, her thumbs stuck in her obi. "You can look at the blossoms later. They'll bloom for two weeks. For now, get busy."

Sen hurried out into the courtyard toward the main keep of Himeji Castle as dawn broke over the castle grounds. Her mistress would rise soon. She needed to be ready.

Passing the west wall, she glanced at the circular tile with a cross on it, nestled near the top of the wall with the other ornamental ceramic tiles. Sen paused, as she did every day, to stare at it. Many tiles lined the eaves of the buildings, tiles intended for good luck to protect against fires, tsunamis, and typhoons. Yet this tile bore the raised image of a cross in its center. How did it get there? Who placed it there? How had it survived the anti-Christian edict?

She pursed her lips and looked around. The courtyard stood empty. Keeping her eyes open, she brought her palms together, but left her hands down as strength flowed within her. She rubbed just below her shoulders and massaged her muscles. Like the symbol of the cross, she would endure. She hoped to have the answer someday to the mystery of how the tile got there. For now, the cross on the wall and the cherry blossoms served the same purpose. Both were signs from God.

But what did they mean?

Did these signs mean she would find a husband here? How? The castle lord was the regent's brother-in-law. This place teemed with samurai who were tasked with enforcing the ban. Why had she come here at all?

Lord Akamatsu.

After the incident in Haibara, Lord Akamatsu and his wife had seen Sen back to Himeji. Upon arriving, she'd learned that Lord Akamatsu had found her work at the castle. She had pleaded to be allowed to go home to her parents, but he insisted it would be better for her here. Why? She was twenty-four, well beyond the age appropriate for apprenticeships and first marriages. Finding a husband willing to marry into her family and care for her parents as they got older would be difficult enough.

Her shoulders had sunk along with her spirit. Finding a Christian husband here would be impossible.

###

Nobuhiro noticed the white flowers as he walked the path along the route to the castle. With each stride, his left foot grew heavier. As a child, he had tried to hide his limp, realizing it made him different. As an adult, he had accepted it, barely noticing any issues in his daily routine. However, as he approached the castle, years of ignored pain weighed on each step.

Himeji Castle was a part of his life, as it was for all the citizens of the city. The three-story structure sat atop Himeyama Hill. If the weather were clear, he could see the castle from the front of the shop at the edge of town, where he worked as a swordsmith's apprentice. When he ran errands in town for his master, he often got close enough to distinguish the castle's features: the stone base, white wood walls, and terraced eaves. However, this was the first time in seven years he had stepped on the grounds of the place he had once called home.

Delivery merchants passed him in both directions. A few familiar nods flickered his way, but he didn't stop. He rubbed the tightness in his chest with a fist as he crossed the bridge that led toward the castle's outer wall. Two prominent samurai walked toward him, and a hard lump rose in his throat. Both men wore typical black kimonos with gray *hakamas*, the skirts extending to the ankles. Both men wore two swords in their belts.

Most people would have found these two men intimidating. However, Nobuhiro was accustomed to them appearing at odd times at his master's shop. His heart swelled at their approach. He breathed deeply and cleared his throat. "You honor me by coming to meet me."

The stocky older one, Ujihiro, laughed. "Dispense with the politeness, little brother. We would not miss your return."

"Yes," the slender one, Toshihiro, commented. "Even if we do remember what a bothersome child you were."

"But Uji? Toshi? What if someone hears I'm on the grounds? Word will reach our father. It may have been a long time, but he will know I'm here."

Uji waved his hand to the side in a dismissive motion. "You worry too much. Rest your fears. You're back home."

How could he rest? Born with a limp, he was a disappointment to his father, a disappointment Nobuhiro never overcame.

Toshi pointed at the long cloth package Nobuhiro carried. "So what have you brought us?"

He looked down and rubbed his hands along the cotton cloth, then laid the item in his eldest brother's outstretched hands. Uji unwrapped it, revealing an intricately carved wooden scabbard. He held it, edge up, and partially withdrew the blade. Both Toshi and Uji gazed at it, admiration gleaming in their eyes.

"Impressive," Uji said. "We've been expecting this. In May, Regent Toyotomi will entertain the emperor at Jurakutei Palace. A group of samurai will leave later this morning for Kyoto to deliver this prize."

Toshi's eyes sparkled like the sun's reflection on the blade. "Your master's work is inspiring. Perfectly balanced, I would imagine. How many times was the steel folded?"

"The core steel was folded five times. The jacket steel was folded fifteen times," Nobuhiro answered, envisioning the process where the metal was heated, flattened with a hammer, and then folded on itself. The process removed impurities and created a stronger blade.

"Can you now craft swords like this?" Uji asked.

"I may be at the end of my apprenticeship, but I'm still a long way from this level of skill. I can fashion standard blades. That's my primary job."

"Did you make any of the folds on this one?"

Nobuhiro nodded. "Several. Master did the rest. We just received it from the sword polisher. Master reviewed the work and signed his name. He then requested I bring the sword here."

Uji's eyebrows rose. "Are you ready to open your own business then?"

Nobuhiro nodded as his mood lightened. "Almost. I will serve my year of gratitude. Then Master will lend me the money to set up my own workshop."

Uji flashed a wry smile. "Your master is the best. He knows your work will reflect on him. He wouldn't help you get established if he didn't think you were ready."

Toshi laughed and slapped Nobuhiro on the back. "It's good we let you live then. I voted to throw you in the river when you were first born."

Nobuhiro froze. He flattened his lips as his brother's verbal arrow pierced his heart.

Uji's voice broke his thoughts. "You are too serious, little brother. Toshi was joking."

Heat flooded Nobuhiro's cheeks. By having a name that meant *family*, Uji understood the joys and responsibilities that term carried. Nobuhiro's actions had shamed his brother. "I know. I beg forgiveness."

Uji placed a firm hand on Nobuhiro's shoulder and stared him in the eyes. "Physical ability is but one part of being a samurai. Striving to improve yourself in all aspects of your existence is a greater challenge and a worthy one for all. You will one day be the finest swordsmith in the region, earning the name of your village as your teacher has done."

Nobuhiro's shoulders slumped. Would earning the name of his village be enough to lift his shame? No matter how many katanas he crafted, no matter how fine they were, he would never wield one like his brothers did. Or like his father.

Toshi shook his head. Did he sense Nobuhiro's thoughts? "Uji's right. You worry too much. You are our brother. That hasn't changed. It's good to have you back, even for a day."

Uji nodded his concurrence. "Let's go," he said in his gruff voice. "The grounds have changed much since you left."

Thankful that his brothers had maintained contact with him through the years of his estrangement from their father, Nobuhiro's mouth spread in the kind of grin shared only by siblings. He rewrapped the cloth around the scabbard, readying the sword for presentation. A blanket of inner warmth from his brothers wrapped his childhood memories the same way. It was a fleeting feeling. His limp had made it impossible for him to become a samurai. His failure disappointed his father. That displeasure resonated in Nobuhiro every day of his life. If only he could prove himself and somehow change his father's mind.

###

Sen crossed the courtyard, feeling the day's warmth on her cheeks. The sun was rising, but the morning dew had yet to evaporate, leaving the ground damp. She gazed at the trees, mesmerized by the beauty of the scenery. The surroundings tugged at her heart.

She closed her eyes and took a deep breath, steeling her nerves.

Focus, Sen. Focus. Remember what Omi said. You need to do your job. You're fortunate to be here. Losing your position would shame your parents and Lord Akamatsu.

Her head clear, she glanced around and stepped back.

Then her foot hit something solid.

She gasped for breath. Her arms flailed. She searched for something to grab on to but clenched empty air.

Strong hands grasped her under her arms and held her until she regained her balance. She turned around and looked at her rescuer, a tradesman dressed in a simple, blue linen kimono. His eyes suggested gentleness and pain. His touch was both light and firm. He must have a kind heart.

"Are you hurt?" he asked.

Her cheeks heated as she bowed. "Ah, *sumimasen*! I'm sorry. I wasn't paying attention."

She glanced to the man's left. Two samurai stood next to him. Her breath lodged in her throat. She opened her mouth, but no sound came out. Instead, she stepped back and bowed again. Her hands trembled as her eyes focused on the ground. "I'm sorry."

"Sen, are you injured?" a deep voice asked.

Her shoulders stiffened. She brought her palms together but couldn't still her quaking hands. *Anybody but them. I am already too much in their debt.* She raised her head slowly and looked back at the two samurai. Two weeks ago, these men had met her, Lord Akamatsu, and his wife in darkness outside Himeji. They'd provided Lord Akamatsu with food and escorted Sen to the castle. Now they stood before her. The tradesman who'd caught Sen bore a striking resemblance to the samurai.

The older of her two escorts nodded slightly. "It's good to see you again."

"And good to see you smiling," the younger escort added.

"Thank you both. I'm sorry, again." Her breaths grew rapid and she looked back down, maintaining her station. "Please forgive me, Samurai-sama. You know who I am, but I don't know your names."

She regretted the question immediately. It was not her place to ask. Impertinence would get her killed faster than religion. The two men had befriended her the night she met them. Lord Akamatsu had promised Sen that these men would take care of her, an amazing promise considering her low status. She trusted Lord Akamatsu.

She trusted these men.

She raised her eyes and the samurai introduced

themselves. Tokoda Ujihiro and Tokoda Toshihiro. Her initial impression that night had been correct. Brothers.

The one called Toshihiro turned and indicated the man she'd tripped over. The man who'd caught her and kept her safe. "And this man is our youngest brother, Nobuhiro."

A cool breeze blew across Sen's face, carrying a mix of floral and pine fragrances, both of which were familiar and comforting. Her lips parted, and she stared for a second. The samurai brothers were both handsome and friendly, but they had the presence of soldiers ready for battle. Nobuhiro was also handsome, but his broad forehead and soft brown eyes gave him the appearance of a peaceful man. Her heart warmed, much like the rising sun. "Are you also a samurai?"

Nobuhiro turned red and studied the ground for a moment before bringing his eyes back up to meet hers. "No," he said, shaking his head as if each little movement caused him tremendous pain. "I . . . I . . . I work for a swordsmith."

Her face grew hot and her skin tingled. Many samurai rose from the ranks of farmers and tradesmen. However, it was rare that one went the other direction if *born* a samurai. Still, her father was a swordsmith, the best in the area. It was an honorable profession.

Movement near one of the buildings drew Sen's attention. Other attendants hard at work. She needed to return to work as well. She bowed before the men. "If it is acceptable, I must return to my duties." Her breath hitched. "I remain in your debt."

The samurai nodded and Sen took a step away. Nobuhiro's face remained in her mind.

"What are all of you doing?" a voice bellowed from behind her.

She turned. An older man whose name she did not know, but whom she recognized as an advisor to the castle lord, approached. His lined face resembled a piece of overripe fruit, wrinkled from the sun. Dressed formally in a *kataginu,* a sleeveless jacket with winglike shoulders, he was not a man to be trifled with.

His eyes flared with anger. "I repeat. What are all of you doing?"

The old man's eyes shifted between her and the brothers. She quivered under his stern gaze like wind chimes in a stiff breeze. "*Sumimasen.* I . . . I just stopped to talk."

The elder man glared. "I wasn't talking to you. Be silent!"

She bowed low, but he strode past her as if she were invisible. She wheeled around to look at the four men. The elder warrior stared at the three brothers, and all three showed glimpses of fear, even Ujihiro, who was half a head taller. The older man glanced at Nobuhiro, who clutched the package he carried, and then shifted his gaze back to Ujihiro.

"What is *he* doing here?" the older man asked, gesturing at Nobuhiro, who flinched and looked away.

"Father," Ujihiro said, "he is here delivering a package for the May festivities in Kyoto."

Father? Are these men really the sons of this grand advisor? This man reports to the castle lord. He even deals with Regent Toyotomi himself. She began to back away.

"You stay put. I will talk to you shortly," the elder samurai said without turning to face her. Instead, he stared at his youngest son.

"Hand the package to me. You are not fit to carry that item any longer than you have."

She gulped air and her fingers grew stiff as Nobuhiro handed over his package.

The elder samurai opened the wrappings and examined the item. "Good. It seems to be perfect, as it must be." He wrapped it back up and handed it to Ujihiro. "Assemble the contingent that will carry this to Kyoto. Leave within the hour."

"Yes, Father." Ujihiro bowed.

A short breath escaped Sen's lips as the old man

nodded and dismissed Ujihiro with a blink of his eyes. No return bow? The man then turned to Toshihiro. “As for you, escort *this man* to the entrance.” He motioned toward Nobuhiro. “He saw fit to leave us seven years ago. He does not belong here now.”

Toshihiro murmured something to Nobuhiro, but it was too low for Sen to hear. He glanced in her direction, his eyes betraying his shame and sadness. She had seen that look before. On Lord Akamatsu when he lost his castle and lands. On his servants when they’d faced the samurai and seen friends killed. She hadn’t before seen such looks of despair at this castle. Her throat tightened.

Toshihiro and Nobuhiro walked away, headed for the entrance. Nobuhiro had a slight limp, yet he walked with the same grace and carriage as his brother.

The elder samurai interrupted her thoughts. “And who are you? I have seen you on the grounds but do not know your name.”

“Goami Sen, sir.” *He’s seen me?* She marveled at his awareness, as there were hundreds on the grounds daily. How did he notice someone as low as her? His aloof eyes drilled into her, though the corners of his mouth drooped slightly and his chin quivered.

“Ah, the new arrival. I understand that the mistress you serve is satisfied with your work. However, you would do well to forget your former associations. Those leanings of yours will cause you trouble if you’re not careful.”

She bowed. Memories of her former master and images of the cross tile flashed through her mind. “Yes, my lord.”

“Also, I saw your exchange with my sons. You would do well to remember your place.”

She trembled and bowed again. Thoughts of Nobuhiro increased the beating of her heart. He might be a swordsmith’s apprentice and have his father’s disdain, but he was still highborn. She was lowborn. Whatever attracted her to him, she needed to forget it. “Yes, my lord.”

"And my name is Tokoda Shigehiro. You would do well to remember me. Get back to your duties."

"Yes, my lord. Thank you for your advice." Again, she bowed low before the older man, squeezing her body together as if she would fall apart. The old man turned and walked away. Her stomach churned at his mistreatment of Nobuhiro. Still, she kept her head down a few more seconds and then raised it up.

Scary old prune.

She turned and headed toward the main keep. In the distance, Nobuhiro and Toshihiro approached the main gate. She smiled. Would she see him again? She would find a way to do so.

A sudden breeze brought stray cherry blossoms down to kiss her face.

Chapter Two

Nobuhiro stared out the window of the workshop into a dark sky filled with stars. Still no hint of sunlight even though the moon had already set. At least two hours till dawn. He rubbed his hands to warm them from the night chill.

So much work to do yet and Master will arrive any minute.

A lantern on the wall illuminated the room, casting a glow on the benches, tools, and forge. Some tea and a half-eaten rice ball lay on a nearby table, a light snack to get him going. Master Goami's wife would prepare a full meal within a couple of hours. He would be fine until then.

He checked the buckets of clay slurry and water to ensure he had sufficient supply. Next, he ignited the pile of pine charcoal in the forge. The fire took on a life of its own, filling the air with the scent of pine. He stirred the fire and then added more charcoal, hearing the words of his master in his mind. *Maintain an even temperature and your fire will serve your work well.* The lessons filled his memory like when he was a young child learning to write characters. Learning required discipline. Discipline was one of the keys to great artisanship.

"You stir that charcoal like someone preparing for a tea ceremony." Toshi's jovial voice jolted Nobuhiro out of his reflections. Nobuhiro nearly dropped the poker.

He glanced over his shoulder to where his brother stood in the doorway. Smiling, silent, and self-assured. How did he sneak up on him? Nobuhiro struck his hip with his hand and wagged the hot poker at Toshi in mock reproach. "It's as precise as a tea ceremony, brother, and to be treated with great care. You should know that."

Toshi nodded. "Something we all learned as children," he said in a you-don't-have-to-remind-me voice. "Father's mentor, an expert at the tea ceremony, ensured that Father mastered the skills. Father taught us well."

Nobuhiro poked the fire hard and sparks showered the dirt floor. Was Toshi trying to provoke him? "Apparently, our *father* is still stuck in the past. He thinks me the child he once abused."

Toshi's eyes flared. "It's been seven years since you chose to walk away. What did you expect? Did you think any hurt he felt would have been forgotten?"

Nobuhiro's stomach tightened like someone who hadn't eaten for days, a feeling he remembered from that first week after he left. "*He* felt?" Nobuhiro shoved his hand through his hair.

"Yes." Toshi's face hardened into the stony visage characteristic of their father and Uji. "Uji and I understood why you left. You never explained your feelings to Father."

"What does he know of feelings?" Nobuhiro spat the words. Inside his mind, confusion raged. How could he have explained his feelings to their father? Samurai didn't talk of such things. Toshi was the only one who wouldn't ridicule Nobuhiro for his thoughts.

"His skills are not limited to the tea ceremony." Toshi's face softened in tandem with his words. "His name, Shige, means *layered.* He embodies that quality. Have you forgotten Father also composes poetry? He is recognized throughout the area for his work. Such a man is in touch with his feelings."

Poetry. Memories of their father writing in the evening flickered in Nobuhiro's mind. He'd left his futon often in the middle of the night and discovered his father alone by the hearth, brush in hand and eyes red. His father had caught him once and admonished him. Still, Nobuhiro found he had no retort for Toshi and nodded his assent.

"And speaking of feelings," Toshi continued, "you seemed to enjoy meeting a certain young woman at the castle."

At the mention of Sen, Nobuhiro's face grew warm. He glanced away briefly before focusing again on his brother. "Yes, she seemed very nice."

"Nice?" Toshi asked. "When you introduced yourself, that nervous stutter of yours arose like a thieving merchant who'd just received a visit from a tax collector. Uji and I struggled to contain our laughter when we heard it."

"But what of it?"

"Would you like to see her again?"

Nobuhiro delayed answering, instead turning to look at the fire and adding coal. It was growing hotter. Coming along nicely. Did he want to see her again? His heartbeat quickened in response.

Wheeling back to his brother, he licked his lips. "Yes, but I don't know how I could arrange it."

"Don't worry. I feel you may see her soon."

Nobuhiro tilted his head. "Why?"

"There are many things you do not know, *Sakichi*," Toshi said, addressing Nobuhiro by his birth name instead of the name he received at his coming-of-age ceremony.

Toshi often used the name to tease Nobuhiro. Nobuhiro sighed. A lecture was coming. He was being chided into listening to it.

"A samurai must be aware of his surroundings. He must understand the motivations of friend and foe alike. Those motivations carry success and failure."

"What does that mean?" Irritation sharpened his response.

Toshi chuckled. "You will find out soon. I must go. Take care, *Sakichi*."

Nobuhiro's upper body tightened. He regretted his harsh words. These family opportunities were few, too few to devalue with pettiness. "My apologies for my earlier comments. Please stay a few more minutes. Would you like some tea?" He walked to the table and grabbed his wooden cup.

"Sorry. I must leave."

Nobuhiro bowed. "Thank you for coming to visit. It's good to talk to you."

No response. He glanced up. His brother was gone, disappearing as if he had been conjured from Nobuhiro's imagination. Nobuhiro walked to the door and looked out but didn't see Toshi anywhere in the distance.

His thoughts were broken by the sliding of a door behind him.

"Was someone here?" a smooth, familiar voice asked.

He closed the outside door and turned. Master Goami stood at the entrance that faced the house.

"No one." Averting his eyes, he returned to the fire. Guilt nagged his conscience at his lie. What would his master think if he knew of the visits over the years by both Toshi and Uji? Would he doubt Nobuhiro's loyalty to this house or his love for the couple who had sheltered him for so many years? But he wasn't ready to discuss the visits. "I thought I heard something and went to check."

"Ahh. Maybe you heard me and just thought the sound was coming from elsewhere. I was up early. I tried to be silent and let my good wife sleep." Master Goami smiled. "Guess I wasn't successful."

Nobuhiro laughed. His master's mood was lighter than usual. It was the happiest he had seen him since before his master had learned of the death of his daughter and son-in-law, many months ago. Nobuhiro only had lost his best friend and fellow apprentice, Jiro. His master had lost his daughter, his heir, and his hopes for his family's future.

With his master in such a good mood, Nobuhiro did not want to broach such memories. "Maybe you *were* quiet. Maybe it was just the wind I heard."

"Whichever. It is good that you have the fire going." Master Goami moved quickly. "We have much work to do today. Later, we need to clean up early. A special guest is joining us tonight."

A guest. That explained Master Goami's good spirits. Later, Nobuhiro decided, he would mention Toshi's visit and reaffirm his own commitment to this family. He rubbed his palms together and went to work.

###

"Kaiken, I will not be led by you." Ishida's voice carried the thunder of more storms to come.

Kaiken stared at the odious samurai, his face puffed up to a bloated state. His red cheeks matched the small red rope that decorated the hilt of his blade. His muscles tensed beneath his kimono. Were he still in shape, he would be a threat. Yet the foolishness beneath his flab robbed his mobility.

"You dare challenge me?" Kaiken stepped toward Ishida. "I lead this group. I alone have received the Master's blessing. We've met with success."

Ishida pounded his fist to his chest. "The Master chose me for this group, too. I spit on your definition of success. We've done nothing for over six months. How are we serving our lord if we do not pursue his goals?"

"We had to suspend our activities. The fire at the factory and the deaths that happened drew Tokoda's interest. Why the old man pursues that incident with such zeal, I do not know. His attention has been relentless."

"You're too cautious. We've accomplished little since then."

Blood pumped from Kaiken's quickening heartbeat. Focusing on Ishida, Kaiken still eyed the other two men in the room, Funaki and Michiba. Neither man moved, content to watch. Ishida's kimono opened, framing a slender patch of skin that led down his chest. He didn't protect his own body. His lack of care matched his lack of wit.

"We've accomplished not getting caught. The day may come where we slit our stomachs in service to our lord, but that day has not arrived yet."

Ishida spat. "You are not one who would take that step."

Kaiken's ears perked up. Voices from outside approached. Had a magistrate heard Ishida's bluster? Possibly. Grabbing the katana's hilt, Kaiken stiffened. Any intruder would be dispatched quickly. The voices passed. Kaiken's shoulders dropped and rose again.

Ishida maintained his verbal assault. "It's regrettable that no one entered. You grabbed your sword. Maybe you could have killed someone and added them to your list of martyrs."

"You didn't grab your sword. You're a fool. Fools do not survive."

"I've been fool enough only to follow you. Placing you in charge is the only unwise move our master has ever made. We list about like a boat with neither oars nor wind."

"Our goals haven't changed. We've created fear in the Christians. We will continue to inspire terror."

Ishida huffed. "What terror? Master struck a blow for our cause when he arranged for Saga and Shimoto to lead the forces against Haibara Castle. They could have slain two hundred Christians that day. Instead, they killed twenty. For what purpose? Twenty lives that didn't matter to anyone. Hundreds dead? Christians everywhere would have trembled. Their religion may be banned, but it still spreads."

Kaiken bristled. It was still there. The *kaiken*, the dagger, the namesake, hidden and held in place under Kaiken's right sleeve. Available to strike. To plunge it into Ishida's throat would bring joy. Later, when Ishida had calmed down, Kaiken could meet him. Alone. Offer apologies. Offer food. Maybe even a geisha for entertainment.

Then Kaiken could stuff Ishida's blasphemous mouth with metal.

Kaiken bit back a smile. Revenge was best when meted to an unsuspecting enemy.

Kaiken studied Ishida, but the fat man hadn't moved. Was he providing an opening or baiting a trap? "We may not understand Master's reason, but we should still follow his plan."

"The Master's plan left Saga and Shimoto dead, two of our most prominent members."

"I admit I do not understand why they had to die, but I won't question it. Neither should you. As the survivors of Haibara attempt to restart their lives, they will rejoin society. The scars on their necks are an indication to other Christians that they're believers . . . and an indication to our fellow followers of people who can be monitored."

"Hundreds can disappear in a country of millions. The story becomes only a myth. To inspire terror, we need more. Churches have been destroyed elsewhere. Other followers are obviously active. Yet we have done nothing since the incident at Haibara Castle."

"The destruction of many churches is a rumor, yet you believe it. The church in Kyoto was demolished. The regent ordered that personally. Some places in Nagasaki have been destroyed, but this religion remains strong there . . . for now."

Ishida scratched his head. "Then what are we doing? What is the true purpose?"

Kaiken breathed slowly. What did Ishida understand about the goal? Their master had entrusted Kaiken with that knowledge. To find the one. "The true purpose is the purview of the Master. For now, though, he wants as many Christians as possible alive."

"Alive?" Ishida clenched his fists and stared at the ceiling.

Kaiken looked across at Ishida. *He left his neck open. His stupidity poisons the air.*

Kaiken stepped forward and Ishida stopped his pacing. "You forget that we know of several Christians in this area. Some have already been eliminated."

"More nameless victims who provided society with no benefit. I can find others to make my shoes and fix my roof. It's too slow. We need decisive action."

A dog barked outside. Kaiken glanced at a low space in the wall, catching sight of a white dog. A silly community dog was the only one to note their presence. Thankfully, it could tell no one. "We need to find the rest of the Christians first, and then we will proceed under my direction. I alone was given the charge. Who are you to question it?"

Ishida took two steps toward Kaiken, bringing himself within arm's reach of his rival. Kaiken coughed, expelling Ishida's foul breath away. *One step and it will be over*, Kaiken thought. *I should have done it when you looked at the ceiling.*

"I am Ishida. The Master may have put you in charge of us," he said as he pointed toward the door, "but out there, I outrank you and you are nothing. Be careful or I will make that permanent."

Kaiken spit in his face. "Back up now or I'll cut out your lying tongue. If you doubt my commitment, you're welcome to challenge me. However, such a fight would be rash."

Ishida laughed. "You're afraid to fight me?"

"You're a good man, Ishida. The group needs you. It needs all of us."

Ishida chuckled, spreading his feet wide. "You do have some intelligence after all." His smooth brow disappeared into a topknot that pulled the wrinkles from his face. "We should get to business as soon as our final member arrives."

Kaiken glanced at the men in the room and listened for the approach of Kitayama, the missing member. More people passed within earshot, but the door remained closed. Kitayama was late again. Kaiken would have to convince him to be on time in the future or else his services would end.

Funaki and Michiba drew closer to Ishida. Had Ishida conspired with them beforehand? Would they support Ishida if Kaiken attacked? Their faces betrayed no emotion. Smart. Definitely smarter than Ishida.

Kaiken inhaled and rubbed moist palms onto the cotton fabric, gaining reassurance from the hidden dagger. Kaiken could step forward, slip it out quickly, and it would be over. "Agreed. We will wait."

Ishida nodded. Dust brushed Kaiken's lips and Kaiken wiped it away.

Kaiken heard a brief click and then a drag of metal on wood, the sound of a sword being drawn. *Boar snouts!* Kaiken's chest tightened like the muscles of a ninja poised to silence palace guards. A flick of the wrist slipped the hidden dagger into Kaiken's clenched palm. Ishida yelled and raised his sword high.

A fool to the end.

Kaiken stepped forward and brought the dagger up. The blade cleaved the fat of Ishida's belly as Kaiken plunged it under his ribs and up to the dagger's base.

Ishida gulped. His lips parted as Kaiken twisted the blade and then shoved upward. Ishida's face cringed. He dropped his sword, which thudded on the ground. Kaiken removed the dagger and Ishida dropped to his knees, his face surprisingly placid. Ishida then fell forward, his head slamming into the rotting wood and soot, creating a cloud of dust.

Kaiken looked at the two remaining samurai. They both backed up and bowed.

Kaiken flicked the blade, casting blood on Ishida's face. The blood's thick smell cut through the air. Kaiken wiped the dagger on Ishida's clothes, then stepped over the body and acknowledged the two men. "I trust there will be no further challenges."

"*Hai,*" they both responded.

A crack outside drew their attention. Kaiken and the two men drew their swords. A smile crossed Kaiken's lips. The dead weight was no more. The remaining members were ready.

Kitayama stepped in, breathing hard.

"You're late," Kaiken said, resheathing the sword. Funaki and Michiba did likewise.

Kitayama bowed. "I beg your forgiveness, but the Christian woman is moving. Her mistress gave her time off to visit her family. We could watch from a distance. The local Christians would know she is from here and may approach her.

"Good work. Your lateness is acceptable. We took care of one issue without you.

Kitayama tilted his head and looked at the ground as Kaiken pointed toward Ishida. "Dispose of the body. Cover it for now to hide it. Return tonight and dump it outside of town where the dogs can benefit."

Kitayama said nothing, but his assent was plain. Kaiken holstered the blade back in its spot. The dagger. The protector. The *kaiken.*

Christians were fools to follow a deity. Skill and weapons were the only true salvation.

###

Sen's steps quickened as the familiar thatched-roof house came into view. The nearby workshop on the left side was encircled by a straw rope from which hung paper streamers, just as at a Buddhist temple. Shadows from the workshop painted the house as the sun drew lower in the sky.

It had been many years since she had been home to see her parents. Her mistress had given her the night off to visit. Her last time at home had been much happier. She had dreamed often of this day and looked forward to the reunion. Would the house feel empty? Haru was dead. A pit the size of a castle cornerstone swelled in Sen's stomach.

She also felt the mantle of her duty now that she was the sole-surviving child. That duty weighed like lead. She paused, knuckles hovering inches from the door. Taking a few deep breaths, she willed herself to chase the issue from her mind and rapped on the doorframe.

The wooden door slid open quickly to reveal her mother. The older woman beamed at her, tears streaming from her eyes. Sen's eyes also misted and tears trickled down her face. She reached out and cupped her mother's elbows in her hands. Her mother did the same to her.

She stared into new wrinkles that were now etched around her mother's eyes. Sen didn't remember the creases from before, but that was ten years ago. Her mother was a young woman. Had Haru's death aged her?

Sen stepped back and bowed, then glanced at the threshold. Her throat tightened. Yes, the place did feel empty.

"What is it?" her mother asked.

"I miss Haru. It's going to be different."

Her mother smiled. "So do I, my daughter, but home is still home. Haru will always be with us."

Her mother's words lightened the load on Sen's spirits. She removed her shoes in the *genkan* and stepped into the house.

She stared at her mother again. The woman was still beautiful. Her black hair was tied in a bun. Her eyes sparkled with more tears that outshone the green kimono she wore. Her mother was of average height. Sen was only a few inches taller but seemed like a giant compared to her.

Sen raised her hands slightly to give her mother a hug but stopped and returned them to her sides. Her lips pursed and grew into a wide smile. "I have missed you." Her voice nearly broke as she said it.

Her mother reached up and cupped Sen's cheeks, then gave her a long hug. "It is good to see you," she said in the same voice that had always reassured Sen as a child.

Sen cleared her throat. "Where's Father?"

"Tidying up a little more. He and his apprentice have worked hard since early this morning."

Apprentice? In her sorrow, she had forgotten. Haru's husband was not her father's only pupil. Another man had come to work for the family a few years after she had left. It was good that her father had someone else to teach. "A rush request?"

"Sen," her mother scolded in a playful tone, "your father crafts the finest blades. Have you forgotten the time this requires? Now come help me in the kitchen. We're serving dinner in ten minutes."

She headed to the kitchen, becoming again the little girl who used to follow her mother around, and assisted her with last-minute preparations. Thoughts of duty receded as they prepared the individual trays.

Sen's mother headed to the door that faced the workshop. "Your daughter is home and dinner is ready. What are you waiting for, you old goat?"

Sen laughed at her mother's words, the teasing that made home wonderful. Then the laughter subsided. She stared at her father as her mouth opened and more childhood memories flooded back, along with more tears.

Then her gaze fell upon his apprentice, the man behind her father. The man who'd saved her from falling at the castle. The man she'd been thinking about for two days.

She froze. "Oh!"

Nobuhiro appeared equally stunned. "Sen?"

"What?" Sen's father smiled as his eyes grew large. "No greeting for your father?"

Sen looked back at her father and glowed inside at the sight of him. She hurried over and bowed low, clasping her hands as she rose. "It is good to see you, Father. I have missed you very much."

"And I, you." He grasped her hands in his and held them tight. "You have been gone much too long. Welcome home!"

He reached over and brushed away a tear, then

stepped back and glanced at Nobuhiro. "It would seem you two know each other."

She looked down as her face warmed and she rubbed her nose. *He's here?* She then faced the two of them. "We've met. He was at the castle two days ago."

"Yes." Nobuhiro's face turned red. "I was delivering a ceremonial sword your father crafted."

She smiled. The coincidence she'd discarded on the castle grounds now rang true. "So, you're the . . . " She swallowed the words *other apprentice*. Another reminder that Haru and her husband were gone. "You're the man my parents wrote about. You've been studying here for a long time."

"It takes years to learn this craft. Your father is the best at what he does."

"And he's learning well," her father added. "He's progressing even faster than I did at his age."

She nodded, afraid to say much more. Being a swordsmith required painstaking attention. If Nobuhiro possessed the patience for the craft, he wasn't deserving of his father's disdain. However, now that Nobuhiro's father knew the name of his youngest son's employer, could it ruin her father's business? How much time remained on his apprenticeship? The sooner he moved on and opened his own business, the better.

The business was only part of it. Nobuhiro's father knew about her faith, the faith she adopted while serving Lord Akamatsu. Sen's parents weren't Christian. Could her beliefs impact her family just as Lord Akamatsu's beliefs had led to the loss of his castle? How could she express duty to family and faith if her religion could cause her parents to lose everything? She rubbed her fingers under the neckline of her kimono, feeling her scars. Two reminders of the choice she had made and how she had been spared.

Might her parents one day have to make a choice between their own lives and Sen?

Chapter Three

Nobuhiro bit his lip and stared at the floor while Master Goami's wife removed the serving trays, the clicking of the lacquer disrupting the conversation. Nobuhiro had met Sen only two days ago, and had thought of her constantly since. Blast Toshi and his ridiculous proverb this morning about a samurai "being aware of his surroundings." Couldn't he have told him who Sen was? Mentioned she was coming tonight? Maybe Nobuhiro could have prepared. Had something to say.

His nerves pricked at him like a heated blade. Why did she have to be Master Goami's daughter? If she had just been a castle servant, he would have never seen her again. He should leave and allow them to enjoy the rest of their family reunion.

"Excuse me," Nobuhiro said, placing his weight on his right foot so he could stand. He worked to not look at Sen. "I . . . I need to go. I left the workshop in disarray. I should go clean it."

"Please, Nobuhiro. Sit down." Master Goami's tone was a polite command. "The workshop is fine. We put everything away."

Nobuhiro paused and then continued to rise. Sweat flowed down his neck and back, disappearing into the white kimono he wore underneath his brown one. He tried to slow his breathing. Slower breaths. Lower tension. Then no nervous stutter. He raised his head toward Master Goami. Anything to avoid looking at Sen. Anything to hide his thoughts. Though Master Goami, discerning Nobuhiro's feelings, wouldn't be much better. "My room needs attention. I should address it."

"Nobuhiro." The old man's tone carried a calm rebuke. "My wife made a favorite treat of Sen's to welcome her home. This is a celebration for us. Besides, you didn't eat much at dinner. I'm sure you're still hungry."

Yes, he was, but he always left dinner a little hungry. When he was younger and had just started as an apprentice, he ate his fill. A product of living on the street after he'd run away. Then he discovered that Master Goami's wife often made additional rice after he went to bed. The rice provided an early-morning snack when he started his morning chores in the workshop. If he didn't overeat at dinner, she didn't have to work late in the kitchen.

A treat did sound good though. He drew a light breath through a closed mouth. "Th . . . that sounds delicious, but—"

"Please stay." Sen looked at him with soft eyes. "I would love to hear about your family. And maybe you could tell me some stories about my parents, things they wouldn't mention on their own. You've known them better than I have these last few years."

He returned her gaze. Her beautiful face was round, almost moon shaped, which showed more distinctly when she smiled. Her black hair, pinned up in the usual style when he met her, was now drawn back tight but then swept over with tendrils resting on each of the shoulders of her greenish-blue kimono. His resolve melted like steel in a furnace.

"Thank you for asking," he said, bowing slightly as he tried not to lose his balance. "I will stay."

Granted, he couldn't have moved if he'd wanted to. When she'd asked him to remain, it was as if his heart reached down and tied his feet in place. The only direction he could go was back to his spot on the floor. He knelt, sitting on the backs of his feet briefly before finally shifting to a cross-legged posture.

Soft footfalls announced the return of Master Goami's wife from the kitchen. She carried a tray of pastries in one hand and a pot of tea in the other. The tray was covered with small plates of various pounded rice cakes filled with sweet bean paste. She offered them to all, then refilled the teacups, and placed the teapot over the hearth in the center of the floor.

"Itadakimasu," everyone said with a nod of thanks toward Master Goami's wife.

Nobuhiro brought the bamboo cup to his lips and paused as the steam from the liquid rose and kissed his face. Sen. What could he say to impress her? Anything? He rubbed his fingers lightly across the lacquer and wished his words were as smooth as the wood, but he had never been good at conversation. He inhaled the tea's bitter scent, hoping it would prod his thoughts. Nothing came to mind. He drank a swallow and then took a bite of the rice cake, as if the mix of flavors would provide a similar complexity to his thoughts.

"Nobuhiro," Master Goami said, "please open the door and let in some air."

Nobuhiro walked over and slid open the door, staring out the back at the garden. Maybe it would provide him with inspiration, but the moon had yet to rise and he could barely see the grounds. The chill from the breeze mixed with the sweat on his neck, slowing the flow down his back into a cold trickle. He shrugged his shoulders, wiping the back of his neck with his kimono. The nights were still chilly. What must it have been like on Sen's return to Himeji?

"How w . . . was your journey coming back?" he asked. "I would have thought it dangerous. Aren't there bandits along the roads between here and Haibara? Wouldn't they have taken advantage of a woman t . . . traveling alone?"

Sen laughed a little and glanced away. The tension in his chest dropped through his body. It must have been an ignorant question. He felt as lame with his tongue as he was with his foot. Another way he didn't measure up to his brothers. They had war stories to tell and could regale others with them. Toshi could chat easily with anyone. Uji could intimidate people with a glance but ease them with a smile. Both could converse with people in any strata of society, rare even for samurai.

The best Nobuhiro could do was ask about her trip home. Foolish words at best. There were many samurai at the castle who could relate similar tales like his brothers. The only thing Nobuhiro knew about was working in the shop, stories similar to what Sen heard growing up. His life story was diminished by his brothers in his family and by Master Goami in her family. If any samurai at the castle ever showed an interest in Sen, Nobuhiro wouldn't have a chance.

A glimpse of Sen's eyes pulled him back to the present. He came back to his place on the floor and returned Sen's gaze.

"I didn't travel alone." Her smile eased his heart. "My former master, Lord Akamatsu, and his wife were headed to Hokuriku. He received word the regional governor there would accept his services. He and his wife provided me safe escort back to Himeji and then continued on their journey."

He sat up straight and steepled his fingers. "Hokuriku? Then he aligns himself with Lord Tokugawa?"

She tilted her head and conveyed a quizzical gaze. "You show the interest in politics I would expect of someone with your lineage."

Lineage. Another family reminder. Given how his

father treated her at the castle that day, it couldn't be a pleasant reference. But yes. He'd learned politics at his father's side. One should be mindful of the travels of well-known, high-level samurai. Others might not follow in body, but their allegiances sometimes did. Lord Akamatsu's followers would always remember.

Nobuhiro glanced over at Master Goami, who smiled but said nothing. Master Goami cared not for politics. He would likely end the discussion soon. Nobuhiro turned back to Sen, who now seemed to be avoiding his glances as much as he had tried to avoid hers earlier. Still, he could at least discuss the topic with intelligence. "If Lord Akamatsu went to Hokuriku, then it implies his support for Lord Tokugawa. Don't you agree?"

Sen shut her eyes briefly and he held his breath as he waited for her to open them. She was beautiful.

"I don't know if he aligns himself with anyone," she said, "other than doing what he needs to do to care for his family and staying true to his beliefs."

His beliefs? Lord Akamatsu was one of the leaders who'd embraced this new religion. He'd surrendered his castle rather than recant. Did he think he could practice his faith freely elsewhere? "Lord Tokugawa might not allow that."

"Though the governor of Hokuriku has ties to Lord Tokugawa, Lord Akamatsu feels he is far enough away there that neither Lord Tokugawa nor Regent Toyotomi would care to notice. Besides, Regent Toyotomi rules the country. He even has the support of the emperor, does he not?"

Nobuhiro wiped his hands on his thighs, rubbing his fingers into the hemp fabric of his kimono. Unfortunately, it didn't absorb like the cotton one underneath. He glanced at Master Goami, who seemed to be enjoying both his tea and the discussion. Odd. Why hadn't he changed the subject? "Having the emperor's support doesn't mean he has the support of Lord Tokugawa. Lord Tokugawa's only loyalty is to himself. As a child, he was a hostage of the regent's predecessor, Lord Oda Nobunaga, when Lord Oda was only a regional governor. As an adult, Lord Tokugawa helped bring Lord Oda to power. Lord Tokugawa even sealed the alliance by executing his own wife and ordering his own son to commit suicide."

Sen stared at Nobuhiro. "Then why didn't Lord Tokugawa take power when Lord Oda was killed?"

Nobuhiro's memory thinned. It was at this point in his life that he'd decided to run away. His father and brothers had been away, fighting. Nobuhiro had left before they returned. Since then, he'd lived on snippets of news from travelers. "When Lord Oda was betrayed and committed seppuku, Lord Tokugawa was away from home. It took many days to avoid the assassin's samurai and return home. By the time Lord Tokugawa reached his forces, Lord Toyotomi had exacted revenge on the traitor and brought himself to power. Now, Lord Tokugawa bides his time and awaits another opportunity."

"So you believe Lord Akamatsu's move changes things?"

No. Little would change with Lord Akamatsu's move. However, Nobuhiro craved to discuss it with his brothers. What did they know? He leaned forward, placing his forearms on his legs. "Lord Akamatsu was always loyal to Lord Toyotomi. If Lord Tokugawa moves against Lord Toyotomi or his successor, people will assume Lord Akamatsu has changed his own alliances."

Sen shook her head. "The governor in Hokuriku has offered refuge to several former Christian daimyos. Lord Akamatsu accepted. However, his only alliance is to Christ."

Christ. The simple, defined way Sen said that name, without hesitation or reservation, came across with conviction. She'd been through a lot prior to returning to Himeji. Did the faith that drove Lord Akamatsu to renounce his lands also motivate Sen? Nobuhiro stared at his last bite of rice cake.

"Y . . . you are a *Kirishitan* then?" he asked. Timidly.

Was he afraid of the answer?

Sen flinched and then took a breath as if steadying herself. The word had stung. She peeked left and right at her parents. Master Goami's wife was looking down and away. Master Goami's smile had evaporated, replaced by hunched shoulders and a blank stare. Sen's gaze drew Nobuhiro's attention back to her. "Yes, I am a Christian."

Every muscle in his stomach trembled. "B . . . but the regent's edict from last year?"

"Yes, I know." Sen rubbed the neckline of her kimono. "But I cannot change my decision."

Nobuhiro's mouth opened and he struggled to breathe. It would have been simple for Sen to renounce her beliefs. Some Christians had. What about this faith pushed its true believers to make the choices they did? A sense of right and wrong? "A brave decision. I'm impressed." The words sounded hollow.

"Thank you."

He rubbed his chest slowly, but the tension remained. "What if the regent knew?"

Sen laughed and it brought back that smile. "I doubt the regent will concern himself with someone as low as me. Lord Akamatsu was made an example because of his status."

Maybe, but commoners can die as an example, too.

"Let's not discuss this anymore," Master Goami interjected. "No regent. No politics. Just family."

"Yes, Father," Sen said. "I'm sorry."

"My apologies, Master."

Nobuhiro's cheeks tightened and he looked back at Sen, losing himself in her eyes. Her decision to stay a Christian was admirable, but was it wise? He drummed his fingers softly on his knees. Were his master and his wife concerned with Sen's decision? Even if not enforced, Toyotomi's edict had already cost people their land and homes.

What if the edict was carried out more forcefully? Would Sen lose her position at the castle? Would Master and his wife be forced to turn her out? It wasn't his place to broach this, but this family had cared for him for seven years. He owed them a debt he couldn't repay.

"Nobuhiro," Master Goami said.

Nobuhiro shook his head as his cheeks warmed. Master Goami's direct gaze bored into him. "Yes, Master?"

"I just remembered I do have things that need taking care of tonight." The old man's eyes glanced in the general direction of the workshop. "I need your assistance. Come."

"Yes, sir."

As Nobuhiro had long expected, Master Goami was finally ending the evening. He must be getting him away so his wife could discuss this religion with Sen. Nobuhiro chewed his lip. He'd thought of protecting this family and he'd overstepped his place. He had shamed himself. One more anchor of shame weighing on the boatload he already carried. Sen's charms had mesmerized him. He regretted his behavior. Master Goami would address it in his time. Not Nobuhiro's.

He smiled at Master Goami, trying to hide his sheepishness. It was for the best. She was beautiful, but she was a Christian.

It was not a good match.

Retainers were the main customers of swordsmiths. Men such as his father and brothers viewed a swordmith's workshop the same way they viewed a Buddhist temple. How would they view a swordsmith in a relationship with a Christian? He had spent these last seven years trying to make his father proud. To prove that he could be of service to people like his father, Uji, and Toshi. Even if Nobuhiro himself couldn't fight, he could produce great swords for samurai. His father would one day see his contributions as beneficial.

Not likely. Christian retainers were no longer welcome under Toyotomi. How would it affect his father and brothers if a member of their own family, even an ostracized one, was involved with a Christian? What would his father think if he knew Nobuhiro's feelings?

###

Sen placed her thumbs under her neckline, running them along the scars and assuring herself that they were still covered. She had spent the evening in fear. She wasn't ready to talk. Her parents wouldn't understand.

Her father and Nobuhiro rose and left the room, Nobuhiro walking a couple of steps behind in a show of respect. His limp, so noticeable at the castle, was still there. However, here, Nobuhiro's steps were light. At the castle, Nobuhiro walked as if he'd been carrying a bag of *tamahagane* steel. She listened for movement as they crossed the garden area and entered the workshop. As a child, she could hear it when her father worked late. However, there was no sound, save that of a few night birds.

"Sen. Stop staring. They won't return anytime soon."

A rush of heat warmed her cheeks as she looked at her mother. "I wasn't staring. I was just thinking about my days here when I was a little girl."

"Oh, yes. I suppose you're next going to tell me you enjoy spending your free time doing laundry or something else equally ridiculous."

Her mother's comments unsettled her, but she didn't know why. "What do you mean? I don't understand."

Her mother didn't answer at first, instead taking the teapot from its hook over the hearth and refilling her cup. She took a sip and paused, also staring at the door, before turning back to Sen. "Well, at least you're listening to me now. Because you might have talked to your father and me tonight, but your eyes were never on us."

Had she been that obvious? Sen rubbed her thumbs together, trying to massage the kinks that had suddenly appeared. "I still don't understand."

"No? I have known you since you were born. When you're nervous, you massage your thumbs."

"I do not."

"You have done so since you were a child." Her

words came in staccato tones. Her mother was right, but not completely. How could she explain?

"I'm not nervous about Nobuhiro."

Sen's mother tilted her head as her eyes softened in that "mother-child" supportive gaze. "I never said you were nervous about your father's apprentice. You like him. That's obvious. But you're also distracted. What's troubling you?"

"Nothing." Sen looked away, trying to shield her face, but her mother's stare bored into her head like the sounds of cicadas in summer. She couldn't escape it. If only she could just delay it for another day.

"I had no sake with my dinner. Like I said, you can't hide your feelings from me."

Sen again tried to look away but felt the soft touch of her mother's hand on her shoulder. Still, she wasn't ready to talk. "There's nothing troubling me."

Her mother pulled her shoulders lightly and brought Sen around to face her. "You can't tell me that and expect me to believe you." Her words were even and soft.

Sen sighed. There was no hiding anything from the woman who could look inside her as easily today as she did ten years ago. The only thing. How to explain it to her. "I'm worried about my duty."

"What duty is that?"

Why was Mother pretending not to know? Why was Sen hesitating? On the trip home to Himeji, she voiced her fears to Lord Akamatsu and his wife. It was through their benevolence that she returned home. But what would her mother think?

"I need to find a husband. Someone who can take care of our family."

"You've been in town only two weeks. I know some women who've been looking for suitable husbands for their daughters for several years now."

Sen laughed at her mother's joke, though the truth struck her gut and tightened it. She stared back. "I don't want an arranged marriage."

"That's fine." She flashed a quick smile. "At your age, an arranged marriage would be difficult anyway."

Sen's entire body tensed. Her mother's jokes rarely intended harm. Yet this one hurt. The challenge was hard enough. Why did she have to mention age? "I'm not that old."

"No, but you've never been married. Other families will suspect something is amiss with you. I would in their place."

Another truth. She was right. She was always right. Still, an arranged marriage would have been problematic. She opened her mouth to respond, but her mother cut her off.

"Your father's apprentice is a nice young man. He has older brothers and will inherit nothing. Such men always marry into families with no sons."

"You make marriage sound like a market transaction." Sen regretted her words but couldn't retract them. Her mother had been through much of late. She was thinking of the family, too. Hopefully, talking about this would ease some of her pain.

"Any new apprentice would likely be much younger than you. Nobuhiro is already your father's apprentice. He works hard and would make a good husband. That should suit you, given how much you stared at him. And he at you."

Back to him again. Not that he'd ever left her thoughts. "I know he's nice, but he's not the right one."

"What *do* you want then?"

Sen paused as memories of the meeting at the castle and Nobuhiro's father came back to her. His charge to her to mind her place. Nobuhiro's father could ruin her family. Even if he accepted Nobuhiro, it wouldn't change anything. Sen's mother meant well, but she needed to tell Mother now. "I want to find a good Christian man to marry and grow old with."

Her mother stared back at her, her tongue wetting her lips like a whip preparing to sting. "While you're at it, would you mind asking for several bushels of rice to fall from the sky tomorrow? I could trade it and find someone to do my daily chores for a couple of years and we'd have enough left to add on to your father's workshop."

"Mother, please be serious."

"That's asking a lot of me."

Admittedly, Sen always loved her mother's quick sarcasm. The last few exchanges reminded her of why she'd rarely traded words with her growing up. She always lost. "My apologies."

"So, how might you do this?" Sen's mother moved next to her.

"Somewhere there are Christians meeting locally, if in secret. I must find them. I could meet someone that way."

Her mother paused, likely weighing her words. "This is a dangerous idea. I agree that there are groups about. It is foolishness to look for them."

"Yes, but you must have some idea, don't you?"

Sen's mother hesitated. She pursed her lips and wrinkled her forehead but didn't respond.

"Mother?"

She scratched her nose. "I've heard nothing."

"That's not true. You do know something."

Sen's mother turned away as if she were the one trying to hide. Sen could no longer see her face, but her response was clear. "Yes, I've heard rumors."

Sen turned to look her in the eye. She grabbed both her mother's arms. "Tell me. Please."

"No, I cannot." Sen's mother shut her eyes and turned away.

"Why?"

"What if the regent's men find out? You work at the castle. The samurai there must follow the dictates and enforce the ban. What will they do to you? What if the regent decides to take harsher penalties against Christians? Lord Akamatsu survived because of his position. You won't be so lucky."

"I need to know."

"No. You do not. I lost one daughter tragically. I will not lose another to this foolhardiness. This religion is dangerous. Following it over your duty to family shows you're only concerned about yourself."

Her mother's words hit Sen like a punch in the stomach. This wasn't sarcasm. Pushing harder was futile for now. "I didn't mean to upset you."

Sen's mother didn't acknowledge the apology. Instead, she maintained her irritated tone. "Your futon is ready in your old room. You should get some sleep. You will need to rise early tomorrow to return to the castle."

"Mother," Sen said, raising her voice. Her eyes teared up.

Her mother breathed deeply and sighed. "Sen, it is our first time to see each other in years. Let's not end a wonderful night this way. For your mother's own heart, let's end this peacefully."

Her mother's disapproval tore at Sen's heart. Her throat muscles constricted, blocking any response but respect for her mother's wishes. She stood and bowed, her hands shaking. "Yes, Mother."

Sadness coursed through Sen's veins when her mother didn't respond. The silence stung, as if Sen had been struck with flat bamboo.

Her mother grasped Sen's hands in her own. "My daughter, my concern is only for you. You're all I have left. Do not push this search. If you want to satisfy duty, then reconsider Nobuhiro. Your father and I are fond of him. He will make you happy."

Sen swallowed back her response and smiled at her mother, who returned the smile. Then, Sen turned and walked silently to her old room, the one she'd shared with Haru for so many years. Shame enveloped Sen over the disagreement with her mother. She loved her mother and wanted her to know.

Yet the choice was stark. Serve her family or serve God. Taking either path meant denying herself.

Marrying Nobuhiro would offer the possibility of destroying both.

Chapter Four

Nobuhiro ambled over to the grounds on the east side, following the noise of the raucous crowds. Events had been going on all day, but the archery on horseback competition had brought out thousands from nearby villages outside Himeji.

His stomach churned as if he'd drunk foul barley water. When Master Goami had suggested this morning that Nobuhiro pick up a package at the castle, a ceremonial sword in need of repair, the possibility of seeing Sen again had raised his spirits. The possibility of running into his father had produced more dread than hope. The previous incident from two weeks ago had put his nerves on edge, raising them to the caution level that he took with hot blades.

The meeting to retrieve the sword was quick. So far, his father had not appeared. Were Nobuhiro's fears of running into him misplaced? No one had mentioned his father. Nobuhiro considered returning to the workshop. However, Master Goami had suggested that Nobuhiro take his time coming back so that he could enjoy the events. He wanted to. His brothers were competing. He hadn't seen them show off their skills since he lived at the castle.

He craned his neck and looked toward the sky, holding his hand to shade his eyes. It was about halfway through the hour of the sheep. A third of the day remained. He would stay for the chance to walk the grounds a few more minutes. The chance to see Sen again. Nobuhiro would risk his father's wrath.

When Sen had stayed at the house two weeks ago, he had hoped to see her in the morning before she returned to the castle, but he had been busy in the workshop. He had tried not to think about her. Only he couldn't. He had thought of her every day since she left.

A conch shell blast drowned out his thoughts and he quickened his pace to the staging area. Time for another contestant. A large *taiko* drumbeat sounded as a rider appeared from the left, galloping parallel to the crowd. He was dressed in light armor with blue and gray braiding. A square, yellow silk flag with the blue outline of the Toyotomi crest flew from the horse.

Childhood memories again roared back for the second time in as many castle visits. Horseback riding. It was one of the only activities in Nobuhiro's life where his limp didn't affect him. He had practiced this skill as a child. It was his favorite activity.

The archer drew his arrow and fitted it to his bowstring. Nobuhiro's hands clenched in recollection of his younger years, a time of harmony between himself and the bow. He stared as the contestant raised his bow and arrow over his head. Then, the contestant pulled back the string, brought both to eye level, and let the arrow fly at the small wooden target fifty yards away.

Perfect!

"Yes," Nobuhiro said, pumping his fist as the crowd erupted. He glanced around to see if anyone had heard him. He needn't have worried over the noise. He sighed and imagined himself back on a horse again, firing a bow. His father had shown him how to hold his posture and maintain his balance. His smiles had punctuated his progress.

Thoughts of a bygone day.

The only reason his father had shown him any respect or love at that time was because, for once, he was finally like his brothers. Did his father ever smile or show approval for anything else Nobuhiro did? Raw frustration surfaced, knotting his shoulders and spiking his insides, reminding him of why he had left. He balled his right hand into a partial fist on the part of the cotton cloth that wrapped the hilt. He had made the right choice.

He gazed over the form of the cloth-wrapped sword he held. Lord Kinoshita had selected Nobuhiro's teacher out of all the area swordsmiths to repair a battle-scarred blade that was the first sword owned by Kinoshita's father. The recognition brought honor to Master Goami's work and home. Maybe Nobuhiro could be known for such skill one day. For being the best swordsmith in Himeji.

"Brother, you are too pensive for this occasion. Wipe that somber look from your face. Enjoy the day."

His shoulders dropped as Toshi's familiar voice erased much of the anger that streamed through him. Nobuhiro turned and eyed Toshi's approach. He was clad in nondescript blue and gray braided armor, similar to what many other contestants were wearing. His grin was larger than usual.

"It's only that I'm thinking of old times," Nobuhiro said. "I imagined myself clothed in similar armor, showing my skill in front of cheering crowds. Representing Lord Kinoshita. Riding with my brothers."

"Yes, you were a natural with a bow. You're likely better than many of the contestants."

The praise warmed Nobuhiro, until his memories brought back a chill. Childhood practice sessions of perfection slammed to the ground the moment he alighted from a horse. A mounted samurai depended more on his arrows in battle than he did on his sword. He dismounted only when his quiver emptied. For Nobuhiro, being on the ground meant death. Quickly. And with little glory.

"Is he lost in his own thoughts again?" a deep voice asked. Uji approached, wearing the same armor as Toshi. Again, the tension that flowed through Nobuhiro dissipated in a sea of sibling recognition and pride in his brothers' accomplishments.

He scanned the simplistic braiding his brothers wore. "I would have thought the two of you would be dressed more finely," he said. "Some of the contestants are wearing a lot of regalia."

Uji shook his head softly in that little-brother-you-have-a-lot-to-learn way. He had done it often when they were young. Nothing had changed now that they were adults. "Such armor is only for show. Cumbersome dress armor would never be worn in battle."

"Besides, it weighs down the horse," Toshi added. "And Uji's horse has enough to carry as it is."

Nobuhiro laughed. Hard. Uji spit daggers with his eyes at Toshi, whose quick wit and sarcasm had long been a bane to both Uji and their father. Nobuhiro missed this most of all.

Toshi used his wit to mask his feelings. Also for protection. As a child, when others made fun of Nobuhiro's infirmity, Toshi was the one who defended him and let others know to keep their criticism silent. Nobuhiro appreciated it back then. However, he dreamed of the day that he could defend himself.

Uji and Toshi exchanged glances, and Uji tilted his head toward the staging area. Toshi nodded and then both turned back to Nobuhiro.

"We both compete in the next group in ten minutes," Uji said. "Stay and watch. We'll try to make you proud before you leave."

Nobuhiro grinned as the two of them strolled away. Make him proud? The comment echoed like a cracked temple bell. He was jealous of his brothers' talents, and he admired them. Could Nobuhiro ride as well as he used to do? One of his neighbors, a man older than Master Goami, owned a horse. Nobuhiro helped the old man care for it, even riding it sometimes. He would never compete like his brothers had today. He would have welcomed the chance to test his skill, though. Only with a bow had he been his brothers' equal.

He walked to the far left of the field, where the next round of contestants prepared. Uji was right. Few contestants were regaled in fine armor. Most wore the same nondescript attire his brothers did.

Glancing around at the crowd, he saw many people staring and waiting for the next contestant. Yet, a lone figure, a graceful woman in yellow, drew his eyes as she moved away.

Sen.

Her pale kimono matched the cheerfulness of both her and the season. He wanted to call out and get her attention, but it wouldn't have been appropriate. His throat swelled as he watched her, making it impossible to call out to her anyway. He gazed at her as she headed toward the western part of the grounds.

"Brother, turn around or you're going to miss it," Toshi called out as he rode past. A pit grew in his stomach. Had Toshi seen him looking at Sen? Just what he needed. Toshi would torment him later, though with a smile. Nobuhiro wheeled back to enjoy the show. There was nothing he could do now.

The competition proved amazing. Both brothers performed well, but one contestant, whom Nobuhiro didn't recognize, was an expert marksman. Toshi's chances fell after round two. Uji followed in round three. The marksman survived to face winners from other groups.

"Who was that?" Nobuhiro asked when his brothers came to see him.

"Michiba," said Uji. "He's the most accurate of us all, though Nishioji is nearly his equal."

Nishioji.

Nobuhiro's blood raced through his veins like a bear chasing its prey. He didn't recall a Michiba from when he'd been here before. Such skill was the result of years or practice. He would have noticed.

Nishioji he remembered, though. The bully had taunted him about his walk. About his inability to be a samurai. He had pushed Nobuhiro into the mud more than once and then laughed at him. The times his father had seen him afterward, he claimed he had slipped so he wouldn't have to admit his inability to defend himself.

"*Sakichi. Sakichi.*" Toshi's voice cut through the grime of Nobuhiro's thoughts.

"Sorry. Yes?" Nobuhiro asked.

"Thanks again for coming to see us. Before you go, you should see the west side of the grounds. The blossoms still linger there."

Nobuhiro winced but kept his lips closed as he nodded. Toshi *had* seen Sen. And he knew Nobuhiro had seen her, too. The name Toshi meant *alert*. He didn't miss anything.

Nobuhiro said his goodbyes and ignored his brother's advice, at least for a few minutes. Instead, he enjoyed the various games and demonstrations at the nearby booths. The most captivating was a candy maker who impressed children and parents alike. The man shaped candy to resemble horses and put the pieces on thin skewers. The joy on the children's faces was amazing. Family was important. Children spending time with parents. That was how it should be.

One day, he would be a parent. He would be a real father, unlike his own father. He would not be a failure.

But what woman would ever want him? Not to mention Sen. She could have any man she wanted.

Yet most men in the castle were watching the festivities.

Sen was headed to the west side of the grounds. Alone

Toshi had advised him to go to the west side. That was a place to start.

He was going to take Toshi's advice. Regardless of its futility.

###

Sen headed for her favorite place, the spot near the wall with the cross tile. A roar erupted from the other side of the grounds and she twisted her neck to listen. Someone must have hit a good shot in the competition. The event would last until dusk. No one would leave to walk around the grounds now.

The festivities of the last official day of cherry blossom viewing were fun, but she needed a respite. She seldom got the chance to come here. The warning from Nobuhiro's father wrapped an invisible mud wall around her every time she got close to the cross. Today, no one would notice her absence.

A light breeze cut across her face, a reminder to enjoy the spring weather before April gave way to months of humidity. The breeze carried the scent of the blossoms. The fragrance graced her nose and she inhaled it. How? She didn't know. Omi was right. Sen shouldn't be able to smell them, but for some reason their fragrance seemed strong to her. The blossoms smelled of life. Their time was short, but they brought beauty to the world while in bloom. People should do the same.

If only Mother thought so.

When she saw her mother at breakfast the next day, Sen didn't mention Christians out of respect for her mother. Breakfast had been pleasant, with one exception: she did not see Nobuhiro before she left.

Her mother was right. He was a handsome man. His smile brought Sen joy. At dinner, she had put her concerns aside, at least for the moment. No worry of duty. No worry of the troubles that brought her back home.

Still, he was not a Christian. That was a problem.

Sen's mother did not want to discuss Christians. That was a problem.

Nobuhiro's father detested him. That was a problem for all.

Another roar sounded in the distance and she looked around again. No one was near. Part of her wished to return and watch, but she needed to be by herself.

Sen's conversation with her mother reverberated in her head, like the thuds she remembered when her father used large hammers to fold his swords. She was missing something. What was it?

Did her mother believe Christians were dangerous? Or was it something else? What was she holding back? Her mother had reproved Sen for her decision. Why would her mother deny her that?

Because she was scared.

Sen's mother mentioned Haru's death as if she were afraid what happened to her might happen to Sen because of her faith. Sen had survived that day in Haibara, but many had survived that day. The regent hadn't executed Christians for their beliefs anywhere else. He just wanted to make an example of Lord Akamatsu.

Yet friends had died in Haibara. Sen glanced down at the ground as she touched her neck. Why had God allowed her to survive?

"Hello, Sen."

She shook her head as she perked up her ears at Omi's familiar voice. She had looked for her this morning, but Omi had risen early. "Hello, Omi. How are you?"

"I'm well. I was looking for you over at the competition. I finally realized I'd find you here."

"Why?" she asked, puzzled by how Omi had located her.

"You're always here." She paused and glanced at the wall. "You seem to like the view."

Sen laughed as she stared at Omi, her black hair pulled tight with a red scarf that allowed people to enjoy her striking facial features. Many thought her somewhat empty headed. However, with her manners and her upbringing she was well-cultured with an understanding of attire, protocol, and place. It made her the favorite staff member of the court ladies.

Sometimes, she would show people that she had a sharp brain, which caught the attention of several of the samurai. But if Omi had figured out Sen's habits, then others likely had as well. Lord Akamatsu had instructed Sen to keep her faith secret. If she kept coming here even when duty didn't call for it, people might suspect it was for more than just the scenery.

"Yes, I do like it here," Sen finally answered.

"It's better than the view near the haunted well," Omi commented.

At the mention of Okiku's Well, Sen inhaled as her body shrunk in fear and sadness, contemplating the fate of a beautiful young lady from over a century ago. Okiku, the maid of a retainer at the castle, foiled the retainer's attempt to overthrow the castle lord. In retaliation, the retainer charged her with thievery of one of ten family dishes. He tortured and killed her, and then tossed her body into the well. Castle residents often recounted times they had heard a woman's voice arise from the well, counting dishes and crying.

"Why were you looking for me?" Sen asked.

"Why do you think? The final round of the archery competition begins in twenty minutes. I thought we might watch it together."

"I'm surprised you left. Shouldn't you be there to cheer for Toshi?"

Omi's face reddened at the mention of Toshi's name, a name Sen would only use around Omi. Many men in the castle appeared interested in Omi, but she appeared to have her heart set on only one.

"I see." Sen leaned forward, full of understanding. "Does this mean he didn't survive?"

Omi smiled as if the words might choke her. "He . . . was eliminated. He is also embarrassed as Uji went further in the competition than he did. The final round will start shortly. We really should go see it."

Sen considered going back but was distracted by the movement of a solitary figure about thirty yards away. The figure limped slightly. Her heart skipped across the distance in an instant.

"Nobuhiro?"

He glanced back and her body tensed before melting into the afternoon heat. He carried a long, cloth-wrapped package. A sword, she presumed. She motioned him over.

"Nobuhiro? Your father's apprentice?" Omi asked. "You ask me questions about Toshi. I should do the same to you. Didn't you just meet him two weeks ago? Don't yell for him. You'll draw someone's attention. Besides, it's embarrassing."

"Be quiet," Sen fired back, though she didn't look at Omi to say it. Instead, she watched as Nobuhiro closed the distance between them. Thoughts of him now warmed her face, even more than the sun. As he approached, the limp seemed to disappear, as if he were floating toward her. What would she say to him? She had been callous the times they had met before. He deserved more respect.

"You weren't going to say hello?" she asked in a light manner that she knew Omi would tease her about later.

Nobuhiro acknowledged Omi with a nod and then looked at Sen. "Sorry. I saw the two of you and I didn't wish to interrupt."

"Don't worry." Omi said, and then introduced herself.

"You're not watching the festivities?" Nobuhiro asked, directing his question to Sen.

"I did for a while," she said. "It's exciting, but I grew tired."

"She's also over here for quiet time," Omi added.

"Quiet time?" Nobuhiro asked. The puzzled look on his face meant she'd have to come up with something.

"Yes, Omi says I come here often."

Sen said a quick, silent prayer, asking for forgiveness. She wasn't denying her faith. But when Nobuhiro had asked her at dinner if she was a Christian, she had hesitated. Thoughts of Peter and how he denied the Lord had rung through her head. She had then confirmed her faith.

Yet flaunting it would be foolish.

Fast-approaching hooves drew her attention, but she didn't see anyone coming. The fear etched on Omi's face made her turn around. Nobuhiro stepped next to her as if to protect.

One of the competitors from the event galloped toward them, his bow displayed. A mask covered the lower portion of his face. The rider pulled an arrow from his quiver and notched it in the bowstring. Her breathing grew shallow. She tried to move, but her feet froze. The rider brought the bow and arrow over his head, then brought it down as he pulled back on the string.

The arrow flew toward the three of them.

Chapter Five

Adrenaline coursed through Nobuhiro's veins as the twang of the bowstring echoed in his ears. He stepped forward and swung the sword in an arc. Cloth met wood. The sword deflected the arrow harmlessly to the side.

"Get behind me," he said.

His breath quickened to match his raging heartbeat. He had been lucky enough to stop the shot, but it wasn't over yet. He stepped in front of the women, placing himself between them and the rider, moving left and right to maintain the barrier as the rider shifted his horse side to side.

In battle, you must do big things to calm your nerves. This will allow you to do the little things correctly.

Where had Nobuhiro heard those words before? He winced as he identified the voice in his head.

His father.

Nobuhiro moved the sword from hand to hand as he tried to slow his breathing. To slow his heartbeat. He would need calm to survive.

He held the sword high and tried to appear menacing. Yet one man with a sword, a wrapped-up one, held little hope against a mounted warrior. He had to outthink him. Did he know who Nobuhiro was? Had he grown up at the castle? If not, did he notice Nobuhiro's limp?

Maybe on the first two questions. Probably on the third. The archer would aim at Nobuhiro's left side. He grasped the hilt with both hands and tried to distribute his weight evenly between his feet.

The masked man took out another arrow. He notched his bow and brought it over his head. The reins were tied taut to his chest.

"Single file. Get down. A little to the right. It will provide less of a target." He hoped the women would trust his judgment, but he couldn't afford to look back.

Steady. Steady.

The rider let the second arrow go. Nobuhiro swept another arc in front of himself. The bump told him he'd hit the arrow. The whoosh of air against his temple told him how close it had come. He held out his arms to steady himself, as his left leg couldn't support him. The extra weight of the cloths made the sword clumsy and unwieldy. However, he had been lucky.

He stared back at the rider, looking for signs that he might identify him from his childhood. Nobuhiro had followed many of the samurai and knew their children. Nothing registered. It was inconceivable that it could be one of his father's men.

The rider returned an intense glare, as if considering another attempt. Nobuhiro held his breath while moving the sword between his hands. Both hands then gripped the hilt.

The rider kicked his heels into the sides of his brown horse and rode off to the north side. A less guarded entrance. Nobuhiro took a step to get a better view as well as to look for signs he might return. Nothing.

Nobuhiro heaved a sigh.

He turned around to see the two women crouched down. "Are either of you injured?"

"I'm fine," Omi responded in loud breaths.

Sen said nothing. Her eyes and mouth were both wide open. He knelt to get her attention. "He's gone. I doubt he'll return. Are you hurt?"

Sen stared back and then nodded. Slowly. "I'm fine, too."

She was lying. The attack had shaken her, but she hid it well.

"We should report this attack," Nobuhiro said. "Can you move?"

Sen nodded again. "Yes. We should go."

He offered his hand to help her stand. She didn't move. Omi came to her side to assist her. Nobuhiro bit his lower lip as Sen stepped back, looking down at the ground. Had she been afraid to touch his hand? Whatever he was feeling, he needed to forget it. He had a bigger problem.

Reporting this incident meant he wouldn't be able to avoid his father.

The walk back to the festival grounds took a few minutes. They quickly found both Uji and Toshi. Nobuhiro's father arrived shortly thereafter. The creases in his face appeared to harden. Apparently, he welcomed this reunion as much as Nobuhiro.

Sen and Omi related their version of events. His father said little, his mouth thinning into a line. Then Nobuhiro gave his report. His father had many questions, as if looking for something Nobuhiro had missed. Nobuhiro breathed slowly through his nose. His eyes fixed on his father. He wouldn't give him the satisfaction of one unknown detail.

"Did you see what he was wearing?" His father brushed his sleeve with the backs of his fingers, as if that mattered more.

"He wore the blue and gray braid, the same that Uji and Toshi wore at the competition."

His father frowned. His eyes flared. "You will address your brothers with the proper respect. Is that clear?"

Nobuhiro swallowed his breath. "*Hai.*"

"Now then. You are certain you saw nothing but the standard braid?"

"That and the reins were tied to his chest."

The old man shook his head. "It could have been anyone then. Even those foolish enough to wear their dress armor for this competition would have worn something similar underneath."

Sen stepped forward, bowing slightly and shrugging her shoulders. "Tokoda-sama, was it definitely one of the competitors?"

Nobuhiro froze and stared at Sen. Most servants would have been afraid to address his father. His father was within his rights to dispatch Sen to her next life. Yet he only waved his hand dismissively, as if her question was as annoying as a buzzing gnat.

"It must be." His eyes glanced her way. "Only a samurai would have been trained in such arts. Anyone else would have fallen from his horse when he pulled back the bowstring."

"Could—"

The cold glance from his father silenced Sen. "You no longer serve Lord Akamatsu. He may have tolerated such impertinence. I. Do. Not."

Sen bowed low and stepped back, keeping her face pointed to the ground. Did she think warrior monks had entered the castle grounds in disguise? None could have done so on horseback. He concurred with his father. It had to be a samurai from the competition.

Still, his father would likely confirm later if anyone suspicious had been noticed on the grounds. Would it have pained him to acknowledge it now?

Nobuhiro tapped his good foot as his chest hardened. Curse the old man's arrogance.

His father stared at him and he looked directly back into the man's eyes. His foot stopped tapping. "How about the horse? Do you remember the color?"

Nobuhiro closed his eyes and replayed the attack in his head. "Brown, I think."

"You *think*?"

"Yes. It. Was. Brown."

His father rubbed the bare path of his own scalp. When he reached the topknot, his fingers tensed. Nobuhiro cringed, but his father's face went blank, despite the flame in his eyes.

"Distinguishing marks?" he asked after a pause, the intensity in his voice rising with the intonation. "Anything to help us identify who might have been riding the horse?"

Nobuhiro ground his teeth, but his cockiness at his actions against the horseman dissipated as he considered his father's question. The old man was right.

"No," he finally said. He breathed slowly. His pride had lost him the battle. He had been so focused on the rider. Looking at the horse? It hadn't occurred to him.

"Regrettable. It would have been . . . helpful."

His father's mocking tone steamed him like the effects of cooling water on a hot blade, erasing seven years in an afternoon. He was a chastised kid again. He vowed to remove that smug look from his father's face.

His father wheeled around and headed toward the entrance of the main armory. "If you *think* of anything else, let us know," he said without looking back.

Nobuhiro felt a reassuring pat on his shoulder. He turned and found Uji, smiling wide.

"Ignore him, little brother. You deflected two arrows with a cloth-wrapped sword. I wish I'd seen it. That must have been some display."

Nobuhiro's heightened tension from his father's derision melted in the praise. Yet, his father and brothers would have noticed more than he did. He had failed again. "He was right. I know horses. I should have paid attention to this one. I'm just relieved that it's over."

"You're too harsh with yourself. When Father has time to think about it, he will be proud of you, too."

"That's good to hear," Nobuhiro said. "In hindsight, though, maybe it wasn't that great an accomplishment."

"Why?" Uji asked, the muscles in his forehead

tightening.

"The archer wasn't that good. Both shots were high."

###

Sen concentrated on the attack again, hoping to remember something else that she could offer, but could think of nothing. She had been scared. Too scared to notice anything. Even safe now, her nerves danced like a rabbit hiding from a fox.

Nobuhiro had saved her.

She wanted to talk with him, to express her gratitude for what he had done. Instead, when he had offered his hand to help her up, she had been more scared than when they were under attack. Afraid to touch him. Afraid to hold his hand. Afraid that she wouldn't be able to let him go.

Nobuhiro and his brother chatted nearby. Their conversation must have ended with a joke, as both men laughed before Ujihiro strode off. How could Nobuhiro be so calm after what had just happened?

"Nobuhiro?" Sen said.

He walked over to her, more slowly than she remembered. His limp caused him trouble, but had he pulled a muscle as well? The laughter that had been there moments before was now gone. In its place was trepidation.

"Yes?" he asked.

"May I talk with you?"

His eyes widened as his body swayed and he shifted his weight back and forth. What concerned him? He had placed himself in danger. He had faced down a mounted archer. He had saved her life. What made him nervous now?

She ran her fingers over her cotton kimono and grasped at it for strength. "Thank you . . . for everything."

Nobuhiro looked around. "I'm relieved you weren't injured."

"Why did you do it? You could have been killed."

He stood straight and still, but his eyes hid passion. "I had to protect you. I owe your parents a debt. They've already lost one daughter. I saw their pain. I couldn't bear for them to lose a second child."

She paused, not knowing what to say. He had done it for her. For her family. For their survival. He had shown more duty to her family than she had. His face reddened and he scanned the room again, as if checking to see if anyone else was present. Sen followed his gaze but saw no one.

His eyes exhibited a rebuke. "You owe it to your parents not to take so many chances."

Chances. Sen didn't understand. Being on the castle grounds should be safe. "What do you mean?"

He leaned closer. "I saw the cross."

Air streamed across Sen's lips as she took in a breath, and her heart beat faster. First, Omi had discovered her habits. Now Nobuhiro had done the same with just one glance. She tried to speak but found no response.

His gaze didn't waver. "Whether there for good or ill, that cross is a trap for you. People here must know about it. It wasn't here seven years ago."

"Are you certain?" Sen shook her head.

He nodded with his eyes closed as if imitating a sage old man and then stared at her again. "Yes, I know every bit of this place. At least I did before I left. An unfortunate result of how slowly I move about. For your own protection and for the happiness of your parents, you should never go near that cross."

Sen reconfirmed that they were still alone. "That cross is a sign from my God. It brings joy to me."

"That cross should be removed." His tone mimicked the self-assurance of his father.

Her mouth tightened and sent tension through her body. "Removed?"

"The regent has outlawed Christianity. Images like that should be taken down."

Sen struggled to maintain a whisper as her throat constricted her words. "How can you say that?" A tear streamed down her face. "You know what it means to me.

My former master lost his lands. Friends of mine died for it."

Nobuhiro's stare remained unchanged. "Precisely the reason to remove it. It's dangerous."

Her eyes teared up and she swallowed hard. "Christians mean no one any harm."

His lips quivered. "I . . . I did not . . . " he sputtered, but that was all he got out.

She opened her mouth to lash out but choked on her own words. Finally, she looked away. "Please . . . leave me alone."

"I did not mean to upset you." He bowed as if that would make him seem more sincere. "I'm concerned for you. For your family."

Her body remained as tense as a drawn bowstring, but she didn't respond. She didn't care. She didn't want to talk to him anymore. She didn't want to see him. In the space of an hour, he had both protected her and insulted her. She rubbed the back of her neck to massage away the pain. It didn't help.

"Just go, please" she begged.

He turned and walked away. She watched him, then wiped away her tears after he left.

He was trying to protect her family.

He didn't deserve her condemnation.

Mother had recommended him as a perfect candidate for a husband. She could satisfy family duty if she followed her advice.

After today, though, she couldn't do that.

She reached up and rubbed the scars on her neck. They no longer bled as they first had months ago. Yet, Nobuhiro's words about the cross had left fresh marks on the emotional wound she had thought healed since leaving Haibara.

To marry Nobuhiro, as her mother had suggested, would not be true to her beliefs. Lord Akamatsu told her to trust in the Lord and He would guide her. Given Nobuhiro's words today, the path to marriage looked to be toward a man who not only didn't believe in Christ but who also thought Christianity a danger. This wasn't the path she had envisioned.

Nobuhiro's name meant *faith.*

How ironic that he had none.

Chapter Six

Kaiken paced in front of Michiba, wearing out the ground in a small circle. The samurai remained impassive, his hands resting on his swords. He didn't move or appear to breathe. The sign of a master samurai.

Being a master samurai was why Michiba had been recruited.

Today Kaiken had expected more.

Crickets chirped in the trees nearby, perforating the quiet of the night. The scent of grasses floated on the breeze, mixing with the light incense that scented Kaiken's kimono. Disappointment overrode both.

Kaiken fumed. "I watched the entire incident. You could have made it look better."

Michiba stared back. His eyes flashed disagreement. "It was sufficient. Any closer and the girl could have been hit. Dead, she is of no use to us. Given the miss, no one will suspect me."

"Still. You let Tokoda survive. Him we don't need. He was protecting a Christian. That marks him guilty."

"Killing him risks war with his brothers. They would never rest until they had their revenge. Neither would his father. I know the Tokodas. You should, too. Our activities would be nullified immediately.

Kaiken mulled over Michiba's words. He had been good counsel. He was the smartest of the group. Still, his actions lacked reason. "You fear them?"

"Any sane man would. Their familial bonds are strong."

"Boar snouts! The elder Tokoda would welcome his lame son's death. His youngest son disowned his heritage. He is an embarrassment."

"He may be estranged, but he's not forgotten. He wielded the sword well, as if he'd inherited his skill. He's definitely a Tokoda."

"Ridiculous. He had scant training as a child. No one can inherit this talent."

"Then he learned as he studied the craft of creation. He's as dangerous as any samurai."

Howls sounded in the distance, adding harmony to the crickets. Kaiken looked toward the stone walls that outlined the borders of the castle. Samurai patrolled the grounds, looking for signs of movement. Could Kaiken and Michiba be seen in the shadows surrounding the building? Attention would not be good. Roughly two more minutes and then a change of patrol. From there, they would have thirty seconds to depart without being seen. They had already been together too long.

"Kaiken, what are your orders then?" Michiba asked.

Asking for orders. Always a good samurai, despite his failure in the arrow attack. "We will meet at the burned-down structure one week from tomorrow. Pass the message to the others. Find a reason to be there."

"*Hai.*" Michiba nodded. "What will you do?"

"My duties allow me access to the woman. I am trying to get closer. She has no idea of my intentions. I will report next week."

Michiba grunted but said no more. They both turned to watch the guards change. Kaiken stared, unwilling to breathe. Wait. Wait.

"Now," Kaiken said.

Kaiken turned, hearing Michiba do the same in the other direction, his steps still audible on the ground.

If you fail me again, I will kill you myself.

###

Nobuhiro glanced constantly at the castle as he approached the market area. He tried to avoid looking, but it was useless. It was like viewing someone else's misfortune. An overturned cart. A sunken roof. You might simply watch. You might try to help. But no matter how sorry you felt for those involved, you couldn't stop staring.

But it was different this time. The disaster was his fault. The castle was his reminder.

It had been four days since the archery competition. Memories of Sen's anger and fear replayed in his mind. Her anger. Her tears. Her dismissal of him with a wave of her hand. It hurt more than when his father had done the same years before. Compared with the pain that still surged through him, jabbing himself with a sword would have been only minor.

Sen, can you forgive me for what I said? I was only thinking of your family.

He had heard that Sen's religion preached forgiveness. Apologies went a long way in salving wounds and saving face. Insulting someone's faith cut deep.

It was best to concentrate on finding that rider. If only he could remember more details. Would finding the attacker take away the pain? Until the attacker was caught, Sen was in danger.

Bumps from passersby brought him to back to the present. The crowd at the market was thick. He would trip if he wasn't careful. The wafting smells of fried octopus, eel, and baked sweet potatoes made his stomach growl. A snack to sustain him would be good. He rubbed his chest and confirmed that the string of coins was there. After the shopping. Duty first.

He headed to a stand of daikon radishes. A small crowd was already at the cart, but he could wait. A tap on his left shoulder startled him. He turned slowly around.

Toshi stood there, his usual smirk frozen in place. He had thought of some comment. Something sarcastic. Maybe Nobuhiro could force the subject and skip over it.

No. Probably not a chance.

"Brother, good to see you," Nobuhiro said.

Toshi nodded, his mouth widening. A playful insult was coming. "I see your techniques are improving. Your master has expanded your duties and you've been entrusted with shopping, though I don't understand how it relates to being a swordsmith. Maybe congratulations are in order. You've been promoted to being a woman."

Nobuhiro laughed for a few seconds. Toshi had probably noticed him earlier and had that comment rolling through his mind, waiting for the right time to irritate him. The laughter felt good and lifted his spirits.

"My master's wife has been ill for two days," he finally said. "I've been doing the shopping while he tends to her."

"I see." Toshi's face changed to somber as he nodded. "Have you remembered any more details on the attack?"

Nobuhiro shook his head. "None. Have you learned anything more yourself?"

"Uji explored something late last night. He woke me when he returned to the house, but I didn't have a chance to ask him."

"He woke you?"

"The floor howled in protest when he stepped on it. Shortly thereafter, I heard him snoring."

Nobuhiro chuckled, though silently this time. "How did you know the snore wasn't our father?"

"Father sleeps mostly at the castle now, buried in his work. I don't believe he has slept well since . . . since our mother passed. Work provides him a respite. Besides, he snores at a lower pitch than Uji does."

"Only you would notice."

A group of people jostled Nobuhiro from behind. A

quick bow between him and them offered the silent apology.

Toshi's grin returned. "I'm happy to see you. Do you have time for tea?"

"Unfortunately, no. I have to finish here in town and then get back to the shop."

"I spoke with Master Goami this morning. You have time."

Nobuhiro looked up at Toshi, expecting another smile but seeing none. "*You* talked with Master Goami?"

"Yes," he said, moving beside Nobuhiro and putting his hand on his shoulder, "and I requested a favor, one he was willing to grant me."

"You're a samurai. He wouldn't refuse you."

"Yes, but he wouldn't refuse a repeat customer either."

Nobuhiro's stomach jumped, and this time it wasn't due to the roasting vegetables nearby. He looked up and down the street, expecting what, he didn't know, but knowing something was coming. "A favor, you said?"

Toshi motioned to his left and Nobuhiro looked that way again. Nothing at first. He strained his eyes a few seconds more and his mouth dropped.

Sen.

She and Omi were headed in their direction, at least he thought it was her. Next to Sen, any woman seemed a blur. He glanced back at Toshi.

"You're trying to arrange a meeting for me?"

He paused, running his hand over his scalp. "What makes you think this arrangement is about you?" He waved his hand in the air, gesturing down the street. "I've been trying to get Omi away from the castle for a while. If Uji knew, he'd give me no end of grief."

Omi? So Toshi was interested in someone. Good. He had been single too long. It was time for him to settle down, though they would have to find a new house. Uji often commented that his wife had enough trouble dealing with Toshi by himself. "So you arranged this to see Omi?

How'd you know she'd bring Sen?"

Toshi chortled. "She thinks she's doing this to bring the two of you back together."

"That explains why you talked to Master Goami." Nobuhiro looked toward the women again. They were still distant. However, every step they made matched the hitches in his breath. He wanted to see Sen, but he wasn't ready for this.

"And you couldn't talk to Omi without my help?"

"I needed someone for Sen to talk to. Omi couldn't meet me alone. Too suspicious." Toshi slapped Nobuhiro on the shoulder. "Thanks for joining me. I appreciate it."

Nobuhiro groaned, both inside and out. He felt trapped like a crab in one of the nearby tanks. He could move a bit, but he wasn't going anywhere. Nobuhiro wasn't ready to see Sen again. Yet he saw her in his dreams.

The two women drew closer. He bounced lightly in his straw sandals, but the solid ground provided scant support to his squid-jelly legs. Several people in the crowded street passed in front of them, but it didn't obstruct his view.

Sen wore a plain yellow kimono with what looked to be birds decorating the front. Omi's was nearly the same. Both women wore geta, wooden shoes with blocks underneath. The shoes kept the dust off their feet. No one ever walked fast in them.

Nobuhiro tried not to stare at Sen. He couldn't help it. Her hair was pulled back tightly. The sun caught a lighter streak in her hair that dazzled him and accented the kimono she wore. The slow pace necessitated by the geta drew out the moment. Each step short. Each step measured. Each step synchronous with the beat of his heart.

My thoughts are nothing compared to being in her presence.

She probably didn't want to talk to him again, especially after his comments about her faith. Why had she agreed to come now?

Nobuhiro surveyed the stores, a line of one-story buildings with narrow fronts. Food. Farming tools. Cloth merchants. Umbrellas. The distraction didn't work. His thoughts were choppy. Like rice through a gristmill, Nobuhiro's husk was stripped away to reveal his feelings. His hands quivered. His body soon followed.

Then Toshi brought him out of it.

"Ah, perfect timing," he said.

"H . . . how can you call this perfect? I'm not ready for this." His voice shook in resonance with the rest of him.

"Simple, you haven't bought any fish yet for dinner."

###

A mother and her two girls crossed in front of Sen in the market area, bringing back memories of her childhood. She used to walk these streets with her mother. The city bustled with the same activity she remembered from then. As a child, she recalled the sounds and the people. As an adult, she noticed the clean streets.

It was a happier time then. A safer time.

Hopefully, with the crowd, it was safe now.

When Omi had asked Sen to join her in a trip to the market area, she had quickly agreed. She hadn't gotten out much since her return to Himeji, except for the visit to her parents. She looked down the street. Getting out was a good idea. People swarmed through the various businesses and side alleys. Traveling merchants, their money scales on their belts, negotiated with shop owners. Restaurant patrons sat along the low walls outside establishments as waitresses took their orders. Dogs yelped on both sides of the street, likely hoping for scraps from both careless and thoughtful eaters.

Sen wiped her brow, surprised at the perspiration that now dotted her head and fingertips. There was only one extra kimono underneath the one she wore, but it was still heavy. If only fashion allowed people to wear lighter clothes before May. Dressing to match the weather made sense on days like this.

Omi grabbed her arm. "Down there, on the left," she said, pointing. "There's a nice place to have tea."

Sen looked where Omi was pointing and wasn't sure at first. The throng of people blocked much of the view. "Where? I don't see any—"

And then there he was. In the distance. Standing with his brother.

Nobuhiro.

She had been set up.

Her heart pulled at her throat with the tension of a drawn bowstring. She couldn't face him. She scanned the other side of the street and gestured to the right. "I see another small shop over here."

"What?"

"This place over here. It looks fine."

Sen glanced at Omi, who ignored her and pointed in the direction Sen didn't want to go. "No, you must believe me. Down there is a great place. Oh, I see Toshi." Omi turned to Sen; her smirk completed her deception. "What's he doing here?"

"Yes, what's *he* doing here?" Sen glared back, letting Omi know she didn't believe her feigned surprise. Still, she was stuck. They both knew it.

The stroll toward the two men passed slowly and Sen fumed the entire way. She tried not to look at Nobuhiro, but her glances strayed to him and she couldn't prevent it.

As they drew closer, she allowed herself to acknowledge him. Light soot stains marked the collar and edges of his kimono. He'd worn these clothes under his ceremonial swordsmith robe. His face and hands were clean, but he had small black streaks on his arms.

His shirt was slightly open at the neck and she looked away so as not to stare. The labor in her father's shop was good exercise. Her father was a strong man. Seven years of similar work had made Nobuhiro the same. His smooth, bare chest showed the definition she had seen in many samurai. However, Nobuhiro appeared more powerful . . .

and handsome.

Put those thoughts aside, Sen, he's not the one for you.

She grimaced at the voice in her head. A slight breeze cooled her nerves but not the feelings within. Nobuhiro had large brown eyes and a cute round nose. He would attract attention from any lady.

"H . . . h . . . hello," he said. "It's good to see you."

That stutter. It arose every time they talked. Why was he nervous? His smile appeared forced, but she wasn't sure. Had he known this meeting was happening or had he been brought here like she was? She didn't have a chance to consider it as the men headed into the shop, expecting Sen and Omi to follow.

A light ring of metal drew her attention, and her gaze drifted to the hanging wind chimes at the entrance. She stopped and read the various blessings that hung on pieces of paper attached to the ends of the chimes. She reached up and fingered one of the metal pieces, feeling the raised writing. The character for "happiness." An omen for the relationship with her mother and for the resolution of her duty? She could hope.

"Is something wrong?" Omi asked.

"Nothing," Sen replied, gathering her distracted thoughts. "I just noticed these chimes and the blessings written on them. This restaurant must be a happy place."

Omi smiled. "Or at least it has good food."

The two laughed and headed in. Windows were open inside, but the heat from the hearths on the floor made the place warm. Tapping their feet, the brothers stood at an open area on a platform that was set aside from the rest of the place. It appeared to be reserved for important people. The owners recognized Toshi's samurai status, which afforded him and his guests a place of honor. Sen and Omi quickened their pace and sat down on the cushions on the tatami mat floor, the men on one side and the women on the other.

Sen swallowed hard as Nobuhiro sat down directly

across from her. At other tables, people were enjoying themselves. Why couldn't she do the same? She rubbed her thumbs, pulling at them. Yet no delays, distractions, or silent prayers would quell the hot rush that hit her face.

The waitress took the order and returned shortly, carrying four dishes. The woman put the first two plates down before the men, then circled around to serve Omi and Sen.

As the waitress bent down, she lost control of her tray, sending two bamboo plates flying. Sen flinched to avoid them.

She needn't have bothered. Both Toshi and Omi extended a hand quickly, each catching a plate.

"Amazing! How did you do that?" Sen asked.

"I'm a samurai," Toshi responded.

Omi smiled. "Just fortunate."

Sen nodded. She expected such from Toshi. Omi's quickness surprised her. Another reason she drew interest from men like Toshi. She glanced across the table. Nobuhiro's gaze remained down. What troubled him? Her resolve against him tempered as she wanted to ease the unknown pain he exhibited. Did being with his brother relax him or did it remind him of the life he wished he had? Did it remind him of his father's rebukes?

She tried to be disinterested.

She failed.

###

Sometimes, Nobuhiro couldn't stand his brothers.

His nerves pulled at him and flattened his stomach. He desired to impress Sen, to make her see him as an alternative to the men she was surrounded by daily.

Then Toshi showed off his skills.

Brother, couldn't you have let the plate hit the ground?

Did it matter anyway? One glance from Sen and he hid his face like an embarrassed child. He rubbed his hands along his trousers and wallowed in his nervousness a few more minutes. If only he could adopt Toshi's attitude, maybe Nobuhiro could deal with unexpected situations like this as easily as he did.

Would the meeting even last that long? Every time he had seen Sen, something intervened. Why would today would be any different?

Nobuhiro bit into his cake as the back of his neck warmed. He rubbed at it to remove the tightness. Toshi stopped chewing and bit on his lower lip. Nobuhiro remembered that look. Toshi was visualizing the room. Some circumstance had changed. The meeting was over.

Nobuhiro glanced toward the door. A second later, Uji appeared at the entrance. Nobuhiro sighed. Another interruption. Toshi had heard their brother's steps from the street.

Uji scanned the patrons and then strode over to the table.

Toshi looked up. Smug. He *had* heard him. "Honorable older brother, what brings you here? I thought you'd be having your midday nap."

Uji rolled his eyes. Nobuhiro laughed and grinned at both of them. Uji acknowledged Nobuhiro. The look on Uji's face said much. He wasn't surprised to see him.

"Ujihiro." Nobuhiro used his older brother's full name in front of others. "In the excitement at the castle, I forgot to ask. How was your trip to Kyoto?"

"It went well," Uji replied. "At times, the regent still tries to impress the emperor."

Nobuhiro scratched at his neck. "Why? Isn't the title of *kampaku* enough? Does he seek to be called shogun?"

Uji leaned his head forward and paused before responding. "Maybe, but I doubt it. The regent knows he's not a descendant of the Minamoto clan. He recognizes the futility of such a hope."

"Regent. Shogun," Toshi piped in with a playful sneer. "As if being in charge of the country wasn't enough. If he wants another title, he could offer to clean the emperor's—"

"Toshihiro," Uji said, glaring as he used Toshi's full

name, an action that mimicked their father's serious nature. "That is not the proper tone for discussing the regent."

"I was only going to say clean his stable," Toshi said. "But it's an accurate statement. After all, there's a reason Nobunaga nicknamed the regent 'monkey.'"

Nobuhiro closed his mouth to stifle a guffaw. Everyone else's engorged cheeks told him they found Toshi's comment amusing. Nobuhiro breathed in through his nose to calm himself and then exhaled slowly.

"What brings you here?" Nobuhiro asked.

Uji shifted his gaze between Toshi and Nobuhiro. "Nobuhiro. Toshihiro. I need to see both of you outside. Your excursion is over." His voice brooked no discussion, only obedience.

Nobuhiro nodded. So did Toshi.

Uji reached into his kimono and pulled out a string of coins. He pulled one off, placed it on the table, and looked at Sen and Omi. "Wait here. Have some more tea." His tone resembled a command and his brusque demeanor surprised Nobuhiro. Uji was a samurai, but he rarely gave orders to anyone but other samurai. He knew what the answer would be.

"*Hai.*" Both women bowed their heads in affirmation and respect. Uji, true to his nature, returned the same. Even when serious, he was still polite. He didn't need to acknowledge the women. He did so out of decency. Another trait where Nobuhiro felt deficient and didn't measure up to his brothers.

Uji even exhibited his affable qualities toward people he vehemently disliked, a quality Nobuhiro had grown to admire more since moving out of the castle. The one time he had met Uji's wife, she had commented that his graciousness was his best trait.

Nobuhiro followed his brothers out of the restaurant and kept going as they turned onto a side street. Finally, Uji turned and faced them.

"What is it?" Nobuhiro asked.

Uji glanced each way, though his head movements were nearly imperceptible. He then stared at Nobuhiro. "What your brother and I have to say can go no further than this street."

Nobuhiro locked eyes with his brothers in unspoken agreement.

"Toshi and I are involved in an investigation," Uji continued. "We fear either one person or possibly a small group of samurai at the castle are targeting Christians in the area."

Nobuhiro's heart stopped and his mind flashed to Sen, his fists clenching. He flinched toward the restaurant entrance.

Uji's gaze held Nobuhiro in place. "Calm down. She is safe for now."

She was safe for now? Did Uji know about Sen's faith? He must. He and Toshi knew Lord Akamatsu well. They must have realized that Sen was a Christian.

Nobuhiro tried to remain calm. "How do you know? She is under scrutiny due to the edict? Is it not connected?"

Uji shook his head. "The regent only requires that Christians renounce their faith or lose their possessions. He's not killing those who refuse. He's barely even following his own edict."

"But the incident in Haibara at Lord Akamatsu's castle?"

Uji chewed his lower lip. "Regrettable. Two samurai overstepped their orders. They have been . . . disciplined."

Disciplined? So the samurai who led the forces at Haibara Castle were now dead, like the Christians who served Lord Akamatsu. What did that benefit anyone?

Nobuhiro wiped his perspiration-covered fingers against the coarse hemp of his kimono. Yet they still felt wet. "So the regent doesn't approve of this? How about our father? Is he not enforcing the ban?"

Both his brothers' eyes flared and Nobuhiro regretted his harsh words.

Uji shook his head. "He oversees the ban, but he will handle it in his way. You know him better than that."

Nobuhiro bowed his head as his face warmed. "Forgive me. I only meant to suggest that, since our father oversees the ban, these actions would benefit his efforts."

Uji rubbed his hand across his mouth. "Father's opinion of Christians is irrelevant. If they behave, he will not trouble them. However, Father is tasked with keeping order. These rogue samurai are operating outside the bounds of the law. To Father, they are a much greater threat than any foreign religion."

Nobuhiro nodded. "Then why the attacks?"

Toshi stepped forward. "Some zealot for Toyotomi's edict may be taking a more aggressive approach. We don't know why."

Footsteps crunching on the road drew Nobuhiro's attention. Were people trying to listen to their conversation? What tradesman would involve himself in the private discussions of samurai? It could mean death.

Uji paused and glanced around, his face like stone. "When Father told me to assemble a team for Kyoto to deliver the sword your master made, I took five people with me: Funaki, Kitayama, Michiba, Nishioji, and Matsubara."

"Our four remaining suspects and a backup," Toshi added. He looked at Uji. "A risky decision. I questioned it."

"A necessary risk," Uji said. "Picked for the trip, they might not realize we suspect them. Away from the castle, they might relax. A little sake, and their tongues might loosen."

Toshi's grin was pocked with annoyance. "I understand why you chose them, brother, but it was not wise."

"Even now you question me. Enough. It was my decision."

Nobuhiro's blood raced through his body. Toshi's concern for Uji was understandable. Uji had returned unharmed, but there was likely a lot he didn't know. It concerned him. "What was the problem then? He is fine."

Toshi licked his lips. "We don't know who is involved or if, possibly, more than one person is behind these events. It was risky. Four suspects. What if all of them had been involved? Death is synonymous with the number four. Uji put himself in a precarious position."

"That's why I asked Matsubara," Uji said, his tone both confident and irritated. "Even if all four were involved, Matsubara and I could address it."

Nobuhiro remembered Matsubara. Uji's best friend. As a fighter, he was of the same mold as his brothers. However, he was more laconic than Uji. *How could two silent people force the other four to talk, unless they broke the silence?* As children, Uji and Matsubara often sat together while studying their lessons or working on their swordsmanship. Father commented once that he'd never seen two people who could have a long conversation with each other and not utter a word.

"Maybe the two of you could handle the other four," Toshi said. "Matsubara was an excellent choice for a backup, and *he* at least heeds my advice sometimes. Plus, he'd made two trips to Kyoto in the last few months. He knows people all along the route."

Nobuhiro nodded and mimicked glancing around like his brothers had been doing, though he didn't know what he was looking for. He thought of Sen, still having tea with Omi. *Is she safe?* A slight breeze greeted his face.

No one approached them, but the usual loud cries of vendors hawking various food wares cut through the conversation. *Food.* He still needed to pick up items for this evening and tomorrow. Master Goami knew Nobuhiro was with Toshi. He had time. He looked at Uji. "Did you discover anything on the trip to Kyoto?"

"Nothing definitive, unfortunately. I suspect Kitayama isn't involved. He was in Osaka the morning of the incident we're investigating. It would have been impossible to get from Osaka to Himeji in the amount of time he had."

"Are you ready to cross him off the list?" Toshi asked.

"Not yet," Uji said. "He could still be an accomplice, providing other information. His actions remain suspect."

"Is there anyone besides these men?" Nobuhiro asked.

Uji and Toshi glanced at each other. Then Uji nodded. "Ishida, but he is no longer a concern. His body was found outside of town. At least we think it was his body."

"We must identify who it is soon," Toshi said. "We don't know how much time we have."

"I know," Uji said.

A drunk man in a loosely tied gray kimono stumbled into the side street. He was dirty and unshaven. His stench suggested he hadn't bathed recently. Bile rose in Nobuhiro's throat, but he managed to keep it down. Uji and Toshi both stopped talking and smiled at the stranger, their eyes focused. Nobuhiro glanced down. His brothers had one hand each on their swords. The drunk man stopped, likely aware he had surprised two samurai. He bowed low and then left.

Nobuhiro stared a few more moments at the street. Passersby continued to mill about, but none took notice of the conversation in the alley. He looked back at his brothers. Uji tilted his head, indicating that they could continue their conversation.

"What do you mean you don't have much time?" Nobuhiro asked. His thoughts flashed again to Sen. "Is someone in danger?" His voice rose to match his worry, but he slowed his breathing to steady himself. Samurai did not betray themselves with their emotions. Yet, once again, Nobuhiro's lack of control over his emotions betrayed him.

"Not yet," Uji said, "but it depends on Sen."

That did it. He straightened his back and clenched his fists, which now matched the tension in his shoulders.

Inside, though, his stomach churned like the water that flowed through the straits between the islands of Japan. "How is she involved in this? She hasn't done anything."

Toshi placed his palm firmly on Nobuhiro's chest. "Calm yourself, brother. She is not involved. Not yet anyway."

Nobuhiro nodded. He should trust more. If there were a concern, his brothers wouldn't be out here. He looked directly at Toshi. "Then why is she in danger?"

"Those behind the incidents we're investigating may be following her to see where she goes. While I did want to get out of the castle, I also arranged this meeting to see who might notice Sen's departure."

"You used her as a lure?"

"You must trust me. She is in no danger. I will explain everything in due time."

Nobuhiro relaxed his shoulders. "Did that happen? Did anyone notice that she left?"

Toshi looked at Uji, whose head bobbed slightly. "Yes. Funaki and Michiba had sudden changes in plans. They left together."

"Are they around?" Toshi asked.

Uji shook his head, placing his thumbs inside his thin belt. "They are not around here that I'm aware of. However, Matsubara is watching them. He will let us know if he discovers anything."

"I still don't understand why Sen may be involved," Nobuhiro added.

Toshi laughed and slapped him on the shoulder. "You've only met her a few times and already she's turned your brains into tofu."

Nobuhiro gritted his teeth. He was missing something. If only he could understand Toshi's point. Uji's lips thinned as he glared at Toshi before focusing again on Nobuhiro.

"She served Lord Akamatsu," Uji said. "She continued to serve him, even after he lost his castle. The people we are looking for may suspect that one of the

Christian groups might try to contact Sen . . . or she may try to find them."

Nobuhiro rubbed his chest while protective feelings swelled within him. Sen was just on the other side of this wall. He should go back in.

Toshi broke his concentration. "Don't worry. She is safe for now."

"You said that before but didn't explain. I would welcome an answer. Is it because she hasn't found any local Christians yet?"

"Only partly," Toshi said. "Whoever it is won't want to try anything now, especially during the day when so many people are around."

"True," Uji said in a gravelly voice. "Scum like this usually appears only at night."

"But the incident at the castle . . . " Nobuhiro said.

"During the day, I know, but they were away from the crowd," Toshi answered.

Nobuhiro inhaled and wiped the perspiration from his brow, catching a familiar scent that he couldn't place. A mixture of musk and sweat. He put it aside. Maybe everything would start making sense soon.

"Still, how can you be so sure she's safe?"

Toshi patted his arm. "She is fine. I assure you. Omi is with her."

Nobuhiro ran his hand over his scalp. "Omi? Now I'm confused. Omi's a servant. She's as meek as Sen. What protection can she offer?"

Toshi flashed his smirk. "Sakichi, have you forgotten? Not all castle defenses are as obvious as floors that squeak on purpose. In the event an assassin may attempt to enter through the women's quarters, several of the women are not the timid flowers they appear."

Nobuhiro's forehead tightened as realization struck him like a bright light in darkness. "She's a—"

"One of the best female samurai I've ever seen," Toshi said. "She almost gave it away in there when she caught the plate. As you may have noticed, she's quick."

"I noticed," Nobuhiro said. He should have ascertained then the truth about Omi. His nervousness about Sen clouded his faculties. "Does Sen know?"

Uji shook his head. "Not yet, but she should be told, and then told to keep it silent."

"I understand, but why didn't Omi do something when we were attacked at the castle?"

"She was going to," Toshi said, "but then you decided to face a masked archer with a cloth-covered sword. How noble of you."

He ignored Toshi's sarcasm as Nobuhiro let out the breath he'd been holding. Omi was a samurai? Had he met her years ago when he lived here? Or would she have been cloistered and trained elsewhere to protect her anonymity until it was time to fulfill her duty? He probably met her once when he was younger. He should remember such things.

"Is she really that good?" he asked.

"She could stun both Uji and Matsubara without working hard," Toshi replied. "After all, she should be good."

"Why is that?" Nobuhiro asked.

Toshi's jovial look turned serious as his gaze strayed behind Nobuhiro. Uji did the same.

"So, why is she one of the best samurai?" Nobuhiro repeated, but both his brothers were now looking through him. The hair on his neck stood up as a slow march of footsteps grew louder, combined with the same touch of musk he'd noticed earlier. Their conversation was no longer private. Like Toshi had done at the workshop, someone had snuck up on him. His brothers weren't moving their hands to their swords. That meant one thing.

"Because I trained her," his father's voice said from behind him.

Chapter Seven

Sen glanced at the door and then back at Omi, who tapped her knee in a silent drumming motion. Was she thinking the same thing? The look on Ujihiro's face suggested that the afternoon was about to end. Maybe it was. Maybe it was her nerves. She barely knew Nobuhiro or his family. His father had already warned her that talking to his family was above her station.

Her fingers stiffened and she pulled at them, trying to ease away the tension. It didn't help. She blew on her palms, but they remained damp. She couldn't believe anything except that something was wrong. Omi's face remained impassive. Nothing disturbed her. Even after the attack at the castle, she acted composed. Could she emulate Omi's demeanor?

"The men have been gone for a long time, haven't they?" Sen asked. "What could they be doing?"

Omi rolled her eyes. "Men always lose track of time. It's a talent they're born with. My mother always said that my father took an hour to complete tasks that should only take thirty minutes. He refused to do things the easiest way."

Sen laughed. "My mother often made similar comments about my father when I was growing up. She said men never do things like they should."

The smile disappeared from Omi's face and she pursed her lips. "Since it seems they may be gone awhile, can I ask you something?"

"Yes, please do." Sen's mind filled with curiosity.

Omi leaned in as her gaze flitted left and right. "I want to ask you about Christians," she said in a hushed tone.

Sen's eyes and mouth flew open and she stared. She never expected interest within the castle walls. Could she trust Omi? Sen had only been in the castle for a few weeks. Omi had looked out for her since Sen had arrived, but Sen still didn't know her that well.

The brothers spoke for her. She must be fine.

Sen glanced around. People appeared engrossed in their own conversations. No one was close enough to hear them. Sen rubbed her fingers across her neck and attempted to relax again. Lord Akamatsu had advised her to be cautious. Time to trust in faith. "Why do you think I would know?"

Omi raised an eyebrow and displayed the playful sarcastic smile that Sen had seen her use on men. "You served Lord Akamatsu for many years. However, your favorite spot on the grounds has nothing to do with what the sunlight does to the view. It's that cross, isn't it?"

Sen managed only a sheepish grin. It had taken Nobuhiro one glance to notice the cross. Omi reasoned out the same after a few weeks. Lord Akamatsu would have been disappointed. Sen needed to vary her habits or else the whole castle would know.

St. Peter's story again rose in her thoughts. Denial was not an option.

"Yes, it's the cross. I'm a Christian."

"I thought so." Omi's eyes opened wide. "Are your parents Christian or did you become one when you lived in Haibara?"

Sen mulled it over. A question about her as much as a question about faith. Was her interest genuine? What could she tell Omi? She could tell her a bit about herself and her life. That would be a start.

God, I place my trust in you.

"In Haibara. Lord Akamatsu believed in Christ, a faith he learned from his father. However, I didn't become a Christian immediately. It took time."

Omi's glance to the right made Sen turn her head. Were the men returning? Instead, it was just a waitress, refilling the tea. Omi waved her off and waited for her to move to the next group.

A few seconds passed. Omi's intense gaze conveyed that she wanted to hear more. "Was it hard? What made you decide to become a Christian?"

Sen paused. The words didn't come quickly. She took a deep breath. "It was difficult. I wasn't raised this way. My parents took me to the local festivals and I followed the rituals, but I was just there for family. But when I first heard about Christ, I felt drawn."

"Why?"

Sen listened for footsteps as she took a sip of tea. "I found it brought me peace. Life is hard sometimes. My faith calms me. When I'm troubled, I pray for help and Christ counsels me."

Omi stared. "He *talks* to you?"

Sen chuckled and tipped her head. "Not like that. But I tell Him my problems, put them in His hands. I know that whatever happens is always the best for me."

"How did you learn?" Omi asked.

A slide of wood grating on wood drew Sen's attention. She paused and looked back at the entrance. Two men walked in. They weren't samurai, as neither wore a sword, but their beige kimonos sported intricate brown lines and cubes. Fine work. They must have been wealthy merchants. The men still hadn't returned. Would she and Omi be asked to move?

Not likely. If the brothers returned, the restaurant

owner would be shamed for his insult to samurai. Such shame wouldn't be remedied easily. The proprietor, dressed in a white kimono, appeared from the kitchen and strolled over to the entrance, passing behind the wooden post that rose in the middle of the room. He greeted the men and showed them to a place close to where Sen and Omi were sitting. Could they hear the conversation from that distance? The restaurant was half full. Was anyone watching? Was anyone listening?

"What is it?" Omi asked.

"I thought I heard the men coming back." Sen's remarks were muted. She wanted to talk openly with Omi, but Nobuhiro's father had already warned her once. He wouldn't approve of her conversation with Omi. Would duty require the brothers to tell their father if they suspected anything? They had already shown Sen kindness that she couldn't repay. Their father's comments suggested as much. She didn't want to seem ungrateful.

Omi shook her head. "Like I mentioned earlier, they're probably going to be a while. You know how men are."

"I know. I know." Sen's reticence surprised her. A quick glance around confirmed that no one was paying them any attention. She could continue.

Sen took another deep breath to slow the flutter in her heart. "You asked how I learned. At first, I just asked questions of other servants. A few missionaries visited Haibara and I asked them questions. The missionaries read from this book and we discussed its teachings."

"That sounds nice."

Sen pressed the neckline of her kimono against her neck. The scars warmed and sent heat through her body. The last service she'd attended was the day the samurai had visited. Just thinking about it brought back pain.

And guilt.

She had survived when her friends had died. The Lord had spared her life so she could help her family. Did every word threaten that now?

She balled her hands into fists and then spread her fingers. “Yes, it was. We often met in people’s homes or in places like this, just to talk.”

“And you weren’t afraid?”

“This was before the edict. There were many Christians in Haibara. No one thought poorly of it.”

Omi turned her hands up. “And do you do that here? Do you meet other Christians?”

Sen bit her lower lip. “Not since the edict.”

“I heard these missionaries carry big books around.”

Sen rubbed her fingers against her palms, remembering the last time she’d held the missionary’s book in her hands. “It’s called a Bible. Lord Akamatsu had one. A gift from a missionary.”

“Do you wish you had a Bible?” Omi asked.

Sen grinned and raised her eyebrows. “I don’t know what good it would do. The writing is in a different language. I can’t read it. I just know the stories.”

A grin grew on Omi’s face. “Is it true what they say? Do the missionaries really drink animal blood?”

Sen winced but also tried not to laugh. Many of the Buddhist sects spread rumors to mock the new religion. She had heard this one before. “They call it milk and they do drink it.”

“It’s disgusting.”

“Don’t worry. Drinking it is not required.”

Omi’s eyes turned sad. “Do you miss it?”

Sen pulled at her collar. “Yes, I do.”

###

Nobuhiro’s father walked around him, adding extra pressure to each step as he circled. “Tell me, my sons,” he said with a measured precision that added the weight of an anvil to each syllable. “Why are you discussing castle business with this outsider?”

His angry breath on the back of Nobuhiro’s neck provided a bellows to the fire within Nobuhiro’s belly. He froze and tried not to let his father bait him. People in the street began to stare as they passed. To them, it looked like three samurai questioning a tradesman. No one would ever dare approach.

After a few moments, Uji broke the silence. "Father, we need him. Nobuhiro works for the Goami family. He can be of great service to us."

Nobuhiro's father completed the circle and stopped to face him, his eyes boring into Nobuhiro like falling stalactites. Initially, Nobuhiro wavered under the assault, but then recalled his childhood. This was his father's typical tactic with subordinates. Many men had wilted under this assault. But Nobuhiro crossed his arms and stared back as he straightened to get in his father's face.

I am not the child you once knew.

"How can he help?" his father asked without looking at either of his older sons.

"Goami may seek to find Christians in the area," Uji said. "Whoever's targeting Christians may realize that. If any Christians contact her, they will likely do so away from the castle, maybe when she's visiting her family. Nobuhiro might know about such things before we do."

Nobuhiro's father scratched his chin. "You think she might ignore my advice about avoiding her former life?"

"I don't know, Father," Toshi responded. "However, Christians show their devotion to their God the same way we show devotion to our duty. If local Christians try to find her, then we need to know that, for their sake as well as hers."

My father dropped his glare and looked toward Uji. "Why were you watching her today?"

Nobuhiro glanced at both of his brothers. Toshi's eyes were fixed on Uji, who lifted his shoulders slightly. Likely, he knew about the date. Had Toshi talked him into something that their father wouldn't have approved?

Nobuhiro's father crossed his arms. "Ujihiro, we're waiting."

Uji swallowed hard and took a deep breath. "When Goami left the grounds this afternoon, Funaki and Michiba suddenly found reasons to also depart. Matsubara is watching them."

Nobuhiro's father maintained his intense focus on Uji. Sweat formed on Uji's brow and appeared poised to trickle down his face. Nobuhiro's heartbeat doubled its speed. His oldest brother feared little. However, their father struck fear in everyone. His discipline made him a formidable foe, regardless of the situation. And somehow, he remained impassive.

His father tilted his head. "Was Goami meeting other Christians today? I see that Moto is with her. Is she trying to include Moto in those meetings?"

Toshi inched in, as if to provide Uji with a break from their father's glare. "No, the two of them were just out for the afternoon. I saw Nobuhiro in the marketplace while I was observing the women. I knew Matsubara was also following, so I decided to put myself more directly into the situation."

That answered one question. His father didn't know about Toshi's arranged date. If he did know, though, Nobuhiro wouldn't have been surprised.

"I see," his father said. His eyebrows rose and pinched the skin above his nose. His shoulders flinched in Nobuhiro's direction. A lump formed in his throat. "So, what brings a swordsmith's apprentice into the market? Shouldn't you be honing your craft?"

Needle-like pain traversed from the base of Nobuhiro's spine to his brain. His father knew his whereabouts. Nobuhiro should have expected this after the meeting at the castle but had hoped that his father was too busy to notice. Nobuhiro had planned for this day. Still, planning did not always beget execution.

And his father was an expert in execution.

"M . . . my master's wife is ill. He asked that I make the daily trip for her to acquire food for tonight and tomorrow morning." Nobuhiro's thoughts shifted to concern for his adopted family. His father had a long memory and an even longer reach. "How long have you known that I work for Master Goami?"

His father lifted his chin and looked down his nose at Nobuhiro. "When you visited the castle with the sword, I realized it. Goami is a master craftsman. He takes no chances with his work. He would not trust the delivery of such a valuable object to the fleet-of-foot express." He paused to look Nobuhiro up and down, his eyes burning disdain into Nobuhiro's skin. "Nor would you be employed for such work."

Nobuhiro inhaled, catching the salty taste of perspiration on his lips. Did his father approve of the choice Nobuhiro had made? Or did he demean it the same way he demeaned everything else Nobuhiro did? His father's simmering look rose to a boil, searing Nobuhiro's cheeks. He wanted to ask more questions, but now wasn't the time. His father's arrogance would eventually provide an answer.

His father shook his head. "Well, it's good that you made something of yourself instead of living on the street, since you didn't have the fortitude to remain with us."

Nobuhiro struggled to keep his mouth shut, choosing to let his father finish his rant.

His father took another breath. "I suppose I should be relieved. A tradesman is at least preferable to other possible occupations. You could have been a novelty act in a traveling sumo exhibition, fighting half-naked female wrestlers."

Nobuhiro's blood pulsed with rage as his father's insults found their mark. He could ignore the novelty act comment, but the implied insult that working for a swordsmith was barely above such work was inexcusable. Master Goami was the most accomplished swordsmith in the area. A swordsmith's workshop was hallowed ground. The equivalent of a shrine, even to a samurai. He considered a response but held his tongue. He represented the family he worked for. An ill response would provide ample support for a rebuke.

One day, old man. One day. You will wake up and understand why I left and why I'm better off without you.

His father turned toward his brothers, and a small sigh escaped his lips. Nobuhiro's head and shoulders sagged, welcoming the release of tension. His father tilted his head back as if he had heard Nobuhiro's muscles move. His father's body then tightened immediately.

Nobuhiro wanted to remove the cocky grin he knew must be there.

"We should return to the castle," his father announced. "After Matsubara returns, we can discuss our next steps in this investigation. Toshihiro, fetch the young women."

"*Hai.*" Toshi disappeared, returning shortly with both Sen and Omi. Sen carried the basket Nobuhiro had brought with him to the marketplace. His father acknowledged their presence with a nod. His father then stared at Sen, whose eyes flew open as she recoiled from the attention.

"Goami," my father said. "I've learned your mother is ill. You will return home and look after her."

Nobuhiro shook his head. Did he hear that correctly? His father made a kind gesture? What was he doing?

Sen's mouth dropped open as wide as her eyes, both of which manifested the surprise Nobuhiro felt. "But my duty at the castle, I—"

"I will arrange things with your mistress," his father said in a gruff voice that restored Nobuhiro's opinion of him, but which was at odds with the favor Sen had received. "Return to your duties when she improves."

"*Hai*, thank you." Sen bowed low.

"And *you*," his father said, turning to stare at Nobuhiro. "Escort Goami home. Can you perform this simple task without error?"

"*Hai*," he said, bowing more out of reflex than respect. His father spun in the other direction without reply, leaving Nobuhiro to stare at his father and brothers as they walked away.

Chapter Eight

Sen stared at Nobuhiro, her hands clenched on the obi wrapped around her waist. The afternoon sun warmed the back of her neck, and cast her shadow in front of her, almost reaching to where Nobuhiro stood. The shadow seemed to inch closer to Nobuhiro with each passing second.

She yearned to do the same.

A fan seller dressed in a light brown kimono with crosshatch markings appeared from the other end of the alley, carrying a pole over his shoulder with fans hanging upside down behind him. The man passed quickly, the fans behind him creating a small breeze. Then it was just the two of them again. Being alone with him was her biggest fear.

She wiped her hand across her mouth as she tried to regain her composure. She was no readier to talk with Nobuhiro now than when she had first seen him in the street.

The long silence grew awkward, but her thoughts turned to her family. "My mother is ill?"

Nobuhiro hesitated, then nodded slowly. "She has

been sick for two days and doesn't seem to be improving. Your father thinks she'll be fine. I'm certain seeing you will improve her spirits."

A hot flush filled her cheeks and she looked at the ground. *Why am I feeling this way? He only said that Mother's spirits would improve at seeing me. Wouldn't any mother feel the same? Why did hearing his voice make it feel like a compliment?*

"I'll take the basket," he said.

"The basket?"

He pointed to the bamboo basket that she held in front of her. She had forgotten that she had brought it out of the restaurant. The light weight suggested he still had shopping to do. She handed it to him, feeling the brush of his hand against hers.

"*Itai*," she said, bringing her finger to her mouth as she sucked on it. She'd pricked her finger against a sharp edge of bamboo. Her tongue provided a salve to the stinging pain.

"I'm sorry. I must have caused that. Are you hurt?" he asked.

She removed her finger from her mouth. The tip of her finger bore a red spot. She pressed against the side and a small drop of blood rose on her skin. She brought her finger back to her mouth.

"I'm fine," she said, embarrassed at her overreaction. She had endured far worse. "Do you have many places to go?"

Nobuhiro didn't answer immediately. Instead, he stared and opened his free hand as if to take her pain into his palm. He shook his head and returned his hand to his side. "Your father suggested squid, but I need to pick up vegetables first."

They left the alley and made a few quick purchases, then walked a few hundred yards toward the fish market area. Sen tried to talk with Nobuhiro. He had offered his hand after the incident with the horseman, but she had refused. He appeared to do it again here but then pulled back. She wanted to reach out to him but couldn't. They were walking together, but they might as well be alone.

The open storefronts, busy with activity, provided a welcome distraction. At one store, an oil seller measured oil through a funnel strainer hanging from his wrist. Farther down, at the front of another establishment, a young girl cut long sticks of incense on a table, while an older woman negotiated with a customer. The fragrances of sandalwood and licorice reached out to her. Across the street, a needle seller passed in front of a much wider store with a deep back. The store offered various cloths. Taxes were paid on store width at the street entrance. This cloth merchant must be rich.

The salty smell broke through her musings. They had arrived. She scanned the various offerings, looking for a place that advertised squid. It was her mother's favorite food, which explained why her father had mentioned it to Nobuhiro. Father would welcome her presence at home, if only because Sen would take over all the kitchen duties.

They found a good place and Sen scrutinized the squid left in the tank. There wasn't a great selection. However, she hadn't seen any other stores advertising squid, meaning they didn't sell it or else had sold off their catch for the day. She picked one and then motioned to the proprietor, a thin, bald man in his fifties with a triangular face and a scar on his temple that blended in with the creases. He wore a gray kimono, stained with ink spots.

The man bowed to Sen and Nobuhiro. He acknowledged Nobuhiro as a familiar face, then looked at Sen briefly, with eyes that seemed to fill with tears. Did he recognize her from childhood? Did he know Haru, and did he see a resemblance?

The old man nodded again, grabbed a hook, and retrieved a choice squid. Once out, the animal emitted a long stream of water that splashed Nobuhiro in the face and chest and then splashed on her.

Sen covered her mouth and tried not to laugh as Nobuhiro wiped the water from his eyes. He chuckled as he dried himself off. His reaction and his smile drained the tension out of her. He was a good man.

"*Sumimasen*," the shop owner said as he grabbed a towel and offered it to Nobuhiro.

Nobuhiro dried his face and laughed again. "Don't worry. It was an accident." His smile widened in a sage-like expression. "Besides, I will have my revenge later."

He continued to clean himself off, pulling his dark blue kimono open to wipe his chest. Like many men, he wore a white cloth underneath his kimono and around his torso. It kept the stomach warm and thereby maintained health. However, his chest was totally bare. Water dripped slowly along his upper body. She licked her lips and stared. Her heartbeat sounded in her ears. She pressed her lips together and struggled to regain herself.

Nobuhiro smiled at her and it melted her resolve. "Shall we go?"

They turned for home. A long walk still. They were half a *ri* away. With her wearing geta, it would take over thirty minutes. Her palms grew wet. Thirty more minutes alone with him. Could she keep her mind where it belonged?

Nobuhiro broke the silence. "Do you enjoy living at the castle?"

An innocent question, but unfortunately no easy answer. "People are nice. Everyone treats me well and I'm learning my duties."

"That's good. May I ask you something about it?"

She hesitated. What could he want to know that he would feel the need to ask permission? "Yes."

"Why did you go to the castle instead of coming home?"

A question she'd asked herself often since her arrival. The answer still troubled her.

"I tried to go home, to live with my parents. However, Lord Akamatsu advised me against it. He obtained a position at the castle for me."

"It must have been difficult."

"It was. Your brothers made the arrangements. We arrived in Himeji late at night. Your brothers met us outside of town, provided provisions for Lord Akamatsu and his wife, and escorted me to the castle."

Nobuhiro's eyebrows arched together. "My brothers? So that's how they knew you when you bumped into us. They didn't mention it. What did they say?"

"They fought together. I know little else."

"Why did Lord Akamatsu not want you to go home?"

Sen recalled that night a month ago, when she had arrived. Lord Akamatsu still wore the same golden kimono that he had worn the day he had lost his castle, the only thing he had been allowed to keep other than his swords. The once fine garment carried several marks of restitching. He had lost everything material in his life.

However, his faith was unshaken.

Sen brushed a tear from her eye. "He was concerned about me. About the edict. 'No one knows how closely the ban against our faith will be enforced,' he said. 'If the authorities are strict? If they suspect you of practicing your beliefs, they may take your parents' home away from them. They could also force your parents to renounce you. If you live at the castle, your parents are safe.' I appreciated his concern. It was all he had left to give."

She glanced at others on the street. Nobuhiro's limp and his status as a swordsmith's apprentice made him stand out. Many here would recognize him. Would they remember her, too? Before Lord Akamatsu left, he had called her a child of Himeji and said that people would welcome her. None of these people had seen her in ten years. If they recognized her, would they, like Nobuhiro, wonder why she hadn't returned home?

Why had fate forced her to reside at Nobuhiro's home and him to reside at hers?

She looked at Nobuhiro. The pain on his face from the time she had first met him seemed etched into him like a scar from a sharp blade. "Do you miss it?"

He stopped, and his eyes shot a puzzled gaze at her.

"What?"

"Living in the castle."

Nobuhiro sighed and looked away as he wiped some perspiration from his forehead. "The castle, not so much, but I do miss my brothers. I was close to them growing up."

"It shows. They care for you."

He shrugged, slowly, as if held down by an unseen weight. She waited for an answer, but none came.

They walked the next few minutes in silence, leaving the storefronts behind them. A light wind glanced off Sen's face, filling her with the scent of the earth. Alongside the road, many men worked hard in the rice fields, buttressing the large square areas with raised dirt. Of course. It was late April. How could she have forgotten? The Good Harvest Festival must have been two or three days ago.

Childhood images again rose in her mind. Images of walking with her mother and Haru to the shrine every year to watch the festival that predicted the impending rice crop. Riders dressed in blue, green, and red costumes circling the field, praying for a good yield. Lots of rice cakes to eat. It was a happier time than now.

"Do you miss living at home?" Nobuhiro asked.

The riders vanished back into her childhood, replaced by the hardworking men at the side of the road. "Excuse me?"

"Do you miss living at home?"

"Yes, but not like I expected. Haru had the responsibility of finding a husband to bring into the family. I served the Akamatsu house so that I might be prepared to be a good wife for someone else's family. Lord Akamatsu and my father were acquainted for many years. It was a proper arrangement."

"And now?"

She bit her lip. "I have been away from home for over ten years. Things have changed much. My parents have changed much. I have changed much. I have no regrets, other than memories I can't revisit."

His mouth tightened. "My father has not changed. He is the same harsh man I remember."

She tilted her head. Chills and warmth clashed within her. The vision of the man who had reprimanded her for talking with his sons clashed with that of the man who had sent her home to care for her ill mother. Something was missing. "Was he always that way?"

He paused and gritted his teeth, but then his lips softened. "No. Not always. I remember him being much calmer and gentler when I was younger."

"What do you think changed him?"

Nobuhiro shook his head. "I don't know."

"What does your mother say?"

He turned his eyes away and stared at the houses before answering. "My mother died when I was young. I remember her being sick often and my father being by her side."

An ill mother. A man grieving a lost wife. Maybe that explained why he allowed her to visit home. "Could that be the reason for the way he treated you?"

"I don't know. I was young then. I remember losing my mother, then crying about it. After that, he was always harsh to me, compared to my brothers."

"What did your father do?"

Nobuhiro slowed. His eyes smoldered. "He told me, 'Samurais don't cry.'"

Sen saw the sad little boy inside Nobuhiro. He was much different from the happy daughter she had been. "What did your brothers say about it?"

He stared into space. "They . . . agreed with me but could do nothing to help. Why?"

She thought hard. She had begun to care about Nobuhiro for several reasons. He worked for her family, and her parents respected him. Nobuhiro's brothers possessed a loyalty to Lord Akamatsu. Enough to meet them all in the middle of the night. Enough to obtain her a position at the castle. Enough to oversee her safety. They were good men.

Christian or not, Nobuhiro was a decent man, too.

She allowed herself to glimpse his face. His warm look and soft brown eyes pulled at the walls of her heart, opening it to possibilities she hadn't considered. She focused on his quivering chin. "I ask because of the look on your face. When you speak of him, you do it in angry terms. Yet your face shows depression and sadness."

"Yes, I guess it does," Nobuhiro said, his voice light in tone but carrying weight. "The biggest challenge is the future. What did you do when Lord Akamatsu's castle was taken?"

She bit her lip. She had spoken enough about her faith. "I worked hard to busy myself, to find work that would allow me to return. It was difficult day-to-day. I also prayed."

"Prayed?"

She took a deep breath. "Yes, I prayed. It provided me comfort."

Nobuhiro tilted his head. "What did Lord Akamatsu do?"

She closed her eyes. "He used his contacts to provide for his people, helped them return home. His hair turned gray these last few months."

Nobuhiro shook his head. "It does not seem like this new religion helped you. Lord Akamatsu lost his castle and lands. You lost your position. You can't even return home to serve your family?"

She broke into a wide grin. "Lord Akamatsu arranged it so I could find a new position. He was able to depend on friends, good friends who cared about his welfare. Those friends assisted him and his wife. They also helped me."

"It does not make sense. If this God of yours is powerful, then I do not see much help."

She winced at Nobuhiro's reply. How could she explain it to him? What could she say?

A warmth enveloped her. "I do not always understand what will happen. But I'm at least in Himeji. Somehow, I will find a way to help my family."

"Your parents are happy you're closer to home. I know that from things your father has said. I see little else. No proof of a God."

She thought back to the first time she heard the word of God. It had been difficult for her to listen and there had been many Christians around. When she finally opened her heart, the missionary had called it a "leap of faith."

How could she convey this to Nobuhiro?

"The choice I made was my own. It was not easy, but it was the best thing for me."

He shook his head. "Maybe for you, but my life is too difficult."

Her chest dropped into her stomach. "You're thinking about it?"

He shook his head. "This God of yours cannot help me reconcile with my father. What does He know about being a samurai? Does this God of yours understand the sacrifice of family?"

Sen bit back her tongue. Pushing Nobuhiro on this issue would only push him away.

The long walk was over. They had reached home. The bushes in the front appeared overgrown. Absent were the vases Sen's mother put out each spring. She had always been so detailed. Spring was her favorite time of year.

She took the food from Nobuhiro and they exchanged bows. She found herself staring again, lost in those gentle eyes that always seemed to carry pain behind them. "Thanks for escorting me home."

"You're welcome."

"May I ask you one thing?"

"Yes."

Looking to see if anyone was close, she kept her eyes on the narrow dirt street. No one was near. Still, she leaned in to whisper. It was best to adhere to Lord Akamatsu's advice. "I know you don't believe, but would you mind if I prayed for you?"

Nobuhiro exhaled and shrugged his shoulders. "I don't believe it would do any good. No power can help me with my father. But you may do as you wish."

He turned and walked away. Sen stepped to the entrance but stopped before knocking. No knocking. Just enter. As her mother had suggested before.

She glanced back at her escort, who had already turned toward the shop. His limp was more pronounced than at the beginning of their trip home. He must be tired. His limp was physical, but he also carried a heavy burden.

Lift the burden.

Lift the responsibility.

Lift the man.

And his spirit would rise with it.

Chapter Nine

Sen cleared the breakfast dishes, taking the trays back to the kitchen area. Her mother relaxed on the floor with the low table still in front of her. The color in her cheeks was pinker than it had been for the last few days. She had even been up early to help cook. However, she tired quickly.

"How are you feeling?" Sen asked.

"You fuss over me too much. I have been ill. I'm not dying."

"How often did you fuss over me when I was sick growing up?"

"That's different. I'm your mother. I'm allowed to fuss."

Sen reached for the pot hanging over the fire in the hearth on the floor, adding the hot water to her mother's cup. "I know, but I'm happy to see you're doing well."

"I can take care of myself, but being sick is worth it to have you here."

Her mother's words cascaded slowly over her like water flowing through the fountain at a Buddhist temple. She had enjoyed the few days she had been here, but her mother's improving health meant Sen would be returning to the castle soon.

And her time to inquire about the church was running out.

The church.

In deference to her mother's illness, Sen hadn't mentioned the church. Today was the time. She knelt next to her mother, handing her the cup, then sat back on her knees. Respectful daughter. Dutiful daughter.

Loving daughter.

"Mother, can we talk?"

Her mother took a sip and set the tea on the table, closing her eyes and clasping her hands in her lap. "What is it?"

Sen breathed slowly as her heartbeat throbbed in her head. "Last time I was here, I asked you about a local church. I know you know something. Please tell me."

Her mother glanced away as she sipped more tea. Her mouth then tightened into a flat line. She parted her lips, licking them slowly before shutting them again. "My precious daughter. Why must you know?" she said in a please-don't-ask-me tone.

Sen sipped her tea and savored the bitter flavor. How to explain? Mother knew nothing of God's word.

"It's important to me. Please tell me what you know or at least what you've heard." Sen leaned forward, looking at her mother. "Please don't keep this from me."

Her mother drew a sharp a breath. It was hard for her. Sen could see that. Sen reached across and grasped her mother's hand. She turned to Sen. "Better that I tell you than for you to take chances looking on your own."

"You do know where?"

"I do not know where a church is," Sen's mother said, glancing toward the window as if staring at Sen would melt a resolve to tell as little as possible, "but I have heard one clue. 'Joy springs from burying your bitterness in the ground.' I have no idea what it means."

Sen smiled as relief spread through her body. She wanted to hug her mother but sensed it wasn't the time.

Instead, she thanked her and then pulled a cushion over and sat back on it. "It's a strange phrase. Who were the people you heard it from? I could ask them."

Sen's mother shook her head. "I'm afraid that isn't possible."

Sen opened her eyes wide. "Why?"

"I do not wish to discuss it. Do not go searching for trouble. It is dangerous, this religion of yours."

"What do you mean?" Sen asked.

Her mother exhaled hard. The lines around her eyes deepened like the designs in a rock garden. She rubbed her temples with her fingers, as if trying to massage away a headache. "I have not looked this way for long. I know you haven't seen me in many years, but my hair turned this gray only during the last few months. I am still a young woman. Your father and I still have years left, I hope."

Her mother's voice trembled and Sen squeezed her hand. "I don't understand. Why are you talking this way?"

Her mother went silent as tears began to flow from her eyes. "It . . . is . . . impossible to ask the person I heard it from. The person who told me was your sister."

Sen's mouth dropped open as she wrapped her thoughts around the news. Her legs shook. "Haru? Haru was a Christian?"

"She was moved by your letters and your conversion to this new faith. She became interested in it, and her husband supported her. Soon, he also embraced it. Both were eventually . . . I forget the term. What's that water ceremony called?"

"Baptism."

"Yes, baptism. They were baptized as Christians. Once that happened, they couldn't have been happier."

Sen rejoiced. *Thank you, Lord. To know that she became a Christian before she died, I am humbled by your goodness.*

"Is something wrong?" her mother asked.

Sen smiled at Mother, but the news still left her

stunned. "I never imagined this. Haru never mentioned it in any of her letters."

"It only happened within the last year. She planned to write you about it soon. She did not know if you would ever come home, but she hoped to tell you in person if she could."

Sen refilled her own cup, then traced the rim of it with her finger, feeling the soft, smooth wood. Bringing the cup to her lips, she closed her eyes and let the sounds of the street drift in. Sip. Savor. Swallow. Memories of Haru—of making mischievous footprints in the rock garden together, of sitting outside their father's workshop hoping he could spare a few minutes to be with them, of Haru telling Sen stories so she would go to sleep—all flowed in with the breeze from the window. The distance of the last ten years erased.

A twig snap broke her thoughts and she stared behind her mother at the window beyond.

"What is it?" Mother asked.

Sen hesitated to say anything, turning her head to focus on the sound outside.

Silence.

She glanced back at the window, expecting the wall to cave in, but it stood firm. She had lived day-to-day for months, serving the governor and his wife as best she could. A dutiful servant. After moving repeatedly, she thought she was safe at the castle.

Then came the attack by the horseman.

Now she was jumping again at the slightest snap.

"Sen, what is it?" her mother repeated.

"Nothing. I thought I heard something outside."

Her mother glanced back to check and then turned to her and smiled, the same smile she had used to soothe Sen's nerves when she was a child. "I'm always hearing sounds outside. It's just a squirrel, most likely."

"You're probably right," Sen said, accepting her explanation. She had been away a long time.

A large thud from outside the house shook both the

wall and the shelves, knocking plates and rings to the floor. Two plates cracked on contact with the floor while the tatami mats absorbed the impact of the rest of the items.

Sen rushed to the window, looking over her mother's shoulder. Her mouth went dry and she brought her hands to her lips.

She saw Nobuhiro and another man were fighting.

She recognized the other man from the castle, a samurai, but she didn't know his name. Dressed in a blue kimono, he was shorter than Nobuhiro, with a flat face and nose.

The man struck at Nobuhiro with a long blade. Nobuhiro parried with a pair of steel tongs used for folding swords. Steel met steel in a cacophony of clanging and sparks. No favor. No rest. Each man turned his weapon into an extension of himself.

Sen balled her hands into fists and searched for something to help. She saw nothing. Grabbing at her clothes, she felt the belt tied around her kimono. She undid the belt and headed for the door.

"No!" her mother screamed. "You mustn't go out there! You could be killed. Find your father."

"Nobuhiro risked his life for me. I have to help him."

She slipped her feet into shoes and slid the door open, then stepped into the area beside her house, hugging the wall as she moved toward the fight. Her breath matched her pulse. Rapid, with quick gulps of air. She peered around the corner, hoping the man wouldn't notice her.

Good. His back is to me.

Her fingers fumbled with the belt as she made a large loop.

Slowly. I can do this.

Afraid of making eye contact and distracting Nobuhiro, she focused on the stranger. Sen reached up and slipped the loop over the stranger's head, pulling hard at his neck.

The man brought his left hand to his throat and

clawed at the belt, trying to shove his fingers between skin and fabric. Sen pulled harder and spread her feet to maintain her balance, but her straw shoes slid along the ground as the man pulled away. A loud ding followed as a piece of sword broke off and spun over her head before hitting the ground.

Nobuhiro could take him now.

Her grip relaxed.

The stranger with the flat nose gulped air, then looked over his right shoulder and stared, eyes erupting with anger. His forehead wrinkled, then tightened. Like a stiff rope.

Too late.

The stranger pivoted and his right elbow struck her in the jaw. Sharp pain flooded her face as she fell to the ground. The attacker stood over her, his right hand clasping the broken sword. He reared back and raised his arm to strike. She flinched and tried to move away, but the ground had no give.

Nobuhiro landed the tongs with a thud into the arm that held the hilt. The stranger grunted, his face contorted with pain and anger. He spun to face Nobuhiro. Despite his pain, he was still a samurai. His moves were graceful. His actions, disgraceful.

"Not in my house. Not to my family. Not again," her father's voice cried out, as he emerged into view, followed by two other men.

The stranger glanced left, his attention focused on her father. Nobuhiro swung down hard, striking the attacker's sword hand. The broken remainder clumped to the ground. The man glared at Nobuhiro and then dashed past him toward the narrow path that separated the house from a neighbor's. Nobuhiro swung the tongs as the man passed, missing him.

The stranger turned toward the corner with Nobuhiro and Sen's father in pursuit.

Sen's vision blurred as the pain redoubled in her head. She pressed her fingers into her temple, desperate to soothe it.

A pair of soft but weighty footfalls soon returned. Her father's measured steps, unchanged since her childhood. The other steps, heavy and light with a drag. They belonged to Nobuhiro. A slowness of steps with no struggle.

"He's gone," her father said.

"Gone?" another male voice asked. "He moves quickly."

"Yes, he does," Nobuhiro said. "He should."

She rubbed again at her temple, shaking her head and trying to clear her vision. "Did you recognize him?" she asked in the direction of Nobuhiro. "I've seen him at the castle but do not know his name."

"His name is Funaki. I remember him from my days there. Other kids used to make fun of the way he looked, but he was strong and agile for his bulk. He was a good fighter when he was a child."

The blurriness receded and Sen found herself staring at Nobuhiro. "What was he doing here?"

Nobuhiro shook his head. "I don't know, but I have my suspicions."

"I know why he was here," her mother spat as she stepped forward.

"Silence," Sen's father said, his mouth drawn in tightly, his eyes brooking no reply. "We can discuss this later. For now, Sen, you must go to the doctor. My wife, please take her. I will be along shortly."

Sen's mother circled behind her and Sen felt her mother's firm hands under her arms. Sen placed her hands on the ground and pushed, looking for support on the soft earth. She didn't have the strength. She rolled to her knees and rose slowly, her mother's hands on her back. Sen licked her lips, catching a salty flavor.

Blood.

Father rushed over and took one arm, insisting again that Sen seek medical attention. She didn't want to go but lost an argument with the pain in her face and the puffiness of her eyes.

She glanced at Nobuhiro, hoping he wouldn't notice.

For a man with a limp who left his home because he couldn't please his father, you fought like a samurai.

What did he think of her clumsy attempt to assist him? Did she just get in the way? All she seemed to have managed was to get herself hurt. If Nobuhiro hadn't knocked the sword out of Funaki's hand, she would be dead.

She would have failed in her duty to her parents because of her own stupidity. She should have gotten her father, like her mother had said.

"I should go to the castle," Nobuhiro announced, looking around at everyone but directing the comment at her father. "My brothers should be informed of Funaki's actions. They will know what to do."

"And what will you do?" Sen's mother asked her father.

"I need to extinguish the forge in the shop. It should take just a few minutes. I will see you at the doctor's place."

"Master," Nobuhiro said. "Please go with your daughter. I'll take care of the forge."

"No," her father said. "You need to go to the castle." Her father turned to the two men. "Will you assist my wife in getting Sen to the physician?"

The men nodded.

Sen could barely make out the two men, much less remember if she knew them. Both were dressed like local merchants with simple white shirts and blue jackets. The man who spoke had white spots on his clothes. Rice flour? Likely a baker. The other man's clothes were free of any spots to suggest what he did.

Sen's parents bowed to the two men. Each stepped to one side of Sen, taking control of an arm while her mother stepped away. Their firm hands gripped under her shoulders. She was grateful for the support. She would have been a burden to her mother.

"One more thing," Father said, placing his arm on Nobuhiro's shoulder. "Thank you, again, for protecting my family. We are in your debt."

Sen's father and mother bowed low to Nobuhiro. Sen did the same as best she could, fighting the pain that throbbed in her head.

###

Nobuhiro stared at Sen as her mother and the two men escorted her toward the road. He wanted to help, but his duty lay elsewhere.

She tried to assist me and nearly died for it. Poor Sen. If I could only move like a normal person, I would have defeated Funaki. Instead of capturing him, I let him escape.

He cursed his limp and his limited abilities. There was nothing he could do. He appreciated Master Goami's kind words, but he would have to admit his shortcomings to his father and brothers.

His brothers would have succeeded.

He had failed.

But why had Funaki been here at all? Was he the man behind the arrow attack? He was never a great archer. It would explain why he missed. But nothing explained the attack.

Nobuhiro recalled the arrow incident. The rider had appeared taller and more muscular. The body type was different from Funaki's. However, it was difficult to be sure since the rider had been seated. Funaki was one of the four suspects his brother had mentioned. Still, if the rider wasn't Funaki, then who could it have been?

That left the three other suspects. Kitayama. Michiba. Nishioji.

Nobuhiro vaguely recalled Kitayama. He was older. Uji's age, with Uji's height and Toshi's build. He could have fit the rider. Michiba? His brothers had praised Michiba's skill with a bow at the archery competition. If he was as good as his brothers said, then the shot wouldn't have been high.

How about Nishioji? His brothers had mentioned him as a possible suspect. Nobuhiro's childhood tormentor was also good with a bow. He would have missed on purpose just to laugh at Nobuhiro, like he did as a child.

He had eventually stopped.

One day as a youth, Nishioji disappeared for a week. When Nobuhiro saw Nishioji again, he had a black eye and a long scab running down his right cheek.

He claimed he had slipped.

The scab had healed into a thin scar.

Had the rider had a scar? Had he worn a mask to hide a scar as much as to hide his actions? Would it be as visible on him as an adult as it had been when he was a child?

"Nobuhiro." Master Goami's voice cut through the speculation.

"Yes, Master?"

Master handed Nobuhiro the two halves of Funaki's blade. "Take these with you. You can show them to your family as evidence."

"I will."

"A very interesting experience, this attack."

Master Goami had questions as well. He crafted swords for many samurai, but Funaki had never been a customer. "How so?"

The old man's eyes lit up like lightning, hinting at the thunder underneath. He exhaled sharply with a huge sigh.

Pride laced with disgust.

There was more here than just the attack.

Master Goami scratched his chin. "A sword carries the spirit of the one who crafts it. The glaze on the metal is from another swordsmith I know. The sword is cheaply made, like the soul of its craftsman. It's good that this man switched to producing guns. He is not worthy to fashion a true sword. Even my tools bested it."

Master Goami smiled at Nobuhiro. "My tools and you," he added.

Nobuhiro again basked in his master's praise, though

he doubted whether it was deserved. Best to focus on the attack.

"There is some food in the kitchen," Master Goami said as he walked toward the workshop. "You should eat before you go."

Nobuhiro nodded, placing the hilt half in his belt. He was not hungry, but the feeling from the battle that sustained him would soon pass. "Please take care of Sen."

And please forgive me for how much I've failed.

Nobuhiro slipped out of his shoes as he entered the house, grabbing two seaweed-wrapped rice balls and a cloth to wrap the blade pieces. The trip to the castle would take an hour or so, less if he hurried.

More time for Funaki to get away and hide.

How I wish I could run. How I wish I could even walk properly.

Chapter Ten

Nobuhiro's trip to the castle took less time than he expected. It was still the hour of the snake when he arrived and it would be some time before midday. He had spent most of the trip worried about Sen. Each step, as quick as he tried to be, still seemed slow.

He wiped the sweat from his brow as he approached the gate. Fresh scents of grass and trees filled the air, mixing with the sounds of business that ringed the edge of the grounds. Thankfully, it was not hotter. It often warmed early in Himeji.

He presented himself to one of the four sentries at the outer gate. All four men were dressed in identical blue kimonos and gray *hakamas*. Nobuhiro didn't recognize any of them, proof of his time away. However, his name still carried recognition as all four raised eyebrows when he mentioned it.

Everyone was familiar with the name of the runaway son.

One of the sentries sprinted to the castle. A few minutes later, Toshi arrived, running as quickly as he could. His characteristic tooth-bearing smile evident.

"Brother, the guard said it was urgent. What brings you here?"

Nobuhiro stared at him and said nothing. He didn't know where to begin.

Toshi's smile disappeared. "Come with me."

He knows.

Nobuhiro followed Toshi, who headed straight for the castle. Both brothers gave a quick nod to the retainers at the entrance, men dressed the same as the ones at the gate, but older. One of them was familiar, but Nobuhiro couldn't place him. The men knew Toshi and allowed Nobuhiro to pass.

From there, they headed to the armory on the lowest level. The odor of oil mixed with powder pervaded the air. Uji was already there, giving instructions to several men. One glance and he dismissed the subordinates before walking over.

"Brother, your face is as blank as an unfinished statue. What brings you here?"

Nobuhiro bit his lip, then brought out the broken halves of the sword, displaying them on the cloth. "We had an intruder at the house about an hour ago."

Toshi's eyebrows rose. He, too, checked his surroundings, though he was always aware of everything, and slid the door to the room shut.

Uji's face went ashen as he studied the blade.

Nobuhiro expected questions and waited for them.

None came.

Just Uji's pronouncement: "Father is in the secondary armory. He will want to know."

The words struck Nobuhiro's gut, but he held back any comment. He pulled at his fingers, but there was no erasing the tension or warming his clammy palms. He had hoped to avoid his father.

His brothers wouldn't judge his failure to capture Funaki.

His father would have no such reserve.

The three brothers left the castle and went to locate

their father. They found their father talking with two other retainers.

Nobuhiro locked eyes with his father, bowing slightly.

His father didn't return Nobuhiro's bow, nor did he acknowledge Nobuhiro's presence.

Nobuhiro's fists clenched, but he kept them by his side.

"A word, Father?" Uji said.

The elder Tokoda dismissed the other two retainers, then looked at his oldest son. "What is it?"

Uji handed the sword pieces to his father, who examined them, turning the pieces in his strong, dexterous fingers.

His father's face did not flinch. "This looks like Funaki's blade. Why do you have it?"

"Nobuhiro brought it to us," Uji said.

The old man turned and finally acknowledged Nobuhiro. Nobuhiro's cheeks seared under the gaze, which soon bored into him.

I am your son. Not your enemy.

"How did you obtain this? Explain," his father said in a quiet voice that indicated only a cold logic in the mind of the speaker.

"Funaki was prowling at the Goami residence, listening at the window. I charged him from behind and slammed him into the wall of the house."

"Go on. Do not leave out any details this time."

Nobuhiro gritted his teeth and recounted the rest of it, staring at his father the whole time. He tried once to look at his brothers and include them in his explanation. The sharp inhalation from his father made Nobuhiro shrink and return to the conversation.

His father pondered the story for a few minutes.

Nobuhiro straightened his back and prepared for the rebuke to come.

"And so you let him flee," his father said. It wasn't a question.

No concern. No caring. No credit.

Just cold.

Nobuhiro had fought hard with the only weapon at his disposal. Yet his past demons resided in the disappointment in his father's words.

Enough.

I defeated a samurai.

I protected the family of the master I serve.

You will not make me feel less of a man for it.

He raised his face to stare at his father. "Yes, he got away. One of *your* men ran away. Have your training methods fallen so much that one of *your* retainers could not stand up to someone lame like me? Perhaps you should retire. Your time is over."

Nobuhiro steeled himself for the verbal barrage to come. He'd challenged his father and in front of his brothers. Such insults would not be overlooked.

Instead, the elder man lifted his chin to the left only slightly, not losing eye contact. "Perhaps." His voice was unchanged. Icy.

His father turned and headed toward the door, carrying Funaki's sword. Before exiting the room, he looked back, his gaze flitting to Nobuhiro like a dagger backhanded at a target.

"Thank you for bringing this matter to our attention," he said. "Ensure that the young lady heals before returning. Make sure she has a suitable escort. You would probably suffice."

He then whipped around and walked out.

Nobuhiro swung back and allowed himself to face his brothers. Both were grinning, trying to contain their laughter.

"There are some plusses to not reporting to Father," Uji said. "Maybe you had a good idea when you left seven years ago."

Toshi nodded. "Fighting Funaki with iron tongs was amazing. But standing up to Father? It would be easier to face ten heavily armed men without a weapon."

Nobuhiro exhaled, letting out his anxiety along with it. “I feared his reaction. But I realized I’d fought well. I wasn’t going to let him belittle what happened.”

Nobuhiro felt a hard slap on his back. It was Uji, trying to comfort him. “Don’t concern yourself with it. Father expects those who serve him to be able to tie down a typhoon. Anything less faces a greater wrath than the weather.”

“I do not serve him,” Nobuhiro said.

“Then, Nobuhiro,” Toshi said, his face adopting Uji’s usual stoic manner, “maybe you should ask yourself why you try so hard to impress him.”

The rebuke struck Nobuhiro hard and his chest tightened. He hated it when his brothers were right. However, they often saw things with more presence of their surroundings than he did.

A trait he didn’t inherit.

From his father.

“We’ll walk you to the main gate,” Uji said. “Please give our regards to Sen. I hope her injuries are minor.”

Sen. How much had the meeting with his father distracted Nobuhiro? He’d forgotten about the woman who’d gotten hurt trying to protect him.

He nodded back to his brothers and followed them to the door.

The walk back to the house would be long.

###

Sen leaned back against the wall, holding a compress to her cheek and right eye. A tray of rice and soup lay to her left. Her mother shuffled in carrying two wooden teacups on another tray. She grabbed the pot hanging over the hearth in the middle of the room, adding hot water to both cups. She handed one cup to Sen and then knelt, sitting on the backs of her feet.

“It’s my turn to fuss over you now. How do you feel?” her mother asked.

Sen pressed the compress to her face and her cheek recoiled in pain. “It hurts.” She grimaced with every word.

The trip to the doctor's place had been a relief. Nothing more serious than a black eye. Her right cheek was bruised. Thankfully, her jaw wasn't broken.

"You're fortunate you weren't hurt worse than you were."

"I know."

The morning's events cascaded through her head. Mother was right. She could have been killed, ending any hope of fulfilling her duty to her parents. They needed her more than Nobuhiro did.

But she couldn't stand by and watch him fight alone.

"You owe Nobuhiro thanks," her mother said.

"I know. I'll tell him when he returns."

"You also owe him a debt."

Her mother's words resonated in her heart. She owed a blood debt to Nobuhiro. Not easy to repay.

She had tried to satisfy one from the incident with the archer.

Now she owed him two.

She took a sip of tea, letting it warm the inside of her mouth as the steam heated her face. Her stomach growled. It had been a while since she had eaten. The rice would be soft, but she doubted she could chew. Miso soup would be good and it wouldn't hurt.

Thinking about her debts to Nobuhiro caused enough pain.

"So, what were we discussing when we were interrupted?" Sen tried to smile but soon brought her hand to her face.

Sen's mother didn't return her cheerful attitude. The good spirits she had shown earlier dissipated, replaced with a pained expression that matched Sen's own.

"I don't know what you're talking about," her mother said.

She's avoiding it. Maybe it's too early to bring it up.

Still, the desire within Sen drove her to push on. "We were discussing the cryptic message you mentioned earlier."

Her mother gazed at the window before turning back to Sen. "I don't wish to discuss it. That man may be around somewhere."

"By now he must be in hiding. There's nowhere for him to go. Once Nobuhiro tells his brothers, I am sure they will catch up with him quickly."

"I don't care. As I've told you before, your sister's gone. I don't intend to lose you to such foolish actions as well."

Sen considered her mother's words. *Foolish actions?* They repeated a theme. "You've mentioned that before. What do you mean?"

Her mother sighed and shook her head. Sen recalled that look from her childhood, at times when she'd begged her mother for things. She was about to give in.

Sen rose and walked toward the window, looking intently to confirm if anyone was there. Convinced, she closed the sliding panes, locked them, and knelt back down. "Are you satisfied?"

Her mother hesitated, trying to shrug as if her shoulders bore an unseen weight. "Do not make light of a mother's worries. One day, when you have children, you will understand. For now, just accept a mother's wisdom."

Sen shook her head. Her mother's resolve had returned. The conversation kept hitting barriers as solid as the mud walls that protected some temples. This was something else. "What did you mean by 'foolish actions'? You've mentioned it twice. What did Haru do?"

Sen's mother rubbed her forehead, something Sen had seen her do many times. She didn't remember if her mother did it while Sen was growing up. It was a habit now.

"Do you have a headache? Can I get you some water?"

Her mother looked as if she was about to burst with sadness. Her eyes moistened. Tears flowed slowly down her cheeks as she buried her face in her hands.

"Mother, what is it?" Sen rose and rushed to her

mother's side.

"Haven't you realized it yet?" her mother asked in a tone that sounded almost disapproving. "Are you so dense? Someone spies on us and it doesn't concern you?"

Her concern for her mother. Her worries for her duty. Her feelings for Nobuhiro. They had all clouded her judgment. "I'm sorry, but I don't understand. Please explain it to me."

Her mother hesitated, as if trying to draw strength from some untapped source. "Your sister's death was not an accident."

Sen's entire body went weak. She put her hand to the tatami floor to steady herself and took several breaths. Her pulse raced inside her, touching nerves and finding them deadened. "What do you mean? Haru and her husband died in a fire. It was in the letter you sent."

"Yes, but I didn't tell you everything. I couldn't. I was afraid."

Sen imagined her sister, dealing with what must have been a painful way to die. To find out that it hadn't been an accident was more than she could bear. "What was missing? What didn't you tell me?"

Sen's mother dried her tears with shaking hands. Then, she grabbed her kimono, tightly balling her fists, as if ready to rip the light blue silk.

Sen put her hands on her mother's shoulders and squeezed tight. "Mother, what didn't you tell me?"

"Haru . . . and Jiro . . . were attending a church service. Someone set the place on fire while they were there."

Chapter Eleven

Nobuhiro rose early, like always, and went to the workshop to prepare it for the day. The spring months, particularly the crisp, cool, early-morning air, usually brought out his best mood.

However, this late April morning didn't lighten his spirits.

Two days had passed since the attack at the house. Life had returned to normal. He had checked on Sen the previous night. She was better and would return to the castle soon. He had hoped to spend some time with her, but her mother doted on her continuously, leaving him little opportunity.

He lit the candle in the lantern affixed to the wall. The shaded panes cast a glow on the workshop that overlaid the moonlight streaming in from the window. A cup of tea and a rice ball lay on a tray on the table. The corners of his mouth turned up slightly.

Sen knew his schedule.

That knowledge lifted his mood in a way that spring could not.

Nobuhiro took a sip of the green tea. Its bitterness

was a sharp poker to his senses. He then lit the forge and sat down for his snack, adding more wood. Within fifteen minutes, the fire was roaring. He got to work.

After two hours passed, his stomach gnawed at him. He considered sneaking into the kitchen and grabbing something but decided now was not the time.

"Good morning," Sen said, walking through the doorway with a tray of food. Her dark hair, tied with a white ribbon, brushed her shoulders. It looked like silk against the linen of her green *yukata*, the summer kimono she wore. A matching obi was tied across her middle. The swelling in her face had receded but was still noticeable.

She was still beautiful.

He put down his tools and bowed as she walked into the room. "Good morning. It's good to see you up and around. What's all this?"

"I prepared breakfast for my parents. I wanted to bring you a tray as well."

"The rice ball was nice. I can eat when your father gets here like I always do."

"My father is with my mother this morning. She is fine, but Father's concerned that she may be tired. He trusts you'll take care of the shop."

Master Goami's trust was appreciated. Nobuhiro had been here many years, but was he ready to go out on his own? He had a lot to learn in his final year.

Sen placed the tray on a low table near a workbench. Dried fish and cold pickles sat on the main plate. Two bamboo bowls, one filled with rice and the other with miso soup, were on the right. A raw egg lay next to them. A pair of chopsticks lay along the bottom of the tray, one end perched on a small stand.

The soup's aroma made his mouth water and his stomach growled in response. "I hope your mother improves. Did she eat at all this morning?"

Sen glanced down, trying to hide an embarrassed smile. "Neither of them had started eating when I left my parents' room, but they asked that I return in an hour and pick up the trays."

"Have you eaten?"

"I'm really not hungry. Maybe later after I clear the dishes."

Nobuhiro knelt, catching a slight frown on her face. "Is something wrong?"

"Nothing. I just realized I forgot the tea. I'll be right back."

She returned shortly carrying a small pot, her slippers making no sound on the wooden floor. His face grew hot. He hadn't touched his food since she left. She grinned and motioned to the tray. "Please eat before it gets cold."

He obliged and asked her to join him. She knelt, sitting back on her feet and sweeping her *yukata* under her knees. The green suited her well.

He cracked the egg and allowed the contents to congeal on his steaming rice. Then, grabbing the chopsticks, he lifted the bowl to chin level and began eating. "It's good your mother is better. I'd asked your father about her, but he didn't say much."

"Father isn't talkative on issues like this. It's not his nature."

He put down the chopsticks. "Do you need to do anything else for them? I don't want to keep you from something."

"You're not. This is the first opportunity I've had to talk with you since the intruder."

He stared into her brown eyes and winced at the fading bruises. Nobuhiro would never forget him. The sight of him striking her. The hatred on his face. It stayed with him.

She tilted her head. Her down-the-middle part held, revealing a few strands of red.

Nobuhiro sat back. "Your hair. You have red hair?"

She looked away and blushed, running her hands through the streaks and burying them under the rest of her black locks. "Yes, just a touch."

"It's rare. I've heard stories that some women have it,

but I can't remember having seen it before."

"More women have it than you'd think."

"Why do you hide it?"

Pausing, she rolled her lips inward, flattening them. "It's not good to stand out sometimes. Red hair is a memorable feature."

He nodded, understanding the implication. The proverb "the nail that sticks up gets hammered down" defined society. Her hair, like her faith, stood out and made her different.

Another thing for his father not to like about her.

Toshi's question came back to him. Why did Nobuhiro care what his father thought?

He had been correct.

Even though Nobuhiro had stood up to his father, the assertiveness was only a start. His father still ruled him.

Whatever it took, though, Nobuhiro would protect Sen.

He took a bite of rice. "The color suits you."

Her face flushed as a smile crossed it. "Thank you." She turned toward the ground. When she raised her head again, the smile had disappeared. "How was it? Did you enjoy your breakfast?"

"Yes, it was good, though I don't deserve a special meal."

"You fought to protect my family. You escorted me home the day I came here. I never showed my appreciation. Also, Father tells me you've been working extra long to allow him time to care for my mother."

His face warmed at her kind words. "That's my duty. I have learned much from your father."

A breeze blew through the room and goose bumps rose on his arms. He looked at the forge. He'd neglected it. He rushed over and added more wood. The smaller pieces caught quickly and he applied the bellows. The heat grew and warmed his frame. Satisfied the fire was growing hotter, he turned toward Sen. "Speaking of duty, if I don't watch the fire, your father will say I've neglected mine."

He sat back down and looked directly at her. "Why do you believe in this God?"

She grabbed a second cup from a pocket in her coat and poured herself some tea, holding the ceramic cup in both hands, staring into space, and not focusing on anything as she wet her lips. She was choosing her words. "Why do you ask?"

"Maybe I'm wrong, but I don't understand how it's benefited you. Jiro tried to explain it to me. Your sister did as well."

"Haru spoke to you about it?" Sen asked, her eyes sparkling.

Nobuhiro recalled his conversations with Jiro. His friend believed, but Haru was the strength behind his faith. "Yes, she did, but I never understood the need for it." His tone perked to match Sen's. He felt duplicitous but couldn't help himself. He would do anything to see that smile. "Perhaps you could explain it to me. From the beginning."

The corners of her mouth turned up as she began the story of the man she called the Son of God. Her smile never wavered with a single word.

"He's brought me peace, Nobuhiro. He has strengthened me inside, to face the trials of life. They have been great of late."

Her faith was amazing. Haru had carried the same conviction.

So had Jiro.

He went back to check the fire and coughed at the smoke. Then, grabbing a rag, he wiped his face and grabbed his cup for more tea. "Would you have faced these trials had you not believed in this God?"

She paused and shook her head. "Hard to say. No one knows what life will bring. The servants still in Haibara may be facing more difficult trials than I am. I have heard no news."

He smiled. "On that we agree."

Sen ran her fingers through her hair and the red

strands poked through again. From now on, he would always look for them. They were rare, just like her. She tilted her head. "May I ask you a favor before I go?"

Nobuhiro's face and back straightened. "You are Master's daughter. I am at your service. You need not request permission."

"You are samurai born. It is I who should show deference."

"I rejected that heritage when I became your father's apprentice. What do you need?"

Sen inhaled and then let it out slowly. "I want to clean the grave. Would you escort me to the cemetery and assist me?"

A hole of shame opened in Nobuhiro's gut. He had not brought food to Jiro and Haru in over two months, hardly a show of respect for someone to whom he owed much. Still, Funaki was out there. If he found them, would he desecrate the holy site?

Nobuhiro had embarrassed Funaki. Nothing would be sacred.

He bowed to her. "I will. Thank you again for breakfast."

"Thank you again for what you have done for my family." She bowed to him. "I must go and look in on my parents."

He nodded and remained silent. She turned and headed to the door. Her steps slow.

He watched, entranced, not that he could have moved.

She closed the door and he heaved a sigh, rubbing his palms together. This faith had brought nothing but trouble. It had killed Jiro and Master Goami's older daughter. It had brought attacks on Sen and her parents. Continued belief meant continued suffering.

He had to find a way to tell her.

She would hate him for his words, but it must be done for the sake of the family. He had to ignore his feelings and dissuade her from finding others.

But did he have what it took to tell Sen?

Chapter Twelve

Kaiken struck Funaki across the face, sending him to the floor, and then kicked him in the head. Foot struck bone with a crack. "You fool. What were you doing there?"

Funaki hacked up blood and spit on the floor. "I was nearby. I knew she was there. I thought to listen at the house. Our previous attempts to discover anything had failed. We needed something new."

"That was not part of my direction. Then you lost a fight with that lame simpleton. How could you let him defeat you? He's not even samurai."

Funaki rolled to his knees, placing his face on the floor and keeping his eyes down. "I have no excuse."

"There is no excuse for you. You are pathetic."

"I am deeply sorry. I regret my actions."

Kaiken kicked him again in the face. "Your worthless apology accomplishes nothing. Your usefulness to our mission is finished. By now, Tokoda knows who you are. He will find you."

Funaki nodded slowly. "Then I have a duty to perform. If you will grant me permission?"

"Granted."

Funaki rose and sat back on his feet. He pulled at his kimono, loosing it from the belt.

Kaiken's rage exploded. "Not here, you fool. Someplace else. By yourself."

"Why not here? It is my right. I am—"

"Boar snouts! You are not worthy of a second. The prolonged pain is your punishment."

"*Hai.*" He knelt back on the floor, bowing low, and then crawled to the door. He bowed again and left.

Footsteps shuffled outside and then disappeared, followed by the low sound of birds chirping. Quiet then filled the air again.

Kaiken tasted the salt and copper of blood. The blood of punishment. "I must have hit him harder than I thought."

Michiba stepped forward. "Blood is a good sign. It can signal death. It can also signal rebirth. Funaki's death is necessary, but what if he's caught before he can complete his duty?"

Kaiken mulled Michiba's words. "He will only be caught if he tries to be dramatic about it. He was clumsy. It cost him this life. His future actions will be a chance to redeem himself. Do it well and the gods may one day allow him again to be a samurai."

Michiba nodded. "If he does it proudly, then it may pull others to our cause. Our numbers dwindle. Once we were seven, a proud band. Now we are three. We need more to continue."

Stepping forward, Kaiken grabbed the necks of Michiba and Kitayama. "Even small numbers can wreak great damage. Soon others will join us. We will survive. For now, we can recommit. Michiba, by chance, are you carrying anything to eat?"

Michiba reached under his kimono and produced a rice ball. "Yes."

Kaiken smiled, took out a small piece of cloth, then laid it on a nearby table and nodded to Kitayama. Kitayama pulled out his short sword slightly, cutting his thumb on the blade and then allowing a drop of blood to fall on the piece of cloth. Michiba followed and did the same. Kaiken completed the ritual. The rice ball was broken into three pieces. The cloth was then burned and ashes sprinkled on the rice. Handing pieces to Michiba and Kitayama, Kaiken then raised the remaining portion in the air. "We will see this through. Our master will be proud."

The ash of commitment tasted sweet.

###

Sen brought her hands together and bowed before the grave. The sun warmed the back of her neck as she bent down, holding the position.

Haru, I wish I'd made it home in time to see you. I miss you very much.

The scent of cedar and dirt drifted on the wind. Crows cawed as if watching from above, adding to the prayers. She rose and stared at the stone marker in front of her. The name Goami was carved deep.

Female voices closed in from the left as two women carrying rakes, other small tools, and a bag approached a grave marker two rows away. More family remembering family. Duty combined with love.

Dragonflies buzzed around her. One alit on the marker. Even insects paid their respects as well. How often had she come here as a child with Haru, with her mother and father, to take care of this marker? Many generations of Goamis had been laid to rest here, cared for by their descendants. The last time she had come here, Haru had been with her.

Now she was cleaning it for Haru.

A clunk of wood sounded behind her, and she turned, her breath in her throat before her nerves then relaxed. Nobuhiro had startled her. Had she forgotten his presence?

No, she had lost herself in thought. Once again, she had forgotten Lord Akamatsu's admonition for vigilance.

He looked solemn, almost upset. "I'll start with the weeds around the marker and then rake the area. Do you want to work on the grave itself?"

Sen nodded and began the process, grabbing a cup of water from the small bucket they had brought with them. She poured the water over the stone and applied a brush. Loose dirt and dust, now moist, streaked the stone and she wiped them away. She applied more and repeated the process, pouring water on the characters, pushing brush and cloth through them.

Sen looked back at Nobuhiro, who was on his knees on the ground. "Have you come here often?"

"I came once a month after they died, though it has been two months since my last visit. Jiro was my best friend. He is the reason I came to be with your family."

She grasped her chest. "How did that happen? How did you know him?"

"He was the one who found me on the street. He remembered me from deliveries he had made at the castle. He gave me food and brought me back to your house. Within a week, I was your father's apprentice."

Sen wiped her hand along her sleeve, glancing at the area around the plot. Nobuhiro had been on the street by himself? He was so young and all alone. At least when Sen had left the castle, she still had friends to support her. Lord Akamatsu gave away his own resources to support others. Who did Nobuhiro have when he left the castle? How long would he have survived? What job would he have found?

"It is kind of you to look after the grave. You care for my parents very much."

"I would die for them. I would have died for Jiro. I would have died to protect your sister. I would have done anything to spare your parents this pain."

Sen's chest warmed at his words. "I know you would. I would do the same."

Nobuhiro inhaled sharply. "If that is the way you feel, then why do you not come home? You do your parents no good at the castle."

"I have to stay at the castle. Lord Akamatsu commanded me to be there. He said it was for my protection."

"And yet you take chances like visiting that cross."

Sen paused. He was right. She'd gone there alone, always alone. Leaving herself open to attack. Why had she done that? She rubbed at the scars on her neck, feeling the thin line. Did she regret the shame of survival? She opened her mouth, but nothing came out.

"Then you attacked Funaki," he continued. "Don't you understand? You must live, for the sake of your family. Nothing is more important than that. Do you wish to die?"

She closed her eyes to hold the tears. She had tried to help him, but he was right. She had nearly gotten herself killed. Why had she done that?

Haru?

Had she done it for Haru?

The samurai who had attacked the house was connected to Haru's death.

Had she wanted revenge?

Possibly.

Revenge for the killings in Haibara. Revenge for Haru.

It was not the Christian way.

"I understand," she said.

She glanced back at the stone, staring at the etched name. A tribute to generations of swordsmiths.

A line that now rested with her alone.

Nobuhiro handed her a brush to continue cleaning. His hand touched her palm, sending warm shards up her arm. His touch, like the first time at the castle, was gentle again. His skin was tough, the effect of years of hard work. She felt his strength, saw it in his eyes. He cared about her. He would do anything for her.

Those who tried to hurt her might hurt him.

She couldn't allow that to happen.

###

Nobuhiro's chest expanded as Sen pulled her hand away from his, her delicate fingers as soft as her features. Her long hair was tied at the top, held by a red lacquer comb. It suited her face and hid the red strands within her dark hair.

He had watched her work earlier. Industrious like her sister and caring like her mother, Sen brushed the base of the grave, scraping away the dirt and twigs that covered it. The afternoon sun reflected off the comb. He tried to look away, but the light brown kimono she wore hugged her curves. He licked his lips.

"Nobuhiro, do you have something you want to ask me?"

He shook his head as the blood rushed to his face. She had caught him staring, another example of the simple-minded person he was. "I was just looking at the marker. I still can't believe it. They were both so young."

"Yes, they were." She paused and shook her head slowly. "Now, they keep my grandparents company."

"Your grandparents?" He stared at the stone. "I did not think about them. Master Goami has never mentioned his parents. They were not around when I was here."

"My grandmother died when I was nine. My grandfather died two years before I left. He trained several swordsmiths, including my father. My father told me he used to spend his days watching my grandfather. They worked together for years."

Nobuhiro stepped forward and traced the etching in the stone. A great line of swordsmiths. Attention to craftsmanship and detail. A gift to receive and a style to carry forward. Was he worthy? Could he ever repay the debt he owed?

Did he deserve this family?

###

Sen watched as Nobuhiro traced the lines of her family name. As a child, she had traced them herself. Never had she touched it with the depth of feeling that Nobuhiro had just showed.

She reached into her bag and brought out two incense sticks, placing them in a small bowl carved into the base. She lit the sticks, using a stone lantern nearby for the fire.

The smell of sandalwood reached out and soothed her nerves. She stepped back. "Nobuhiro, would you say a prayer with me?"

Nobuhiro sidled next to her, his arm brushing against her sleeve, the warmth of his touch flowing through the kimono. He reached in his kimono and brought out a rice cup and dried fruit, laying them next to the incense. A fitting complement to what she brought. Not a Christian but no less an offering. "I do not know a Christian prayer. I would not feel comfortable saying it even if I did."

"You honor your beliefs. I will honor mine."

He raised his eyebrows but did not respond, instead turning to face the marker, clapping twice, and then bowing. She clapped twice herself and bowed her head, keeping her hands together at her waist as she prayed.

After a few seconds, she opened her eyes and looked at Nobuhiro. He seemed to be waiting for her. "Again that look. What is it?"

"You do your sister proud. I am just nervous. My father charged me with your safety. Yet even he has no idea what is happening. Maybe Lord Akamatsu was right. You have more protection at the castle."

"Your brothers can't stay with me all the time."

"Not just them." He paused. "Omi protects you, too. She is also a samurai."

"Omi's a samurai?"

"Yes, and she will look after you, too."

Nobuhiro's face grew calm. He trusted his brothers. He trusted Omi. Yet, Nobuhiro had shown himself to be capable.

Now the only thing he showed was that he didn't believe in himself.

Chapter Thirteen

Sen greeted her last morning at home with mixed feelings. Heading back to the castle meant she and her mother were both healthy. For that, she was grateful. She had been away for too long. People might suspect favoritism. Jealousy would make her life more difficult.

A change of scenery would help her concentrate on the clue about the local church. She had thought about it ever since her mother had told her the clue. Nothing had come to mind. Leaving, though, meant she would leave home, the place she had wanted to come to originally when she first returned to Himeji.

She would miss her parents greatly.

She would miss Nobuhiro more.

Separated, she could pray that he would reconcile with his father. Allowing her time to care for her family meant that Nobuhiro's father had a good heart, if only he would show it to Nobuhiro.

Away from Nobuhiro, she could keep him away from her heart.

She headed toward the kitchen, stepping softly on the smooth wooden floor. The warm smell of miso soup flavored the air as her mother finished breakfast preparations.

"Good morning, Mother." Sen bounced toward her. "Let me help you with that."

"Sit down," her mother said. "This is your last day here. Let me take care of you."

She seated herself as her mother put her breakfast before her, then bowed her head and said a quiet prayer. The steam from the rice rose to meet her face, warming her as it had when she was a child.

"A simple *itadakimasu* would have been sufficient, I think," her mother deadpanned. "By the time *you're* finished, your deity must be starving."

"Oh, Mother." Sen gently shook her head and smiled anyway. Christianity scared her mother. Sarcasm likely hid her fear. Sen glanced up as her mother sat to join her.

"You're going to look for it, aren't you?" her mother asked.

Sen had hoped to avoid this topic. Still, she couldn't lie. Especially to her mother. "Do we have to talk about this?"

"What? You've been attacked. Spied on. Yet it's me you're afraid of?"

Sen tried to avert her gaze. It didn't last. "Yes, I will look for the church. I will find it. God will protect me."

"Your deity will do no better job of protecting you than he did your sister." Her mother flung her left hand outward, as if tossing something away. "How do you know He'll do a better job this time?"

"Why must we fight when it is time for me to leave?"

"If you weren't so unreasonable, maybe we wouldn't have this problem."

Sen sighed and rubbed her fingers on the worn bamboo plate in front of her, trying to clarify her thoughts. After what happened to Haru, Mother wasn't open to talking about it.

How would Sen feel in her mother's position?

The door slid open and Sen's father walked in.

"Excuse me, everyone," he said, his smile brighter than Sen had seen since her arrival. "Hope I'm not interrupting anything."

"Nothing," her mother said. "We were just spending a last few moments catching up while we can."

"Good to hear it." Her father wheeled slightly and looked at Sen. "Are you ready to leave? Nobuhiro is waiting outside. He is prepared to escort you back to the castle."

Sen shook slightly and gulped. She had forgotten Nobuhiro was going to walk back with her. Her body quivered at the thought of being with him for the trip.

She bowed to both her parents and stepped outside. There stood Nobuhiro. Though she had seen him nearly every day, he looked different. Polished. He hadn't worked at the shop this morning.

"Good morning, Sen. Are you ready?" he asked.

"Yes. Thank you for agreeing to accompany me."

She turned and said one last goodbye to her parents, who had followed her out the door. From there, Sen and Nobuhiro were off.

Despite the early morning, the humidity draped over Sen like a heavy coat, bringing sweat freely. She glanced skyward. Storm clouds were growing. Along the road, many men worked in the rice fields. Soon they would irrigate in preparation for planting. The heat would only get worse. The men's faces and chests were covered in dirt. The rain would be welcome to both her and the workers. Somewhere nearby, women must be tending the rice seedlings, preparing them for planting. The pit grew in her stomach. She should be with those women. She should be serving her village, not the castle.

Her stomach churned harder. Lord Akamatsu must have been wrong, requiring her to stay.

They walked for thirty minutes before they reached the edge of the market area that led all the way to the castle. Sweat continued to trickle down Sen's neck and back. The walk had been mostly in silence with few passersby. Now more people gathered. The crowd was light, but the bustle of the businesses was a welcome respite. Still, they blocked any breeze.

The air grew thick with the warning of impending rain. Sen noticed two straw merchants nearby. Both were displaying rain jackets in front of the stores. They were about to get busy.

"Would you like to stop for tea before we get there?" Nobuhiro asked.

Sen considered the proposal. The rains would come soon and they needed to hurry. Still, the silence with Nobuhiro had been unbearable. "Are you thirsty?"

"No, I'm just concerned that I'm taxing you. I have been worried about you since your injuries."

She glanced at the ground as heat sped to her cheeks. "That's very kind of you. Did you have a place in mind?"

Nobuhiro didn't answer. Instead, he jerked his head slightly askance and indicated for her to glance in that general direction. She looked but didn't understand at first.

"There," he said, motioning with his hand.

Sen took a second look and then smiled. It was the place they had been before. "I don't know," she said, laughing. "What do you think Toshi and Omi would say if they knew we went without them?"

"It won't irritate them too much, I'm certain." Nobuhiro grinned in a way that calmed her. He had a good smile, indicative of his warm heart.

As they stepped toward the entrance, Sen saw the hanging medallion she remembered from the last time she was here, the one indicating happiness. She brushed her fingers over it. The metal was cool to the touch. A dog barked nearby and she withdrew her hand, noting a little white dog with short hair at the bottom of the steps. The dog seemed to smile at her. She smiled back and entered.

They took their seats and ordered. The server brought tea and mochi quickly.

"I know you enjoyed being home, but are you looking forward to returning to the castle?" Nobuhiro asked.

Sen sipped her tea. “Yes, it will be good to get back to work. I have not been here long enough to have been gone so long from my duties.”

Nobuhiro nodded his concurrence. He understood duty. Did she? She looked about. The place was mostly empty, but that could change at any time.

It had to be now.

“Nobuhiro, there may be a church somewhere in town.”

His lips thinned into a line. “Even with the edict. Even after what’s happened. You believe that Christians would still gather? Where is this place?”

“I don’t know. Mother had a clue about where one might be, but she didn’t know anything else.”

Sen related what Mother had told her as Nobuhiro sat rapt. “What do you think?”

“Joy springs from burying your bitterness in the ground,” he repeated. “It makes no sense.”

“I know, but it’s the only clue I have. Will you help me find it?”

He inhaled, taking the air through his teeth. Whatever his answer, he believed she wouldn’t like it. She clenched her teeth as her nerves danced like an apprentice geisha. Spice scents wafted through the air, but her mouth was dry.

“I will help you,” he said, “but I agree with your Mother. This religion. It has brought sorrow to your family. As I said at the cemetery, I fear more will come.”

Sen stared at the floor, absorbing his rebuke in her gut. Her jaw tightened, but she steeled herself to stay placid and looked back at Nobuhiro. “If you don’t believe it, then why would you help?”

“Jiro would have wanted me to help. Your sister would have wanted me to help, to look after you.”

“And what do you want?”

A foursome of men took seats near them and Nobuhiro did not answer. Just as well. It was time to go.

She needed to get back.

###

Nobuhiro accompanied Sen the rest of the way. Both had said little since they left the restaurant. Approaching thunder filled the silence. His leg winced in response. Many people on the street carried raincoats. It would be a long walk back.

They stopped at the castle's outer entrance at the edge of the stone wall that buttressed the grounds. Sen broke the tension first. "Are you going in to see your brothers?"

He cleared his throat. "I am, but I wanted to say something I can't say inside."

Her soft eyes did little to mask the pain in her face. "What is it?"

His shoulders tensed. "I'll keep my promise. I'll help you look for the church."

She bit down on her lip as she shook her head. "It's not necessary. If you don't believe, then it's best you don't help. I can look on my own."

Her refusal ripped at his gut. He tried to think of a response. A woman's voice interrupted his thoughts.

"Sen, welcome back!"

Omi, dressed in a tight yellow kimono, approached at a fast pace. He and Sen both walked toward her.

"Good to see you, Omi." A wide smile stretched across her face.

Omi responded in kind, her smile emphasizing her dimples. Her black hair was pulled up tightly into a bun with red sticks poking out, and her perfume smelled like honey. She was an attractive lady. Toshi was a lucky man.

"How did you know I was here?" Sen asked.

"We saw you coming from the castle," Omi said.

"We?" Nobuhiro asked. "I only see you."

Omi's cheeks reddened. She flashed a sheepish smile and glanced down. "I was with Toshi," she said. "We saw the two of you from one of the strategic windows."

Nobuhiro looked at the castle, its white structure now framed by dark, billowy clouds. Thunder echoed again as he studied the portals that faced the front entrance, windows with small apertures that opened wide, allowing archers to shoot invaders with little fear of a return volley. As a child, he had walked the castle with his father, who showed him how to aim properly and produce the correct angle. As a child, he had fantasized about saving the castle from attack and his father had laughed.

As a child, he had walked the castle with his father and his father had laughed . . . with him.

He rubbed at his chest as he turned to the ladies. “Your eyesight is remarkable,” he said, impressed.

Omi nodded. “It’s the limp. Toshi’s familiar with it. You have a distinctive gait.”

Nobuhiro glanced back at the windows and imagined his brother chuckling at him. He would never be able to approach an enemy with stealth. He had accepted that. “I should’ve known.”

Omi looked toward the castle. “Your brothers wish to talk to you. There’s been some news.”

Nobuhiro inquired, but Omi added nothing further. It must be private and not for Sen. As they neared the main keep, he saw Uji bounding in their direction.

“Brother, good to see you,” Uji said as he smiled. “And you, too, Sen. Welcome back.”

Nobuhiro watched as Sen and Omi walked toward a building that housed the women’s quarters. He had wanted to say goodbye to Sen before she left, but the presence of Uji and Omi erased his opportunity. Every step Sen took along the worn dirt path pulled at his heart, as if he would never get this close again.

“Even were I blind,” Uji said, “I could see what is in your heart, little brother. She is a beautiful woman and appears to have captured your interest.”

“Yes, but what would our father think?” Nobuhiro answered.

Uji stopped and crossed his arms. “The last time you were here, you did not seem to care.”

Nobuhiro looked at his brother. What should he say?

He thought of Sen. A couple of drops struck his forehead. He wanted to move.

He wanted to talk.

He could trust his older brother.

"I care what our father thinks." The admission struck him hard as he groped for the words. "I've always cared."

Uji grinned. "It's good to hear. But why would he not approve? Though samurai often marry for political reasons or to satisfy obligations, it is possible to marry a woman like Sen. You forget that my wife was an attendant, like Sen. My wife is a bright woman. She runs the house. The fields. The workers. Besides, you are a swordsmith now. Sen would be a suitable match for you."

More drops fell on Nobuhiro, trickling down his face. He glanced about. Various samurai and attendants were passing around them, moving quickly so they wouldn't be caught in the squall. No one was close enough to hear them.

No one was close enough to learn Sen's secret.

"It's not her station in life. It's her beliefs."

Uji wrinkled his lips. "Oh, she's a Christian." He whispered the last word in a mocking tone as the two started walking toward the main building. "That is not a choice one makes lightly."

"I know. Sen discussed it with me. Her older sister and her husband, before they died, also discussed it with me."

"Are you considering it?" Uji asked, arching one eyebrow.

Nobuhiro gaped at the ground before turning back to his brother. "I told Sen that I wasn't interested."

Uji smiled. "You didn't answer my question."

Nobuhiro's throat tightened. "I listened to what she said. You find that strange?"

"I don't," Uji said. "Growing up, you always viewed things in a different way. Toshi and I inherited Father's manner. You inherited Mother's."

"I wish I could remember her."

"You would have been her favorite."

Nobuhiro gazed up at his brother. "She would have considered what the Christian missionaries, or those Japanese who converted, say?"

Uji pursed his lips and shook his head. "She would have listened well and understood. However, I don't think she would've agreed."

Rain sprinkled in a constant patter. It would drench them soon. Nobuhiro ignored it. "And you? Have you listened?'

Uji paused. "I have. It is the duty of a samurai to open his mind to all the possibilities in the world, so long as it does not impact his service to his master."

"Then what do you think?"

Uji looked up at the sky as if measuring his own words. "It's not for me. I have many issues with it."

"Such as?" Nobuhiro asked.

"I heard accounts of how these Christian missionaries first arrived forty years ago. They came on large ships, along with men who wished to trade with us. These men claimed to be from halfway around the world."

Nobuhiro chuckled. "I have heard the stories."

Uji ran his hand over his head. "These men were a study in contrasts. They brought a new religion in tandem with their goods. They also brought guns. One does not need to be skilled to kill with such a device. There is no honor in fighting with it."

"Yet samurai now use these weapons," Nobuhiro said.

"Yes, it's slowly replacing the way we've always done things. The number of swordsmiths dwindles as some of them turn from making swords to producing guns. Within a few years, samurai will fight as easily with a gun as with a sword. I fear this religion will sweep our country the same way."

Nobuhiro stopped, tapping his toe on the ground. "From what I've learned, these men possess different tools. I've heard stories of their ships. Have you seen any of them? Are they as huge as rumored? Maybe they have things they can teach us."

"Yes, I saw their ships during the campaign last year down south in Kyushu. The technical knowledge of these foreigners surpasses ours. Despite this"—he softened his voice—"the motivation of their leaders matches ours."

"What do you mean?" Nobuhiro asked, tilting his head.

"Last year, one of the missionaries offered their largest ship to the regent so he could take Kyushu."

"I didn't know that."

Uji's face darkened, matching the clouds. "The missionary thought to provide himself with a way to establish a permanent place in Kyushu for his religious efforts. However, this was a man of politics, not of religion. Such a man is no better than those members of certain Buddhist sects who take money for protection or sexual favors. Within a week of his victory, the regent ordered all missionaries to leave the country."

"And now Christians live in fear."

"Not everywhere. Their faith is still practiced openly in Kyushu, especially in Nagasaki. The missionaries even have houses in Osaka and Kyoto. They just remain quiet. The regent hasn't eliminated it. He's as addicted to the money from trade as the man who lent him the ship."

"Do you doubt their beliefs because of this one man?"

"No, I doubt them because I have yet to meet someone who can put the high ideals of their religion into practice."

"So, you admire their ideas then?" Nobuhiro asked.

Rain pelted Uji's head and shoulders. "*Hai.* I admire the ideas. However, I don't know if they can be applied here. I would have to meet a Japanese person who embodies these beliefs."

"As I have met Sen?"

Uji grunted his assent but added nothing further.

Nobuhiro nodded his head slowly. "Why not one of

the foreigners? Why would talking with them not help?"

Uji laughed. "They are uncultured barbarians and they let their dogs sleep at their feet."

Nobuhiro grinned in response, but he didn't feel good about it. He respected Uji's opinion. However, his own feelings for Sen were strong. He had told her not to bother with him. Was that a mistake? If he showed more interest in her faith, would it be for himself or just to please her?

"Omi mentioned there was news," Nobuhiro said.

"Yes, but we should wait. Father and Toshi will be along any moment. It is best to do it all together. What has Sen said to you about her faith?"

"She said she will pray for me. I believe she prays for my relationship with Father."

Rubbing his hand across his forehead, Uji grinned widely. "Her prayers seem to be working."

Nobuhiro eyed his brother. "What makes you say that?"

"That's the first time I've heard you acknowledge Father as *Father* instead of *our father*. It's a good beginning. She should continue with the prayers. Her heart is kind. She offers these prayers not for gain but for grace. It is a thoughtful gesture."

A chill wind blew through the courtyard, raising the hairs on the back on Nobuhiro's neck. Had he really said Father? He shivered and hunched his shoulders, then wiped his forehead. The light rain had stopped for now. "But you do not believe in this faith? Why accept the prayers?"

Uji shook his head lightly. "I would welcome the benevolent intervention of her deity, even if I do not believe He exists. It is foolish not to accept such genuine help and I'm not wise enough to know everything."

Nobuhiro fingered the rough hemp edge of his jacket. "Neither am I."

"Good," a terse, authoritative voice responded from nearby. "It is gratifying to see you have learned that. Young men think they know everything. It is only age that makes them realize how irresponsible they once were."

Nobuhiro wheeled to face his father, who strode toward them. Toshi followed, a few steps behind him in a show of respect. Was his father commenting on his decision to leave when he was young? Likely. He considered a response but bit his words. *Let Father say his piece without rebuttal.* "I understand there is news."

"Yes," Father answered. "Toshihiro."

"We found Funaki," Toshi said, "or rather he turned himself in."

"So, you are questioning him?" Nobuhiro asked.

Toshi chewed his lower lip. "Not exactly."

"Toshihiro," their father interrupted, his eyes flashing disapproval, "this is not the time for your humor. Move on. We have much to do."

"Yes, Father," Toshi said. "Funaki returned to the castle last night. He committed suicide on the grounds. We found his body this morning."

"Where?" Nobuhiro asked.

"The suicide gate," Toshi said.

Nobuhiro made a low whistle. The suicide gate. The spot on the castle grounds where people were brought when ordered to take their own lives. "I thank you for telling me."

"You earned the right to know," his father said. "Your actions in facing Funaki were"—he tilted his head slightly—"impressive."

Trying to mask his face, Nobuhiro stood there silent. *Impressive?* It was his father's first word of praise that Nobuhiro could remember.

At least since Mother passed away.

Uji's voice brought him back to the present. "Father and Toshi have reported this to Lord Kinoshita. They've been ordered to journey to Kyoto and deliver an update on our progress in this investigation. This news is too important to trust to a messenger service."

"Progress? It's not over?" Nobuhiro asked.

"We don't think so," Uji said. "There's still a

possibility that more than one person is behind what's been happening. We have not eliminated the other suspects. Kitayama is still a possibility, though I am convinced he is not involved. Michiba and Nishioji remain suspects as well."

"Is the Goami family in danger?" Nobuhiro asked.

"We do not think so," Uji said. "However, there is one rather odd item."

"What is that?" Nobuhiro asked.

Uji went silent. Nobuhiro looked at his father, whose stonelike face betrayed nothing. Finally, Toshi piped in.

"He killed himself like a woman."

"Excuse me?" Nobuhiro said, turning to face his other brother. "Are you saying he slit his own throat?"

Thunder sounded overhead as if mocking the silence of his father and brothers. Nobuhiro rubbed his chest. "Why?"

"We don't know," Uji said. "Stabbing one's self in the gut is painful, especially without a second to end your suffering. Perhaps he flinched at the pain."

"He carried a short sword with him when he ran," Nobuhiro said. "That would have been sufficient for the traditional way, wouldn't it?"

"Yes," his father said.

"Well, at least he was kind enough to do it at the suicide gate," Toshi added.

Nobuhiro turned to Toshi. "Why do you say that?"

"The haunted well is nearby. No one drinks the water anymore, because of the stigma. However, it makes for an easy clean-up."

Chuckling at the joke, Nobuhiro noted that even Uji was smiling.

His father, stoic, silenced their laughter. "It is time we readied ourselves for our trip to Kyoto." He stared at Nobuhiro. "Your duty remains. Protect the Goami family."

Nobuhiro met his father's gaze and then made a slight bow, thinking about the progress that might have been made. Maybe Sen was right about there being hope for his relationship with his father. However, Nobuhiro's chest clutched as he watched his father's feet turn in the wet ground before Nobuhiro raised his head.

Still, he would do more than protect.

He would find the people targeting Christians, even if his father couldn't.

He would find whoever killed Jiro.

Chapter Fourteen

Nobuhiro spent the next month rarely leaving the workshop and grounds. Work varied during the day, but his nightly activity did not change. After work was over, he stored his traditional robe in a closet, making sure there were no spots on the ceremonial garment. He washed his face and hands, wiping away the dirt and soot and then drying himself off.

Some small tools lay on a workbench. He shook his head. He thought he had put everything away. He must be too distracted. Master Goami taught him early in his apprenticeship that the workshop of a swordsmith was like a temple is to a samurai. It was the reason swordsmiths wore fine clothes while working. The reason swordsmiths handled their trade with respect. The reason they imbued each creation with a piece of their soul.

Yet at the end of the day, Nobuhiro focused on one task that no other swordsmith did.

His day done, Nobuhiro sat on a workbench and pulled out a piece of parchment from his pocket. The parchment fibers were weak from the number of times he had folded it. Fingerprints and dark smudges covered the paper.

On the parchment were written the words Sen had told him.

Joy springs from burying your bitterness in the ground.

He traced the letters, his fingertips feeling the ink. He meditated on the phrase every night before going to bed, as if it brought him closer to Sen.

A bead of perspiration trickled down his face. The late May heat in Himeji made for occasionally sweltering nights, but they were not too intolerable. He wiped his head with a nearby towel, pulling the wet cloth to the back of his neck. It cooled him down.

Trace remnants of pine pervaded the air, mixed with the smell of fish. Master Goami's wife was preparing dinner. His stomach growled in anticipation.

Soft footfalls from outside broke his concentration. He straightened.

Uji's voice broke the silence. "You study that parchment like a schoolboy preparing for an exam." Nobuhiro turned and saw his brother in the doorway, smiling at him. "What makes you focus so hard after such a long day?"

Nobuhiro folded the paper, putting it in his pocket as he rose and bowed to greet Uji. "You are losing your step, brother. I heard you coming."

Grinning, Uji nodded. His face was an exhibition of mock disbelief. "If you were an enemy, you still couldn't have stopped me."

"We'll never know."

Uji entered slowly, surveying the workshop as he did. His reverence for the solemn interior evident on his face. Nobuhiro's chest swelled. His brother respected and admired his craft. "What are you studying so intently?"

Nobuhiro showed him the parchment and filled him in on the details. Uji steepled his fingers and considered it.

"What do you think?" Nobuhiro asked his brother.

Uji licked his lips, his face blank. "I'd like to hear

your musings first."

Sighing, Nobuhiro expelled a rush of frustration. "I've been trying words, reforming them, substituting different options. However, nothing has provided me with any plausible solution."

"I believe you should modify your approach," Uji said. "It sounds like an ideograph riddle."

Nobuhiro stared at the phrase as he massaged the sudden tightness in his neck. An ideograph riddle? Did Uji think him a child?

He clenched the parchment in his fingers and his feelings calmed down. No. Uji just wanted to discuss the possibilities. Hear it out loud. Maybe something would arise from discussing it. "What do you mean?"

"Have you thought of it as a picture? Think back to how you learned characters. Combine two characters and come up with one new meaning."

Nobuhiro shook his head. "I thought about that, but I know of no ideograph that can be split up to create anything with any semblance to this riddle. I've also tried substituting characters for the sounds but not the words. Still nothing."

Uji stepped close and lightly tapped his own forehead. "You're thinking like someone born in this country. That may not work in this case."

Nobuhiro stared at Uji, not knowing what to make of his brother's comment. "Excuse me?"

Uji sported a chiding smile. "This is a foreign religion, Nobuhiro. It's likely the riddle was developed by a missionary, based on a foreign interpretation of one of our written characters."

"Are you suggesting that I start splitting ideographs by something other than their root characters?"

"That would seem logical."

Nobuhiro rolled his eyes. "Logical but mad. Which of the thousands of ideographs available should I start with?" he said in a mocking tone.

Uji laughed. He had an answer there, too. "I suggest

that you start with the biggest foreign symbol of these missionaries . . . their cross. It is the cross that brings these Christians eternal joy."

Nobuhiro gritted his teeth and ran both hands over the top of his head. "There are many characters that have something resembling a cross in them. We're talking about an intersection of two lines."

"I would also suggest starting with the ideographs for *joy*, *ground*, and *bitterness*," Uji responded in his typical measured tones. "Split up those characters differently. That would be an apt place."

"You make it sound easy," Nobuhiro fumed. "I've been at this for a month."

"Such is not my intent. I do not know the answer myself."

Nobuhiro chewed his lower lip. He had shamed himself again with his temper. He must learn better control. "I know. You're trying to help. I appreciate it."

Uji smiled and nodded and the tightness in Nobuhiro's chest dissipated. Finally relaxing, he walked over to the door and looked outside. The nearly full moon lit the neighborhood. He closed his eyes and drew in a large breath of the fresh night air to clear his head.

"What is it?" Uji asked.

"Nothing," Nobuhiro said. "Ever since the incident here, I've gotten into a habit of surveying the outside. Every rustle. Every sound I don't recognize I investigate. I don't know what I'm looking for, but it makes me feel better."

"You're looking for serenity. It's understandable after what happened. More important, you're protecting the house you serve by syncing yourself with your surroundings. Even Toshi would be impressed."

Nobuhiro stretched him arms, feeling the wooden door in one hand and the stone wall with the other. "This has been my home for a while. Why would I not do my utmost to protect it?"

"I agree. You serve this house, but it has been your

refuge," Uji said. "You still have a home if you want it."

"I can never return to the castle if I cannot serve as a samurai. I can never return as long as my father does not welcome me back. I can never leave here if it would put my master and his family in danger.

But I would do anything for Sen.

Nobuhiro closed the door and wheeled to face Uji. "So, to what do I owe the honor of your visit, elder brother?"

"There is more news in our investigation."

###

The smell of dried ash mixed with the heavy, humid air. If the place was ever put to use again, it would have to be a Buddhist temple. The incense would be necessary. Kaiken stepped over a piece of rotting wood on the floor. The ash darkened the *tabi* socks, the ankle-length socks that separated the big toe from the rest. A shame. They would have to be discarded.

Michiba stood nearby. Normally, he would kneel but soot on the kimonos would be bad. More to explain. More to discard.

"Where's Kitayama?" Kaiken asked.

Michiba glanced up, his expression blank, and said nothing.

"Boar snouts! Didn't he get the message?"

The rustle of the door indicated Kitayama's arrival.

"You're late," Kaiken said.

Kitayama bowed low. "My apologies. I was delayed by Lord Kinoshita. He requested I find the elder Tokoda for a meeting. I could not refuse a request from the head of the castle. There is an unexpected guest from Kyoto."

Kitayama's face registered a smile combined with fear. Who could bring that mix of emotions? Something was wrong.

Kaiken's body went rigid. "The master is here?"

"Yes, I saw to his comforts."

Kaiken swallowed hard. He was here. Perhaps there was news or a new impetus for the group. A chance to recruit more followers. Would a meeting be possible? Why was Kitayama afraid? Kaiken and Kitayama needed to talk.

In time.

"Your lateness is acceptable. Learn to anticipate unforeseen events and leave earlier if possible. Our success depends on our meetings being limited. The longer we are gone, the more people will piece together our movements. The plan is this."

###

Sen glanced up at the moon. The castle grounds glowed with its light. It reminded her of the night she first returned to Himeji. Even with only a sliver of moon that evening, the reflection from the castle's white walls shone a great distance. She shivered, remembering the chill wind that blew that evening. It matched her fear then.

It signaled her trepidation now.

"I'm not sure if this is a good idea. We shouldn't be leaving the castle like this."

Standing by her side, dressed in a yellow kimono with red flowers, Omi shook her head as if finding Sen's concern amusing. "We have worked hard since this morning and we are spending the evening in town."

Sen recalled the attacks at the castle and her house. They had found Funaki dead, but the brothers were still concerned about others being involved. "I'll accept that, but why are we going?"

"Why not? The charity sumo exhibition is tomorrow. Many people have come to town to see it and the local inns are full. The market will be festive with treats and street performers. We'll get something to eat and rest. The local saunas will be open late. We may get to take baths every day but when's the last time you went to a sauna? It'll be fun."

Her last excuse rebuffed, Sen acquiesced. Besides, Omi was a samurai. She could defend herself against any brigand. Sen's nervousness wasn't warranted.

Sen followed Omi to the entrance and the two of

them left the grounds. It would take a while, but they were in no hurry. Torchlights along the street led to the light noise that beckoned to be joined. The air was heavy and warm. It would be hot at the festivities. Fireworks rose in the air, signaling the revelry as Sen's cheeks warmed at the display. There was one for the magistrates. Flash powder was controlled by the government and its usage was monitored. An errant explosion could set any of the wooden buildings on fire. Whoever set the fireworks off was dull or in hiding.

The noise of the crowd grew, indicating they were getting close. The aromas of the cooking coming from the street vendors and their various offerings filled Sen with a gnawing hunger. She bent down and smoothed her green kimono, feeling the fine weave. It had once been her best garment. She had saved it each week for services. It had grown worn, marking the number of days she wore it since leaving Haibara and her former employment.

She brought her hand to her throat, feeling the scars just below the neckline. Feeling the bumps of blood on the fabric, bumps that wouldn't go away. Feeling for the friends who gave their life for the faith.

Would she ever feel safe again?

Fragrances wafted toward Sen, assaulting her with a mixture of fried and roasted aromas. She moved through the crowd, feeling the press of people around her. Each jostle startled her and her body tensed. Would it always be like this?

Omi pointed out a nearby *yakisoba* vendor who had a long trail of people in front of his cart. The two of them got in line, watching the entertainment nearby. Flute players and *rakugo* storytellers competed for audiences and brought smiles to many. Buddhist priests chanted in front of businesses, hoping also for a generous crowd.

They reached the front of the line as Sen and Omi both ordered a plateful of yakisoba noodles with mushrooms and octopus. Sen ate quickly, enjoying the tangy flavor. Omi finished hers a little later and then motioned toward a side street. Sen followed Omi's lead, stepping around a candy maker as they got away from the din.

"You look like you want to talk," Sen commented as they found a quiet place to sit.

Omi fiddled with her obi, readjusting it around her waist. The yellow belt looked perfect, but Omi looked uncomfortable. She pursed her lips and grew still. "I want to talk a little more about—"

"Jesus Christ?"

A dog barked from the end of the alley and ran past the two of them, stopping at Sen's feet and licking her toes. The dog's fur was white with a couple of black spots, likely dirt and grease from the alleys. Sen wished she had a little food she could give the dog but found none after searching her pockets. The dog seemed to sense it and headed to the main street.

"You didn't move. Why?"

"He's just a little dog living on the street looking for a meal. I know that feeling well."

"From the time before you arrived back in Himeji?"

She recalled the day she left Haibara Castle. The samurai had allowed her to leave along with many other servants on whom they'd conferred mercy. Some had returned to their homes. Some disappeared. Some like her went into the woods outside the city. Servants who had recanted and kept their station now braved death to bring them food. They begged for forgiveness.

It was hard to forgive. None of them dared look anyone in the eye.

Omi nodded, her face showing concern. "My apologies. I did not wish to bring up any sad memories.

Sen brushed a tear away with her finger before it could form. "Do not worry. I have been through a lot. The Lord made me strong enough to face these challenges. You wanted to talk?"

Smiling, Omi moved closer. "Yes, I've been thinking a lot about it lately. We had to get away from the castle though. There are too many people around, and samurai are too adept at walking around silently."

Sen spent the next few minutes explaining her faith, her heart growing with every word. It was the second time she had had such an opportunity since she'd arrived in Himeji.

Omi peppered Sen with various questions. Sen did her best to answer them.

Sen clasped her hands on her lap. The exhilaration coursing through her veins placed her entire body on alert. "Have you tried praying?"

Omi tilted her head, her eyes conveying a quizzical gaze. "You mean like they do in the Buddhist temples, where they clap twice, bow once, and then clap once?"

Sen chuckled and then shook her head. "That's not quite what I mean. In prayer, you talk to God, tell Him your problems, and thank Him for the good things in life and ask that He be with you. It's not a ritual. It's an opportunity to get closer to Him."

"Sounds like you're meditating on a koan."

"It's not a Zen riddle, but there are mysteries we don't understand."

"What do you do when you don't receive understanding?"

Sen licked her lips. "You accept the mysteries and the teachings on faith."

"It sounds hard."

"Yes, it is, but it is wonderful."

Fireworks erupted with a bevy of explosions. Sen glanced skyward as a mixture of red and blue light rose into the air. Cries from the nearby crowd grew louder. A soft scrape behind them raised the hair on the nape of Sen's neck. She looked around.

Nothing.

She glanced toward Omi. "I think we should be getting back."

"Probably a good idea, let's get—Aiiih!" Omi crumpled to the ground.

A flash of movement in the dark startled Sen. She turned. A masked man stood in front of her. He raised his arm as if to strike. She lifted her hands to block the blow. He grabbed her wrists and held them over her head in one vise-like hand.

"Let me go. What do you want?"

"You," the man replied as he struck her on the right temple.

Pain rushed to her forehead. Her knees buckled. She fell forward. Her world turned dark. Fabric ripped. The impact shot pain through her knees. She smelled honey, plum, and a fragrance she couldn't place. Then, nothing more.

Chapter Fifteen

“Kitayama’s dead.” Uji stood in the doorway to the workshop, gripping the doorframe stiffly. His lips squeezed into a tight thin line.

“How?” Nobuhiro asked, his eyes searching for good signs from his brother.

“Poison, we think.”

Nobuhiro chewed on his lower lip. “Who would want to kill him? I thought he wasn’t involved.”

Uji lowered his gaze, then looked up as if searching for words. The case worried his brother. It was obvious. Nobuhiro had even heard Uji approach the workshop earlier, as his brother had made no attempt to even mask his steps. “We believed so. Still do. Kitayama accompanied Father and Toshi to Kyoto to report the news of Funaki. They took him to get him alone. Father queried Kitayama about his activities. He was convinced of Kitayama’s innocence.”

“Maybe he knew something.”

Uji rubbed his chin. “Possibly. Two days ago, Kitayama requested a meeting with Father. They were supposed to meet yesterday at dawn. When Kitayama didn't show, Toshi and I went to look for him. We found him dead."

Sweat trickled from Nobuhiro's brow and he wiped his forehead with the sleeve of his kimono. The heat from the day's work still weighed heavily within the room. He opened windows on each side. Cooler night air greeted his face, along with the smell of grass. Crickets chirped in the background, their nightly song disturbing an otherwise silent evening. It was later than he thought. How long had he been in the shop?

Nobuhiro indicated a raised platform at the rear of the shop, suggesting that Uji sit down. Uji gave a quick nod and obliged.

Another suspect dead and no closer to the truth.

Nobuhiro walked over to a small hearth, where a pot of water sat warm over a bed of hot coals. He removed the pot with a wooden hook and prepared tea for his brother. Uji had already sat down. He hoped that meant he had time. Nobuhiro prepared a second cup for himself and then walked over to the platform, handing the cup to Uji.

Uji nodded his thanks. His normally stone face dropped its hard edge.

Nobuhiro seated himself, sloshing drops of hot liquid on the back of his hand. He winced but kept it to himself. "Does Father know you're here and that you're telling me this?"

Uji leaned back and shifted to a crisscross sitting position, which for Uji meant he was stretching his legs. "Father is aware of it. He approved Toshi and me keeping you abreast of everything."

The answer stunned Nobuhiro. He sat up straight and looked intently at his brother. "I'm . . . surprised. In our last conversation, he only grudgingly admitted I might be able to assist. What has brought about this change in him?"

Uji shook his head. His eyes conveyed undisguised disdain. "You ask too much sometimes, Nobuhiro. Father has been impressed with your actions. He has shown it the only way he knows how."

Nobuhiro's jaw clenched, matching the tension in his body. *The only way he knows how?* The phrase brought back the barbs of countless shameful displays of a man who only knew how to display embarrassment. "His few words mean little. His manners indicate nothing has changed."

"*Hai*," Uji said, his voice again showcasing a gruff timbre. "He has his issues, but so do you. You are headstrong. Stubborn. It is the one quality of Father's that you *did* inherit. True change is achieved over time. Even the slow-moving stream wears smooth the rocks at its bottom. You need to give him more time."

Nobuhiro's jaw hardened, matching the stiffness in his heart. "I was gone seven years. Wasn't that—?"

"And you also need to grow up." Uji's eyes opened wide and his voice carried fire. "There are reasons some Buddhist monks meditate by sitting under a waterfall. The same could help you concentrate. Your thoughts and feelings cloud your judgment."

Nobuhiro stared at Uji. His brother seldom lost his temper.

He never lost his reason.

Uji's comments settled in Nobuhiro's gut hard, reminding him of when he had first left. Three days passed before he ate his first meal. He had downed every morsel rapidly, but the food settled like stones in his stomach. He had grown sick and thrown up. He had considered going back. But he had made his decision to leave.

He had needed to move forward then.

He needed to move forward now.

Wasn't that the reason he left in the first place? Yet the child in him still waged a battle with the old version of his father. He had said farewell to that life when he accepted the role as a swordsmith's apprentice. Accepting a new station in life meant learning to see with different eyes. Applying those eyes now was required.

Have I been too hard on . . . Father? Did he suffer back then as I did? Am I too hard on his actions now?

Nobuhiro studied Uji. Perspiration beaded on his forehead, poised to stream down his cheeks. His face was impassive. The angry color gone. Uji acted from duty and common sense, but also from an understanding of how his actions were interpreted.

Nobuhiro must learn to do the same.

He took another sip of tea and pursed his lips. "You are right, brother," Nobuhiro said as he allowed himself to breathe, "but I don't know if sitting under a waterfall is the way I want to spend my time."

Uji grunted, using the sleeve of his jacket to wipe his forehead. "When this humidity gets worse, it might not be a bad idea."

The brothers chuckled, but Nobuhiro considered the point. He needed to meditate, to sort out his thoughts.

He still had not talked with Master Goami, to reaffirm his commitment to his service for another year. He had affirmed it in his actions. He had progressed greatly since the day he had abdicated his samurai life. Prayer offered hope, regardless of his station. Zen, though, offered no answers for his plight.

Where to begin? Where to look? Where to find answers to the meaning of a relationship with his father?

Sen flashed to his mind. Her words. Her beliefs. Her conviction.

Maybe she was right.

Maybe the wisdom in the relationship he sought was something that could be understood by meditating on this Christian God.

Maybe the love of Father and Son from that foreign religion could help him with his own life.

Nobuhiro walked back to the open window and looked in the direction toward town. The marketplace was a sizable distance away, but he heard the low murmur of the night and imagined it was the crowd, milling about the night before the sumo exhibition. The voices sounded happy.

However, Nobuhiro could have sworn he heard a

scream.

###

Sen awoke with a pounding headache and her arms numb from being tied behind her. She moved her wrists but felt little slack in her bonds. Her cheek rubbed against a column that had the texture of smooth wood.

Her lips caught the salty taste of dried sweat. Her left temple throbbed from where she had been struck. She longed to massage her head but felt pain each time she pulled her hands to free herself. The rough hemp chafed her hands and she winced as the twine cut into her skin.

She sat up and looked around the room, using her eyelids as best she could to flush the blurriness from her eyes. Partially opened windows allowed in a little light from the full moon outside. A small hole through the ceiling allowed moonlight as well. Still, the remaining darkness grayed her ability to see her surroundings.

Rotting wood and ash saturated the air, overlaying the musty smell of a room that had not been opened often to the outside world. Dust choked her breath, drying her face and throat.

"Uhhhn," a pained voice said behind her, catching her attention.

"Omi, is that you?"

"Yes," she responded, her voice dragging out in a low tone.

"Are you badly hurt?" Sen asked, her voice coughing out the words.

"I feel like I collided with a giant Buddha statue. What happened?"

Sen related what she remembered, but it wasn't much. Omi's scream. The masked man. The cold edge on the one word he uttered. Pain clouded the few facts that darkness had failed to hide. "Are you tied up also?"

The sound of rope moving against wood cut through the silence. "Yes, and it's tight. My wrists hurt and I can't feel much. You?"

"The same."

"Can you move at all?" Omi asked.

Sen inched forward, sliding along the ground. Her arms pulled back. "I can move a little, but I'm tied to the column."

"So am I," Omi said.

Sen struggled against her bonds to no avail. She scanned the room again as her eyes adjusted slightly. Blurry shapes now had dark outlines. Thin rods protruded from the walls in a diamond-shaped pattern. Likely for storage, though nothing indicated what items that might be. "Do you have any idea where we are?"

Omi drew a large breath and then expelled it loudly. "My eyes are still getting used to the dark. There are machines in front of me, but they're so burned I can't tell what they were used for. A fire did a lot of damage to this place."

Sen coughed again as the dust and moldy ash clogged the air. "What should we do? Do you think anyone would hear us if we yelled?"

"Possibly. Do you hear anything?"

Sen strained her ears to concentrate on the outside. Soft voices echoed, but she couldn't discern anything other than occasional distant laughter. "Sounds like they're too far away. Besides, what if that man is close by? He might be the first to respond."

Omi grunted. "We can't just sit here and wait for someone to find us. I know you can't reach your own ropes. See if you can reach mine."

Sen inched back toward Omi and stretched her fingers out, seeing if she could grab on to Omi's bonds.

"*Itai.*" Sen drew her hands back. Her forefinger pulsed in tandem with the pain.

"What happened?" Omi asked.

Sen gritted her teeth. "I touched something sharp. Before this night is over, I'll be covered in blood and bruises."

"You probably touched something that fell and broke in the fire. Be careful."

"I have an idea." Sen moved her hand back slowly in the direction where she had drawn it from earlier, finding the sharp-edged object. She fingered it and found a smooth side. "Got it."

"What do you have?"

"Whatever it is I cut my finger on." As best she could, Sen raised the object toward what she hoped was the bonds that held her to the pole.

"*Itai*," Omi said.

Sen stopped, relaxing her wrists. Soreness ran through her shoulders and upper arms. "Sorry, I must have poked you."

"What are you trying to do?"

"This thing I picked up is sharp. I thought I might be able to use it to cut my ropes."

"Good idea. But since my hands are close by, try mine. Keep it still. I'll see if I can find it again."

Sen held her hands motionless, waiting for some signal that Omi had found the target. Fingers brushed along the back of her hand, flowing out to her fingers. A muffled gasp followed.

"Found it," Omi said.

"Keep your voice down," Sen replied, irritated.

"Let me poke you and see how *you* keep your voice down," Omi retorted.

Sen closed her eyes, holding the object in one hand. Omi's fingers brushed Sen's hand again, guiding the object toward the rope fibers.

"Got it," Sen said and held the fibers tight.

She ran the sharp edge along the rope weave for several minutes, holding her breath as if that would help her concentrate. Her arms grew tired and she willed herself to keep going. The pressure in her head multiplied the pain of each stroke.

Sen's breath came in gulps. Sweat trickled down her face. She pushed her heels into the ground to gain more pressure, the smell of the room turning her nose. After a few minutes, she exhaled with a loud rush. "Sorry, I don't know if I'm making any progress."

"We are, I think. I'm trying to spread my hands and they're getting farther apart. You're getting there. Hurry."

Sen reached out again and felt the rope. It was tight. Omi was pulling on it to increase the tension. Sen went back to work.

"Keep going," Omi said. "I can feel the rope weakening."

Sen continued to press, hearing light sounds as tiny strands seem to snap in a slow succession like icicles cracking as the sun melted them. She applied more pressure and—

Crack.

Sen's hands slid. Whatever she'd held in her hands likely broke.

"I'm free," Omi cried.

"Great," Sen whispered.

The tension in her bonds loosened. Omi was trying to free her. She moved her hands closer to provide extra slack. Soon, Sen was free as well.

"Thanks." She rubbed her wrists where the ropes had chafed them. Her breaths came more easily. She looked up and smiled at Omi, who had come from around the other side.

Her friend smiled back. "Can you move?"

Sen put her hands on the floor and tried to push herself up. The stiffness in her muscles hampered her efforts. Omi knelt next to her and put her own hands under Sen's shoulders to help her stand. She flinched at the pressure.

"Did you see a door?" Sen asked.

"Over on my side. Let's go."

The two of them tiptoed to the door, knowing by the light coming from the nearby window that the door led outside. Sen listened but heard no sounds. If there was someone outside, they were being quiet. She knelt and cracked the door open to peer outside. Seeing no one, she nodded to Omi. They slid the door completely open, the scrape of wood on wood adding to their unease, and ran toward the sounds of the city.

Chapter Sixteen

Nobuhiro pushed the bellows, providing more blasts of air to the already hot forge. The scent of pine greeted his nose, as potent as the incense of any temple. The heat waged a battle with the breeze blowing in from the windows. The sweat on his brow told him the heat was winning.

A rush of cool air reached his back. Nobuhiro turned to see Master Goami. The old man's smile resembled that of a Buddha. It decreased the years in his face.

"Hard at work, I see. Very good," Master Goami said. "You worked here late last night and are here early today. You are a dedicated apprentice."

Nobuhiro recalled Uji's visit last night. He and his brother had talked a long time. He had felt like family again, like the times when he was young and had followed his brothers everywhere, wanting to be like them. He still admired them greatly.

But he was happy with the path he had chosen.

Still, Master Goami believed he had been working. Nobuhiro had hidden the visits of his brothers for a long time, afraid it would show a lack of commitment. Afraid it would show he hadn't left his old life. Afraid that Master

Goami would reject him.

Fear of uttering words that his own ears had never heard him say out loud.

“Good morning, Master. It was not that much work. Just taking care of the shop. Making sure that everything was in working order. That the tools and equipment were clean.” His chest tightened. It hurt to hide the truth from the man who had guided his steps all these years. He would apologize for his dishonor later. “I didn’t think I was up late.”

“I saw the shop from my room. It was nearly the hour of the rat.”

“It must have been later than I thought.” Nobuhiro looked at Master Goami, hoping that his response would end the discussion. However, the old man’s gaze was drawn toward the platform on the side. Nobuhiro turned and his knees wobbled. Two of the honored chairs were still out as well as a tray with two ceramic cups. He was tired last night and neglected to clean. This morning, he’d failed to notice it.

Master Goami stared at him. “Nobuhiro, who was here last night?”

###

Sen took a sip of water, placing it on the tray in front of her. The liquid cooled her thoughts as well as her throat. Footsteps, fast and slow, sounded in the nearby hall. The castle was busy with activity, as always.

Nobuhiro’s father sat across from her. The old man rubbed the sleep from his eyes and ran his hands over his scalp. Small streams of light peeked in from the open portal behind him. It would be daytime soon.

Toshi sat close by, questioning Omi. Concern radiated from his face, though he tried to hide it. He would be tending to Omi if not for the presence of his father nearby. If only the man had struck Sen first. Omi could have used her skills to fight back.

Had the attacker known Omi was samurai?

“Is there anything else you remember?” Nobuhiro’s

father asked. His normally gruff voice was softer than Sen remembered.

She went over the events again in her head, knowing even the tiniest detail could be important. Her head throbbed with the remnants of pain from the blow she took from the masked man. "Nothing."

Toshi approached, his left hand over the swords stuck in his belt. "There have been a few fires in the last year. There was a large fire in the silk garment area, a fire that burned more than one building. There were also some smaller ones that were better contained. Do you think it was could have been the silk district?"

Sen recalled the building, the ash smell, the pegs on the walls, the moonlight . . . through the ceiling. "I don't think so. The building had no second floor for the silkworms."

Toshi flattened his lips. "Do you think you could take us to where you were?"

Sen nodded slowly, her attention shifting back and forth between the two men. "I remember where we came out in the market area. I think I can find it."

"I think so, too," Omi added, her eyes half closed.

Sen stared at Omi, thankful her friend wasn't in worse shape.

"Very well," Nobuhiro's father said, rising to his feet. "Let's go now. Time is precious. Are you ready?"

Sen gave a half smile. "It's my duty. I'll do whatever I can."

###

"Who was here last night, Nobuhiro?" Master asked again, his voice rising in tone, though not sounding angry.

Nobuhiro stared at the cups, then he turned toward Master Goami and looked at the ground. His entire face flushed as he dealt with the shame. He should have mentioned his brothers' visits long before now. To have Master Goami discover them was not the way Nobuhiro wanted to address this, but the time for planning was over.

It was time to admit the truth.

Nobuhiro kept his head facing the floor. “My older brother visited last night. We talked for a while.”

“I see.” Master Goami’s voice was flat. “A surprise visit from family. Why did you keep this information from me?”

“I did not mean to do so. I . . . I worried you might doubt my commitment. That you might think I wished to return to my old life.”

“Is this the first time one of your brothers has visited?”

Shaking his head, Nobuhiro inhaled and steadied his nerves. “No, they have visited many times over the years.”

Master Goami nodded, but his expression remained flat. “I see. Should I doubt your commitment then?”

Nobuhiro raised his head. “No, Master. It’s just—”

“When you asked to be my apprentice seven years ago, my only requirement was that you renounce your title. I could not be your master and treat you like the son of a samurai. A master does not address a pupil as *sama*.”

Looking down, Nobuhiro said nothing. Maser Goami’s next words could change Nobuhiro’s life.

Master Goami exhaled slowly, cutting through the silence. “However, I never demanded that you abandon your family. Family is important. Besides, what properly thinking merchant would do anything that eschews potential customers?”

Nobuhiro’s chest relaxed. He had worried too much, creating much angst within himself. He inhaled. The scent of a fresh pile of rice straw reminded Nobuhiro that the day lay ahead of him. Time to work.

###

Sen replayed the incident in her head several times as she walked back toward the festival area in silence, looking for landmarks and trying to retrace her steps. The walk had taken twenty minutes. The men and Omi had moved quickly, and Sen struggled to maintain pace. She regretted her fear of the night before. She had forgotten everything. Omi was more helpful, though she did appear a little confused.

The main market area, the site of last night's celebrating, bustled with early morning activity. Several merchants and their employees were hard at work, taking in deliveries as they arrived. Other merchants swept their storefronts, likely cleaning up from last night's activities. Sen thought back to the previous night. Did any of these people see who attacker her and Omi?

Nobuhiro's father and Toshi walked on either side of Sen and Omi, as if blocking them from attack. Toshi walked on the right side of Omi, their relationship a secret no more. What did his father think of them?

Sen peeked at Nobuhiro's father, who walked stiffly on her left, his proud manner drawing gazes from passerby. His right hand remained close to the hilt of his sword. The twinges of emotion that had breached his stoic defenses at the castle now lay hidden behind the wall of his stony face. His gait kept him a half step ahead of her.

A half step?

He was a samurai. She was nothing. She should be several steps behind. Even a lady of the court would be behind.

Why did he allow her to get this close?

Why had he not reminded her of her place?

He was protecting her.

Nobuhiro's father was maintaining a protective stance. No wonder the people in the street stared. They were giving a wide berth.

"Moto. Goami." Sen's back stiffened at the old man's crisp tone of voice. At what time do you recall reaching the main street that leads to the castle?"

Sen focused on the banners in front of the various stores. Were any of them familiar?

A low gong sounded from the Buddhist temple down the street on the right. Black-robed men with shaved heads walked about, attending to the temple walls. Another stood in front of the temple, chanting prayers and asking for donations, his face partially covered by a pointed, straw hat.

Had they passed that temple? Was this the first temple they saw when they reached the main street?

Her stomach rumbled in response. Something about the temple had made her hungry.

A whiff of sweet air then reached her nose. She followed the aroma and saw a familiar face from the day of the attack at her house. The baker who had helped her and her parents when that rogue samurai had attacked knelt in front of his store, which was across from the temple. The baker petted a fluffy little white dog with a tail that curved over its back. Sen didn't recognize the breed, but the dog looked familiar, too. A community dog perhaps. One that stayed in the neighborhood and the local shopkeepers had adopted as a mascot.

The baker fed the dog something. He was a nice man. Duty and gratitude demanded she express her appreciation for his actions on the day of the attack, but now was not the time.

They had reached the place.

"Here, I think," Sen said, pointing to a side street next to the temple.

Omi concurred and the foursome headed down the alley. Sen remembered the wall of the temple being to her left as she ran past it in the darkness that morning. Now, she scanned other storefronts, looking for any recognizable feature from last night. Trash from the previous night still lay on the ground. The local wards soon would mobilize workers to clean it.

Several times Sen looked at Omi as they noted other places they had passed the night before. They had picked the larger roads, hoping to see other people in case their attacker chased them. Bigger roads had stone streetlamps lighting the area.

The group crossed two more streets. Sen scanned the shops. Did anything look familiar? Images flickered through her mind. "Over there. This is it, I think."

"Are you certain?" Nobuhiro's father asked.

"I am," Omi said, pointing to the left. "I remember that dark green awning from when we exited the place."

They turned the corner and the charred building came into view. Sen stared at the building. Bile rose in her throat. The exterior appeared gutted and rotted. The heat had long since died, but the smell of the remnants lingered like garbage left out in the sun. A tremor ran over her body, sending cold chills up and down her back.

"What happened here?" Sen asked in a hurried, excited voice. Stress clutched her chest. She breathed in short gasps of air. Did she want to know the truth?

Toshihiro blinked slowly and looked in the direction of his father. The elder man pursed his lips and nodded his head.

Toshihiro's jaw tightened. His usual grin, gone. "It was a garment maker. It burned down several months ago. The owners died in the fire."

Sen's pulse raced. Who had been here? She wanted to ask Toshi, but it was difficult to question him like this, especially in front of his father. Both men were samurai. Toshi would tell her. In front of his father, though, her impertinence would be reason for punishment.

It was not her place to ask, but she needed to know the truth. She inhaled softly to strengthen her nerves. "Is there something special about this place?"

Toshi again glanced at his father before looking back at her. The old man said nothing. The meaning was clear.

The place carried importance for her.

Toshi licked his lips. "This place doubled as a location where Christians met."

The words struck her like a spear in the chest. She brought both hands up, covering her face for a moment. She turned back to stare at the ruins before continuing. "Is this . . . where my sister died?"

"Yes," Nobuhiro's father said. "I am sorry for your loss."

Sen turned to face him and saw a gentle mist in his eyes. Again, the hard-edged warrior disappeared. He was now different. His features had softened, indicating the part of him few ever saw.

The part that knew grief.

Sen fell to her knees and cried, not caring who saw.

Chapter Seventeen

Sen said goodbye to Toshi and Omi at the entrance of her parents' house. Nobuhiro's father had suggested Sen go home and rest a day before returning.

Why?

The recommendation puzzled her. Duty demanded that she return to work. The old man's concern belied his outward gruff appearance. Why did she warrant the kindness of a man of his status? Why the protectiveness?

Either way, she didn't feel like resting. During the walk home, she had thought of nothing but the church. Was there a clue in the rubble about the local Christians? Was there a clue there about who had killed her sister?

Sen paused at the doorstep and looked around. Perspiration trickled down her face as the late May humidity strengthened its grip. A month had passed since her last visit to her parents' home. The bushes appeared more overgrown than before. Flowers wilted for thirst, though some showed signs of life. A layer of dirt blown in from the road dusted the porch, marking her steps. Sen's mother prided herself on taking care of the home. Maybe Sen could come out early in the evening and tend to the front garden?

Like a dutiful daughter should.

A baby's cry broke through the silence. Sen searched for the source of it but the voice disappeared. The echo tugged at her heart. A reminder that she needed to find a husband, and soon. Whoever attacked the night before could have ended any chance of that.

"Mother, are you here?" she called out after she slid the door open. Every time she visited made it feel more like home.

Sen's mother appeared a moment later. Her face worn but her smile wide as she stepped out from the kitchen. Sen bowed and then hugged her mother, pleased to see her again. The woman flinched slightly, and then Sen felt the gentle pats of her mother's hands.

"What brings you home?" her mother asked.

Sen glanced at the floor. This wouldn't be easy to say. She inhaled to steel her nerves and then apprised her mother of the attack, the meeting at the castle, and the visit to the place where Haru had died. She braced herself for a verbal onslaught on the dangers of her Christian faith.

Instead, her mother said nothing. Her faced showed relief. The concern of a parent for a child. "I'm glad you're safe," she said. "Why don't you take the kind old samurai's advice? You should rest awhile."

"Mother, I can help you in the house."

"You can help me later. For now, just rest."

Silenced by the lack of a rebuke, Sen went to her old room. The heavy air greeted her with a mixture of straw and a slight touch of incense. The room had been cleaned since her last visit, suggesting a hope that she would return soon. However, it needed fresh air. She opened the windows, allowing in a small breeze that fought against the outside heat. It felt good.

She stopped at the closet door, tracing a picture of a few birds in flight over a river with her finger. She had looked at the scene every night as a child.

She had lived that scene often as an adult; in the

months before returning to Himeji, she had often slept outside on the nights when the kindness of strangers wasn't available. Sleeping near a river had reminded her of home because of this painting.

She opened the closet and pulled out a futon, spreading it on the floor and running her hand across the cool fabric. She removed her outer kimono, laying it in the closet. Her mother arrived a few minutes later, setting out a tray with tea and then leaving. Sen sipped the tea, inhaling the green scent that steadied her still-shaken nerves.

Then, the tea drunk, Sen lay down on the futon. The soft fabric and padding felt good on her back. The silence provided a welcome respite. Birds, real ones this time, chirped from outside the window.

An hour later, Sen lay awake on the futon as sleep proved futile. Thoughts of Haru and the place where she died gnawed at Sen's heart. She might have escaped whatever fate her captor had planned for her, but she couldn't escape the stench of charred wood and moldy ash.

After a half hour of trying to rest, Sen rose and headed to the kitchen. "Mother, I'm going to step outside and get some fresh air."

Her mother smiled. "That's nice, little one. Nobuhiro's in the workshop."

Sen frowned at Mother's reference to Nobuhiro, but she kept her response to herself and just shook her head. Her mother just didn't understand. Instead, she stepped out the back door and glanced at the workshop, coming to a stop. A series of clinks resounded through the air, the sound of hammers on steel. Each tone pulled at her, dragging her closer to the shop.

No.

She had to stay away. She couldn't avoid him while she was visiting her parents, but she shouldn't go seeking him out either. Seeing him at dinner would be difficult enough.

She sighed and headed for the rock garden. As a

child, she had traipsed through it once, making several piles with the pebbles. The horror on her mother's face told her to never do it again. As she grew older, she learned how to help maintain the garden. Her mother showed her how to smooth the garden with a rake and how to repair designs marred by storms. The smoothing of the rocks provided her mother solace.

Today, though, the garden appeared rough, dotted with twigs and leaves. Weeds grew through the rocks. Sen's mother had not tended it in months, probably since Haru's death.

Someone should. Sen. A dutiful daughter. For her own growth, she needed work, not sleep.

She walked to the stand where the garden implements hung, waiting to be used. Then, she knelt at the edge of the garden and ran a hand across a mound of tiny rocks, feeling their hardness. Calmness enveloped her as she smoothed the tiny crystals flat, but that wasn't the way to begin. The garden required cleaning. She reached for a weed near the edge and dug her fingers into the rocks until she hit the soft dirt underneath. She grasped the base of the weed, making sure to avoid sharp points that might stick her, and then pulled it out. Fragrances of earth and plants filled the air as she tore the weed from the ground, spreading clumps of dirt everywhere. That would be next, after the weeds and twigs.

Sen traced the scars on her neck with her forefinger. She had been spared so that she could help her parents. Even if she could not return home, she could make home a better place. Tending the garden would offer her time for reflection . . . and prayer.

###

"Kaiken, you've done well. I'm impressed."

Kaiken stared at the ground, back straight with hands and knees on the floor. The two kimonos provided some relief against the wooden surface. Kaiken could handle the pain when it didn't.

Michiba occupied a similar position on the right. A

new recruit of Master's knelt on the left. *Carpenter,* Master had called him. He wore a simple brown kimono.

He was not a samurai.

The man had talents, Master had said.

Bathing obviously wasn't one of them.

Push those thoughts from your mind. Master knows what he's doing.

The slow breaths of Michiba and Carpenter resonated in Kaiken's ears while the wood smell of the floor filled Kaiken's senses. White *tabi* socks paced in front, partially covered by a purple kimono with a peculiar cross-hatching of lines. Kaiken desired to understand the meaning of the design but dared not look up at Master until asked.

Just respond to Master's praise.

"A servant's greatest gift is a master's appreciation," Kaiken said.

"Well spoken," Master responded. "Rise."

Kaiken stood, gut churning with a mixture of fear and pride, and stepped forward, raising a glance. Carpenter and Michiba remained on their knees, their kimonos as unmoving as they were. Master walked forward and addressed them. "You two are dismissed. You will get your orders later."

"*Hai*," the two men responded as they lowered their shoulders, their foreheads nearly touching the ground. Both men rose and headed to the door. They slid it open, turned, and fell to their knees, bowing again and sliding the door closed behind them.

Kaiken turned to face Master, shoulders square as the tension that held them tightened with the closing of the door like a rope being pulled taut. Master was impressed. There would be no more issues. All that mattered was the goal. With dedication, it would be met.

Master stepped closer. "You should have no further problems. It's good that I was close and able to visit as I can't come often. Kitayama's deception surprised me. Thankfully, it was caught before he met with Tokoda."

Kitayama's deception. How had Kaiken missed that?

Despite a lower status, Kaiken had been placed in charge. The followers might have grand designs, but they needed guidance and planning for true subterfuge. Kaiken had done well recruiting Saga and Shimoto but their deaths had caused doubts. Kitayama's treachery could have destroyed the group.

He was now silenced.

Numbers did not matter. Kaiken would go it alone if necessary.

But what next?

Kaiken studied Master's purple kimono, noting again the odd mixture of lines that seemed to represent half of a design. What was the other half? *Focus, Kaiken. Focus. Master will explain everything when it's time.* "Your presence is always welcome. It has been a long time."

Master licked his lips as his face reddened. "My movements are at the mercy of the regent, at least for now." He turned to study the garden scene on the closet. "One day that will change. With your help."

Kaiken's chest swelled at the words. Master in charge of the country. A grand day indeed. Perseverance was paramount. So was understanding. "It is regrettable about Saga and Shimoto. They served well."

Master smiled as he nodded in agreement. "It was necessary. I gave the orders to the men who led the forces at Haibara Castle. The regent's true orders never included the deaths of anyone if Akamatsu surrendered the castle, but I wanted to put fear into the Christians. I succeeded with the deaths of the twenty, marking the remaining servants for the rest of their lives."

"Does marking them really help?"

"Yes. Anyone who sees the marking will know its origin. Akamatsu was a fortunate choice. His samurai hail from many areas. They will disperse widely with their marks a testament to our beliefs."

"Why did Saga and Shimoto commit seppuku?"

"Because they followed my orders. Eventually, it would have been discovered that the order to kill was false. Saga and Shimoto would have been questioned. They took their own lives to prevent discovery. They died to protect the cause. They will be remembered when I take control."

Kaiken glanced at the window. Modest shouts of boys at play dotted the otherwise serene view. "Will the Christians, the ones who hide, really seek them out?"

"They will. These Christians risk their lives for their fellow believers."

"Do you think some of the Christians will renounce their ways?"

Master scratched his chin. "A few, maybe, will renounce this faith. The intelligent ones. Those who've had time to consider the scars on their necks and the pain their intransigence brings others. However, these Christians seek the support of their own kind. They will search for kindred spirits for support. As they do, we will root out more of them. Those missionaries in Kyushu haven't left the country. They've just moved their accursed school to a less obvious place. The missionaries in Kyoto and Osaka still maintain their houses, while they seek a change of heart from the regent."

"Will the regent change his mind?"

Master gripped the hilt of his sword and squeezed it. The answer troubled him. "He is soft unfortunately. These barbarians who claim to be from a land half a world away, they should not be intermediaries between us and the Chinese. We should not be on our knees, grateful for their service. Yet, the money from their trade has the regent dependent on these foul outsiders. We have the power to force the Chinese to trade with us directly. Send the Christians into hiding. Make them the source of any problems. One day, being a Christian will truly mean banishment from society, instead of the regent's empty proclamations."

Kaiken smiled. "I will welcome that day."

Master nodded. "So will I. Eventually the people will turn away from this foreign infestation, these strange-looking men." He laughed and shook his head as his eyebrows arched. "Some of these *yabanjins* even have blue eyes like the monsters in children's stories. They are an abomination."

Kaiken's stomach roiled. "My team and I will continue to serve you."

"You should have no more problems. Remember, your role is part of a larger agenda. There are many groups in many cities. All groups must perform their duties well."

Kaiken rose and stared into the master's eyes, eyes that sparkled like jewels. One day the master would lead, and then the master would be known and feared throughout the sixty-six provinces. "Master, will we meet again before you return to Kyoto?"

"It is best that we not. One meeting can be innocent. Two meetings and people will suspect conspiracy or other adventures. In addition, I must return to the castle. Lord Kinoshita may wonder where I have gone and he may suspect me."

Kaiken knelt and bowed before the master again, placing forearms on the floor. Duty. Responsibility. Glory. Sheathed for now, but ready when needed.

And the possibility of failure.

Boar snouts!

There was no failure. Threats had been eliminated before. They would be again.

Else, Kaiken would die.

###

Nobuhiro laid his hammer on his work bench and then grabbed a towel, wiping the sweat from his forehead. He then grabbed a cup and took a sip of water. The heat from the forge radiated out, bringing more perspiration with it. It would only get worse as summer approached. The one benefit of winter was that it was easy to cool off, though Master Goami had warned him years ago that he would get sick if he cooled off too quickly. He rubbed his stomach, feeling the loincloth underneath that was kept tight to maintain health. Normally, his stomach was quiet,

but
today it churned with something other than hunger.

Nobuhiro rubbed his shoulders and then his chest, as if some balance between them and his stomach had broken. No change.

"You seem tense," Master Goami said. "Is something troubling you?"

Nobuhiro turned to look at Master Goami, who was dressed in one of the fine robes required for this work. He owned several, proof of his abilities and accomplishments. Nobuhiro hoped to be half as successful. He might never be the old man's equal as a craftsman, but he at least had an opportunity. That was inspiration enough.

"I can't explain it," Nobuhiro said. "I feel different."

Master Goami smiled. "Your techniques have continued to improve. Maybe you're finally becoming one with the blade. Craftsman. Forge. Hammer. All are necessary for creating the best blade." The old man paused, as if the next words carried extra weight. "Your brother Toshihiro would be proud. You're becoming more aware of your surroundings."

Nobuhiro glanced to the ground as shame enveloped him. *A samurai must be aware of his surroundings.* Toshi's words from that morning conversation a month ago resounded in Nobuhiro's head. He bowed low. "You sound just like Toshi." Nobuhiro inhaled. "My apologies again, Master. I should have told you about my brothers' visits. I have—"

"Yes. Yes. Yes, I know. Your brothers have visited several times over the years. When I think about it now, the times I thought I heard conversations in this room, I left you alone. Maybe I knew. Then again—" Master Goami smiled "maybe I walk in my sleep."

Nobuhiro laughed and the tightness in his chest dissipated. Still, a shift in the air remained. He couldn't place it, but it did not worry him. An answer would arise soon.

###

Sen pulled the last of the weeds from the rock garden and viewed the discarded greenery that lay along the garden edges. Hard work. Yet it only took care of half the job. Raking the pebbles until smooth was next. From there, she or her parents could choose a design.

She wiped her brow with the sleeve of her kimono and then grabbed the rake. Light strokes to smooth the holes left by the weeds and then use of a brush to even it out.

Glancing at the workshop, she listened hard for the clinks from earlier. None came. Were they taking a rest? If there was a time to disturb them, this was it.

She put away the rake and made straight for the workshop, stepping around the rope and then heading to the door. Stepping inside, she found both Nobuhiro and her father dressed in red and yellow robes that were cinched at the waist with a sash. Both were drinking something. Hopefully, it wasn't barley water. That couldn't be good at a time like this. How did they not melt away in those clothes? Her mother always complained about the smell of those robes after a hard day.

"Excuse me," she said.

Both men looked up. Her father's face erupted into a smile. Nobuhiro's face went blank and he dropped his cup.

"S . . . s . . . sorry about that, Master." He picked up the cup. "I'll clean up the mess. It will only take a moment."

Sen looked at the floor. Barley water. Warm drinks to go with the hot robes? It made no sense. Nobuhiro looked handsome in his robes. She wouldn't mind cleaning them.

"Nobuhiro, wait," her father said. "At least say hello."

He pursed his lips but maintained his blank expression. "Hello, Sen. It is good to see you again."

"Hello, Father. Nobuhiro. Sorry to surprise you."

Nobuhiro glanced back and forth between Sen and her father, his eyes wide. Her father stared at her and then walked over, touching her temple. Pinpricks of pain shot through Sen.

The cuts from the attack.

Sen's face grew hot. She hadn't looked at herself in a mirror since the attack. Then the dirt and sweat from her time in the garden. She must look horrible.

Her father gave her a hug and then stepped back, holding her hands in his. "I'm happy to see you, my daughter, but what brings you here and what happened to you?"

Sen sighed, glancing at her father and then Nobuhiro. Where should she begin? Her father pointed to the raised platform at the back of the shop. Nobuhiro grabbed a bench and took it to the platform, the muscles rippling in his arms. He motioned for her to sit. She gasped.

"You did that for me? I am unworthy. You are samurai."

Nobuhiro's face reddened. She'd embarrassed him again.

"As I have mentioned before, I am not samurai. Not anymore. And you are Master's daughter. You sit on the platform."

Sen seated herself and nodded as her father and Nobuhiro joined her. Her chest heaved as her hands sank to her lap.

She took several deep breaths. Her father leaned forward, his hands on his knees. Nobuhiro stroked his chin.

She retold her story.

Her father's eyes flew open and his mouth dropped before he closed it again. Was he recalling Haru's death? Nobuhiro's face grew taut and his lips compressed. Was he blaming her faith?

Sen's father's eyes narrowed as he looked directly at her. "So, why aren't you taking that good samurai's advice and getting some rest, especially if you don't have to return until tomorrow?"

"I just don't feel like resting. I'm not tired."

"Well then, maybe assisting your mother would be a

good idea. You could help her in the house."

Sen smiled. Her mother had declined her help once. Still, she could try again. It would rest her mind.

But only for a short while. She had been given time off until tomorrow. And now she had a mission. She had to return to that church.

But this was no longer about finding local Christians. There might be clues there as to who killed her sister. Clues she would notice that non-Christians might miss. But what if she were discovered?

Did it matter by whom? There were more dangerous things to fear.

If the man who had imprisoned her and Omi in the church found her, she could be killed.

Which option scared her more? Death or dishonor? Did it matter? She had to know what happened to Haru.

And what if Sen's search brought death? She had been shot at by an archer. She had been imprisoned. Her family had been attacked. Death, it seemed, was already seeking her.

She had been lucky so far. If her efforts brought death, it was still preferable to dishonor. Seeking the church and the truth about her sister was the only path to honor and survival. To wait for death, when it wasn't inevitable, was the decision of a coward.

And she was not a coward.

Chapter Eighteen

Nobuhiro stood in the small grassy area behind the house later that day and wiped the sweat from his forehead with his sleeve. A few hours remained to work and the humidity was already unbearable. The time left would be worse.

Sen's question still resonated in his head. What to say?

She paced in front of him, then stopped and looked into his eyes again. "You offered to help, Nobuhiro. I'm asking."

He glanced at the rock garden. The weeds were gone. The surface was smooth. Had Sen or her mother tended it today? Living here, he had always loved the tranquil garden. It soothed his nerves. His master's wife and Haru had tended it over the years. However, his master's wife had not touched the garden since Haru's death. Weeds had overrun the garden. Wind, rain, and neglect had left it in disarray.

He had planned to work on it himself, to restore some of the happiness of this place. His efforts in the front yard had restored some flowers, but there had been no time for the rock garden.

He studied the dirt marks on Sen's face and the scratches on her hands. Her bruises from the attack were a day old. The dirt was fresh. She had tended the garden.

She did understand something of her duty to her family.

She had declined his first offer of help. Now she sought it. He stared at her. "It's still madness . . . going back to this church."

She stared back. "I have to go."

He bit his lower lip. Sen's wrists had red streaks from her bonds to go along with the welt on her temple. "You had a nasty injury. Your second one in a month. You should rest."

Sen shifted her weight back and forth and rubbed her hands together. "I can't rest."

"You just escaped from that place. Someone beat you and tied you up. You could have died. Now you want to go back? Why?"

Sen clenched her jaw. "This isn't just about me. It's about my sister as well."

He rubbed the back of his neck. It provided a break and another chance to dissuade her. "I'm certain my father and Toshi searched the place. They are thorough and would have noticed anything important."

Her eyes smoldered. "They did search. They found nothing."

He looked toward town. Twice he had protected her. Twice he had been fortunate. Twice she had been fortunate. Only fools continually tested the favor of the gods. "At least let me get my brothers' assistance."

She shook her head. "There's no time. It must be us. We only have today. Tomorrow, I return to the castle. I want to find Haru's killers as much as I want to find the church. Don't you want to know what happened to Jiro?"

His stomach tightened as if cut across the belly. He had as much reason to look as she.

A door slid open and Master Goami stepped outside. His gaunt eyes appeared red. He licked his lips but left his mouth open. "Excuse me, children. I didn't mean to interrupt."

Nobuhiro stiffened and opened his hands. Finding the killers would lift his master's burden. What burden could he lift from his master's shoulders? He looked at Sen, who had straightened. "How can I help you?"

Master Goami smiled and his gaze darted between them. "My daughter, your mother mentioned that she might work on the flowers this afternoon. She noticed some of the blooms had spruced up recently and she praised the rain. She could use your assistance. You will probably finish in an hour, maybe less."

Sen nodded. "*Hai.*"

The sound of feet spinning on the ground followed by the shuffle of footsteps faded. A sparrow trilled in the tree above the garden. Two men carrying a palanquin approached along the road and then passed. This was a serene place. Sen's actions would bring more danger.

Master Goami rubbed his eyes with his fingers. "She will go by herself if you don't go with her. You know that, don't you?"

Nobuhiro inhaled. She was still his master's daughter. He debated his words. "Forgive my impertinence, but she is stubborn and invites trouble."

The old man pursed his lips and nodded. "Yes, she inherited that trait from her grandmother. One day, I will tell you a story. Regardless, she is my only remaining daughter. I can't bear to lose her." His eyes misted. "Please go with her and protect her. It is preferable to the alternative."

Nobuhiro looked at Master Goami. His cheeks sunken. "I will do as you ask."

Master Goami stepped forward and slapped Nobuhiro's shoulder. "Very good. However, there is one task I need your assistance with in the workshop." He paused and smiled. "It will take an hour, maybe less."

###

The walk back to the place where Haru had died was

short.

The silence between Sen and Nobuhiro stretched the minutes.

She was happy to have Nobuhiro join her, whether he approved of her actions or not, but his stern face voiced his displeasure.

Sen ran her fingers through her hair, hoping to alleviate the tightness in her joints. Nothing soothed the stiff feeling that spread through her body. Between the rock garden earlier today and helping Mother, she had finally been the daughter duty required for the first time since returning to Himeji. The time with Mother had passed quickly. She had not mentioned her faith but would do so again soon. She rubbed her finger in the cotton of her kimono, pressing it against one of her scars. Her parents still didn't know she had chosen duty to God over duty to them.

Sen studied the rice paddies along the road. The flooded paddies stretched back into the distance. Numerous small paths built up through the area provided access to all the farmed plots. Women in straw hats shaped like large upside down bowls worked in ankle-deep water, planting the cultivated seedlings. Neat rows of thin green plants rose from the water in nearly half of the plots. There was still much work to accomplish.

I should be living at home and helping in my village, not hiding at the castle.

"So, where is this church?" Nobuhiro asked.

"Jiro never told you?"

Nobuhiro shook his head. "No, he didn't. After the magistrates announced the edict, they moved meetings to a secret location. I . . . I didn't want to know."

His eyes misted and a daikon-sized hollowness formed in her stomach. How much had Jiro's death affected Nobuhiro? He had served Sen's father and devoted himself to her parents. Since becoming an apprentice, he had worked every day with Jiro. Nobuhiro's pain was as great as her own.

The number of people on the street grew as they approached the market area. The crowd was larger than she expected. Of course: the sumo exhibition. She had forgotten all about it. That would help. With more people around, it would be more difficult for anyone to notice their movements. They could blend in with the crowd.

The Buddhist temple came into sight. Two monks clothed in black with hats covering most of their faces stood at the entrance. They chanted constantly, each shaking a small jingling cup in one hand, asking for donations. Their voices both soothed and annoyed her.

She wiped the sweat from the nape of her neck and glanced down the road, looking beyond lines of vendors. The bakery was there. She still needed to visit and thank the man again for his assistance to her family. The debt needed acknowledgement.

Nobuhiro scratched his nose. "You are certain that you wish to search this place?"

Sen rubbed her palms together. "Yes, I have to do this. Why?"

He exhaled and glanced down. "This p . . . place carries painful memories. It is best not to stoke them."

"Then you know this place?"

His eyebrows arched but he said nothing, pausing to look around. A passerby bumped him and he bobbed his head in contrition. Then, he came to a stop. "I've seen it before."

Sen's knees wobbled. His few words carried tones of harsh rebuke but masked his concern. He must have come here after the fire. She had only heard about the deaths. Did he see Haru's and Jiro's bodies? No wonder he didn't want to be here. Sen wiped her hands on her kimono. Nobuhiro's face begged reason. She wasn't ready to be reasonable. She needed answers.

They arrived at the building. Her pulse quickened and she breathed deeply to slow it down. Nobuhiro's chest rose and fell like waves washing ashore. He held out his hand to stop her, proceeding to the door first and then motioning her inside. He protected her again like his father had done.

Sunlight provided the visibility she hadn't had the first time she was taken captive. The fire had gutted the place, and what she thought were broken windows were instead holes in various walls, some clear through and some held together with thin strands of wood that appeared ready to disintegrate.

"You were here?" Nobuhiro asked.

"Omi and I were tied up against one of the support beams."

He moved in front of her, as if to put himself between her and the room. "Were you scared?"

"No, Nobuhiro. I was expecting to be served miso soup and rice."

He laughed, his warm smile loosening the strings of her tension. "There's no reason to be angry."

"Then what's so funny?" Her voice carried an edge as blood rushed to her face.

His shoulders drooped. "You're behaving like your mother, or at least the way she was before your sister died."

She exhaled, regretting her harsh words. He provided support through his protection. She stepped forward, reached out, and grasped his hand. She ached to hug him, to thank him for everything he had done, but couldn't raise her arms. "My apologies. What happened was so senseless."

He inhaled and grasped her hands in his, giving them a gentle squeeze before letting them fall. "Again, what do you think you we will find here?"

Sen scanned the room. She hesitated to burden Nobuhiro further, though they had become friends. "I don't know. Somewhere in here, I hope, there may be an indication of where I can find a local group of Christians. I have to find out."

"You are fortunate then."

"Fortunate? About my faith?"

"This building should have been demolished.

However, it has become something of a memorial to the dangers of fire. Either someone is keeping the property from being turned over or merchants who might use this property fear tempting fate. For some reason, the building remains."

"Forgotten."

"No. Sometimes food is left on the steps."

Food. An offering to the spirits whose souls might still reside here. It could be local Christians remembering their fallen or family members remembering their friends. No real memorial had been erected in front. Was it fear of angering the fire's perpetrators or acknowledgement of Christian deaths?

Sunlight filtered through the cracks in the walls, providing an eerie hue to the debris on the floor. Light. Shadow. Shades of gray in between. Nobuhiro would have no idea what would be important. For this, she was on her own.

"What's that?" he asked, pointing to a small pile of rubble near one of the mains beams.

She walked to the pile and knelt, running her fingers across the small ceramic shards. The sharp edges cut lines into her fingertips. "This must be it."

"What?"

"This is what I used to cut Omi's bonds. It held together just long enough to do the job before breaking."

He bent down and picked up a couple of the pieces, examining them. He squinted and moved over to one of the holes in the wall to view them in the light. "It's got some markings on it, though I can't make them out."

She walked to his side and peered at the item but couldn't see the markings well. "What do they look like?"

"I'm not sure. On one side the pieces have parts of an ideograph."

"Which one?"

Nobuhiro turned the pieces over one at a time and studied them, the sweat pouring off his brow. "Hard to tell. It could be any number of things. It's like a puzzle."

"Is there anything on the other side?"

He wiped his face with the sleeve of his kimono. "I don't recognize anything." He handed the first piece to Sen.

She held the shard in her palm and traced the design with her finger. At one time, the item had possibly been oval or maybe rectangular with rounded edges. She fingered the edges, reminding herself of how she had escaped.

Perspiration dripped down her cheeks and soaked into the *yukata* she wore. She coughed and pulled out the collar of her garment but still gasped on the hot air. Not even the holes in the wall offered any hope of catching any breezes.

"Are you feeling well?" he asked.

"Sorry. I got distracted. It's hot in here."

She looked up at Nobuhiro, who stared back, his gaze focused on her chin. Did he notice the scars? She hunched her shoulders and turned to avoid his gaze, focusing on the markings on the decoration. She flipped it over and stared at the other side. Nothing.

He handed her another piece. Her forehead tightened. The lines were familiar. Where had she seen them? What were they?

Letters.

A few of the missionaries who visited the old church in Haibara had similar medallions. They had called the letters "Greek." Whatever this shard was from, it had belonged to one of the Christians who had been here that day.

"What is it?" Nobuhiro asked. "Is this important?"

"I think so. What about the other pieces?"

He shook his head and handed her another shard. "This one makes no sense."

"Why do you say that?"

"It looks like the back end of a fish."

Her eyes flew open and she held her breath as she studied the next piece. He was right. A fish. Her hands shook as she rubbed the pieces in her fingers. She placed them inside her kimono. "Let's take the pieces back to the house. I think this may be what I'm looking for."

"Are we finished here then?"

She glanced at him. He had his hands on his hips and one foot toward the door. She had imposed on him long enough. "I think we should leave. The sun is low and I don't want to be in this place after it gets dark."

He nodded but didn't respond. She put the pieces in her belt. She didn't know what the character on the front was, but was certain that, with help, she could assemble the fish on the back. One step closer to her goal.

###

Nobuhiro sat hunched on a stool, his head over the workbench, gingerly clamping the pieces of the tile in place. He chewed on a millet stalk. Its light sweetness helped his concentration. A cup of oolong tea sat nearby.

The trip back from the church had taken longer than he thought it would. The heat had slowed them down. They had stopped once to rest, finding some shade on the path by the rice fields. Yet it had done little to cool them.

He wiped his face with his sleeve and focused on the puzzle in front of him. Did these lines go together? The jagged edges had lost flecks, making the fit imperfect.

"Do you think it will work?" Sen's rapid breaths matched the beat echoing in his head. Was it his heart or hers? Maybe it was both. Were their hearts beating in unison?

Nobuhiro caught the scent of alderwood and turned his head. Sen was leaning over, trying to see. His breath lodged in his throat. *Scars? Who did that to her?* Her gaze met his and he coughed and turned back. "It's difficult to say if it will work. This is a small item. Also, I haven't worked much with clay."

"Be careful you don't damage the design on either side or we'll never know what it says."

Nobuhiro ground his teeth and stiffened his arms. He didn't need the criticism. It reminded him of his father. "I can do this."

Her eyes flew open and she stepped back, crossing her arms.

His lips rolled in. His voice had carried an edge that he hadn't intended.

Her eyes drooped, along with her shoulders. "I was just trying to—"

"S . . . sorry. I sometimes pass by that place but have not been inside since the day Jiro died. I thought I had made peace with his fate. I overreacted." He hoped his words would calm her. He had gone with her out of his promise to his master. He had never expected to find anything.

Now he might be one step closer to finding Jiro's killers.

He glanced at her again. She moved closer, a hesitation in her step.

He tilted his head. The scars she tried to hide slipped into view. Whoever did this to her could have killed her. Still, she was loyal to this foreign religion. If her parents did not stop her, then it was not his place. He would have to marry her to get her to listen.

Marriage. He balled his hands. He would hurt whoever did this to her if he could. Was that the way a husband would feel?

He looked at the ceramic pieces, starting with the tail portion in reassembling the carved fish they had found. Next, he examined the letters. He had never seen them. Sen recognized them but didn't recall any special order. The outline of the fish helped in that area. The process was slow, but as he added each section, more options occurred to him. Each time, he flipped the piece back to see what was on the other side.

He looked back at Sen. "It resembles a few characters so far. I'm not sure yet which one it might be."

"We'll get it. Just a few more to add."

Nobuhiro's heart pounded, and each pulse resonated in his chest with the measured rhythm of the three drummers in a four-man Noh ensemble. Each piece brought a new clue into place and a different drum pitch. However, until he understood the puzzle, he was missing the flute player.

Another ten minutes passed and Nobuhiro added the last piece he and Sen had found. It looked like a pendant, though it was hard to be certain. There was still a piece missing.

"Finished?" she asked.

He turned it over, eyeing the ideograph on the other side. "Yes, for now."

Sen looked over his right shoulder, her breath caressing his neck. Their closeness broke his concentration.

"What do you think?" he asked, trying to keep his eyes on the puzzle.

She leaned closer. A loose tendril of hair brushed the bare skin of his arm. She smelled of plum and alderwood.

Sen said nothing for a moment, only staring at the partial medallion. "It looks like the character for bitter, and that fits into the clue, though the character is missing one of the marks. Then there's also that horizontal line on the top."

He viewed the piece, rotating it for ideas. Nothing came to mind. "I think you're right. The last piece will provide an answer."

Sen stared at him. He looked into her eyes and then lost track of his thoughts. She was beautiful. Despite the bruise on her temple, despite her disheveled appearance, despite the scars on her neck, she was the most beautiful woman he had ever seen. He leaned forward and closed his eyes as his lips found hers in an exchange even better than he had imagined.

Chapter Nineteen

Sen pulled away. Her body tingled. Her mouth opened. Her eyes closed. The soft touch of Nobuhiro's warm lips reverberated inside her like the dancing at a festival.

She had often thought of kissing him but hadn't known what to expect. When she was younger, she had kissed a boy in the neighborhood out of curiosity.

This was different.

She opened her eyes.

Nobuhiro's mouth was rounded. His eyes focused on her. His face, startled. "I . . . I am sorry. I did not mean to do that."

Her chest lurched. He didn't mean to do that? What did he mean to do?

The partially closed door to the shop slid open and her father stepped in. Thoughts of Nobuhiro dissipated as heat flooded her cheeks.

Father beamed at them. "Your mother was wondering if either of you wanted something else to eat, since neither of you ate much at dinner. She could prepare something."

She looked away but in truth looked nowhere. Had her father seen Nobuhiro kiss her? What did he think of it?

Her mother had suggested Nobuhiro as a suitor. Her father appeared happier than she had seen him in a while. He likely approved. Still, it didn't make sense to her, since Nobuhiro wasn't a Christian.

Yet he was everything else.

She glanced away, as looking at Father proved difficult. She saw the ceramic medallion in Nobuhiro's hand and reached for it gingerly, fearful she would break it again. "Father, we've assembled what appears to be a medallion with a monogram of some kind. We're not sure what it means, as it's missing a piece. Perhaps you might have an idea."

She handed him the medallion. He turned it over in his hands. His face blanched and he staggered. She and Nobuhiro both rushed to his side as her father reached out and pressed his arm against a wall.

"I'm fine. I'm fine." Her father took a few slow breaths and rubbed his chest as if his airflow was constricted. Nobuhiro grabbed a stool and brought it over for her father to sit on.

Sen and Nobuhiro grabbed under her father's shoulders and eased him down. She then rubbed his shoulders. "Father, what is it?"

The old man continued to stare at the object, rotating it in his fingers. "I'm sorry. I must be tired. I'm not sure what it is and I may be wrong. It's just . . . "

Confusion lapped at Sen's brain like waves on a shore. "I don't understand."

Her father handed the medallion back to her and then widened his stance as he rose. Nobuhiro moved to grab his arm, but Sen's father waved him off. "Follow me." He motioned to them and then turned and headed for the house.

She went to the door and then looked backed at Nobuhiro to confirm he was coming. The care he had shown her father just now when he had faltered to the protection of her family when attacked, Nobuhiro supported her family. He behaved more like her parents' dutiful child than she did.

She would find no better man than him.

Sen's mother sat at the table, enjoying tea and staring at the hearth. She looked up. "Ah, good. You pulled them from the workshop. You both must be hungry."

Sen's father looked at her mother with cautious eyes and her mother set her tea on the table. "The children have assembled a most interesting item. Perhaps it's nothing, my wife, but I thought you should see it."

Sen's mother nodded but didn't respond, instead remaining seated cross-legged on the tatami mats. Sen walked over, her feet scraping the soft straw, and handed her mother the medallion fragment. "Mother, this is what we put together."

Her mother's mouth flew open, and she covered it with her hand.

"What is it?" Sen asked.

"Wait here." Her mother glanced at the shrine for Haru and then headed toward the room she shared with Sen's father. Birds chirped outside, their songs broken by the sound of wood sliding against wood, the opening and closing of a closet. Sen's mother returned, carrying a small chain necklace with an odd-shaped shard hanging off the end. "Here," her mother said.

She handed the necklace to Sen, who ran her forefinger across the sharp edges. The imprint drew her gaze.

On one side was the head of a fish.

On the other side, a cross.

Sen extended her open hand. "Mother, may I have the fragment I gave you?"

Her mother handed the item over, and Sen put the two parts together.

They fit.

Sen held out the pieces to Nobuhiro. "What do you think?"

He examined them and nodded. The corners of his mouth turned up slightly, though his eyes conveyed a heavy burden. A bit of hope breaking through despair. How could this pendant do that to him?

Nobuhiro handed the pieces back to her. She stared at the cross as she ran her finger across her neck, tracing the scar underneath her kimono. Her breathing quickened. "In the workshop, I mentioned I thought the bottom part resembled the character for *bitter*."

Nobuhiro paused. "Does it fit the clue then? The clue uses the word *ground*. The cross on your mother's part of the medallion has nothing to do with that."

Sen smiled back at him. "The cross is *true joy*. However, there's a line above the character for *bitter*. Put the cross over the line—"

"And you create *ground*," Sen's mother offered.

Sen's insides churned. Her mother offered help. Were her feelings changing toward Sen's search? Sen recalled her last day in Haibara. She had chosen the Lord over her parents. Was the Lord preparing them for the day she would tell them? "Yes, and the whole thing assembled—"

"Resembles the ideograph for *happiness*," her father interjected, "though it's missing a mark."

Sen raised her head, staring at her father, though not really looking at him. "You are right. It is strange. Who would have created this clue? When you look at the character for *happiness*, you think of the top half as the character for *ground*."

Father stepped forward. His sensei-like gaze overpowered the room. "No Japanese person would have created the clue. None would have thought of it either when they saw the medallion."

Sen glanced toward her mother, who stared back at her, though her eyes blinked into nothingness. "Mother, why do you have this cross?"

Her mother coughed, her eyelids flitting away tears that pushed to flow. "It belonged to Haru. She was wearing it when they found her."

Sen's hands shook and her throat went dry. Haru's. The pendant was Haru's.

Nobuhiro reached out and clasped her trembling fingers. His gentle touch provided support. Just like he did. “Does it help you, Sen? Have you seen this symbol before somewhere?”

She exhaled, the tension ebbing from her face. “Yes.”

“Are you certain?”

She breathed deeply. “Yes.” Her voice echoed the certainty that flowed within her. She closed her eyes and rubbed the symbol in her hands. Her body tingled at the thought of meeting other Christians again. She had found a clue. She knew where to go next.

However, getting the Christians to reveal themselves was another challenge. Should she even try? She didn’t know who had attacked her and Omi.

If she found the Christians, would she be bringing trouble to a group who wanted to remain hidden?

Just as she was bringing trouble to Nobuhiro if she continued to bring him along with her?

Chapter Twenty

Sen inhaled the crisp morning air while listening to the rustle of the nearby trees. A few crows cawed in the distance. Clouds still covered the morning sun, remnants of the rains from the night before. Some merchants, their bags over their shoulders, walked the streets. Others carried goods of cloths and vegetables on pushcarts. It was a good day to be outside, unlike yesterday during the search of the church ruins.

"Nobuhiro, you did not have to come. I told you that before."

He grunted but did not look at her. "You are my master's daughter. I would give my life to protect you."

Master's daughter? Was that all she meant to him? She licked her lips, remembering his warm touch from last night. She had prayed about it but had yet to hear an answer. "Is that why you're here?"

Nobuhiro stopped, his soft gaze glancing down. "No, it is not the only reason. I wanted to apologize for last night. I should not have—"

"Should not have what? Should not have kissed me?" She regretted her outburst but couldn't pull it back. The constricted look on his face revealed his pain. Furtive looks from passersby caught her attention, but they soon turned back to their business. She had been loud. Rudeness reflected poorly on her.

Nobuhiro leaned in. "Do not think that way. I don't regret what happened. I am concerned, for your welfare as much as your parents'. I protect you as much for me as I do for your family's future."

Her chest warmed. He cared for her. Why did it matter so much to her? She had prayed often to God to help her find a Christian man, but Nobuhiro did not believe in God.

He did believe in her, though. He believed in her feelings and believed in her future. Would God lead her to a non-Christian?

"I am humbled by the care you have given me."

He swallowed hard. "You have been touched once by a sword. I would do anything to prevent that from happening again."

She grabbed her throat, massing the fabric just above the scars. "How long have you known?"

"I have noticed the scars on your neck several times, but always just at a glimpse so I wasn't sure. Then I realized there were two straight lines. You had swords there. Why?"

Sen took a deep breath and then recounted the day. It was the first time she had discussed the incident with anyone who hadn't been there. The words came slowly.

Nobuhiro nodded but said little other than to indicate that she should continue. Her feet grew heavy as she recalled each step toward the front of the line. She craved water now like she had then. Nobuhiro's body flinched with each sentence. Her scars tingled. Her shoulders scrunched together.

He moved closer, as if he feared her falling. "So you renounced and survived?"

She inhaled through her teeth.

She could not lie.

"I professed my belief in God."

His face contorted as his cheeks grew red. "How could you do that? You knew what that confession might do. You knew your sister was dead. You knew your duty to your family."

"I knew my duty to God. I trusted in Him to protect my parents."

He stared back, his eyes wide open. "I don't see how it benefited you."

"I survived to return to Himeji. I can still help my parents."

"Have you told them? Do they know the choice you made?"

Her stomach twisted like weed roots. "Nobuhiro, I'm sorry."

"It's not me who deserves an apology."

"My apology was for placing you in a difficult position with my parents. However, I will tell them."

His face remained stern, but he said no more as he turned down the road, pausing only to stare back at her. She started forward, keeping her gaze on the road.

Fifteen minutes passed, and Sen and Nobuhiro approached the restaurant where they had stopped twice before. He had said nothing to her during the walk, but she hadn't talked either. When would she see her parents again and have the chance to admit her actions?

Sen paused at the restaurant entrance. Her heartbeat quickened, as optimism and fear argued within her. A dog barked, but Sen glanced around and saw none. Probably a neighborhood dog behind one of the buildings.

"This is it," she said. "I hope we're right."

"It makes sense."

Nobuhiro's voice startled her. His anger still radiated.

The place was closed. A sign on the door thanked potential patrons for coming and said the place would open at the hour of the horse, just in time for lunch. Nobuhiro stepped up onto the porch and knocked. A window on the side of the building slid open and then closed quickly, but no one came.

"Let's go," Nobuhiro said.

She closed her eyes and strained her ears. Someone had at least looked. "Wait. Please."

Soft footfalls on a hardwood floor sounded from inside. The door opened and a petite woman, aged fifty or so, stepped to the entrance. She wore a simple blue kimono. Her black hair reached her shoulders. Her smile was wide. Her look firm.

"I'm sorry, but we're closed right now," the woman said. "Thank you for stopping by. We'll be open soon. I would happily welcome you early, but we're not ready for customers. Please come back."

Sen put her hand out, palm down, and stopped the woman from leaving. She bowed low. "We're sorry for disturbing you. We were hoping you could help us."

The woman stared and then turned aside as if she wanted to say something but dared not. "Maybe another time. Please come back when we're open." She gave a slight bow.

"Wait, please," Nobuhiro said as he stepped forward. "Can you tell us where true joy springs from?"

The woman hesitated for the second time in the conversation. She closed her eyes. "From burying your bitterness in the ground."

Sen inched forward. "You can help us?"

The woman inhaled. "You are Haru's sister, are you not?"

Sen's skin tingled as joy leapt into her throat. A tear slid down her cheek. "Yes, I am. You knew her?"

"Come inside," the woman said. "Quickly."

###

Nobuhiro's heart beat louder in his ears as he stepped through the entrance. Where was this leading? He was here to protect her for his master and his wife. Why had he stepped forward to ask that question? It would have been easy to press on, but then Sen might have returned without him.

How would these people greet him? He was not a Christian.

"Please sit down." The woman motioned to one of the tables. "I will only be a moment."

Nobuhiro looked around. They were the only ones in the room. The tables sparkled. Cushions were available for customers. Rear and side windows had been opened to allow a breeze. He focused on the solid floor, sliding his feet along the wood. His muscles tensed as if expecting a problem.

The woman returned with a man dressed in a white linen kimono, the man who had greeted them at the door when they had been there before. Like the woman, he was also in his fifties. His hair was gray and his face round. His clothes had smudges of food on them. His wide grin showed kindness. Nobuhiro's shoulders dropped, the tension easing out of them.

The man rubbed his palms together. "I apologize for my appearance. I have been preparing to open. My name is Yoshi. This is my wife, Naomi. Welcome, sister of Haru. We offer our condolences for your loss."

The older couple bowed low before Nobuhiro and Sen. Nobuhiro returned it, seeing Sen out of the corner of his eye as she bowed as well. His hands trembled and he placed them against his thighs to steady them.

His throat grew dry. Should he say something? These people had known Sen's sister.

They had also known Jiro. Jiro had trusted them. That was the only support he needed. He decided to keep quiet and let Sen ask questions.

Sen smiled back at the couple. "Thank you very much. I am—"

"Sen," Yoshi answered. "We heard about you often from your sister. She spoke fondly of you. Again, our sympathies."

Sen's lips drooped as her eyes glazed over, likely recalling past joyous times. "I wish I had made it home to see her."

Naomi stepped forward and grasped Sen's hand, patting the top of it. "Nevertheless, you are home. Your parents must be happy." She paused, looking at Nobuhiro. "Is this a relative?"

Nobuhiro coughed and brought his hand under his chin to stop the hard lump from rising into his jaw. He stroked his chin and took a breath. "My name is Nobuhiro. I am an apprentice in the Goami household."

"Wonderful. Then the Goami style will extend more generations." Naomi turned toward the kitchen but looked over her shoulder. "Please rest. I will fetch something to drink."

Yoshi grabbed some cushions and brought them over, handing one each to Nobuhiro and Sen and then pointing to a table. Sen sat next to Nobuhiro while Yoshi sat across from them. Yoshi entertained Sen with a couple of stories about Haru. Sen's eyes lit as she listened to both tales. Her smile was beautiful. Just like her.

Naomi returned shortly, carrying a tray of cups with steam rising from them. She served them and then sat next to Yoshi.

Yoshi glanced between Sen and Nobuhiro, his face a blank stare. "How did you find us and how can we help you?"

Sen's lips thinned, but she said nothing. Nobuhiro waited and then leaned forward, his hands open and his muscles tight. "Sen is looking for a place to meet other Christians. Can you help her?"

Yoshi and Naomi looked at each other and nodded. Yoshi then glanced at Sen. "Yes, we can. Sometimes, we meet here."

Sen's eyebrows raised. "Here? How could you meet here? This is in the market area. Won't people notice a large group coming in here? Wouldn't they be suspicious if you're closed?"

Yoshi smiled. "We often host private gatherings for large groups, so it is not uncommon for groups to be here. Also, the meetings are not always here. We are discreet and move it often, something necessary given the regent's unfortunate decree." Yoshi's eyes glowed and accented his smile. "Smaller groups meet in homes. Besides, the way someone worships is a private matter, is it not?"

Sen nodded her head slowly. "What if the magistrate suspects something? Has the place ever been searched?"

"No, it has not. But if it is, then we are just a private meeting of friends. We do have special items, reserved for if a missionary were to visit, but these things resemble elaborate cups. If the police saw these items, they would not know what they were. We're more likely to lose them due to taxes than to our faith."

"Missionaries have visited here?" Sen asked.

Yoshi sighed. "Only one since the decree. I heard that after the edict was announced, the missionaries were given twenty days to leave. Some left, but most are still in the country. Unfortunately, they live with other Christians and need to keep themselves quiet."

"Did the missionary stay with you?"

Yoshi's smile was matched by Naomi's. "Yes, we were honored to have him. However, he told us of the destruction of the church in Kyoto and other places. Our hearts ached."

"The church in Kyoto was destroyed?" Sen's mouth and eyes flew open in shock.

Yoshi rubbed the back of his neck, the joy on his face from celebrating his faith gone. Naomi squeezed his hand and the two of them exchanged supportive glances. "Yes, it was disheartening."

Sen's gaze fell and she did not respond.

"What is it, Sen?" Nobuhiro asked.

"Do you know what happened to Lord Akamatsu and his first castle? With your upbringing, I supposed you'd be familiar with the story."

"I only know that he surrendered it to show his allegiance to the regent's predecessor. What else is there?"

Sen's lips thinned. "He surrendered it for his faith. In exchange, the missionaries were permitted to build a church in Kyoto. It was important to have a large presence in the capital. Now it's gone. Lord Akamatsu proved once before that he could practice his faith without betraying the government. Still, the regent made an example of him."

The looks on the faces of the couple matched Sen's. What was it about this faith that strengthened and drove its converts?

Naomi turned to face Nobuhiro. "I am curious. You said Sen is looking for services. How about you?"

Nobuhiro coughed and considered his answer. He did not wish to offend the couple, but he didn't wish to lie. What should he say? This faith's adherents impressed him. Better to tell the truth. "I'm not a Christian. I'm just supporting my friend."

"Then may God bless your efforts. So, who are your parents? Do we know your family?"

Nobuhiro dragged his fingers across his mouth. "My mother passed away many years ago." His heart still ached at the thought of his mother, the few memories that remained. "My father is Tokoda Shigehiro."

Their shoulders snapped straight. "Your father has a surname?" Yoshi asked. "He must be as great an artisan as Sen's father to have earned such a title."

Nobuhiro avoided their looks. The couple's words were to mask their concern. They were words of hope. Great craftsmen could earn a last name. However, surnames were reserved for samurai and ladies of the court.

The type of people this couple would most fear.

"He is a senior retainer at the castle," Nobuhiro said.

Both Yoshi's and Naomi's nostrils flared. Each sat back, as if to avoid getting closer. Yoshi finally voiced their concerns, concerns Nobuhiro knew well. "Your father serves the regent?"

Nobuhiro crossed his arms and lowered his chin. "I am not my father. However, he protects the castle, its residents, and the city."

Yoshi squinted and stared at Nobuhiro. "The regent's

brother-in-law is the castle resident. Everything he does, he does on orders. He is responsible for the fire that claimed Sen's sister and her husband, just as much as those who set it."

Nobuhiro balled his fists, putting them on the table. "My father may act on orders, but he is an honorable man." His jaw clenched as the hair on the back of his neck rose. "Jiro was my best friend and I want whoever did this punished, but my father had nothing to do with the fire. He and my brothers are searching for the true perpetrators."

"Searching?" Yoshi asked, his voice gaining volume. "Like they soon will be searching every house in Himeji."

"What do you mean?" Sen asked, her voice soft and calm.

Nobuhiro looked at her, her eyes pleading calm. His ire subsided. He lowered his arms.

Yoshi looked at his wife, his eyes aflame, and jerked his head in a direction behind them. "Please show them."

Naomi rose and walked to the back of the room, returning shortly with a rolled-up piece of parchment. She handed it to Nobuhiro.

He unrolled the scroll and read aloud. "By order of the regent, all swords and guns, except those owned by the samurai class, will be confiscated. Surrender your swords to any retainer who visits your house or establishment. All properties will be searched. Individuals who do not surrender all their weapons will face severe punishment."

Sen's hands shook and she gasped. "Can this be true?"

Nobuhiro studied the document, looking for anything telling. "It looks legitimate." He stared at it further, stunned by its implications. What was the reason for this order? What were they trying to accomplish?

"It is legitimate," Yoshi interjected, his eyes raging but his voice dropping. He tapped his forefinger on the table, creating heavy pings that vibrated through the wood. "The regent fears revolt. This is a pretext to ensure that only those within his control have the means to protect themselves."

Nobuhiro rolled up the document, feeling the soft, heavy paper and the heavy weight of the ink. "Thank you."

Yoshi slammed his fist on the table. "For what? For allowing you in? For telling you our secrets so you can inform your father?"

"Your secret is safe with me. As I said, I know my father. He was not involved in the fire and he is not trying to harm Christians. His only concern is protecting the populace." He stared Yoshi directly in the eyes. "Whoever did this is a criminal. They will be punished."

Yoshi hesitated. Had Nobuhiro convinced him of his father's intentions? Sen had searched for Christians. Nobuhiro couldn't bear causing them to flee.

The proprietor bit his lower lip and nodded his head in assent. "I believe you, but I do not know if I trust your father."

"His father is an honorable man," a deep voice called from another room. "We have nothing to fear from him."

Slow, ponderous footsteps sounded on the wooden floor as a tall, dark man entered the room. The top of his head was shaved, samurai style, with his hair in a topknot. He wore a white shirt and a gray kimono. He was half a foot taller than Nobuhiro and muscular, with arms that could break a man like a toothpick. A scar marred his right cheek.

The sight of him raised the hairs on the nape of Nobuhiro's neck. He had seen him at the archery competition for the first time since he had left the castle seven years ago. His presence alone intimidated Nobuhiro. As a child, he had been a bully. As an adult, he was a force.

The nemesis of his existence stood in front of him.

Nishioji.

Chapter Twenty-One

Sen's breath lodged in her throat as the brawny Nishioji approached the group. His black hair was tied in a topknot. His gray kimono did little to hide his broad shoulders and biceps. The samurai admired him as the strongest man at the castle. She had never met him, but she knew who he was.

So did every female attendant at the castle. His sparkling brown eyes had melted many hearts.

Nobuhiro grunted under his breath, though it was nearly inaudible. Sen turned to look. Nobuhiro frowned, his arms locked across his chest. His eyes focused on the samurai.

The entire group stood to greet the brawny man. Why was he here?

Nishioji stopped within an arm's length of the group and drew himself to his full height. "Pardon my interruption. I thought it best to add my thoughts to this discussion."

Yoshi stared at the man and nodded his head, though he glanced downward. A sign of respect accorded Nishioji's status. "I'd wished to protect you, Nishioji-sama. It wasn't necessary for you to reveal yourself, though I always value your sage counsel."

Sen couldn't take her eyes off the imposing figure. "Are you really a—"

"Christian?" Nishioji widened his smile. "Yes, sister of Haru. I am."

Sen's heart swelled. There was another Christian in the castle. Did he know about the mysterious cross tile on the wall? Did he know how it got there? Maybe. Could she ask?

Forget that. He was a samurai. She wouldn't be able to approach him at the castle. She wouldn't be able to approach him at a gathering. He would have to mention the cross.

"I . . . am . . . surprised to find you here." Nobuhiro clenched his fists but left them at his sides.

Nishioji took a long breath and exhaled slowly. "Yes, Nobuhiro, I suppose you would be. I treated you poorly when we were younger." He bowed to Nobuhiro. "I beg your forgiveness."

Sen looked back at Nobuhiro. His shoulders and face relaxed. His eyes glanced toward her. How much pain had he endured as a child? How much teasing from bullies? He had no support from his father and no love of a mother. Was that why he left the castle?

"I . . . appreciate your words . . . in support of my father." His expression was a light grimace.

Yoshi shook his head. "I believe both of you." He looked directly at Nobuhiro. "But I still don't know if I trust your father."

Nobuhiro lowered his head. "Then please trust your Father, the one to whom you pray. No one in my family wishes to harm Christians."

Yoshi smiled, his arms raised slightly, palms facing out. "Asking for the trust of my God? You have learned much. If there is more you wish to know, I offer my guidance."

"Thank you," Nobuhiro said.

Yoshi bowed and extended his hand outward. "Go with God's blessing." His tone was reverential. "May He smile upon you."

Sen smiled and her entire body tingled. "He already has. He has led us here to find you."

###

Nobuhiro didn't know what surprised him more, having found other Christians or discovering that Nishioji, the tormentor from his childhood, was one of them. For Nishioji to apologize for actions he committed as a child was unexpected. Nishioji's station was far above his.

This religion had changed him. It had made him a better person.

Was there substance to Sen's beliefs?

Nobuhiro and Sen left the restaurant, waving farewell before turning toward the castle. He moved closer, narrowing the amount of space between the two of them. He didn't expect trouble. Still, given the attack on her and Omi, and his father's charge that he protect the Goami family, he rose to his duty.

The midday sun made the air feel heavy. The streets were lively with people sampling the various offerings of the street vendors and businesses that bustled with customers. A grunt from behind made Nobuhiro shift left as two men carrying a palanquin hurried around him. The men's posture indicated the lacquered vehicle carried a passenger. A difficult job in this weather. They reached the intersection ahead and turned right at the square pole that marked the street names. A statue of a smiling Buddha rested on a pedestal next to the pole.

A burning feeling filled Nobuhiro's chest, but it wasn't painful. Sen avoided his gaze, her beautiful face casting a permanent frown. He wanted to talk, but any discussion would have been difficult out in the open.

As they neared the castle, the land turned grassy. Sen broke the silence. "What does it mean, this new order?"

A low-pitched temple gong sounded in the area, adding weight to the heavy air. "I don't know, but I'll ask as soon as we return to the castle."

Sen dipped her head. Her lips were thin and slightly parted. "So, you plan on speaking to your brothers?"

He glanced at the wall that surrounded the castle grounds, then turned back to her. "Yes, the minute I can find them. What is wrong?"

She glanced away, her eyes a mix of hesitation and fear that she tried to hide. "You know where the church is now. I trust your brothers, but I'm still concerned. Omi and I have no idea who locked us in that old church."

Nobuhiro tensed, the muscles in his forearms stretched taut. "I'll be vigilant."

Sen lowered her chin. "I'm not asking only for that. The place needs to remain a secret." She held out her hands, palms up. "Nishioji's faith needs to remain a secret."

His stomach began to roil. She was protecting him. He understood the need for secrecy. Keeping Sen safe meant keeping Nishioji's secret quiet. Here she was, protecting Nishioji. It was hard to bear.

Nobuhiro said nothing as he and Sen passed through the entrance, nodding to the guards, who appeared pleased to see him. He said goodbye to Sen and his thoughts turned to his brothers. He put his foot squarely on the ground and began walking, crunching the small pebbles on the road beneath his feet.

He would find out about the edict, but what would he do next? To not tell them about the church could place Sen in danger.

But if he spoke about it, Sen would never forgive him.

Chapter Twenty-Two

Nobuhiro found Toshi on the grounds, demonstrating fighting postures to ten young boys. His brother eyed him and nodded before focusing back on his charges.

The boys were lined up in two rows behind Toshi. Each carried a bamboo sword and wore a light jacket, with pants that reached his knees. Each boy also wore *tabi* socks and sandals. *Hakamas* were the proper attire for kendo as the long skirt hid leg movement. Toshi probably had the boys dress in knee-length pants so he could inspect their footwork.

The boys were practicing two-strike techniques, striking body level to catch an opponent's hand and then up to strike the face. Poised on toes. Sword out. Glide forward. Strike and strike. Repeat.

Nobuhiro brooded as he watched his brother's polished performance and saw the boys repeat the moves. As a child, he couldn't even handle this. He always dragged his left foot. Would these boys have heard stories about him? What would they think?

After thirty minutes, Toshi ended the class, stating, "Before you begin your game, I have a special guest I'd like you to meet."

Nobuhiro's pulse raced as he heard these words and saw his brother motion him over. He froze, not sure what to do.

Toshi called out to him, "Nobuhiro, come over. These boys want to meet you."

They wanted what? Nobuhiro puzzled over this but walked to where his brother waited. He looked at the faces of the boys and saw something he didn't expect, eagerness and flashing eyes.

Toshi handled the introductions as each young man walked up to greet Nobuhiro, bowing low and glancing up at the same time. The introductions then completed, Nobuhiro looked at Toshi and shook his head as the boys headed out to begin their game. "I don't understand. Why were those boys excited about meeting me?"

Toshi laughed, as if surprised he needed to explain. "For someone with tofu in your head, you should absorb more of what's around you. These boys admire you."

"Admire? Why?"

Toshi's eyebrows rose, and then he slapped Nobuhiro on the back. "You took on a mounted archer with a cloth-covered sword. You faced Funaki with an iron clamp."

Nobuhiro stared at his brother. "I survived. There was no glory in it."

"Not true. Remember, the cloth-covered sword belonged to Lord Kinoshita's father. Word reached Lord Kinoshita about the *activities* of his father's sword. Lord Kinoshita was impressed."

Nobuhiro tried to hide his grin and at least keep his mouth shut. He had come to the attention of the castle lord? Would Lord Kinoshita make such a comment in the presence of his father? "I am humbled to hear that."

Toshi beamed. "You should be. You battled both men to a standstill. Both ran. A samurai must be prepared to use whatever he has available to defend his honor and the honor of those he serves. It is simple to explain that concept. It is a challenge for them to learn it. Your actions helped them understand. They will not forget."

Nobuhiro's heart swelled. Young charges now admired his actions. It was difficult to comprehend after a lifetime of feeling inadequate.

"What brings you here?" Toshi asked.

"The edict on the confiscation of swords. What's this all about?"

Toshi didn't respond, instead staring out at the grounds. Nobuhiro turned as well. The boys were now playing a game of *kemari* with an eight-inch deerskin ball, kicking, passing, running, and catching. Shouts of "*Ariya*" erupted when players kicked the ball high into the air, combined with "*Ari*" for each pass. Another game Nobuhiro was unable to participate in as a child.

"Let's walk," Toshi said. "We can talk on the way."

###

Sen cleaned up her area in the women's quarters and tidied the rest of the room. She surveyed the room after she was finished. No dust on the tatami mat floor. She walked over to close the futon closet, sliding the door to reveal a tiger painting. On the opposite wall hung a large horizontal scroll with handwritten seasonal poetry. To the side, two paper screens were open, allowing in fresh air. An alcove was between the two windows. On the raised stoop sat a vase with arranged flowers.

"You've been back nearly an hour and you still haven't come by to see me," Omi said, startling Sen.

Sen flashed a smile. "I have a lot to think about."

"You're always thinking about something." Omi's playful look relaxed the tension in Sen's shoulders. "If work helps you think, I have to wipe down the walls and screens in the mistress's quarters. You can do that for me."

"No thanks. I'll leave that to you."

"What are you thinking about? You look almost happy."

Sen looked around to see if anyone was close by. Should she trust her? Omi was the best friend she had here and had twice expressed an interest in Christianity. Still, she didn't know her that well.

She decided to take the risk.

"I found a group of Christians in town." The words sprang from her lips, matched by the wide smile she knew she now showed. She couldn't contain her excitement.

Omi grasped Sen's hands. "That's wonderful. I'm so happy for you. When can we meet them?"

Sen's eyes widened and she smiled. "We? You really want to meet them?"

"Yes, I do. I have watched how your faith sustains you. Even when we were locked up, you never wavered. I was impressed."

Sen's heart thumped against her chest. She had found a place to join other Christians. Now, she had someone to share it with. It was truly a special day.

Then she grasped the edges of her kimono, rubbing the fabric in her fingers. One thing would make the day even better. Would Nobuhiro want to join them?

Likely no.

She loved Nobuhiro. He was the man for her.

But he was not a Christian.

A nonbeliever held her heart.

###

Nobuhiro and Toshi entered a room adjacent to one of the samurai quarters. It was sparse with a wooden floor. A battle scene was painted on the closet, with words of exhortation on scrolls that decorated the walls. Toshi motioned for Nobuhiro to take a seat as he walked to the window and stared outside. Nobuhiro declined, heading to the window himself to stand beside his brother. They had discussed minor things so far but not the topic on his mind.

He looked out the window and saw the courtyard that led to the entrance. Parties of samurai and servants moved across the grounds, neither intersecting with the other. The servants swept the paths, falling to their knees and bowing their heads to the ground when a samurai came near. Other servants scrubbed outer walls and climbed to the top of the gate, buffing it with rags. A typical afternoon, at least as he remembered them.

He walked back and sat on the floor, crossing his legs in front of him. "What is it? What are you waiting for?"

His brother stood motionless except for a light-tapping toe and slight flinches of his neck. "I was looking to see if Uji was coming. However, I don't see him."

"Are we going to talk about this?"

Toshi looked back. His lips thinned as his face tightened. He stretched his arms and then walked over and sat on a raised platform nearby, crossing his legs like Nobuhiro. Whatever his concerns, he hid them well. He took a deep breath and then leaned forward. "The new edict? Yes, it's true."

The simple words cut deep into Nobuhiro's flesh. "Why?"

"The official reason is that the regent wishes to melt the swords of the people to create precious artifacts for various temples."

Nobuhiro shook his head. "And the real reason?"

"He fears revolt."

Nobuhiro groaned inwardly, his gut sloshing like a stormy river. Yoshi had been right. "Revolt? From whom?"

Toshi coughed as if the words would choke him at the source. "Any who would challenge his authority. Nobunaga also faced revolt from the people."

Nobuhiro rubbed his fingers across his forehead. "The regent actually thinks the populace capable?"

"You forget. The regent is lowborn. He earned his name when he came to power. If he could rise from a peasant status, so could another leader."

"Then this has nothing to do with Christians?" Nobuhiro rubbed his chin. The contradiction of action and words remained incomprehensible.

Toshi grinned and shook his head, reaching across to grab Nobuhiro's shoulder and pat it. "Christians are only a pretext. The regent fears them because the missionaries take their orders from foreign countries. That was the logic behind the expulsion. However, it's just political. Homegrown threats are greater. If it meant staying in power, he would build Christian churches in every city. As with any leader, the regent's only concern is self-preservation."

Nobuhiro looked at the wall and then at his brother. "Then his fears of an uprising are local. Without arms, it would be difficult for the people to mount a threat."

Toshi nodded. "Yes, it would be. The people have been through much. People are susceptible at these times. It is why the Christian message has been so well received. Some Buddhist sects offer peace, but fears of renewed militancy remain. These Christians offer a new way of peace without preconditions."

"Then why the edict? Why attack the Christians?"

"Because then the regent can focus on the true problem, the regional governors. The regent doubts the loyalty of several of them. They continue to quarrel with one another, fighting for position like family members fighting over too little money. This breeds violence. Nobunaga took his own life to deny an assassin. The regent fears the same."

Nobuhiro massaged the back of his neck, applying some deep pressure. "Then why not just apply this sword edict to the regional governors?"

"By mandating this charity that people surrender their weapons, the regent can forestall numerous threats to his rule. More importantly, he can disarm his most vocal opponents without losing any of his own men. Weapons are costly. Sometimes it is easier to bankrupt an enemy than defeat him in battle."

Nobuhiro nodded in agreement. Toshi spoke the truth. It didn't make the words easier to digest. They carried a taste more bitter than tea leaves.

Heavy footsteps from behind caught Nobuhiro's attention. He turned, pausing to place them. A moment later, Uji entered, his face more dour than usual. He did not wish to convey the news he carried. Nobuhiro stood to bow to his oldest brother.

Uji acknowledged him and waved his hand, indicating that Nobuhiro should sit. He joined them on the floor and then glanced at Toshi. "Have you told him yet?"

Toshi exhaled and paused, looking still as if his thoughts carried a new burden. "Not everything."

"About the sword hunt? I've heard. Will the two of you lead any of the searches?"

Uji scratched his arms. "All of the retainers will be involved. I do not agree with it, but it is our duty and we will carry it out."

Toshi and Uji both wore pained expressions. Both would follow orders. Nobuhiro's fury about the edict now carried a twinge of pity. If he were a samurai, he would be following the same orders, experiencing the same regret.

His older brothers glanced at each other and then looked away. Neither made eye contact with him.

Nobuhiro's chest tightened. He rubbed it to relieve the stress, but the pull within increased, drawing tension from his brothers to him. "Is there something else?"

Uji nodded. "Yes. It concerns our Father."

"What is it?"

Uji drew a sharp breath through his teeth. His stoic resolve now timid. The news had touched him. The proper words proved difficult. "Father met with his former supervisor this morning. He received some disquieting news. His supervisor has been ordered to take his own life. He met with Father privately to let him know."

Nobuhiro's mouth dropped open, but little air passed through his constricted throat. Their father had served this man for many years. He had been a friend to the family. Nobuhiro struggled to regain his composure. "That was kind of him. Father must have been moved. Was it a final goodbye? Did he offer Father the honor of serving as his second?"

The corners of Uji's mouth turned up slightly before flattening into a thin line. "Nobuhiro, you left home a man in age only. You still possess the idealized view of being a samurai."

He stared at his eldest brother. "What do you mean? A second stands beside the one taking his life. Sword held high. Ready to end the pain of a friend who has made the ultimate choice in life. It is a moment of supreme honor. It is to be revered."

Toshi stepped beside him and placed his hand on Nobuhiro's shoulder. "Nobuhiro, it is a moment of honor only for one person. There is no honor in being a second at a seppuku. Only everlasting embarrassment if you miss."

Nobuhiro studied Toshi's face. He had made a joke in a tense situation, yet he did not seem to be lighthearted. His jaw was tense and muscles tight, more serious than Nobuhiro had ever seen him. Uji, normally a calm presence, appeared to have trouble breathing. Sweat beaded his forehead.

Nobuhiro licked his lips. "There's something else, isn't there? What aren't you telling me?"

Toshi glanced at Uji. Uji nodded. Permission to speak granted.

"It's the reason his mentor had to commit seppuku. Apparently, he made a plea to both Kinoshita and the regent on Father's behalf. It was this plea that brought about the suicide order from the regent."

"What was the plea about?" Nobuhiro asked.

"We don't know," Toshi said.

Nobuhiro exhaled softly, feeling a weight on his body that foretold what Uji had yet to utter. "So he feels responsible. Is he going to—?"

Uji nodded. "Yes. As soon as the investigation is complete, Father plans to take his own life."

Chapter Twenty-Three

Sen, with Omi in tow, approached the restaurant. She paused at the entrance, running her fingers through her hair, and then glanced at Omi, who bounced on her toes while scratching her forearms at the same time.

A week had passed since Sen's discovery of the church. Earlier today, Nishioji had pulled her aside to mention some rooms that needed attention. Then during the conversation, he had informed her that there would be a meeting of Christians at the restaurant this evening. She had thought of little else as she had attended to her duties.

The sun was setting over the mountain. It would be dark soon. Perspiration dripped down her face and back. She hoped the evening would be cooler.

Not likely.

The hot, early-June weather felt as heavy as some of the elaborate kimonos her mistress wore for festivals. She and Omi would have to contend with getting cleaned up as best they could before they returned to the castle.

Barks rose from the back of the restaurant. Moments later, a little white dog appeared, the same one she had seen with the baker. The dog panted and pranced and seemed to smile as it stared at her. It then bounded toward the entrance and pawed at the door. Sen laughed. The little dog seemed to know where it could find food, as any good community dog would. Sen stepped toward the entrance and knocked on the doorframe.

The door slid open and Naomi stood there smiling. "Come in. Come in." She waved them in with quick motions, indicating they should hurry.

Sen and Omi stepped inside. Sen bowed to Naomi. "Nice to see you again."

Naomi bowed back and then grasped Sen's hands. Naomi's warmth and happiness flowed to Sen. "You also." She smiled and tilted her head toward Omi. "I see you have someone with you."

Sen introduced Omi and related her story. Omi's cheeks turned red as Naomi's infectious smile and welcoming manner brought a smile. Good. At times, Omi seemed tense and too serious. Whatever troubled her at the castle, maybe she could find peace here.

Sen stepped toward both of them. "I like your little dog outside. He's as friendly as you are."

Naomi stared into space as if visualizing the outside. "Ah, yes. Boon. Very special dog. Very discerning. He understands people."

Tables had been moved out of the way to create a space in the center. Sets of cushions were stacked on the floor with some laid out in rows in the center of the room. Twelve people had already gathered, including her parents' next-door neighbor and a prominent umbrella maker and his wife. Two other servants from the castle were also in attendance. Did Nishioji tell them as well or did they get messages about this meeting from another source? How many Christians were part of this group?

The baker stood in the corner of the room. Naomi's comment about the discerning dog took on new meaning. She recalled the day she had walked through town and seen the baker playing with the dog. Did the dog recognize Christians? She smiled at that. Discerning indeed, if that was possible.

The baker was talking to a tall man. Sen only saw his back but knew who he was instantly. She glanced at Omi, wanting to point him out, but Omi appeared engrossed in the whole scene. A gathering of people from different strata of society. It was one of the true joys of believing. Christianity brought all types together. All were equal in His sight.

"Nishioji-sama? He's here?" Omi's voice rose to a high pitch after he finally turned around. "He's even more handsome close up. Maybe there's something to this Christian thing after all."

Sen laughed at Omi's newfound interest. "I thought you only liked Toshi. What would he say if he heard you say this?"

"It doesn't hurt to look. Besides, how do I know if Toshi's the right one unless I compare him to others?"

Yoshi, dressed in a green kimono, asked everyone to take a seat. Sen knelt and bowed her head to pray, then sat cross-legged. Omi sat beside her.

Yoshi began the meeting with a song and followed with a prayer. He then opened a metal box and pulled out a raft of papers. Was it a partial Bible? Was it written in Japanese? Did one exist? The missionaries, even those who had arrived in the country as young men, found the language difficult. Was it written in the missionaries' language? Could Yoshi read it? Joy washed over Sen as Yoshi recited three different passages. From there, he locked the pages back in the metal box and began to preach.

A bark from Boon silenced Yoshi. The hair on the back of Sen's neck stood up. Yoshi went to the back of the restaurant, returned a few moments later, and continued.

Sen clasped her hands and continued to pray, enjoying every minute of the service. Her head was still bowed when Boon again began to bark loudly.

Voices from outside soon grew loud. Yoshi again stopped the service, holding his hands out to silence the group. Could the people outside hear the singing and prayers? What was causing the commotion? A few seconds later, whispers of smoke touched Sen's nose.

Fire.

###

Nobuhiro finished sweeping the workshop. He wiped his brow with the sleeve of his kimono, but sweat still poured across his face. He removed the cloth tied around his head. It was soaked.

"That looks fine, Nobuhiro." Master Goami hung various steel tongs on the wall. A column of swords was placed on the wall, blades to the sky. Even unfinished, the swords were placed ready for battle.

Bags drooped under Master Goami's eyes. Did his own face exhibit the same exhaustion? He looked forward to eating a light dinner and resting. The two of them had worked hard the last few days.

"Yes, Master. I will just look over the shop again and make sure I didn't miss anything."

His master nodded at him with a smile and wished him well, exiting by the door that led to the house. Nobuhiro bowed and resumed his duties.

His thoughts turned to Sen. It had been a week since they had visited the restaurant and met the proprietors. He was happy for her and wished her well.

In the last week, though, he had done more than just think about her. His meeting with the couple at the restaurant weighed on his heart. He recalled the old man's words. "May God guide you in your steps," he said. No pressure. Just the good wishes of a well-intentioned man. A man comfortable in his faith. Just like Jiro had been, up until the day he died. Just like Haru, too. Their faith had been an outpouring of their love for each other. Their faith made them happy. Their faith made them able to face life.

When he found Jiro, he was holding on to Haru. Both went to their deity with smiles on their faces.

He envied their peace.

Could this Christian deity be the way for him?

Sen would suggest he try to pray.

He clasped his hands together and went to the door that led outside.

Words failed him from there.

Dusk approached. He glanced at the rock garden. The tiny pebbles had been smoothed even more since the work Sen had done. New furrows had been dug in, creating detailed curved lines. He smiled at this. His master's wife was restoring the garden to life.

He looked in the direction of town, when suddenly his happy thoughts vanished and his body began to quiver. Long tendrils of smoke rose in the distance over what looked to be the market area. He guessed Sen was at the castle, but couldn't escape the feeling that lodged in his gut.

It would take him too long to get there if he walked to town. He ran to one of the neighbors and rapped on the door. A tall, thin, gray-haired man opened the door. He wore a light white shirt, dusty from work. The old man bowed, but his eyes opened wide, as if feeding on Nobuhiro's intensity.

"Nobuhiro, good to see you. What brings you here?"

Nobuhiro swallowed hard and looked down. "I apologize for asking, but I need to borrow your horse. It's urgent."

###

"Fire!" The baker rushed to Yoshi. Both of them ran to the front door. Yoshi tried to slide it open, but the thick door was stuck. Both men rammed their shoulders into it. Still, the door wouldn't budge.

Sen felt the touch of a hand on her shoulder. She wheeled about to see Naomi.

Naomi's eyes were alert and fearful. "Let's try the back. Come with me."

Sen and Omi followed the older woman through the kitchen. The flames engulfed one wall, creating thick, acrid smoke. Sen coughed and lifted her sleeve to cover her mouth. Naomi did the same.

Nishioji and another man were already there, trying to break open the door. It was stuck, too. The two men slammed their shoulders into it.

Oomph.

Oomph.

Crash.

Wood splintered as the jamb gave way. The men fell through the opening into the street. The door hung askew and off its railings. The men lifted it out. Omi stumbled out first. Sen pushed Naomi to the opening, but the old woman coughed hard and didn't move. Sen's face tightened. "You need to go."

The woman's red-rimmed eyes wept from smoke and sadness. "No, I have to get my husband and show him the exit. He might not have gotten out." She turned and headed to the front.

The two people from the castle and the umbrella maker and his wife passed by, along with another. Neither Yoshi nor the baker were there.

"I'm going with you."

Naomi grabbed Sen's arms. "No, child. You go outside. I'll be fine. I can show my husband the way."

Sen shook her head. "You'll never make it back without my help."

The old woman smiled, albeit through more coughs. "You are truly Haru's sister."

"Sen, come on," Omi yelled from behind.

"Stay there. We'll be right back."

Sen followed Naomi to the front of the shop. They found Yoshi and the baker lying on the floor.

Naomi knelt and shook Yoshi. "Husband, wake up."

Sen knelt beside the baker and tried to move him. But he, like Yoshi, was unconscious. She put her arms underneath the baker's shoulders and brought him to a sitting position. She tried to bring him to his feet, but the man was too heavy. She slapped him hard on the back twice. Wet coughs racked his body. His head lolled as though he was still unconscious.

Lord, please help us. Please see us through this.

Sen heard coughing behind her and saw a large figure crawling underneath the smoke. *Nishioji.* He came around her and put his strong arms underneath the baker. "Help Naomi. I'll take care of our friend here."

Sen relinquished her hold. Nishioji's strong arms easily lifted the baker, whom he carried toward the kitchen. Sen turned her attention to Yoshi and Naomi.

Yoshi, roused by his wife, wheezed and coughed up streams of soot. Naomi knelt on one side of him, while Sen moved to the other side. They pulled him to his feet and began to drag him toward the kitchen.

Smoke filled Sen's lungs. She gasped for breath and forced her feet to move forward. The heat and flying ash burned her eyes and brought tears that poured down her cheeks.

Nishioji then appeared at the door and rushed to their aid. He took Naomi's place and tilted his head toward the door. "Go! Both of you. I'll get him the rest of the way."

Sen and Naomi took his advice and moved. They turned the corner. The back door was off its rails, offering air.

Just a few more steps.

The two women clutched each other for support as they hurried outside and inhaled, breathing in great gulps of fresh air. The rest of the church members were already outside. All were fine. Several of them had faces covered with soot. Their clothing was singed. Others worked with townsfolk to put out the fire, throwing buckets of water on the walls. The restaurant was beyond hope. Stopping the blaze from spreading to other buildings became the concern.

The baker lay on the ground, his head propped up with someone's coat, but he was awake. Another member attended to him. The little white dog sat next to the baker, his tail wagging excitedly. The baker didn't move much but gently scratched the dog's head.

Sen knelt next to him, smoothing out his kimono.

"Can I get you anything to help you?"

He looked at her and smiled. "I remember you trying to help me in there. Thank you very much."

She nodded. "You did the same for me. I remember what happened at my parents' house. I owe you a debt."

He paused. "I would do the same again, for the love of Christ and the memory of your family. Your brother-in-law, Jiro, gave his own life to save mine. Now I am in your family's debt again."

Sen bowed and then looked back at the door. Naomi was on her knees, clasping her hands in prayer. She no longer cared who knew her beliefs. Nishioji carried Yoshi in his arms and laid him next to her. He coughed a bit. He was still alive. Naomi bowed low, her forehead kissing the dirt. Nishioji placed his hand on her shoulder and then looked back at Yoshi. He then removed his outer kimono and placed it under Yoshi's head. The umbrella maker's wife came over, bringing something to drink to the couple. Both drank it quickly, their faces marked with gratitude.

Sen looked at the restaurant, now consumed with flames. More townspeople had arrived and worked on putting out the fire. A light wind blew and licked at the flames. All in the crowd quickened their pace, as if concerned that pieces might blow to other buildings. Sen wanted to join them, but her legs burned. She spit up soot, sick from the smoke, and sank to the ground.

Omi sat next to Sen and gave her a friendly grin, the kind shared by two people who had escaped death. "How are you feeling? Are you all right?"

Sen exhaled hard, hoping to purge remnants of the fire from her lungs, and spat soot. "I'm fine. Just tired." Still, an unanswered question gnawed at her like a dog chewing on a bone.

"You don't sound like it. Everyone seems to be fine. You should be happy."

Sen looked at the building but stared beyond it. The sounds of the crowd meshed in her ears, a mixture of dissonance that overrode the insect tweets that normally filled the night air. "I'm just wondering who would do such a thing. These people aren't a threat. Why did this happen?"

Omi mumbled a response, but Sen couldn't make out the words. She rubbed the back of her neck. The tension remained and shot pain through her muscles. "Only one other person knew about this place. I didn't even tell you where it was until we got here."

Omi eyebrows rose high. Who? Nobuhiro? You can't mean that. He wouldn't do this."

Sen waved her hand, hoping to calm Omi. "Yes, I know he wouldn't, but he may have mentioned it to someone. I have to ask him."

Shaking her head, Omi clasped Sen's hands. "There are many people who knew about this. One of them could have let it slip. Maybe someone who wasn't here tonight."

"The people who knew are here. There has to be another reason."

"That dog is a message. Someone else in the community might have noticed, someone unfriendly to Christians."

Sen stared at her hands, pulling at her thumbs. Sorrow replaced her relief at being safe. Had Nobuhiro told someone, despite her concerns and pleadings? It was only through the grace of God that everyone was all right.

Nobuhiro's face appeared in her mind and her stomach tightened. The next time she saw him, she would have to find out. Whatever happened here had nearly cost all these people their lives. She scrunched into a ball, clasping her hands tightly around her legs, then buried her face into her knees, dampening the voices of those around her. The sounds of the night, the ones that she had grown accustomed to those evenings under the stars, reached her ears.

And over those sounds she heard the approaching hoofbeats of what sounded like a lone rider.

Chapter Twenty-Four

Sen looked again at the building. Ash and smoke permeated the air, but the fire was now contained. Sen had survived death again. Why did she deserve to live? She had as much as brought this trouble to them.

Omi walked toward her, her normal gait now timid. “Sen, the officials will be over shortly. They’re going to ask you questions.” She sounded as if she were asking for a favor, and it hurt to phrase the question.

Sen didn’t feel like answering anyway.

She rubbed her face in her hands, seeing the black streaks on her palms and realizing her cheeks were probably streaked with black as well. “What did you tell them?”

“Everything, though it’s not much. I heard that Yoshi and the baker are both fine. They will need to rest a few days. A doctor who lives nearby is here. He is looking everyone over.”

Sen laughed softly. “Great. Everyone is being told to get a bath and drink some strange Chinese herb. That should help a lot. Is anything else happening? Did the magistrate or his men find anything about who did this?”

"They found shards of wood covering the front and back entrances, pieces that didn't belong to the building. Someone jammed the doors from the outside, intending to burn us all."

Sen's hair stood on end. "Are you serious? Wasn't burning the building enough? Why did someone have to do that?"

Omi glanced down, licking her lips while her foot tapped the ground. She didn't meet Sen's gaze. Her silence signified her confusion, or was it more? "What is it? Is there something you're not telling me?"

"Nobuhiro's here."

Sen gritted her teeth, inhaling sharply, as blood coursed through her veins. It masked the pain. She searched the crowd and saw him, talking with her neighbor who had been at the service. "Why didn't you tell me?"

Omi's voice soothed her nerves. "Sen, he had nothing to do with it."

"I still have to ask." She took a deep breath and calmed herself. She needed to be lucid when she saw him. She didn't have long.

Nobuhiro walked over a minute later. "Are you injured?"

She stared into his eyes, puffy and red. Could a man cry? Had he shed tears for her? Had they been tears of worry or relief? Sensitivity marked his personality, a trait her parents probably admired. It made him a good swordsmith. "I'm fine." She glanced away, stiffening her spine. The rage of the night brimmed within her. "Nobuhiro, I need to ask you a question."

His eyes blinked rapidly, while the rest of his face went rigid. "Yes?"

She pressed her palms into her hips. "Did you say anything about this place to anyone?"

He tilted his head with his mouth open wide. "No, I said nothing. This was our secret. I . . . I promised you that. I would never break my word."

"You're the only other person who knew about it. I

didn't tell anyone, not even Omi, until I brought her with me today."

Nobuhiro stared into her eyes and held his palms out. "I . . . I didn't say anything to anyone. I wouldn't do that."

Sen's shoulders relaxed, her arms dropping by her sides. He had saved her life twice. Had he been early, those who did this might have hurt him.

Yet her heart ached for him. She had asked the question and slighted him. Nobuhiro felt wronged. "I know. I'm sorry for not trusting you."

He nodded, though the corners of his mouth drooped. "I understand. How is everyone?"

"Everyone made it out safely. Yoshi and the baker both inhaled too much smoke. They are resting behind the store."

"Let's go see them."

They walked around to where Yoshi and the baker were recuperating. Naomi tended one of them. Another woman oversaw the baker. From the way she doted on him, she was likely his wife. She hadn't been at the meeting. Yet she was here now. How had she known?

She jabbed herself in the hip. That thinking was wrong. Nobuhiro lived farther away and he was here. She was looking for a conspiracy and was creating one instead. There had to be a simple answer. She needed time to think.

Nobuhiro squatted next to the two men. The baker had his eyes closed, but Yoshi was awake. "How are you?"

Yoshi looked at Nobuhiro and struggled to sit up, pushing himself into place.

Naomi placed her hand on her husband's shoulder. "Lie back down. Rest a few for minutes."

His face drained of color as his eyes widened. "I cannot." He faced Nobuhiro. "This is your fault."

"M . . . my fault? What do you mean?"

Yoshi gestured to the building. "This fire. Your father is responsible for it."

Nobuhiro's face blanched and he shook his head. The

look on his gentle face registered disbelief. He closed his eyes and breathed slowly. The muscles in his arms and legs pulsed in rhythm like a heartbeat. "I said nothing to anyone, not even my father."

Yoshi shook his head and pointed to the building. "The proof is in front of us."

Nobuhiro studied the building. His body vibrated like the cloth head of a drum. He said nothing to anyone. It was not his fault. He turned to face Yoshi. "I . . . I understand why you say it. But I promise I didn't do anything to cause this."

"Then why are you here?"

He stared Yoshi in the eye. "I came here because I saw smoke. I was concerned. I had a feeling something might be wrong."

"That is your conscience. You should listen to it."

Naomi patted Yoshi's hand. "Husband, calm down. He speaks the truth and I believe him. You had a rough time in there. You're not thinking with reason."

Nobuhiro coughed and wiped his mouth. He thanked Naomi with a bow and then turned to Sen. "I need to tell your parents. What should I say?"

Yoshi groaned and rolled over on all fours, grinding his feet into the ground as he rose slowly. He declined Naomi's assistance at first but then took it when he couldn't stand straight. "You can tell them their apprentice almost made them childless."

Sen looked at Nobuhiro, who returned her gaze. His moist eyes appeared to hold back tears. The pain of loss registered in his face. The fire had opened feelings within him as it had in her. She missed Haru. He missed Jiro.

Nobuhiro faced Yoshi. "I am sorry."

"Sorry for what you did?"

He shook his head. "No. I am sorry you feel this way. I hope, one day, to convince you otherwise."

Nobuhiro walked away without another glance. Sen crossed her arms, squeezing them with opposite hands. She tried not to cry but failed. Nobuhiro was a good man.

He was the man of her dreams.

For Nobuhiro, though, Christians were only trouble.

###

Nobuhiro grabbed the reins of his white-and-black spotted horse and rubbed the animal's nose. The horse rested its head on Nobuhiro's shoulder as if in support of Nobuhiro's sad heart. When he returned home, he would tell Master Goami that he had seen Sen and that she was fine. He exhaled, his lungs deflating to match his feelings. The taste of smoke soured his lips, just like the conversation with Yoshi.

"Nobuhiro, wait," a low voice called out.

He turned and saw Toshi. Nobuhiro was so lost in thought that he hadn't recognized the sound of Toshi's voice when he called his name. How long had he been there? How could he not have known? He stared at him, unsure of what to say. "Brother." It was all he could muster.

"I saw what happened back there. We were fortunate any real tragedy was averted, but how can the restaurant owner believe you had something to do with this?"

Nobuhiro rubbed his hand across his face. "He knows Father's position and the sword hunt. He does not trust him because of the edict."

"Regrettably, that makes sense. How does Sen feel? Does she agree with him?"

"She doesn't. I promised I would keep the church a secret and Sen believes me. However, if the restaurant owner thinks otherwise, then others may believe him."

His brother eyed him. "Of course you wouldn't break such a promise, though I do wish you'd told Uji and me."

"I couldn't."

"I understand. At the same time, do not let love blind you to issues of safety. We could have protected them and done it quietly. You took much on yourself. Do not forget that family shares burdens."

Dissonant voices merged in the night. The people were coming together to help those less fortunate. In the middle was Sen, now tending to others who had been hurt. Someone tried to kill her tonight. Again. Yet she maintained her strength. A strength propelled by faith. She was strong. She deserved someone who could care for her. "It is my duty to protect her. Yet I failed."

"She is safe. You may rest. If you didn't say anything about the church, then tonight's activities are a coincidence. Whoever did this must have learned another way. You cannot worry about what has happened, only how to change the future. Do you agree?"

"I think so." His body relaxed as Toshi's firm voice provided support. "However, someone betrayed these people and now they may think I'm to blame."

Toshi looked him in the eye. "I know of the restaurant owner. He is a respected local leader and his voice carries weight with other merchants."

"That could cause problems for my master's business . . . and for mine when I begin in a year."

"Do you have any ideas then?"

He paused and closed his eyes. "None. There is no reason for this attack." He scanned the area. "Where's Uji?"

"He and Matsubara are investigating something to do with Michiba. Matsubara followed Michiba earlier this evening but lost him."

"Do you think Michiba is responsible?"

"Likely, but there is still no proof. Besides, he couldn't have been the archer. He is the best we have."

"So we still don't know?"

Toshi shook his head and said nothing.

Nobuhiro pressed his fist against his chest. Pain and relief remained. His body tensed, working up from his calves. "It is lucky that everyone got out safely."

Toshi's gaze swung back to the scene. "Yes, though I understand much of the thanks goes to Nishioji. He saved several people's lives. Sen was also brave, I hear."

Nobuhiro nodded. Sen's heroics underscored what he knew to be true about her. "Does Nishioji's presence have anything to do with the reason he's a suspect in your investigation?"

"Yes. In keeping many of his activities hidden, he caused us to think he might be involved. It appears he converted to Christianity last year during the campaign in Kyushu. He spent some time in Nagasaki and saw drawings of a printing press the foreign missionaries hope to bring here. He understands well how machines work. Nishioji says he can use what he learned from those drawings to improve the printing techniques that Buddhist priests use to print prayers. He hopes to use this new method to spread this faith."

Toshi's words cut Nobuhiro like the edge of a blade. Didn't Toshi understand that Nishioji, his childhood tormentor, was now a hero? Nobuhiro was now a villain. He hadn't been needed here and showing up had made things worse for him.

Nobuhiro's horse whinnied slightly, as if vying for his attention. "Then he's no longer a suspect?"

"No, he is not," a stern voice uttered from behind them.

An odd calm rinsed his nerves. His father? He should have expected his arrival. He should have prepared.

Nobuhiro pressed his hands along the sleeves of his kimono. Oddly, the stiffness remained steady instead of increasing with his father's approach. Did he no longer dread being with him? Did he even welcome his presence? Then what caused Nobuhiro's apprehension?

Nishioji.

Nishioji's fate raised Nobuhiro's tension. Would he be stripped of his samurai status? Would he have to start a new life? "What will happen to Nishioji, now that everyone knows of his beliefs?"

Father's face remained unchanged. "He will retain his samurai status. People think him a hero. We would not cast such a man out of our ranks, but he could be demoted."

Nobuhiro tilted his head and glanced askance at

Toshi. "Demoted?"

Toshi nodded. "His annual allotment of rice would be reduced. However, it should still be sufficient to support his parents."

Parents? Nobuhiro scratched his chin. He had never thought of Nishioji having a family. The demotion would be a loss of face. "Would a samurai accept demotion?"

His father shook his head. "It depends on the reason. However, Nishioji's father has been ill for a long time and requires his mother's constant care. He is devoted to them and his parents depend on him for support. He is also a Christian. If he is true to his beliefs, as I understand them, he will report to his post tomorrow morning."

"If he is not?"

Father went silent for two seconds, looking through Nobuhiro instead of at him. "Then, unfortunately, we may need to prepare for his funeral."

Nobuhiro swallowed hard and nodded. The life of a samurai was difficult. Despite his history with Nishioji, Nobuhiro wouldn't wish this situation on anyone. Nishioji's faith, like Sen's, was powerful. Whatever his faith, Nishioji had found a way to provide for his family, like any dutiful son.

Like Sen was trying to do.

Would this God find a way to let Sen care for her parents and remain true to her faith, when duty seemed at odds with faith?

Nobuhiro found himself wishing Nishioji well.

"Nobuhiro," Toshi said, his voice quiet. "I will visit you in a couple of days. Please return to the Goamis and let them know about their daughter. Maybe by then, the restaurant owner will have reconsidered his hasty words."

Nobuhiro agreed. He stroked the neck of his horse. "Let's go home." Nobuhiro put his right foot in the stirrup and stepped up, swinging his left leg over, thankful that his defect still allowed him to mount a horse properly. He had once heard that these foreign visitors mounted horses from the left side. It didn't make sense. Little did.

He picked up the reins and rubbed the cord in his hands. It had been a rough day. He had gone to town because he had feared for Sen's life. Now, some people believed he might be responsible for the fire. Could it get any worse?

He prodded the horse into moving but didn't push the pace. The up-and-down *clop, clop* of its motion mixed the acid in his stomach. He hadn't talked to anyone. He was sure Sen hadn't either. But then how did whoever set fire to the restaurant know about the service?

Could he convince everyone that he hadn't betrayed them? If not, then what would be his station at the house? Master Goami and his wife had known him for years. They would believe him. Others in the city might not. He would have to leave to save their business.

If that happened, he would have nowhere to go. He couldn't return to the castle. If he ran from his situation again, people would believe him guilty.

If that transpired, he would have only one option for restoring his honor. He would need to make the ultimate sacrifice.

And not even Sen's God could save him.

Chapter Twenty-Five

Sen glanced at the sky as clouds covered the late-afternoon sun, providing a brief respite from the sun's intense glare. It was a good time to go inside. The bathhouse was normally full, since it was attached to a well-known inn. It was also popular with locals.

She and Omi crossed the threshold and entered the building. Two bathing areas were at the end of the hall, one for men and one for women. As the rooms had different ambiences, they were rotated twice a day to allow guests to enjoy both rooms. Large signs denoted the gender of each spa, to avoid any potential embarrassment to guests.

She slid the door open to the women's entrance. Steam billowed from the room, bringing sweat to her brow. She wiped her face as her shoulders relaxed. "Ah. This is what the doctor should have recommended two days ago after that fire. We've endured much."

Omi shook her head. "You still need to go slowly. The doctor was worried the smoke might have affected you more than you think."

Sen put down the bag that carried fresh clothing for

after the bath and surveyed the bathing area. Three customers sat nearby in the area reserved for washing and rinsing off. Each of the women wore light, sheer underskirts that extended to their ankles. Attendants scrubbed the backs of two of the customers. The third woman held a wooden bucket, pouring water to rinse her own legs.

"I'm fine, just tired. Tired of being injured. Tired of dealing with surprise visitors in my life." She laughed at her own words, but her insides tightened like a court lady's hairstyle. The latest attack had left her frustrated at all that had occurred. If Nobuhiro hadn't told anyone, then did that mean she was the source? Had she made a mistake? Had someone followed her? She felt responsible for the fire but didn't know why.

She stripped to her underskirt and placed her clothes and bags in one of the straw baskets next to one wall of the room. Omi did likewise and headed to one of the small wooden rooms in the bathing area. Sen followed, ducking below the top of the frame and stepping into the room. No one else was there. Steam rose from underneath the wooden floor.

Sen felt the sweat trickle down her face instantly. She sat on the bench inside and closed her eyes. Omi sat next to her and sighed. Fifteen minutes should be enough time to loosen the dirt.

Sen rubbed both her hands through her hair. The steam allowed her to sort through her feelings. About the fire. About Nobuhiro. He was a gentle, noble soul. No matter what the restaurant owner said.

"What's wrong, Sen?" Omi asked. "Your face looks like the time you had to help clean up tatami mats after Lord Kinoshita's wife was sick the night before."

Sen pursed her lips. "I was thinking about Nobuhiro."

"Aren't you always? Though that face doesn't exactly exhibit fondness . . . "

Omi's light teasing eased Sen's tension. She smiled back at her. "I was thinking about what the minister said earlier. Nobuhiro had nothing to do with the fire. He would never have mentioned it to anyone."

Omi's eyes flew open. "You haven't heard the news? I guess it's being kept quiet. It was Michiba. He was responsible for the fire. Ujihiro caught him. He confessed yesterday."

Sen sat up, lifting her back away from the wooden wall. Sweat now flowed down her arms and legs. "He confessed. If it's a secret, how did you learn of it?"

Omi looked down but said nothing.

Sen smiled. "Oh. Toshi told you, didn't he?"

Omi's cheeks reddened and she looked away. "Y-e-e-e-s."

Sen tilted her head. "That will make Nobuhiro happy. It will erase the comments about him and his father."

"Why would you or anyone believe Nobuhiro's father was involved anyway?"

Sen's throat tightened and she rubbed at her scars. "I Didn't. Still, he twice warned me about my former associations and, by that, he meant Christians."

Omi shook her head. "It sounds more like a warning to me. It's just concern or fear. He's really a harmless old man. He tries to frighten people to maintain order at the castle." Omi wiped her forehead. "His harder job was raising three sons alone. I've talked with Toshi about it. His father took his mother's death hard."

She stared at Omi as pity again crept into her opinion of Nobuhiro's father. Just like the day he had escorted her to the kidnapping site. He stayed close to her for her protection, not her confinement. "What happened?"

Omi closed her eyes for a second, as if thinking. "The family used to live in a house about one *ri* from the castle. After his wife passed away, Tokoda basically moved himself and the boys to the castle."

"What did they do with the house?"

"They maintained it. Servants took care of it and the rice fields. When Uji married, he moved back into the house. Uji's wife now manages everything." Omi displayed a devious grin. "Toshi has a room there where he rests sometimes, though Ujihiro's wife thinks Toshi is there to annoy her."

Sen clasped her hands on her lap. The slip she wore was now soaked. "And Tokoda still lives at the castle. The whole thing must have been difficult."

"He cares for all his sons, I think. He has probably always known where Nobuhiro was. He may have even looked in on him, though he would have kept his distance out of respect for Nobuhiro's decision."

Sen nodded but didn't respond. More sweat poured down her body. How long had it been since they entered the room? Fifteen minutes? Twenty minutes? She had had enough and jerked her head to the entrance. Omi nodded and the two women stood.

Sen placed her hand on the wooden door, ready to push it out. "Still, how did Michiba find out about the meeting?"

Omi's lips curled in and she looked down before facing Sen. "I've been thinking about that. It could have been us."

The words struck Sen like a punch to the gut. Had Omi had the same thoughts she had? "What do you mean?"

"Well, when you talk about your faith, you always look around to make sure no one is close enough to hear. Maybe this time Michiba was close by and you didn't see him."

Sen's knees quivered and she pulled at her thumb. Lord Akamatsu had warned her about keeping her faith secret. Nobuhiro's father had warned her as well. Now Omi suggested she hadn't been careful enough. Her own experience in Haibara had not been enough. She had managed to endanger people here. How could she be so concerned with herself? Had she thought of her parents' welfare? She had survived Haibara. Her guilt had led her to put others at risk. She had failed. She had failed everyone.

Omi grabbed Sen's hand and squeezed it. "Don't worry about it anymore. Michiba has been caught. It's over."

They left the sauna. The three customers who had been there previously were gone. However, five more women had come. It would get even busier later. The best time was when it was still warm but after the temperature had cooled in the evening. A third attendant had joined the two who had been there before.

Sen and Omi walked to the washing area and sat down. Two attendants approached. One appeared to be in her sixties, with gray hair and lines etched in her face. The other looked about ten years younger, with salt-and-pepper hair and a smooth round face. Both women wore similar white *yukatas* with yellow trim. Each carried a small bamboo scraper.

The older woman pointed to buckets of soapberry and volcanic ash with small bowls next to them. "Please turn around."

An attendant lathered Sen's back, applying pressure to massage the muscles, and then scraped the soap and dirt away. The massage and scraper relieved stiffness. Sen ran her fingers down her thighs and slowly exhaled. Omi was right. She no longer needed to worry.

After her back was done, Sen held out her hand and was given the scraper. She nodded. "Thank you."

The older of the two attendants then reached into her pocket and took out an egg. She grabbed a small bowl nearby, cracked the egg, and separated it, putting the egg whites in the bowl. She scooped in some ash and mixed the two, handing the bowl to Sen, who poured the mixture on her hair and rubbed it in. The attendant filled a small wooden bucket with water and rinsed Sen's hair.

Sen held out her hand, palm outward. "I'll finish it." Omi did likewise and they were left alone, as alone as one could be with three attendants and now seven customers as two more women entered. She wanted to continue her earlier conversation with Omi, but the place had echoes.

Sen rubbed soapberry on her arms and legs, scraped it off with bamboo, and then rinsed her legs. The water cooled her down. She poured more on the back of her neck, sending waves of relief through her body. It was time to go. The sooner they left, the sooner she and Omi could talk more. Omi's first meeting with Christians hadn't gone well. Would she hesitate to think about it again?

Sen dried herself and walked to the basket area where she had stored her clothes. She donned fresh linen and stopped as a whiff of incense from Omi's bag reached her. "What's that fragrance?"

Omi glanced between Sen and her own bag as if she didn't understand for a minute, for her eyebrows flashed. "Oh, it's *kyara*."

"So that's what *kyara* smells like. It's nice but heavy. Where did you get it?"

Omi's eyes lit up. "About a month before you arrived, the mistress invited a few of us to play the incense game with her. I won. *Kyara* was the prize. I sometimes fragrance some of my clothes with it. Not often."

Sen giggled. "You're lucky. It's rare, isn't it?"

"Yes. You've never smelled it before?"

She shook her head. "Lord Akamatsu's wife received some once as a gift, but I don't know if she ever used it."

They finished dressing and then left the bathhouse. The day was nearly over. Soon, lanterns would be lit to mark the street. Sen always enjoyed people watching. Today, though, she spent more time looking at the ground than at the shops.

"What's wrong now?" Omi asked.

"Just wondering how Lord Akamatsu and his wife are."

Omi smiled. "They're fine. I'm certain of it."

"How do you know? Have you heard something?"

"No, but that's why I am sure. Lord Akamatsu is a prominent samurai. If something had happened to him, we would've heard by now."

Sen nodded. Omi's words made sense. Always that bright spark of reason that made her so popular, even more so than the looks that garnered many stares.

Omi held her hand out and pointed to some street vendors. "Ahhh, that's what I'm looking for. Let's get something. Michiba's caught. We need to celebrate. We also need to talk a little more about Nobuhiro."

"Why Nobuhiro?"

"Because it's over and because he took care of you. I don't understand this religion of yours yet, but I wonder if your God didn't put him in your life for that purpose. You owe him your gratitude."

A smile creased Sen's lips as the aroma of frying octopus reached her. Much had changed since her arrival in Himeji. She had lost a lot before coming, but she had gained more. Like Lord Akamatsu, she needed to look forward.

Nobuhiro had been there for her. He would die for her. She would die for him. Marrying Nobuhiro might be the only way her parents would forgive her for choosing God over them.

She would find no better man.

###

"Michiba confessed."

Nobuhiro's mouth gaped at Toshi, whose words still resounded in his head. *Confessed?* His brother had told him after the fire he would see him in two days and he had kept his word. Still, Nobuhiro hadn't expected this news.

He removed his headscarf and wiped his brow. The scarf, saturated with sweat from the long day, helped little. He wiped his sleeve across his forehead and then rubbed his eyes. "He was responsible for the fire?"

Toshi nodded and took a sip of tea, wiping the ends of his lips with his thumbs. "The fire, the kidnapping, even the arrow shooting at the castle. All him."

"How did you find him? Did someone see him outside the restaurant?"

"One of the magistrate's men found a ripped piece of

a dark blue *yukata* near the scene. Also, while interviewing potential witnesses, Uji and Matsubara got a description of a stranger and it matched Michiba. They found and questioned him, found the *yukata*, and matched the torn piece to it. After that, Michiba told us everything."

"Did the magistrate take umbrage with Uji's and Matsubara's involvement?"

"Doubtful. Uji is well known locally and respected for more than just his rank. Likely, the magistrate was happy to cede everything rather than question a samurai."

Nobuhiro chewed on his lower lip. Toshi's compliment of Uji without even light sarcasm hung over his words. "What about the first fire? Did he say anything about that?"

"He blamed Funaki for the fire that killed Sen's sister."

Nobuhiro rose from the bench and walked to the window. He stared out into the growing darkness and massaged his neck, but the knot that appeared there refused to leave. The gentle voice of crickets and cicadas chirped for the full arrival of night, their voices carried on the wisps of wind. He should feel peace. Sen would be safe for now, at least from the attacks. Images of a little white dog barking excitedly and wagging his tail tried to bring a smile to his face. They failed.

He should feel relief. His name would be cleared among the people. There would be no effect on Master Goami's business and nothing to stop Nobuhiro when he opened his own shop a year from now. Yet neither peace nor relief found a willing home within him. Something gnawed at him, the same way the last vestiges of night clawed at the dawn.

He turned to Toshi. "Does that mean the investigation's over?"

Toshi walked over and joined him at the window, staring out instead of looking at him. "Yes, it's over."

Nobuhiro's shoulders tightened. He tried to loosen the tension, but his palms were sweaty. He coughed once and cleared his throat. Nothing dulled the edge in his body. The realization of what was to come explained Toshi's unusually dour mood. "And Father?"

Toshi put both his hands on Nobuhiro's shoulders, rapping the right one twice and then squeezing. "Father's seppuku is two nights from today. He has requested your presence."

###

Sen again checked the placement of the cups and whisk on the tray. Her hand shook as she edged a cup to the left, then moved it back to its former place. How many times had she done that? Six times? Seven? She needed to leave the cups where they were. A tray of sweets lay next to the cups. She reached out to move the sweets, only to draw back her hand and rub her chest.

Omi had reviewed details of tea ceremony with Sen, much of which Sen had forgotten since childhood. Her father had maintained the teahouse behind the family house for customers, a must for entertaining samurai. She had watched him and her mother and mimicked their actions. That was years ago.

Sen pulled at her thumbs, but Omi's words circled in her mind. Nobuhiro's family was samurai. They were well acquainted with tea ceremony. However, to learn that Nobuhiro's father had studied under the nation's master drew out her breath. Everything had to be perfect.

A flower arrangement rested on a pedestal in the room. She had tended it as well as she had tended the outside. She scratched her head as she surveyed the room. Everything was in place.

A rap on the frame drew her attention. It was time.

She went to the door and dropped to her knees, opening it two-thirds of the way and bowing, then opening it completely.

"Welcome, Nobuhiro. Thank you for coming."

Nobuhiro climbed the steps and entered, depending on his right leg as he did so. He had likely made the steps to assist her father. "It is my pleasure."

He wore a simple blue kimono, one without stains from his work. He probably saved it for guests. She wore a light green kimono decorated with flowers. It had belonged to Haru. Her mother had thought it appropriate. Would he like the way she looked?

He gestured outside. "You did wonderful work on the garden. Your parents must be appreciative."

"I'm humbled by your approval, but I only did my duty. I was inspired when I noticed the plants in front of the house sprouting new life. Life brings more life. I felt I should support it. Please sit."

Nobuhiro glanced away and then smiled back at her. Family obligation mattered. She had proved her loyalty to him. It had taken too long.

"Your mother is getting out again, more than just shopping. Your presence has been soothing for her and your father."

Sen tilted her head. "That is good to hear. Is that the only thing?"

Nobuhiro's cheeks reddened. "I . . . I . . . I admit I have enjoyed seeing you as well."

Sitting on her knees, Sen handed a mochi to Nobuhiro, who nodded and accepted it. She then reached for the ladle, pouring a scoop of hot water into the *chawan,* the serving bowl. She grasped the whisk and stirred slowly, checking its tines as she did. Her right hand trembled, and so did her breath. She placed the whisk aside, then picked up the chawan, tilting and rotating it so that the warm water could warm the bowl. Drops of water jumped from the bowl and landed on the mat.

Nobuhiro reached out his hand and placed it under hers, grasping her hand and wrist. His gentle, steady touch calmed her. "There is no reason to be nervous."

She stared into his brown eyes, eyes that had never wavered in their love. Her heart pounded against her ribs. "Omi told me that your father trained you in tea ceremony and that your father was trained by Sen no Rikyu."

Nobuhiro smiled and rubbed her arm, sending heat

through her frame. "Yes, I met the tea master twice when I was a child. He has a teacher's manner. He is a great man, but even he would be impressed by your care. He preached simplicity. You are adhering to that."

Her cheeks warmed at his comment and she discarded the water into a separate bowl. Time to make the tea.

She placed one and a half scoops of bitter green tea into the chawan. Then, she ladled more hot water into the bowl and mixed it with the whisk, creating a green froth. It matched the churning in her stomach. She loved Nobuhiro. If he would have her as his wife, she would agree.

She handed the serving bowl to Nobuhiro, who took it in his right hand. Her fingers stiffened as he turned it three times so that the flower on the bowl faced her and then drank it, finishing with a slurp.

Sen smiled and sat back on her feet as the weight in her stomach dissipated. He liked it.

He turned the bowl, then handed it back to her, brushing her fingers as he did so. Again, her heart pounded in her chest. Waves of heat shot through her arm and went to her face. Would his touch always feel the same?

"I was flattered by your invitation, but why did you go to this much trouble?"

"Because of the fire. You have done everything for me and my family. Yet I doubted you. My faith was weak when it should have been strong."

He shook his head. "I don't understand."

"You were right, Nobuhiro. You were right. I've let Lord Akamatsu's commands blind me to my duty to my family. I understand that I'm supposed to be here. I took irresponsible chances. I placed my parents and you in danger."

"From what I see, you've learned your duty. You've begun to look after your parents."

Sen rubbed her neck as her body shook and then steadied. "But I didn't at first. Back in Haibara, so many died, but I was spared. Those people had families, too.

They did not get to return home. To their parents. To their children. None ever saw them alive again. Why did I deserve better?"

He rubbed his chin. "Is that why you took the chances you did? You acted as if you wanted to die yourself."

Sen glanced down and said nothing as her chest tightened. Her eyes held back tears as she shook her head. Her dry throat choked her words.

"At least you will get to share it with them," Nobuhiro continued. "My father's seppuku is tomorrow night. There is so much more I could have learned from him, time I could have spent with him. You still have time. More than I."

Sen moved closer. Nobuhiro would soon know grief. If only she could be there to support him. "I want to come home."

His eyes opened wide. "That would be wonderful. You should do it."

"I cannot. Not yet. Your brothers are protecting me. What if there are others besides Michiba?"

Nobuhiro squeezed her hand. "I can protect you. My brothers know this. My father knows this. Else, you would not be here. You can leave your position. You can come home."

Sen smiled. "It will take some time. I will work with Omi on the matter. She has a new position at the castle, but she can talk with your brothers."

"Please give them some time. My brothers will not be ready to discuss this so close to Father's ceremony. After a couple of weeks have passed and all family duties have been addressed, then that will be the time."

She inched her face closer to his. "Nobuhiro, I'm ready to become the dutiful daughter I should be. If my parents approve, I know a way to extend the family, if someone will have me."

Nobuhiro smiled and leaned forward, planting a kiss on her lips. It was sweeter than before. A kiss to carry forward.

Chapter Twenty-Six

Nobuhiro entered the barn close to Uji's house and tied up his spotted horse. He was thankful his neighbor had let him borrow it again. He didn't look forward to walking back after his father's ceremony. Master Goami and his wife would be asleep before he got home. He didn't wish to wake them. Three other horses, two brown and one white, were already there, including Toshi's. However, Uji's horse was noticeably absent. Nobuhiro stepped back outside. The moon had waned to less than half but still lit up the ground on the clear night.

A light breeze blew across his face as he walked along the path that led to the front door. The stoop spread across the narrow front of the house. Shrubbery flanked both sides. It was well manicured. Uji's wife kept the place looking neat. Nobuhiro would have enjoyed seeing her again but knew she wouldn't be here this evening.

His stomach growled, but he ignored it. He had tried to eat dinner earlier but found he had no appetite. His dream had been to reconcile with his father on his own terms.

How regrettable that true reconciliation would not

occur until the day of his father's death.

He rapped on the doorframe. It slid open to reveal Toshi. His usual smile gone. "Where's Uji?"

Toshi glanced over him and down the road. "I don't know. He was to follow me within a few minutes after I left the castle. He should've been here over thirty minutes ago."

Nobuhiro licked his lips. "Where's Father?"

Toshi exhaled slowly. "He is meditating alone. He asked that we enter after all of us had arrived."

Nobuhiro nodded but said nothing, rubbing his waist to stem his unease. Rapid hoofbeats thumped along the dirt road from the left side. He and Toshi turned to see Uji approach.

Uji brought his horse to a stop and dismounted, tying it to a post on the stoop. He ran to the door. "Where's Father?"

"Inside," Toshi said. "When I left him, he was kneeling in front of Mother's shrine. He's been there since I arrived. What kept you?"

Uji glanced back at his horse and then jerked his head toward the entrance. "We need to talk. All of us."

###

Sen lay on her back on the futon, worn out from the day's activities. Omi had been promoted to supervision over the mistress's kimonos, a lofty position, and had brought Sen with her. Sen welcomed the change. Still, Omi began her work day before dawn and expected the same from those working under her. Sen needed sleep. Omi would have her up even earlier tomorrow.

Something had happened in the castle that evening. Yet she still didn't know what it was. Servants had gone about their duties with their eyes more downcast than usual. The samurai walked together, speaking in hushed tones as if they feared being overheard. What was happening? She asked some of the attendants, but none of them knew. It wasn't her place to ask the samurai. Even if it were Nobuhiro's brothers or Nishioji, she couldn't overstep that boundary.

Instead, she tried to ignore it. When it was appropriate for her to know, she would know. She closed her eyes and tried to get some sleep. Her nerves, however, remained on edge. She gently massaged her temples. Nothing. She clasped her hands and pressed against her stomach. Nothing. Something nagged at her. Something seemed wrong. Something raised her suspicion.

Omi had yet to arrive. Sen had laid out her futon for her. Maybe they could talk when she arrived. Maybe sleep might help. What question was still unanswered?

###

Nobuhiro and his brothers entered the back room at Uji's house, the room that housed their mother's shrine. The back doors of the room were open, showing a yard lit by torches. Their mother had enjoyed sitting out back on warm evenings. The location for this gathering was appropriate.

Father knelt in front of the shrine, his right side to his sons. He wore a white kimono, the folds of which reached the floor and covered his legs. Over the kimono, he wore an off-white *kataginu*. The garment's stiff shoulders made him appear regal.

A long, thin stick of incense burned on the altar. Nearby lay a short sword on a small, flat wooden platform. Their father's best sword, a katana with a dragon's head on the scabbard, lay on a pillow. A bucket of water and a wooden cup on a long stick sat outside the rear door. Everything was ready.

"Michiba's dead," Uji said.

Their father cocked his head slightly. Yet his eyes remained on the ornate, dark brown wooden memorial. "I'm not surprised. Wasn't he searched when he was arrested?"

Uji moved to his father's side and bowed low. "He was. Somehow, he got a small sword. We do not know how it happened."

"It's not important. Lord Kinoshita could have

ordered one tossed in to rid the castle of the problem. He admitted his guilt. No reason to delay justice."

Uji cleared his throat. "Agreed, but he slit his own throat."

Their father stood up. His kimono shifted, revealing a black *hakama* that stretched from his waist to his ankles. He stared at all three of them, his eyes wide open. "That doesn't make sense. Two dead retainers. Both cut their throats instead of slashing their stomachs."

Uji nodded. "I agree. There is no logic to these actions."

"How about the lack of a second?" Nobuhiro asked. "After all, the traditional way is painful."

Toshi shook his head. "Impossible. It's not the samurai way. There must be another reason."

"It's not the first strange thing," Uji said.

Their father stared at Uji. "What do you mean?"

Uji turned to Nobuhiro. "Nobu, do you remember what you told me after the arrow attack?"

He thought for a second. "I said I was lucky because the shot was high."

"High?" Father asked. "Michiba was the best shot. That would suggest he missed on purpose. Why?"

###

Kaiken paced the castle grounds, hoping for solitude in the darkness. Solitude offered little in the way of solace.

Once they were seven and they created terror.

Now Kaiken was the only one.

Just Kaiken.

Captured, Michiba had confessed. Now he was dead by his own hand.

Michiba, the most loyal of all, had saved Kaiken from that traitor Kitayama. Michiba had noticed Kitayama's hesitations, his conversations with Tokoda, his second thoughts and brought them to Kaiken.

Then, Michiba, following Kaiken's orders, had addressed the traitor.

Poison was no way for a samurai to die, but Kitayama

had no longer deserved a samurai's death.

Now Michiba was dead, too. The Carpenter had disappeared and was useless. Solitude was the only result.

The revelation of Nishioji's faith at the fire would bring comments. Maybe there were others who would voice their displeasure at these Christians. There was time, time to pull back and recruit.

Images of Michiba's lifeless body flashed through Kaiken's mind, the blood pooling from his neck and congealing.

Boar snouts! The neck! Michiba? You betrayed me, too?

A silent rage exploded within Kaiken's chest. Michiba used his death to send a message. Like Funaki. Would the Tokodas understand?

Did it matter?

Did anything?

Kyara. Curse me for a fool as well.

Even if the Tokodas remained unaware, the swordsmith's daughter would soon figure it out. She must.

Kaiken must leave. Tonight. The brothers were away, attending their idiot father's seppuku. It was fortuitous timing.

Kaiken's life was over.

No chance to say goodbye to Toshi.

No chance for one last shared moment of love.

No chance for one last night as a woman.

She would flee tonight to Kyoto to see her master. There was no other option. She might be required to pay the ultimate sacrifice. It was no matter. Death in the service of one's lord was the highest hope for any samurai, even if it came at the lord's command.

Yet before Kaiken's death, one more Christian would die tonight.

###

Their father's question rolled around in Nobuhiro's head. He was right. There was something missing. Some detail they had overlooked. Sen and Omi were attacked by the archer. Sen and Omi were attacked by Michiba in town. Sen and Omi were attacked at the church. His chest tightened. “Father, maybe it’s a message.”

Silence fell, the void filled only with the buzzing of nearby flies and the chirping of nighttime insects attracted to the light outside. Light sweat trickled down Nobuhiro’s face. His undershirt was damp already, owing to the hot night.

His father nodded, his eyes showing interest. “Continue.”

“It’s something I remember Sen mentioning earlier about the attack in town.”

“You’re just telling us now?” His father stepped closer, unblinking. His breath singed Nobuhiro’s face. It made the night heat seem cool by comparison.

He drew himself up to his full height and inched closer to his father. “I am responsible for my own actions. You questioned her first. I assumed she had told you.”

His father eyed him. “Continue.”

“Before she fell unconscious, she said she thought she smelled honey and plum on the attacker.”

“On Michiba?” his father asked. “Only a woman would wear such fragrances.”

“Not always,” Uji said. “However, it wouldn’t be on purpose. For a man to have that scent indicates recent company with a woman.”

“You can be plainer than that,” retorted his father. “It could just mean Michiba visited a prostitute before the attack. Nobuhiro, are you suggesting something more?”

He nodded. “Perhaps it means there is another member of this conspiracy, other than Funaki and Michiba. Both used a woman’s method of suicide. Maybe a woman is involved. Behind the scenes.”

Father pursed his lips. “Possibly. Toshi, you’ve been silent for a while. What is your opinion?”

Toshi stared into space, not looking at any of them. His face radiated death. “My opinion is that I’ve been a fool.”

###

Sen lay her head on her pillow and closed her eyes. Thoughts of the attack in the marketplace swam through her mind.

"Probably a good idea, let's get—Aiiih!" Omi crumpled to the ground.

A flash of movement in the dark startled Sen. She turned. A masked man stood in front of her. He raised his arm as if to strike. She lifted her hands to block the blow. He grabbed her wrists and held them over her head in one vise-like hand.

"Let me go. What do you want?"

"You," the man replied as he struck her on the right temple.

Pain rushed to her forehead. Her knees buckled. She fell forward. Her world turned dark. Fabric ripped. She crashed to the ground. The impact shot pain through her knees. She smelled honey, plum, and . . . kyara.

Sen sat up from her futon. Heat surged through her body, erasing her grogginess. She looked at Omi's usual spot, but the bedroll was empty. Where had she gone? No time to think about that now. She had to find Nobuhiro's father or brothers, offer her lowest bow, and tell them everything.

She rose, stepping softly as she exited the room. She looked both ways at the door but saw no one coming. Turning right, she walked quickly, the floor squeaking with every step. The men, if they were back yet, would be in another building. She would have to cross the grounds. Hopefully, she wouldn't run into Omi before then. She knew too much. Omi would recognize that.

Sen turned a corner in the hall. The building's exit was in sight. Her steps quickened. Her pulse raced.

A sliding door made her look back. A hand grabbed her throat and pulled her back. She gagged. No scream.

The door closed behind her. The hand on her throat relaxed but didn't release.

An arm slid across her chest and held her arms

against her sides. She couldn't move. She couldn't breathe.

Cold metal found her neck and dug just under the skin right at one of her scars. A warning.

Omi whispered in her ear. "No talking. No screams. Or your parents and your precious Nobuhiro will die."

Chapter Twenty-Seven

Nobuhiro stared at Toshi, whose face grew red. Omi's treachery. He wanted to support his brother.

He wanted to find Sen. She was still in danger.

"Uji." Toshi's voice carried an edge. "Your *hachimaki*. It is needed."

Uji reached underneath his kimono and withdrew a thin, white piece of cloth. He offered it to Toshi, who shook his head and then angled it toward Nobuhiro. Uji turned toward his youngest brother, walked over, and held the *hachimaki* out to him. "Your time, little brother."

Nobuhiro took the thin fibrous cloth and rubbed it in his fingers. He glanced at Toshi, who took out his own *hachimaki* and wrapped the cloth around his scalp, finishing it with a knot behind his head.

Nobuhiro followed suit, tying Uji's around his own head. The feel of the knot on the back of his head cleared his thoughts. He now possessed only one goal.

Uji removed his two swords and held them out to Nobuhiro. "You will need these."

Their father held up his hand, his face a mixture of solemnity and pride. "No." He walked over to where his own swords both lay, picked up the blades, and offered them to Nobuhiro. He licked his lips. "Take mine."

Nobuhiro grasped both swords, holding the hilts in each hand.

He had grasped swords before in his life. Only now, wielding them with a purpose, did he grasp the honor of doing so.

He placed them crosswise in the belt he wore and then bowed to his father. His father returned the gesture and Nobuhiro's heart grew in stature. He locked eyes with Toshi and each nodded. "It is time."

###

"Stop struggling. You'll only make me use more pressure," Omi said.

Sen inhaled and caught a whiff of kyara, the same scent she had noticed earlier at the bathhouse. She fought a little longer but knew she was powerless against the much stronger Omi, who had been trained as a samurai. She gave up the struggle.

"That's good," Omi said. "It will make things easier. You're not going to die . . . yet, but you will."

Omi relaxed her grip, allowing Sen to turn. She looked into Omi's eyes. They radiated cold, like the gray steel of a blade. The warmth that showed during what Sen thought was their friendship was no longer there. The true Omi had taken her place.

Omi had used her.

Omi held Sen's arm tightly, removing the blade from her neck and waving it in front of her eyes. It sported a drop of red. Her own blood.

"Your own blood shouldn't scare you. Didn't you see enough of it back at Lord Akamatsu's castle in Haibara? Now let's go. Slowly." Omi's voice was as sharp as the blade. "Not a word from you until we're outside. Do you understand?"

Sen flinched her head and swallowed hard.

"Good. Time to go." Omi turned Sen around and placed her hand over Sen's mouth. The knife once again pressed against her neck. She stiffened, afraid to breathe lest the blade go deeper.

"Slide the door open," Omi said.

Sen complied and the two of them stepped into the hall. They walked slowly through the exit into the open air. There was no one in sight, but guards must be patrolling nearby. If only she could find them. She needed to get Omi to talk. To waste time. To relax her guard. "Why?" Sen tried to say with her mouth muffled.

"Why what?" Omi sneered. "Why am I doing this or why did I pretend to be your friend?"

"Mhoth."

"Both, huh? I guess you deserve the answer. I did it for duty."

"Mhat mhuty?"

"Can't understand you. I'll lower my hand, but no sudden moves. Remember, it's the only way your parents and Nobuhiro stay alive." Omi lowered her hand, but the respite was short-lived, as Sen's arm was jerked hard. Omi stayed behind her, holding Sen's left arm in a crooked position that guaranteed she couldn't move. The knife was still at her throat.

###

Nobuhiro and Toshi galloped toward the castle. Each one bent down to increase his pace.

"Where do you think they'll be?" Nobuhiro shouted.

"We'll check the women's quarters first."

They slowed their horses to a trot as they arrived at the gate. Toshi signaled the guards. "Arrest Moto Omi on sight. Let everyone know." The guards nodded and allowed the brothers to pass.

Nobuhiro's stomach clenched with nervousness. Hopefully, Sen was safe. If she was hurt, he didn't know what he would do.

Chapter Twenty-Eight

Omi stared at Sen and smiled. "Good girl. You've listened well."

"Did I have a choice?"

"No. You didn't."

"Why are you doing this? What did you mean by *duty*?"

A smug look crossed Omi's face. "The regent fears this new religion. When he took Kyushu last year, he saw how many converts there were and it frightened him. It's why he banned it. Here, the emperor is a god. Citizens don't need to look elsewhere, especially not to some foreign land."

"But he's not killing Christians. He only required that they renounce their faith. He hasn't done anything publicly since the castle and the destruction of the church in Kyoto. Lord Akamatsu served him well. He was not a threat."

Omi cackled and threw back her head. "No, but he was convenient. There is one who believes in a more aggressive stance. The Christians are first. Himeji is only one place, but there are many groups in other places. My master will restore the nation to true beliefs. There remains but one missing piece and then the nation will return to the only way."

Sen breathed in huffs. "Christians are peaceful." She tried to turn but felt the sharp edge dig into her skin.

Omi flipped her around and stared with an unblinking gaze, her face curled up in grim delight. She leaned closer and lowered her voice. "The most peaceful person is a dead one."

Unable to look away, Sen listened intently, hoping for something that might draw Omi's attention. Nothing. Only the rustle of wind. Where were the internal sentries? One should pass soon. "When did you realize I knew?"

"A whiff of kyara on my clothes reminded me that you had noticed the scent at the bathhouse. I remembered it being on Michiba when he locked us in the warehouse."

Sen shook her head. "Why did you plan that? Why the arrow attack?"

"I was worried you wouldn't trust me enough when you found your church. People who've endured harrowing situations together grow a bond. I created one." Satisfaction covered Omi's face, the satisfaction of control.

Sen slowed her breathing. "So, Michiba and Funaki felt the same way about Christians you do?"

"They said they did, but they were indifferent. Besides, they're men." She rolled her tongue around her lips. "I was able to persuade them in other ways."

Chills coursed through Sen. "That explains why Michiba had your scent on him."

Omi's nose wrinkled. "The fool should have bathed."

"You're disgusting and pathetic." Sen's face tightened as feelings of hate rose inside her.

"As if I care about your opinion."

"Where are we going?"

Omi smiled. Her expression resembled a cat ready to pounce on a bird. "Where else? The well. It's about time poor Okiku had someone to help her count dishes."

Sen's knees shook. What could she do? She just

needed one opening. One chance. She closed her eyes and cleared her thoughts, trying to see a way out.

Lord, please look after Nobuhiro and my parents. Keep them safe. Keep them—

A slap forced her eyes open. "Prayers to your God won't help you now." Omi's face twisted like her mind. "Your life is in my control."

###

Toshi closed the door to the women's quarters in one of the servants' barracks and stepped back into the hall, shaking his head. "Omi's not here. Neither is Sen."

Nobuhiro glanced down the corridor. "We came in one entrance and didn't see them. Maybe they went out the other."

Toshi nodded. "Let's go."

The two of them exited the building. Nobuhiro watched as his brother moved his head about. He had always thought Toshi could commune with the elements. Today, he depended on that talent. Toshi would sense. Nobuhiro would follow. Toshi would obtain revenge.

Nobuhiro would save Sen, the daughter of his master.

The holder of his heart.

Toshi changed course and started to run, headed in the direction of the well. A grunt escaped his lips as he hit the ground hard.

Nobuhiro knelt beside him. "Toshi, are you hurt bad?"

Toshi pushed against the ground to bring himself to a sitting position. With each inch, he appeared to swear under his breath. "I'm fine. I stepped in a hole. Just give me a second."

Nobuhiro studied his brother's face. Toshi dug his hands into the soft earth, clenching the ground as if trying to draw strength from the soil. A glance at Toshi's left leg told Nobuhiro why.

Toshi's calf was bent above the ankle. Fortunately, the skin wasn't broken.

Nobuhiro patted Toshi's shoulder. "Rest easy,

brother. The night is over for you. I will send help as soon as I can."

###

Her prayer interrupted, Sen looked at Omi and narrowed her eyes. "You will be discovered. If you hurt Nobuhiro, his brothers will not rest until they've found you."

Omi laughed out loud. "They haven't discovered me yet. Why would that change?" She threw her head back. Finally, she wasn't looking. Sen charged, throwing Omi off balance and knocking her over. She jumped on her and began pounding her face, her fury taking over.

"You will not get away with this. I will stop you! Aiii!" Sen winced. A kick in the back of her head stunned her. She rose into the air as Omi threw her off, and landed hard on her side.

She tried to rise, but Omi was quicker, dagger drawn and ready to finish what she started.

"You made it interesting." Omi's snicker conveyed death. "I'm impressed. I thought you would go quietly, my friend, willingly sacrificing yourself like a dutiful daughter."

Sen exhaled and tried to catch her breath. "I am not your friend. I can't believe I trusted someone like you."

"I guess your God doesn't protect you from everything. Oh, well, we all make mistakes. Yours was your last." Sen's heart dropped as Omi approached her menacingly, waving the dagger in her hand.

###

The scream captured Nobuhiro's attention. He stood and glanced in the distance. Two figures struggled in the moonlight.

Sen?

The other must be Omi. Nobuhiro sped up as Sen pounded the person about the face. The prone figure kicked Sen in the head and threw her to the side.

A dagger flashed in the moonlight. He ran as if on air. Limp in rhythm. Stride for stride.

God of Sen, if You do exist, please help me protect her.

Chapter Twenty-Nine

Sen eyed the gleaming dagger and scanned the area, searching for another opportunity to escape. Omi wouldn't make the same mistake again.

"It was nice knowing you." Omi chuckled and glanced at the well. "Thanks for your help. I now know many Christians in the area. Their lives will change. I couldn't have done it without you."

"Stop, Omi!" rang a male voice that brought warmth to Sen's heart.

A figure in shadows approached. He was dressed like a tradesman but wore two swords. The mark of a samurai. Despite his off-balance stride, he appeared to be running on air. A mixture of pride and love swept through her soul.

You made it, Nobuhiro. I knew you would.

A feeling of relief washed over her like a cool breeze that made a humid night more tolerable. "It's over, Omi. Your day and time are done."

Omi glanced as Nobuhiro closed the distance. "Him? I should be frightened of him?" She rolled her eyes. "Your faith makes you believe in the impossible even more than I imagined."

###

Nobuhiro had yet to feel Omi's blade, but she'd already delivered the first blow with her derisive remarks. She was a trained samurai, an expert at fighting.

He was a trained swordsmith, but until today he had never understood what it meant to hold a sword.

He took a breath. "Why? Why attack Christians?"

Her lips curled. "I see you at least learned one lesson. When facing a superior foe, get them to talk. It doesn't matter. You haven't a chance." She inclined her head toward Sen. "If you want your answers, you can ask her. If you get through me, that is."

Nobuhiro's gaze darted toward Sen, but his focus never wavered. His face tightened as he prepared himself.

He had faced samurai before.

He had defeated them out of sheer will.

No matter her training, this one would not defeat him.

He unsheathed his father's sword; the familiar draw of metal on the scabbard perked his ears. He held the blade out to the side as the strength of the steel flowed into him.

"It is over. Your terror ends now. In the name of my father, you are under arrest."

Omi flipped her dagger to her left hand, drew a sword from her side, and brandished it with gritted teeth. "Your father? You left many years ago. What have you learned since?"

He grasped the hilt with both hands and extended it toward Omi. "We may have had the same teacher, but you obviously did not grasp his lessons."

Footsteps on pebbles sounded to the left as Sen stood. Omi waved the point of her sword toward her. "Are you so eager to meet your precious God? Do not worry. I will make your death swift."

Nobuhiro's stomach twisted tighter. "Sen, stay back." He would protect her, even at the cost of his own life.

Omi snorted as she placed her dagger in her clothes. "You are brave to face me alone. You will not succeed." She held her hand out and waved her fingers toward herself. "Come, if you dare."

Nobuhiro raised the sword and held it level over his shoulder. "I am ready."

Omi moved first, swinging her sword in a sideways arc. Nobuhiro angled his weapon, catching it as the blades slid down to the hilts. She shoved him back and pirouetted, bringing her sword down hard again. He deflected the blow as she stepped back.

Nobuhiro took the offensive. Two angled thrusts produced only loud noise.

Omi sighed. "Why are you even trying? Were I to be serious about this, I could dispatch you easily."

His face flushed. *Ignore her taunts.* He shifted his feet for better support and balance. He swung his sword up and down quickly, stepping forward. Omi strode sideways and extended her blade, waving it directly at him. Nobuhiro swung hard, shoving her blade to the side. She stepped back to give them distance.

He raised his sword over his head and circled around. Omi glided forward. He struck down, hitting Omi's extended blade. Omi parried, moved her sword level, and slashed him on the leg. He glanced down. A light cut only. It stung, but he would be fine.

Omi turned around and raised her sword high over her head. "I drew first blood. A sign of the outcome."

Nobuhiro moved forward and extended his sword at belt level. He swung in an arc. Omi blocked. Their blades sparked as they advanced close and pressed against each other.

"You fight well," Omi said. "I'm impressed."

Nobuhiro breathed in. "I do not care for your assessment. Keep your opinions to yourself."

She smiled and shook her head. "What's the matter, *Sakichi*? Are you sad? Did you dream of a future with Sen?"

Nobuhiro didn't blink. "My feelings and future are not your concern. You must be worried. You're not thinking about the battle at hand."

He shoved the long hilt into Omi's face, stunning her. She recovered quickly and kicked him in the shin.

He retreated and then pressed forward again. Omi swung hard, but Nobuhiro deflected her blade to the side. She brought out her dagger suddenly and slid it down the length of his blade. Then, she cut Nobuhiro's arm and brought her sword handle square into his leg.

Nobuhiro winced. He extended his sword to hold Omi at bay. The pain in his knee cost him his balance. He staggered and fell to his knees.

###

Sen's heart crashed as Nobuhiro hit the ground. Blood oozed from his wounds. She moved toward him.

Again, Omi smiled wide and motioned her sword toward Sen. "You stay put. Don't worry about your poor Nobuhiro. Worry about yourself. As soon as I'm done with him, it'll be your turn." She flashed the dagger in her sleeve. "Make a move to run and this will be in your back."

Sen clasped her hands and prayed.

Lord, please be with him.

Nobuhiro surged to his feet. Omi slashed a feint at belt level and then brought her sword over her shoulder. From there, she stepped forward, bringing her blade down. He sidestepped, holding his blade level. Their paths crossed. He slashed her arm.

Omi grimaced as her eyebrows rose. "Congratulations, you actually cut me. I'll wear it as a mark of honor."

He shook his head. "I've yet to be beaten by words, but I look forward to silencing you."

The twosome circled as swords clashed high several times. Omi turned to step away. Nobuhiro stepped with her and sliced her back.

Omi's face went red, like a volcano about to explode. "This ends now," she screamed and stepped toward Nobuhiro, bringing her blade down hard. He brought his weapon up and blocked the thrust. She raised her sword for another strike. He advanced into the small opening and sliced across her side and hand. She staggered back toward the well and dropped her sword, falling to her knees. Her hand caught the edge of the well and she steadied herself.

He held out his sword, pointing it at her. "It is over. Officials have been alerted to your treachery. You will come with me to answer for your crimes."

Relief washed over Sen. She looked at Nobuhiro. Her hero had come through.

Nobuhiro sheathed his sword. Omi tried to stand, using the well to balance herself. Sen stared at the blood oozing from the wounds. Her eyes moistened.

Omi flicked her hand. Steel flashed in the thin, pale light. Her dagger. Her kaiken. She stood at an angle, knife tip in hand, her cold eyes locked on Sen. "Under arrest? I don't think so."

Sen's hair stood on the nape of her neck.

Omi brought her arm sideways. Sen's vision was blocked as a white-robed man darted between her and Omi. The figure lunged at Omi and shoved his full weight into her midsection. The force knocked her off balance and threw her backward. She fell into the well, her scream echoing all the way down.

Sen ran and hugged Nobuhiro. The white-robed figure appeared to stare into the well, as if he expected Omi to climb back up. His breaths were heavy and loud.

She stepped toward the man and bowed low. "Thank you, sir. I am forever indebted to you."

The white-robed figure turned around and bowed in return. Sen rose to look at her unknown benefactor.

Nobuhiro's father.

Ujihiro appeared and rushed to his father's side. The elder Tokoda dropped to the ground. It was then that Sen saw it.

Omi's knife was lodged above the old man's heart.

Chapter Thirty

Sen watched as Nobuhiro and his brother laid their father on the ground. Samurai began to assemble around them. Where had they been before? One barked orders to bring a stretcher and rouse a doctor. Another called for assistance at the well. Nobuhiro told one man about Toshi and his broken leg. The man gave more directions and assured Nobuhiro he would take care of it.

Sen glanced at the well, which moments before had echoed with Omi's scream. It was now silent. Okiku's actions were noble. She likely didn't welcome the newcomer.

Sen's gaze fell on Nobuhiro, who was receiving pats on his shoulders and back from the other samurai. A hero celebrated by his heroes. The moment he had dreamed about, ever since the day he had left the castle.

Then he looked at Sen and stared. He was her hero, too.

He walked toward her. "I seem to say this often. Are you injured?"

She shook her head as her tears fell freely. "I'm well enough, thanks to you. You saved my life. Again."

His face grew red. "I only did what anyone would. I could not bear to see something happen to you."

"You're my angel. When Omi was leading me out to the well, I prayed for a miracle. You came." She leaned forward and whispered. "You are a gift from God."

Nobuhiro glowed and shuddered at the same time. Then, Ujihiro came up and tapped Nobuhiro's shoulder. "The doctors are tending to Father and Toshi. We should go."

###

Nobuhiro fell in step behind Uji, who followed another samurai. Uji had said Father's wound looked bad, but that he was alive. Nobuhiro would have time to make it up to Father for leaving years ago.

Sen's words replayed in his head. *You're my angel.* Should he tell her he had said a prayer as well? He didn't know why he had prayed. Maybe Uji's words that any good help offered should be accepted. The pain from his injuries was minor compared to what he would feel like if he had lost Sen.

Nobuhiro and Uji entered the room. Toshi was sitting up near the entrance, his left leg in a splint. His usual grin grew broader and he laughed. "That's always the way. Become a hero and you forget about everyone else."

Nobuhiro chuckled. He was glad to see his brother in good spirits. He remembered the bend in Toshi's leg when he fell. He would be in a splint for a while. "You've never looked better, in my opinion."

Toshihiro crossed his arms in front of his body. "My leg feels like what a sword must feel when caught between a hammer and an anvil."

Nobuhiro nodded at his brother. "I'll remember that the next time I'm in the workshop and you annoy me. How's Father?"

Toshi jerked his head. "He's over there. He's talkative, but his breathing sounds labored. He's coughing a lot."

Father lay on a futon. Nobuhiro walked over and

knelt by his side. The knife had been removed and the wound on his chest cauterized. The old man tried to sit up.

Nobuhiro grabbed his father's shoulders and tried to support his back. "Please rest. You'll be better soon."

His father's face turned grim, the likely result of trying to sit up, but he didn't lie back down. "The pain does not matter. I am not long for this world."

Uji walked over and knelt on the other side of his father. A sound of dragging caused Nobuhiro to look back. Toshihiro was holding his leg aloft and pushing himself along the tatami mat.

The paper door to the room slid open. Nishioji stood before them. He bowed low. "Excuse me for disturbing you, but we pulled the body from the well."

"Did she survive?" Uji asked.

"She broke her neck in the fall."

Toshi grunted. "A pity she did not live for a trial. Such scum does not deserve to die fighting."

"Nishioji, find Matsubara," Uji said. "Search Omi's clothes and personal effects. See if there are any clues as to others involved in this conspiracy. Keep it to yourselves. Report only to me."

Nishioji bowed again. "*Hai.*" He closed the door and left.

A hacking cough drew Nobuhiro's attention. He turned to his father, who stared back. "I see that you have forgiven Nishioji for the transgressions of his youth."

"What makes you say that?"

"Your shoulders relaxed when he entered. That would not have happened when you were a child."

Nobuhiro smiled. His father was right. Whatever edge had always risen in Nobuhiro at the sight of his childhood tormentor had vanished into the past. "Father, you don't miss anything."

Despite his pain, his father's face radiated serenity, just as it did when he wrote poetry. He was at peace. "My son, you make me proud."

Nobuhiro froze. His father's words, words he had

longed to hear, resonated within his head like the clang of the large bells at a Buddhist temple. "Proud?"

"Yes, proud. I know you think me harsh all these years, and maybe I was. But there were reasons for what I did."

"What were—" Nobuhiro began, but his father raised his hand. Nobuhiro fell silent.

"My son. I have always been a samurai. But my true strength was your mother. When she died, I became morose. I turned inward. You were the youngest. I ignored you when I should have been there to support you."

Nobuhiro nodded. "I understand."

His father coughed again. "I moved the three of you to the castle so I could look after you while I worked. However, I saw how you struggled and knew your life would be difficult. I pushed you not to chastise you but to help you to be your best. Unfortunately, I pushed too hard."

Nobuhiro looked away before turning back. "Be my best?"

"Yes, Nobuhiro. When you were young, you chased your brothers around like any little brother would, but you could not keep up with them. I saw in your face the hurt you felt. My heart ached for you."

Nobuhiro rubbed his chest. "It never seemed like you cared. Your words were often harsh."

"Your mother was the one who could provide you with the care and understanding you needed. All I could do was push you to make you better. When she died, I had no idea how to be both mother and father. I have trained men to be samurai for years. I have studied the arts and poetry and can impart wisdom about those things. Yet I do not understand how to show love. It was not part of my training."

Nobuhiro considered his father's words. The years. The anguish. It all came flooding back. "So you pushed harder after Mother died?"

"Yes, it was the only thing I knew."

Nobuhiro fumbled for a response. "But if you cared, then why didn't you seek me out?"

The old man's eyed softened and he shook his head. "Do you think I didn't watch you? It was my job to know everything that occurs in the city. When you left here, I knew where you'd gone almost immediately."

"But how did you—" Nobuhiro glanced to his front and right without turning his head. Uji tilted his head down to avoid the gaze. Toshi flashed a quick smile through his pain. Nobuhiro again looked back at his father but remained silent.

"I have known your master for many years," his father continued. "Goami is the best swordsmith in the region. Why would I not be acquainted with him?"

The question was more of a statement. The logic of his father's words washed over Nobuhiro like an icy bath. His father had looked out for him. "I thought—"

His father again held up his hand. "You thought you remained hidden. Yes. Out of respect for your departure, your decision to make your own way, I never contacted you. But you are still my son. I always knew. Goami has told me many things. He believes you have a gift. From what I've heard, I concur."

"All this time?"

Nobuhiro's father's eyes fluttered and he brought his hand up to his chest. "Yes, Nobuhiro, all this time, but I regret it has taken us this long to once again be father and son."

Nobuhiro's hands shook. "Father, you survived death tonight. It is a sign you should live. Do you still plan to take your own life?"

His father stared at him. "It is not necessary anymore. The heaviness I feel in my chest tells me the doctor's efforts were to no avail. I have seen similar situations on the battlefield. I have a few more minutes. Maybe an hour at best. And I have repaid the greatest debt in life."

Nobuhiro scratched his head. "The suicide of your supervisor?"

His father shook his head. "The death of Goami's elder daughter and son-in-law. I requested long ago to your master that he look after you. I repaid his kindness by training someone who killed his children. Until tonight, for this failure, there was no absolution."

"Why were you going to commit suicide? What request did you make?"

His father wet his lips. "I asked the regent to rescind the official ban on Christianity."

Nobuhiro said nothing. He glanced down but did not close his eyes. His father had risked his life, given his life, for Sen.

His father placed his hand on Nobuhiro's shoulder. "I have always been with you, but I go forth to the next life. May the goddess Amaterasu allow me to watch your life with great joy."

Nobuhiro squeezed his father's hand. "No, let us call the doctor back. Maybe there is something else that can be done."

His father wheezed loudly. Uji shuffled closer on the other side, while Toshihiro dragged himself next to Nobuhiro. His father continued. "One day, in the future, we will have time as father and son, the time that our miscommunication denied us these last seven years."

Nobuhiro bowed and touched his forehead to the floor, then looked up. "Yes, Father."

His father looked at all of his sons and displayed a smile of satisfaction.

"An old tree withers.
Its branches thrive
In the dawn of a new spring."

And with those words, their father died.

Chapter Thirty-One

Sen wiped her eyes, losing count of her tears over the last two days. She had tried to hold them inside, but the beauty of the elaborate funeral brought them forth again. She brushed her hand down her chest, but the tightness remained. Many guests had paid their respects to the brothers. Nobuhiro had mentioned there would be a private ceremony later where the brothers would reunite their father with their mother.

Sen approached the front and bowed low. Duty demanded she hold it out of respect, but gratitude held her there. Nobuhiro's father had looked after her as well. She rose and looked Nobuhiro in the eye, hoping to send support for him at this difficult time. She ached to talk to him. She would have to wait.

She would see him again tomorrow.

She woke early the next morning. The events of the last three days still seemed like a dream. Nobuhiro saving her life. His father dying to save her and Nobuhiro. Nobuhiro saying goodbye and finding out that his father did love him.

During that time, she had had a chance to talk with

her parents, to finally admit what she had done.

She also admitted that she loved Nobuhiro. Christian or not Christian, he was the angel in her life. Her mother was right. Nobuhiro was the perfect man for her.

She had work to do today. Yet she had a little time before she would have to report. Before work, she would go to the cross.

###

Nobuhiro walked toward the west part of the castle grounds and the location of the cross on the wall. He stared at the tile for a minute. What to do? What to say? His family accepted his actions. It made his decision easier.

He was not a Christian. He would not be one. Too much to understand. However, something dragged him here to offer thanks.

Nobuhiro clapped twice and bowed slightly to the tile as he let his thoughts flow. *God of Sen, I am in your debt.* He straightened and clapped one more time.

"Nobuhiro? What are you doing here?"

Nobuhiro turned and his breath stuck in his throat. Sen approached with widening steps.

###

Sen pursed her lips and smiled, laughing inside as she approached. "I saw your clapping and bow. It's not necessary."

He laughed. "It's necessary for me. I will never understand your faith, but if you will have me, I will do my best to support you as your husband."

Ujihiro walked up; his normal serious gaze was almost relaxed, as much as it could be for him anyway. "I thought I might find both of you here. Especially you, Sen, as you seem to come here."

She glanced down, her face warming. Another person who noticed. She looked back up at the kind and gentle samurai. There was nothing she could hide from any member of Nobuhiro's family. "Yes, I do."

"It is just as we planned. It would bring Lord

Akamatsu joy if he knew."

"What do you mean? What does he have to do with that cross?"

Ujihiro grinned widely. "Do you remember the night Toshi and I met you outside of Himeji? Lord Akamatsu handed me a package that night and asked Toshi and me to 'put it where it would do the most good.' The package contained this tile."

Sen looked at the cross and then back at Ujihiro. "He carried this here? Why? It must have been heavy. I never knew."

Ujihiro shook his head. "Actually, it doesn't weigh that much."

"Why did he do it?"

Ujihiro took on the wizened expression of a teacher. "He was fulfilling a debt to Kuroda, the former castle lord. Do you remember him?"

Sen nodded. "Yes, the castle was much smaller when I left ten years ago. Two years later, Lord Kuroda remodeled it. Lord Akamatsu and Lord Kuroda were close, so drawings and paintings of the castle made it to Haibara. I looked at them every day. It reminded me of home."

Ujihiro nodded. "Indeed. Home. Family. Very strong bonds. You have an excellent understanding of duty."

"I remember that time well." Nobuhiro turned to Sen. "Father served Lord Kuroda then and assisted with the renovation. When it was completed, Lord Kuroda presented the castle to the regent as a gift. The regent lived here for five years before moving to Kyoto and turning the castle over to Lord Kinoshita."

Sen leaned forward. "Forgive me, please. I understand what happened here, but I don't understand how it relates to the cross."

Ujihiro stroked his chin. "When the regent took over Kyushu last year, Kuroda was with him. He was so moved by the faith of the Christians there that he became one. He even installed a cross in his family crest."

Sen's mouth dropped open. "But Lord Kuroda

renounced Christianity after the regent's edict. He even gained lands in Kyushu for his decision. Lord Akamatsu lost all of his holdings."

"Lord Akamatsu is an idealist. Lord Kuroda is a realist. He was concerned over what actions the regent might take toward the faith. It pained him to do so, but he renounced his faith. He believed he could best counteract problems from a position of strength."

Sen stared back at the tile. "What does that have to do with the cross?"

Ujihiro swept his outstretched hand over the grounds. "Remember, this castle was Lord Kuroda's home. He wanted a piece of himself to always be here. He had the tile fired and asked Lord Akamatsu to carry it to Himeji on his journey. The package was marked with the seal of the regent and guaranteed your safe passage, at least as far as Himeji. Toshi and I affixed it to the wall after you went to bed that evening."

Sen scratched the back of her neck. Everything had been planned? "Are you saying the regent approves of Christianity?"

Ujihiro clasped his hands in front of his belt. "Approve or disapprove is irrelevant. The regent will believe whatever is necessary to maintain power. However, he owes debts to Kuroda. Allowing the tile to be displayed at this castle was one way of repaying them."

Debts. Everything in this society was about debts and obligations. Obligations transcended feelings, transcended politics, transcended everything. She held her breath. She had one more question but had already pushed too far. Could she ask it? What would Nobuhiro say? "Do you approve of Christianity? Are you a Christian, hiding like Lord Kuroda?"

Uji glanced at Nobuhiro. She had overstepped. She knew it. She wished she could see Nobuhiro's face but she refused to look. She bowed. "Forgive me, please. I've forgotten my place."

Ujihiro waved his hand, palm outward. "It is not a

problem. No, I'm not a Christian, but I also owe debts to those who are. Some of those, like the one to Lord Akamatsu, are blood debts. Repayment of those supersedes even my life."

Sen nodded, understanding. She owed this family a debt, too. She owed her parents a debt. She owed Nobuhiro three times over.

Uji turned to Nobuhiro. "Nobuhiro. Sen. Please visit me at the main armory in thirty minutes. I could use your assistance."

Nobuhiro glanced at Uji with eyes wide open. "The armory? Is there something wrong?"

Ujihiro's face went stern. "I have been promoted to father's position within the castle. Omi's comments to Sen about this being the beginning of the conspiracy and a connection to the regent concern me. I wish to discuss it again."

Sen's pulse raced at the thought of that night. It was over here, but other Christians still faced danger, likely in many cities if Omi was to be believed. Her chest tightened. She would keep them in her prayers.

Nobuhiro ran his hand over his head. "Any plans?"

Ujihiro nodded. "I need people I can trust in other locations. I have already arranged for a few transfers. Nishioji will go to Osaka. Toshi, once he is healed in a few months, will move to Kyoto. I am still debating where to send Matsubara. I may have him join one of them. That seems the best way to start."

"Why there?" Nobuhiro asked.

"When we searched Omi, we found a black eyepatch sewn with red thread. It made no sense, so we split it open. Inside was a note referencing those two places. I don't know what we'll find, but something is amiss."

Ujihiro turned to go but quickly doubled back to the couple. "I almost forgot. Sen, welcome to the family. You are a lot like our mother and a perfect match for Nobuhiro. It will be good to have a relative who is an esteemed swordsmith. We may need it in the days and months ahead."

Sen's jaw dropped and she bowed quickly. "Th . . . thank you."

Ujihiro walked away as Sen turned to Nobuhiro and stared. "Welcome to the family?"

Nobuhiro turned red. "I asked his permission this morning. I will try to be a good husband. Will you be my wife? We'll have to wait a year until the mourning period for my father is over. Also, Uji did request we hold the ceremony on a *daian,* saying that we should still respect local tradition."

Sen thought it over. A *daian* occurred every six days on the Buddhist calendar. It would be easy to schedule.

She yearned to hug Nobuhiro, but now would be inappropriate. Instead, she reached out and brushed the tips of his fingers. "That will be fine. However, I won't wait any longer than the first or second one after a year to become your wife. A year will be good. It will give us more time to know each other."

And somewhere in the distance, a little white dog wagged its tail and barked.

Epilogue

Kyoto, Japan—Three days later

Eijiro sipped his tea as he tapped his fingers on his legs, wiping light beads of sweat on the silk fabric. Silk. A special fabric reserved for those with means and the will to deliver change.

He would deliver change.

His underling bowed before him on all fours, his head parallel and inches from the ground. His fingers quivered. A decent show of respect.

Scared, Yamashiro. You should be. But today is not your day. If the time comes, you will know.

He placed the tea on a table next to his chair. "Yamashiro. Report."

Yamashiro raised his head and bit his lower lip, swallowing hard as he sat back on his calves. "Kaiken is dead, my lord."

Eijiro's chest twisted and he flattened his lips. The news was not unexpected but not welcome either. "How did it happen?"

"She broke her neck, falling into the well at Himeji Castle. She fought Tokoda Shigehiro and one of his sons.

The elder Tokoda is dead. His son still lives. Another one of Tokoda's sons broke his leg. An epic battle, it would seem.

He took another sip of tea. "She died honorably and loyally. It pleases the soul. Any more word on the Christians in Himeji? Is my disloyal runaway wife Iri hiding with them?"

"It would not seem so, my lord. Few of the Christians in the group are the right age. Those who are do not bear any resemblance to your descriptions."

Eijiro rose, his face red. "My descriptions were of a young girl, barely of the age to even produce a child. Do you not understand? The last time I saw her was years ago. We are speaking of an adult woman."

Yamashiro cringed but then straightened and held his ground. "Yes, my lord. I understand. Yet Himeji would seem the wrong place."

"Then our work there is done. With the death of our entire group in that area, we need concern ourselves no more. Kaiken died fighting. She would not have breathed a word of our existence. The Tokodas will believe a madwoman died. We need to shift our assets. There are other places. Other groups. Other possibilities. This woman, my wife, must be found."

Yamashiro looked away. "Was there anything else in the divorce document from the empress? Anything that gave you a hint of where your wife might be?"

"None. It's not right. The empress's rules on divorce are specific. I'm supposed to be given notice. A place to meet. Knowledge of her location. Why am I being treated differently from anyone else?"

"The only divorce temple is in Kamakura, I thought. Has it been checked?"

Eijiro grabbed a mochi from the tray on the table next to him. "The document from the empress states she is not there, but our associates went there anyway. Nothing."

"One temple cannot serve an entire country. Maybe the empress designated others."

"My wife would not trust them."

Yamashiro looked up and tilted his head. "Do you have an appeal? You have friends. Can they plead on your behalf?"

"I cannot risk it. Besides, if a ruling has been made, I must abide. When the time comes, I will have the power. The imperial family will bow down to me soon enough. Then I will rule."

"So we continue to pursue Christians then?"

"Yes, she has always leaned on these foul wretches since the day she escaped me. The search alone will bring me joy. Christians caused my mentor's downfall. I will see that they pay for their insolence."

"Very good, my lord. What of the messenger we hired? He knows of us."

Eijiro looked up and studied the ceiling. "Ah, yes. Carpenter. He was a good idea. With her dwindling numbers, I knew Kaiken had scant time remaining. Pay him his money. Thank him for his service and tell him we have another job for him. When he sits down to discuss the job, kill him."

Yamashiro laughed. "It will be done, but what if he has other contacts?"

"I hired this one for his reputation. He will not be missed."

Yamashiro nodded and turned to leave. He paused at the door, knelt, and bowed. "You are the way."

Eijiro grunted. "Don't forget to retrieve the money after you're done with our guest."

Yamashiro closed the door behind him. His footsteps brought chirps from the nightingale floor. *A good man, Yamashiro.*

Eijiro walked to the window and stared out from the top of the hill. Sweat dripped down his face and soaked into the edge of his kimono. He rubbed his cheek against the cloth and shook his head as his gaze fell over Kyoto and wandered into the distance. Crowds milled about in the streets, unaware that life would change for the better.

He would bring that change to fruition.

A movement of one drew his attention, but he tossed it aside. Even from this distance, he would know her in the crowd. A shuffling of black robes stood out among the people. Talk of temples stayed with him.

Iri, my wife and my love. You cannot hide from me forever. I will find you. On our togetherness rides the fate of a nation.

Author's Historical Note

I thank you for reading my book, *The Samurai's Heart*. As the epilogue shows, it is the first in a series. If you enjoyed the secondary characters here, such as Toshi, Uji, Matsubara, and Nishioji, they do come back again, with Nishioji's story the focus of the next book and then Toshi having the final chapter.

I have endeavored to make my stories as historically accurate as possible. Please e-mail me with any mistakes you find. Some items are noted below for explanation.

Himeji Castle–The history of Himeji Castle offered the greatest challenge. The current castle, a white, six-story structure meant to represent a heron in flight, is a UNESCO Cultural Heritage site and one of the best-known structures in Japan. Himeji Castle, as it stands today, is the result of a remodel dating to 1601–1609. This story takes place in 1587–1588. At that time, Himeji Castle was only three stories tall. It also may not have been white. Many castles in that area of Japan used black lacquer, as it withstood the humidity better. White castles would be found in less humid areas like Tokyo (where Tokugawa Ieyasu resided from 1590). And, as Ieyasu sought to eradicate Toyotomi Hideyoshi's influence after Hideyoshi's death in 1598, remodeling the castle as a white one instead of a black one would have sent a message that Tokyo was in charge. As I could find no reference to definitively support that the castle was black at the time of my novel, I left it white.

Haibara Castle–The incident in the prologue is based on the conglomeration of two events involving Takatsuki Castle and its Christian daimyo, Takayama Ukon (the basis for the character of Akamatsu Fumio). Takatsuki Castle was besieged by the forces of Oda Nobunaga in 1579. Ukon shaved his head and, with the help of his father, managed to save the local Christians from persecution, and impressed Nobunaga enough to be reinstated at the castle. In 1587, Regent Toyotomi Hideyoshi ordered Christian daimyo to renounce Christianity or surrender their lands. Ukon surrendered the castle again and adopted a life of poverty.

The Himeji Castle Cross–The cross tile at Himeji Castle exists today. It was installed when the castle was a three-story structure and is one of the few items to be included in the remodel. There is a plaque near its location, stating that the origin of the cross is unknown. The blogosphere offers that it was a tribute to former castle lord Kuroda Yoshitaka, himself a Christian who later renounced Christianity when the religion was banned. History suggests that Kuroda's decision was a pragmatic one and that he continued to work to support Christianity, believing discretion would allow him to protect more lives. The religion would eventually be driven underground in the seventeenth century by the grandson of Tokugawa Ieyasu and was punishable by death. However, the cross was allowed to remain.

The May Festivities in Kyoto – In the first meeting between Nobuhiro and his brothers, Ujihiro mentions the "May Festivities in Kyoto." This refers to a visit by the Emperor to Hideyoshi's palace. The visit was in May 1588 and lasted for five days. It was a lavish celebration and Hideyoshi gave the Emperor many gifts.

Lord Kinoshita–The castle lord of Himeji Castle at the time of my story was Lord Kinoshita Iesada, brother-in-law to Hideyoshi. Since he never appears, I left him there. Also, with regards to Lord Kinoshita's father (and his sword), I found one oblique reference that suggested he was an *ashigaru*, a part-time foot soldier. I ask that anyone with more information please email me the sources.

Politics at the Dinner Table–The Goami household political discussion was historically accurate, even with regard to the fictional Akamatsu going to Hokuriku. His real-life counterpart did the same. The biggest dinner challenge was how to refer to Japan's leaders in private conversation.

Oda Nobunaga, Assassination or Ritual Suicide–History records Nobunaga's death as an "assassination" by one of his generals, Akechi Mitsuhide. However, knowing he had no chance of survival when Mitsuhide's forces surrounded his temple location, Nobunaga took his own life.

Monkey (and Weasel)–The reference to Hideyoshi as "Monkey" refers to a nickname that Nobunaga attached to him. Though not mentioned in the book, Nobunaga gave the nickname "Weasel" to Tokugawa Ieyasu.

The Haunted Well at Himeji Castle–The well does exist, and the story of Okiku's ghost is one of the best-known ghost stories in Japan. There are numerous versions of the story, some that happened before and some that happened after the time period covered in this book. For my purposes, I've accepted it as having happened in an earlier time.

The Suicide Gate at Himeji Castle–The current Himeji Castle does have a "Suicide Gate." However, I don't know if the three-story version did.

The Banning of Christianity–Christianity was banned in 1587. However, the government took several public actions as a show against Christianity while continuing to allow whatever was necessary to promote trade. Some Christian properties were destroyed, but the overall effect was to make Christians downplay their missionary efforts. Later edicts would produce more devastating results.

Tokoda Shigehiro's Death Poem–Death poems were common among samurai, and many of them are moving. The elder Tokoda, noted in the book as a poet, would likely have been able to compose a tanka, a 5-7-5-7-7 structure that was prevalent in the day. However, to do it properly in this work would have required me to produce a tanka in Late Middle Japanese and then translate it to English. Instead, I composed the words as I wanted free from the 5-7-5-7-7 structure. My mother-in-law was kind enough to translate my thoughts into something resembling the style of the period. Her words are below.

老木枯れ逝ゆけど
出でし若枝いきいきと
光り輝き 春来たるなり

Acknowledgments

I started this novel several years ago. When my initial attempts to find a publisher failed, I worked on other projects. Still, I kept the storyline of this book, and the later ones in the series, close to my heart. Now that the book is published, the biggest fear I have as I write this page is forgetting to thank people from whom I've received advice. I'm grateful to everyone.

Thank you to Melinda Leigh, Lindi Peterson, Tosca Lee, and Kit Wilkinson for reviews and insights on my draft.

Thank you to Haywood Smith and Dianna Love for all of your help, suggestions, and mentorship.

Thank you to my writer's group, Georgia Romance Writers. The opportunities and support you provide are amazing. Special thanks to both Anna Destefano and Jennifer St. Giles for inviting me to join.

Thank you to the wonderful women of Seekerville, my favorite writing blog, for your numerous suggestions and guidance on everything writing related. Special thanks to Debby Giusti, with whom I had initial conversations that led to this story, to Tina Radcliffe, who helped me design my Kindle Scout campaign, and to Myra Johnson for last minute grammar assistance.

Thank you to my aunt, Jeanne Robertson, for being a continuing inspiration in my writing career.

Thanks to my online groups, WritingGIAMx3 and Authors of Asian Novels, for your continued support and good wishes.

Thank you to Yoshinori and Naomi Ishihara for your assistance with research materials and comments on historical Japanese culture. Special thanks to your little white dog, Boon-*chan*, the model for the little white dog in the story.

Thank you to my in-laws, Kazuo and Takiko Umeda, for their discussions with me on the intricacies of historical Japanese politics.

Thank you to Amy Knupp at Blue Otter Editing for the original edits.

Thank you to historians Dr. Stephen Turnbull; Michael Cooper, S. J.; and John Dougill for your books on Japanese history. Thanks also to authors Sato Kanzan and Colin Roach for your books on Japanese swords. Additional thanks to James Gillam, professor emeritus, Spelman College. Any historical or technical mistakes in this book are the fault of the author.

Thank you to Professor Carl E. Creasman Jr. and Amber Stokes for your overall insights.

Thank you to veteran Federal law enforcement officer and childhood friend, Kyle Cummings, for discussions on combat mindset.

Thank you to Amazon and Kindle Press for the wonderful opportunity the Kindle Scout program provides authors. Special thanks to my editor, Ellen Hurst, for the final edits.

Thank you to Ciara Knight for answering my questions on putting out a book in paperback.

Thank you to everyone who voted for me and who shared my links on various social media, helping me to make publishing this book a reality.

Lastly, thank you to my wife, Motoyo, and to my sons, Andrew and Christopher, for putting up with me when I'm writing.

About the Author

Walt Mussell lives in the Atlanta area with his wife and two sons. He works for a well-known corporation and writes in his spare time. Walt primarily writes historical novels, with a focus on Japan, an interest he gained during the four years he lived there. He refers to his work as "Like *Shogun*, but the heroine survives." He is currently working on Books 2 and 3 in his series, *The Samurai's Soul* and *The Samurai's Strength*, which take place in Osaka (late 1589) and Kyoto (early 1591).

Outside of writing, his favorite activity is trying to keep up with his kids. As one is away at college and the other is in high school, this is proving more difficult each day.

You can follow Walt on Twitter at @wmussell. Please visit his website Daddy Needs Decaf at waltmussell.blogspot.com and sign up for his newsletter. Please check out his Facebook page at "Walt Mussell - Author."